Match Wits with The Hardy Boys®!

Collect the Original
Hardy Boys Mystery Stories®
by Franklin W. Dixon

Celebrate 60 Years with the World's Greatest Super Sleuths!

THE FIREBIRD ROCKET

The launching of the Firebird Rocket is endangered when a famous rocket scientist disappears without a trace on his way to the Woomera Monitoring Station in Australia. Assigned to the case, Fenton Hardy tells his sons he needs their help. And Frank and Joe must turn down a request that they find the missing son of a prominent senator.

The search for the scientist begins at the Princeton Space Laboratory, where the boys realize they are being hunted by an unknown adversary. Clues lead them to Australia, and again they are followed.

Then suddenly their lives are in danger!

Someone in an automobile tries to run them over; and, later, at dockside, a heavy cargo bale falls and just misses them. Disregarding the danger and warnings of worse to come, the boys follow the trail to a cattle station in the Australian Outback.

With courage, wit, and clever detective work, the young detectives begin to close in on the enemy, only to discover that the tables have been turned. Captured by their cunning adversaries, the Hardys face certain death!

Will they escape? Will the Firebird Rocket ever be launched? Read this exciting mystery about Frank and Joe's most difficult case.

"Your nitwit contraption smashed my hen house."

The Hardy Boys Mystery Stories®

THE
FIREBIRD
ROCKET

BY

FRANKLIN W. DIXON

GROSSET & DUNLAP
Publishers • New York
A member of The Putnam & Grosset Group

PRINTED ON RECYCLED PAPER

Copyright © 1978 by Simon & Schuster, Inc. All rights reserved.
Published by Grosset & Dunlap, Inc., a member of The Putnam & Grosset
Group, New York. Published simultaneously in Canada. Printed in the U.S.A.
THE HARDY BOYS® is a registered trademark of Simon & Schuster, Inc.
GROSSET & DUNLAP is a trademark of Grosset & Dunlap, Inc.
Library of Congress Catalog Card Number: 77-76131 ISBN 0-448-08957-2
2000 Printing

CONTENTS

THE
FIREBIRD
ROCKET

CHAPTER I

A Frantic Warning

FRANK and Joe Hardy were performing a chemical test in the laboratory over their garage. The boys were checking out a clue for their father, famous private detective Fenton Hardy.

Frank held a test tube up to the light. In it was a dark-colored solution soaked from a torn piece of cloth Mr. Hardy had sent from the Space Flight Center in Florida, where he was working on a new top-secret case.

"If Dad's hunch is right," said Frank, "that cloth was stained with the invisible dye he uses to trap suspects."

Joe nodded. "The methyl test will tell us."

He picked up a plastic bottle labeled METHYL YELLOW. Unscrewing the cap, he tilted the bottle until a trickle fell into the solution.

Pufff! A burst of acrid vapor shot up into the boys' faces. They staggered back, clutching their throats! Frank dropped the test tube, which smashed, and the bottle fell from Joe's nerveless fingers, clattering onto the wooden floor! The two boys rubbed their eyes, fought for breath, and felt giddy.

"The bottle!" Joe croaked. "It contains the wrong chemical!"

Desperately Frank groped about on the floor till his fingers closed over the plastic container, which was still oozing a wisp of vapor. He managed to screw the cap back on. Joe opened the window, and they collapsed on the sill.

Fresh air poured into the lab, dispersing the fumes and clearing their heads.

"That stuff was liquid tear gas, or I'm a monkey's uncle!" Joe exclaimed.

Frank examined the bottle. "It's supposed to be methyl yellow," he declared. "That's what the label says."

"Somebody switched it!"

"That's possible. But who? And why?"

"Let's talk to the guy at the chemistry shop who sold us the bottle," Joe suggested, always eager for a mystery.

Joe Hardy was blond and seventeen. His dark-haired brother, Frank, was a year older.

As they were clearing up the mess from the broken test tube, the Hardys heard the doorbell, which was wired to ring in the garage as well as the house.

"Aunt Gertrude will answer it," said Joe.

"She can't. She went out shopping with Mom," Frank told him. "We'd better go see who it is."

Hurrying out of the garage, they went through the house and opened the front door. The caller was a well-dressed, portly man, clutching an ivory-headed cane. He peered at the boys through gold-rimmed pince-nez, which he held in place on his nose with thumb and forefinger.

His gesture called their attention to the ring he was wearing. It was set with a huge red ruby.

"Is this the Hardy house?" he inquired in a deep booming voice.

"Yes, sir," Frank replied.

"I'm Oliver Ponsley," the man announced. "I would like to consult Fenton Hardy on an urgent matter."

"Dad's away on a case right now, but would you care to come in and tell us about it?" Frank said politely. "As soon as we hear from him, we can give him your message."

"Thank you. I would appreciate a chance to explain my problem."

Frank led the way into the living room. Their visitor settled himself on the sofa, which groaned under his weight, and clasped his hands over his ivory-headed cane. Frank and Joe sat down in easy chairs and waited for him to speak.

"You boys often assist your father on his cases, do you not?" Ponsley inquired, sizing them up with a shrewd glance.

"That's right, sir," Frank replied.

"And we've solved a few mysteries on our own," Joe added, grinning modestly.

"So I've heard. Well, then, perhaps you can help me with this one, at least until your father returns."

"We'll be glad to do whatever we can, sir."

"Fine! My problem is this—a young man named Michael Moran has disappeared, and he must be found. Quickly!"

"Have you notified the police, Mr. Ponsley?" Frank asked. "They should be able to help you on a missing persons case."

"Not on this one," Ponsley retorted sharply. "We can't risk the publicity. Michael Moran is the son of Senator Jeff Moran!"

He reached into his pocket and produced an old snapshot, which he handed to Frank. The Hardys saw a clean-cut youth, not much older than Frank, holding a baseball bat on his shoulder.

"That's the last photograph of Michael before he left home," Ponsley told them. "He's been gone for over a year now."

"A *year?* Good night! Hasn't his family tried to locate him at all?" Joe asked.

"No. They felt he wanted to go away and think things out for himself, and that he'd come back when he was ready."

"Then why are they looking for him now?"

"Michael used to work for the Mid-County Bank. As you may have heard, the bank was recently broken into and robbed."

"Gosh, yes. I remember hearing about that on the news!" Joe exclaimed.

"The next day, the police caught the two crooks who pulled the job," Frank recalled.

"That's right." Ponsley nodded. "What you may not know is that the culprits are now trying to incriminate Mike Moran."

"How come?"

"The bank's alarm system was tampered with, which convinced the FBI that the robbers had inside help. So now those two scoundrels are saying it was Mike who gave them information on the wiring of the alarm system."

"Is there anything to support their accusation?" Frank asked.

"Mike studied electrical engineering before he quit college to work at the bank. And a bank employe named Thurbow remembered that Mike showed some interest in the alarm system while he was there."

"That doesn't prove anything," said Joe.

"Certainly not!" Oliver Ponsley boomed. "So far, the FBI has made no official charge against Mike, but his family is very upset, especially since Senator Moran is running for reelection. A scandal could wreck his political campaign. He's sure Mike is innocent, and wants him to come home and clear his name."

"Mr. Ponsley, how are you involved?" Joe asked.

"I'm on Senator Moran's staff and a friend of

the family's. I want to prevent any bad publicity before the news leaks out. That's why I came to see your father."

"Tell me," Frank said, "when and where was Mike last seen?"

"Leaving the bank one day last February. But he never arrived home that day."

"Has he written?"

"Yes, a number of postcards from Chicago. The last one came about three months ago, saying he was leaving the country. After that—silence."

"Any other clues?" Joe asked.

"Just one." Ponsley slipped the ring from his finger and held it up to the light so the boys could see it better. Sunshine slanting in through the window seemed to bathe the room in the gem's lustrous red glow.

"Michael always admired this stone," Ponsley said. "He was fascinated by rubies, so his parents bought him one as big as mine and had it mounted in the same kind of setting. Find a ring like this, and you'll find Mike Moran."

The Hardy boys examined the gem and felt sure they could easily spot a duplicate.

"Now then," said Ponsley, slipping the ring back on his finger, "I want you to get on the case right away. Fly to Chicago tomorrow and see if you can pick up Michael Moran's trail. Make your first report to me by the end of next week. Speed is essential!"

"But we can't leave town right now," Frank

"Find a ring like this, and you'll find Mike Moran."

said. "We're waiting for a phone call from our father. He may need us to help him with his own case."

"We'll let you know as soon as we're in touch with him," Joe added.

"Hmph." Frowning, Ponsley rose to his feet and adjusted his pince-nez. "Very well. If that's the best you can do, I'll just have to wait. You can call me at this number."

He handed Frank his business card and the boys escorted him to the door. They watched him lumber down the steps, squeeze behind the wheel of an expensive car, and drive off.

Frank and Joe returned to the living room.

"How about that ruby?" Frank enthused.

"Big as a pigeon's egg!" Joe said. "Boy, that stone must be worth a bundle!"

"Say, could thieves have gotten to Mike Moran?" Frank said suddenly. "Maybe they did him in for his ring!"

The two boys exchanged worried looks. Joe felt cold chills prickle up and down his spine.

"A ruby that size would sure attract crooks!" he agreed. "I wonder——"

He broke off at the sound of brakes screeching out in the street. Tires grated harshly against the curb in front of their house, and a car jolted to a stop. Its door opened and slammed shut. Someone raced up the steps and pounded on the door.

"Open up!" a man's voice shouted. "You Hardy boys are in danger! You may be killed!"

CHAPTER II

The Runaway Rocket

"Who the dickens is that?" Joe blurted.

"Search me, but he sounds pretty worked up!"

The doorknob rattled violently, and the thumping continued. Then their caller began ringing the bell.

"Take it easy! We're coming!" Frank yelled.

He yanked open the door. The man outside tumbled in and had some trouble regaining his balance.

"It's Mr. Oakes from the chemistry shop!" Joe exclaimed, recognizing his face.

The man was gasping. He stuck his hand into his pocket and pulled out a long plastic bottle. The label read METHYL YELLOW.

"My assistant made a terrible mistake," Oakes said, panting. "He put the wrong label on a bottle of liquid tear gas and sold it to you as methyl yellow. This is what he should have given you. If you use that other stuff in the wrong kind of chemical experiment, it could even blow up in your faces!"

"We know. We found out the hard way," said Frank. "We already had an accident."

"Great Scott! Was anyone hurt?" Oakes inquired anxiously.

"No, luckily we reacted as soon as we inhaled the fumes, and Joe got a window open fast."

"Thank goodness!" The man sighed with relief. "My store phone's out of order, so I hopped in the car and drove here the minute I discovered what Bob had done. You both have my deepest apologies. I'm terribly sorry."

"That's all right, Mr. Oakes," Joe said. "We were just about to come back to your place and find out what happened."

"A mistake—a dreadful mistake! Would you please give me that wrong bottle now?"

"Sure," Joe said. "I'll go get it." He took the methyl yellow out to the laboratory over the garage and returned with the liquid tear gas.

"We supply this stuff to various security guards around town," Oakes explained. "In fact, one of them came into my shop to get some just before I told Bob to fill your order. I suppose that's how the mix-up occurred."

After repeating his apology, the manager of the shop left with the dangerous chemical.

"Well, that solves one mystery," Frank said as he shut the front door. "Now we can concentrate on the Mike Moran case."

"Unless Dad needs us," Joe reminded him. "But listen. Suppose we do get a chance to look for that guy. How would we trace him in Chicago?"

"Good question. For one thing, we'd have to find out more about him—what his interests are, how he spends his spare time—stuff like that."

Frank broke off as the telephone rang. Joe hurried to pick it up, heard his father's voice, and gestured to Frank to come and listen in.

"Dad, where are you calling from?" he asked.

"The Space Flight Center in Florida," Fenton Hardy replied. "This case is turning out to be even tougher than I feared."

"Can you tell us anything about it?" Frank put in.

"Not on the phone. The investigation's being conducted under airtight security."

"We goofed on testing that scrap of cloth you sent us," Joe said. He told his father about the accident in the lab.

"That's all right. No harm done," said Mr. Hardy. "I identified the wearer by means of a polygraph test. I had him figured as a prime suspect in this case, but he cleared himself. Now I've got another job for you, at Princeton."

"You mean Princeton University?" Frank queried. "In New Jersey?"

"Yes. I want you and Joe to go there tomorrow morning. Talk to Professor Arthur Young at the Aerospace Laboratory. He'll clue you in on the case, and I hope he'll give you a lead to work on. Report to me after you see Professor Young."

"Dad, how do we get in touch with you?"

"You can reach me through a hot line to the Space Flight Center. The number is the Center's initials followed by the first four digits—SFC-1234. Got it?"

"Got it," Frank said.

Mr. Hardy's voice became tense. "Be careful," he warned. "This job is too important for any slips. NASA is involved. An international incident could be in the making."

"We'll be careful," his sons promised, then Frank told his father about the visit by Oliver Ponsley.

"He wants us to find Mike Moran."

"My case has priority," Mr. Hardy replied. "After we've cracked it, you can look for young Moran. So long." He hung up.

Joe replaced the phone and the boys began to talk about their trip to Princeton.

"The home of the Princeton tiger!" Joe said with enthusiasm. "Wow! Maybe we'll get a chance to see some of their athletic teams work out."

"I think we'd better just stick to the Aerospace Lab," Frank said. "We're on a case, remember? I wonder what Professor Young knows about Dad's investigation. Maybe somebody stole a missile!"

"Yeah, sure." Joe grinned. "Like maybe a crook slipped an interplanetary rocket up his sleeve and walked out unnoticed. If you ask me——"

He was interrupted by a series of loud reports in the street. A clanking sound drew near.

Frank grinned. "Chet Morton's coming."

Joe peered out the window at the approaching jalopy. "Looks like he's got the whole gang with him. Let's go see what they're up to!"

As the Hardys grabbed their jackets and ran outside, Chet's fire-engine-red car pulled up to the curb. Its roly-poly, freckle-faced driver applied the squeaky brakes and brought his car to a jolting halt that threw his passengers forward, then bounced them back in their seats.

"Should we call a doctor?" Joe inquired. "Or are all of you still in one piece?"

"Wait'll we check," said Biff Hooper, a husky six-footer. He was crowded into the back seat with Chet's pretty sister Iola and Tony Prito.

"No broken bones—yet," Tony reported. "The question is, will we be able to walk away from this moving wreck?"

"What I'm worried about is my back," groaned Phil Cohen, who was sitting up front beside Chet. "I think I slipped a disk when we stopped."

Frank laughed at the driver's indignant look. "What's that you were telling us, Chet, about your rebuilt shocks and the smooth suspension you were engineering on this job?"

"So it's got a few bugs." The stout youth shrugged. "I notice that doesn't stop these wise guys from thumbing a ride in my racer whenever they need a lift. You'll have to admit it's really sharp looking!"

"Pedestrians call it the *Red Menace*," Phil wisecracked.

The car's body metal had a worn, battered look but gleamed with a fresh coat of paint.

"Not bad for an old heap," Joe said, grinning. "When are you going to install a refrigerator?"

"Hey, that's an idea!" Chet said, snapping his fingers.

The Hardys' plump pal had helped them on many investigations. Even though he preferred food to danger, Chet never let Frank and Joe down when they were in a tight spot.

"Hop in, you two. We're wasting time!" he went on. "We can talk about food supplies later. Right now we're on our way to Bayport Meadow."

"What's going on there?" Frank asked.

"The most exciting scientific event of the century!" Chet exclaimed. "Up, up, and away! Don't miss it."

"Chet just finished his rocket," Iola confided. "He can't wait to try it out. It's in the trunk."

Laughing, Frank and Joe crowded into the car, practically sitting on their friends' laps. By now they were used to Chet's mania for new hobbies. His latest was rockets, and he had been working on one in his basement for weeks. He intended to enter it in a national high-school science contest.

The jalopy sagged under the extra weight but began to move. Chet drove it noisily through Bayport and headed for the meadow outside of town, while the others chatted and joked about the contest.

Joe had managed to squeeze into a place next to Iola. He usually dated her when the gang went to picnics or dances.

"Chet just might win," Iola told him. "He's really worked hard on this project."

"We'll all be cheering him on," Joe promised.

In a few minutes they reached the meadow, a large open area covered with dry brown grass. The soil was still slightly frozen from the winter's cold.

Chet parked and they all got out and checked the area to make sure no one was in the way of the test.

"Looks like you've got a clear firing range," Tony observed.

"As long as he aims straight," said Frank.

"Don't worry," Chet boasted confidently. "I've designed a foolproof steering system."

He opened the car trunk and lifted out his rocket. It was a two foot long cylinder with a pointed nose and tail fins. For a launching pad, Chet stuck two pipes in the ground, mounted a cradle on them, and placed the rocket in it. The

missile tilted at an angle with its upper end pointing skyward. Then Chet attached a control wire
with a switch at one end.

At last the tubby teen-ager stepped back
proudly to survey his handiwork. "Ah! Ready for
the countdown!"

"Man, that looks like a space probe to the
planet Mars!" Frank joked admiringly.

"Powerful enough to carry an astronaut to the
moon," Joe suggested.

"Any astronaut but Chet," said Biff. "With a
payload that heavy, even a Saturn rocket would
never get into orbit."

"Quiet, you guys!" Chet commanded. "The
Morton Moon Grazer is about to be launched.
My electrical igniter will do the trick. Here goes!"

He pressed a remote-control switch. There were
a flash and loud report, followed by a burst of
smoke. The rocket shuddered, left its cradle, and
shot high in the air. Chet's friends were impressed
and burst into applause.

Chet bowed. "It'll land at the far end of the
meadow," he predicted.

They all shaded their eyes and watched. Suddenly the missile began to wobble and veer off
course.

"Oh, oh! It's looping over to the right!" Joe
blurted.

The rocket appeared to be zooming down beyond the strip of woods fringing the meadowlands.

"There are farms on the other side of those trees!" cried Biff.

"What happened to your foolproof steering system?" Frank inquired.

Chet gulped and turned pale. "S-S-Something must have gone wrong!"

"No argument there. Come on! We'd better find out where your Moon Grazer lands!"

The boys and Iola ran around the edge of the meadow and headed through the stand of trees.

"Must've come down on Old Man Jessup's farm!" Phil guessed. "Boy, that guy's a real crab!"

Chet shuddered. It took them several minutes to cover the distance, and he was puffing and panting anxiously by the time they approached Jessup's farmyard. He turned even paler as the loud squawks of frightened chickens with an angry bellowing voice reached their ears from the other side of the barn.

"Oh gosh!" Chet exclaimed. "Sounds like we're in real trouble!"

"What do you mean *we?*" said Biff.

The words were hardly out of his mouth when the barnyard noises were drowned by the shrill hoo-haw of an approaching police siren!

CHAPTER III

The Blow-Up

A SCENE of wild confusion greeted the teen-agers' eyes as they rounded the barn. Feathers were flying as white Leghorns and Rhode Island reds hopped, cackled, and fluttered about the yard. Chet's rocket had smashed their chicken coop.

Enoch Jessup, a gaunt, bushy-browed man in overalls, was shouting orders to his farmhand, who was trying to round up the frightened fowls and calm them down by scattering feed.

Just as Jessup's glance fell on the young people, a police car with flashing lights screeched to a halt near the farmhouse. A burly man in a brass-buttoned uniform jumped out and strode toward the scene of the disaster.

"Oh, brother! It's Police Chief Collig himself!" muttered Tony Prito.

"What's going on here?" Collig demanded.

"You've got eyes! What does it look like?"

18

Jessup retorted. "These young scamps just wrecked my chicken coop with their blame-fool contraption! Scared the wits out of my best laying hens!"

Turning to the high-schoolers, he growled, "Which one of you's responsible for this outrage?"

"W-W-We weren't aiming at your chicken coop, Mr. Jessup," Chet stammered. "It was j-j-just an accident. . . . I mean, that is . . . well, I—I guess *I'm* *s*ort of responsible."

"*Sort* of responsible, my foot! Your nitwit contraption smashed my henhouse, didn't it?" Shaking his finger in Chet's face, Enoch Jessup proceeded to bawl out the trembling youth.

"All right. All right! Take it easy," Chief Collig cut in. "We got a CB call from some motorist who saw you kids about to fire a rocket. Good thing I grabbed a squad car and came myself. I might've known you'd be at the bottom of this mess, Chet Morton. You and your harebrained hobbies!"

"Actually, Chet made the rocket for a high-school science competition, Chief," Frank Hardy spoke up. "I know the test went wrong, but he's worked hard on this project. I think he deserves credit for making a model that flew as well as this one did. After all, our country *needs* rocket engineers, and they have to start somewhere."

"Tell you what, sir," Joe added. "If Mr. Jessup won't press charges, we'll all pitch in and repair his chicken coop. We'll even help out with a few chores."

"Sounds fair enough," Collig agreed. "What do you say, Enoch?"

The farmer's scowl relaxed. "Why not? Makes more sense than wasting time in court."

Biff Hooper borrowed Chet's car keys and hurried off to get some fresh lumber, while the others cleaned up the debris from the wrecked coop. Luckily the coop had broken the missile's fall, so that the rocket itself was not much damaged.

"Boy, you Hardys really saved my neck," Chet said as they drove back to Bayport.

"Forget it. It was fun," Joe said.

"Think you can still enter your rocket in the competition?" Frank asked their chubby pal.

"Sure. I can make repairs tonight and turn it in tomorrow morning."

Although spring vacation had started, Mr. Palmer, the science teacher, had promised to be on hand at the high school to receive last-minute entries.

Frank and Joe found their mother and aunt just back from the supermarket. Aunt Gertrude was their father's sister.

"Where have you boys been?" she demanded tartly.

"Watching an unidentified flying object, Aunt Gertrude," Joe told her with a grin.

"What's *that* supposed to mean, young man?"

Her eyes flickered suspiciously over her two nephews.

The tall, sharp-tongued spinster was extremely fond of Frank and Joe and secretly longed to take a hand in their detective work, although she could seldom bring herself to admit it openly.

"Chet fired a homemade rocket," Frank said, and he described the crash landing.

"Good heavens! I'm glad no one was hurt," Mrs. Hardy exclaimed.

Aunt Gertrude sniffed. "That boy Chet needs a firm hand."

"Someone like you to help fire his rockets?" Joe teased.

"He could do worse," Gertrude Hardy snapped. "Apparently you two didn't help him steer it right."

The boys laughed, and Frank said, "Score one for Aunt G.!"

He told them about Oliver Ponsley's visit and their father's call. "We have to go to Princeton first thing in the morning," Frank added.

"Oh dear," his mother said. "I hope you're not going to get involved in anything dangerous." Mrs. Hardy, an attractive woman, worried whenever her husband and sons took a new case.

"Well, what's dangerous about going to a university?" Aunt Gertrude scoffed. "Might learn a thing or two there at Princeton, as long as they don't start playing any foolish college pranks."

"We won't," Joe promised, chuckling.

"You're going alone?" Mrs. Hardy asked, still a bit concerned.

"We were," Frank replied, "but now that you mention it, we might ask Chet to come along."

"Hey, good idea!" Joe said.

He rushed to the phone and called their overweight buddy. Chet was delighted at the suggestion and agreed at once to accompany them.

"Pack an overnight bag," Joe advised. "We may have to stay a day or two."

"That's okay with me," Chet said. "I was just thinking it might be a good idea to stay out of sight the next few days. Chief Collig will probably have every cop in town breathing down my neck for a while."

Joe then called Mr. Ponsley and told him that they could not start searching for Mike Moran until they knew more about what was expected from them in their father's case. Ponsley agreed to the delay. "Call me as soon as you know more," he added.

Early next morning, the Hardys got into their sleek yellow sports coupe and picked up Chet Morton. Then they headed for Princeton. Threading their way through traffic, they reached the highway, where Frank stepped on the gas and kept the car whizzing along at the speed limit. Once the rush hour was over, they made good time under the brilliant sunshine.

"Get your rocket fixed, Chet?" Joe inquired.

"You bet. Handed it in just in time. I think I've really got a chance to win."

"I sure hope so. We'll keep our fingers crossed."

At a fork in the road, Frank turned onto Route 206 and soon they saw signs indicating that Princeton lay straight ahead. When they ran into Nassau Street, they knew they were at their destination. Shops lined one side of the famous Princeton thoroughfare, and university buildings occupied the opposite side.

"Now I know why it's called Ivy League," Chet quipped. "Look at the ivy on the dorms!"

"I wonder where the Aerospace Lab is," Frank said. He stopped for a red light near a couple of high stone gates flanked by iron railings. Beyond the lawn they could see Nassau Hall, the main building of the campus. Its slender tower rose toward the sky and was topped by a weathervane.

A student carrying a couple of books under his arm started to cross the street with the light. Joe leaned out the window and asked him the way to the Aerospace Lab.

"Go down Nassau Street and turn right onto Washington Road," was the reply. "The lab is near the football stadium."

Frank followed the directions. They passed the psychology and biology departments, and arrived at a science complex, where Chet spotted a sign reading: PRINCETON AEROSPACE LABORATORY.

Frank parked and the young detectives went in.

They found themselves in a rotunda, where a model of a Saturn rocket stood upright in the middle of the floor. Around the walls behind glass were exhibits of dramatic moments in the history of space exploration.

Chet pointed to one of them. "The astronauts on the moon!" he said.

"And there's Skylab in orbit!" Joe exclaimed.

"And Telstar!" Frank marveled. "They bounce signals off it out in space, and the signals are picked up by TV systems around the world!"

A guard approached and inquired what they wanted. When Frank explained their mission, he escorted them down the hall to a door bearing the nameplate: PROFESSOR ARTHUR YOUNG. The guard knocked and went in. A moment later he returned and announced that Professor Young would see them.

They entered a study lined with books, graphs, mathematical equations, and blowups of major rocket launchings. The professor rose from his swivel chair and shook hands with the visitors. After introductions were made, he made a motion indicating that they take three chairs near his desk, and sat down again. He was tall, thin, and slightly bald. He looked intently at the boys as he tamped tobacco into his pipe and lit it.

"Your father phoned me and told me you were on your way," he said with a smile. "I'm very glad to see you and your friend. We need fast action."

"Professor, what is the problem?" Frank asked in a puzzled tone.

"How much do you know about the case that has developed here at the lab?" Young countered.

"Nothing," Joe admitted.

"Well, I'll give you all the information I have. First let me show you around the place, so you get an idea of what we're doing. Then you'll see what we're up against and why we need your assistance."

He led them out of his office and through the building. "Everyone here is devoted to the exploration of space," Young commented. "This lab is one of the best in the world when it comes to interplanetary probes and the study of the solar system."

The group passed a lecture hall, a library, two seminar rooms, and several offices belonging to famous scientists. Then they arrived at the lab itself, a maze of rooms in which experts were carrying out experiments on everything from liquid fuels to the problems of weightlessness in outer space.

"Boy, this sure beats Bayport High!" Chet exclaimed. "I could make myself a real rocket here. Maybe I'll apply for a job after I win the state science competition."

Young laughed. "Glad to have you aboard,

Chet. Just be sure you get clearance from the Space Flight Center when the time comes. You'll have to be okayed down there because we work for NASA. What we discover goes on the drawing boards at the Center."

"No wonder Dad said the case was hush-hush," Frank put in. "This lab must be filled with top-secret stuff."

Young became solemn. "That's the whole point of the investigation you're undertaking."

They arrived at a room where a youth was working at a modified atomic reactor. Young introduced him as Smoky Rinaldo, a senior at Princeton University.

"Smoky can show you around from here on," the professor said. "When you've seen enough of the lab, meet me back at my office and we'll discuss your assignment."

He walked off and Smoky informed the visitors that he was doing research for a term paper.

"I'm into rockets, myself," Chet spoke up. "Fact is, I've got my own missile."

Frank chuckled. "You almost didn't. It flew straight—straight to earth."

"What are you talking about?" Smoky asked.

"Oh, nothing," Chet said hastily. "Why don't you show us the rest of the lab? I can't wait to see it."

The young people wandered through the last row of rooms, which were assigned to scientists experimenting with the shape of nose cones and tail fins for partly developed rockets.

Suddenly a movement caught Frank's attention. Looking out of the corner of his eye, he noticed a man behind them. He was tall and lanky and wore a black beard and tinted glasses.

Frank paused before a blow-up of a Saturn rocket. Joe and Chet joined him. The man stopped at a workbench and furtively glanced at them.

"I think we've got a shadow," the older Hardy informed Joe and Chet in an undertone.

Joe traced the curved line of a nose cone with his finger, pretending to be interested in it. "Are you sure?" he asked.

"No. It could be a coincidence. Let's go on and keep an eye on him."

Joe turned as they walked farther, catching a glimpse of the man. "Beard with glasses?" he asked.

"Right."

Smoky was slightly ahead of the group, explaining the interesting features of the lab. When they left the last room and walked back to where they had started, Chet asked, "Who's that guy with the beard over there?"

Smoky turned around to look. "I've no idea. Matter of fact, I've never seen him before."

The man obviously realized that the boys had noticed him, and instead of following them far-

ther, he entered a door with the sign OFFICIAL
PERSONNEL ONLY.

"He must be on the staff here," Smoky went on.
"Would you like to see the reactor I'm working
on? The interior is hot enough to handle uranium."

They walked over to the instrument. "We can't
see the interior," Joe pointed out.

"That's because it's running," Smoky said.
"Just follow me, and you'll find out what's in
there." He led the way to a diagram on the wall
representing a slice through the reactor from top
to bottom.

"This is how the machine is put together," the
student explained. "The core in the center
marked A is where the uranium goes. The letter
B stands for the pressure vessel, and C is the
casing. These tubes extending from the core to
the top are the fuel——"

A loud sputtering noise broke out. Red sparks
flashed through the air around them. Chet turned
pale and shouted, "The reactor's going to explode!"

CHAPTER IV

A Strange Disappearance

CHET dived to the floor, crawled under a workbench, turned around on his hands and knees, and stared at the other three. Frank, Joe, and Smoky remained standing.

"You guys want to get blown up?" Chet quavered.

"False alarm, Chet," Smoky said.

"How do you know?" Chet demanded.

"Because that wasn't the atomic reactor," Smoky explained. "It has a failsafe protection. If anything goes wrong, the motor shuts off automatically. And besides, this is a modified reactor. It doesn't have enough power for an atomic explosion."

A man in overalls came over. He was wearing a plastic eyeshield and carrying a blowtorch. "Sorry about that," he apologized. "I'm working on a wire coil with this torch. The coil's too soft for the flame, and that's the reason for the noise and sparks."

"That's okay," Smoky said. "Don't worry about it."

As the man walked off again, Chet crawled out from under the workbench and got to his feet. He looked embarrassed. "Guess I overreacted," he said sheepishly.

Frank soothed his feelings. "It's better than taking chances. Well, we've seen the lab. Let's report to Professor Young and find out about our assignment."

The Bayport youths left Smoky Rinaldo tinkering with the heat shields on the atomic reactor. They rejoined the professor, who shuffled some papers, placed them on the desk, and leaned back in his swivel chair.

"How do you like the Aerospace Lab?" he inquired genially.

"We like it fine, Professor," Frank declared, "except for one thing."

"What's that?"

"We were being followed." Frank told him about the man who seemed to be shadowing them through the lab.

Young frowned. "I've never seen anyone who matches that description, but I'll try to find out who he is. The lab is strictly off limits to unauthorized personnel."

He ordered through the intercom an immediate search of the premises. Then he turned back to his visitors. "Now," he said, "let me tell you about the mystery."

The boys leaned forward in their chairs, eager to hear every word.

"It concerns Dr. Adrian Jenson," Young went on. "You may have heard of him."

"The rocket scientist," Joe said. "He's been working on space probes ever since the astronauts landed on the moon."

"And he won a prize for his math on trajectories," Frank added. "The path of reentry from outer space into the earth's atmosphere."

Young smiled. "You know your rocketry," he complimented them. "Well, Dr. Jenson and I have been working on a revolutionary new engine powered by nuclear energy. We call it the Firebird, and it's due for a test flight in a couple of weeks. Dr. Jenson flew to Australia three days ago to follow the flight of the Firebird at the Woomera Monitoring Station."

"Australia?" Chet spoke up. "Why there?"

"When a rocket is fired into orbit from our Space Flight Center, its path over the Southern Hemisphere is followed at tracking stations south of the equator. Woomera is one of the best of these installations. We are cooperating closely with the Australian government in monitoring our missiles, and our people go there frequently."

"But why the mystery?" Joe asked.

"Dr. Jenson never got to Woomera. He hasn't been heard of since he left Princeton!"

Frank let out a low whistle. "Did he actually get on the plane?"

"Yes. We checked with the airlines. He arrived in Sydney and picked up his luggage. There the trail ends. We also searched his desk for clues, but found nothing."

"And you've notified the Australian police?" Joe asked.

"We did that immediately and they've been working on it ever since. However, both we and NASA wanted a top-flight investigator assigned to the case at this end—especially since there were indications that the plotters had been after him in this country. Our project's top-secret, so the investigation has had to be kept under wraps, and your father seems the ideal man to handle it. But so far we have no real clue to Dr. Jenson's whereabouts."

"Maybe enemy agents kidnapped him!" Chet exploded. "Maybe they're brainwashing him!"

"That's possible," Young admitted. "The Firebird Rocket is classified. Dr. Jenson and I are the only scientists who know the secret of the nuclear engine. If enemy agents kidnapped him, he may have revealed the secret. A foreign power could be building a Firebird right now!"

Frank said, "You mentioned that someone had been after Dr. Jenson in this country."

Professor Young nodded. "A neighbor noticed a car with Florida plates parked outside his house after he left. And the police discovered that his home had been broken into and ransacked. Also, telephone company records show that a call was made from there that same night to a pay phone in Florida near the Space Flight Center."

"So that's why Dad's been concentrating on the case down in Florida!" Joe said.

"Exactly. But he wanted all aspects of the case covered and decided his sons could handle the investigation here at the Aerospace Lab. So here you are."

"And we've brought Chet," Frank said. "He's helped us many times before and is reliable."

"That's fine," Young said. "I trust your judgment."

Chet grinned and said he would do his best to help the Hardys crack the case.

The professor continued. "Your task is to investigate all possible leads at the lab and see if you can find the clue you need to solve the mystery while your father does the same at the Space Flight Center. I have some information that might help you."

"Oh?" Frank asked. "What is it?"

Young's answer surprised him. "Jenson and I received a warning letter and threatening phone calls. Here, I'll show you."

He reached into a drawer and took out an envelope. Removing the letter, he handed it to Frank. Joe and Chet craned their necks to see it. The message was crudely pieced together from words out of a newspaper.

It said: *Kill the Firebird or else!*

"Someone's trying to sabotage your rocket!" Joe exclaimed. "They don't want it to be launched."

"That's right, and whoever wrote the letter means business."

"Professor," Frank said, "do you realize that you may be in great danger yourself?"

"Everyone here is aware of that. I have been assigned a personal bodyguard, without whom I do not leave the building. I don't want you to worry about me. Just find Dr. Jenson!"

Frank was about to say something when he heard a noise outside the door.

"An eavesdropper!" Frank thought. Leaping out of his chair, he strode to the door and swung it wide open.

Smoky Rinaldo was standing there!

"Hi," Frank said. "Are you interested in our conference?"

Smoky looked surprised. "I didn't know a conference was going on in Professor Young's office. When I heard voices, I stopped momentarily to see if I should come in or not." Glancing past Frank, he addressed Young. "I can't tell if the fuel is getting hot enough. Would you mind checking it when you have a chance?"

"I'll be right along, Smoky," the professor promised. Then he said to the boys, "I'll phone the Nassau Club and make arrangements for you to stay there while you're in Princeton. It's on Mercer Street."

Young made the reservations, then went with Smoky to the atomic reactor while Frank, Joe, and Chet drove to the Nassau Club. The driveway curved in a semicircle past the steps leading up to the front door of the stately building.

Frank parked the car. "Do you think Smoky was eavesdropping?" he asked as the boys got out.

"I'm inclined to think he's honest," Joe said. "But we'll keep an eye on him."

The boys entered the building and went to the front office to see about their room. Frank inquired while Joe and Chet looked around.

A hallway led through the first floor to a coatroom at the rear. Members of the club were seated in the reading room to the left, scanning the latest newspapers and magazines. Two portraits hung on the opposite wall, flanking the entrance to the main dining room.

"I wonder who those old geezers are," Chet whispered to Joe.

The younger Hardy walked closer, surveyed the inscriptions under the portraits, and came back. "They're two presidents of the United States," he said. "Woodrow Wilson and Grover Cleveland."

Frank strode out of the office and announced that they were set for the night. The three drove to the rear of the club and left the car in the parking lot. Walking toward the back door, they examined the building, which had plenty of corners and angles, tilting roofs and high eaves.

"The club would make a good haunted house,"

Joe suggested. "All we need is a spooky face at the window. Frank! There he is!"

"Who?" Frank asked, glancing in the direction his brother had indicated.

"The guy from the lab!" Joe gasped. "He was right there, looking out that window. The fellow with the tinted glasses!"

"I don't see him now," Frank stated, "but let's go inside and see if we can catch him!"

The boys hurried up the wooden steps and through the coatroom door. Seeing nobody, they hastened down the hallway into the reading room, through the dining room, and to the front door.

A footfall on the carpet made them whirl. Their shadow was trying to tiptoe down the stairs to the basement!

The boys rushed after him. As they reached the bottom of the stairs, they saw him run into the bar. By the time they got there, he was exiting by another door.

The pursuers went pell-mell up the stairs to the first floor, and then to the second floor, where Chet was too exhausted to go any farther. He sat on the top step and watched the Hardys race along the corridor to where the man was climbing out the window. The fugitive slid down the fire escape to an alley at the bottom, and hurried around the corner into Nassau Street.

When Frank and Joe reached the spot, the man had vanished!

CHAPTER V

Night Visitor

"No SIGN of him," Joe said, looking up and down the street. "He could be anywhere by now."

Frank nodded glumly. "You're right. We lost him."

The boys returned to the club and picked up Chet, then went to their room. It overlooked the alley and had a fire escape under the window.

"Good," Chet declared when he noticed the exit. "We can get out of here in a hurry if we're cornered by crooks. Say, how about chow? I haven't eaten since breakfast. I might faint."

"If you do, you'll shake up the club," Joe quipped. "It wasn't built for your weight."

Chet looked pained, but Frank came to his rescue. "I'm with you, Chet. It's dinnertime anyway."

The boys freshened up a bit, then went to the dining room. After giving the waiter their order,

Chet leaned back in his chair. "Well, Hardys," he grinned, "do you have a plan for solving the big mystery yet?"

"We're working on it," Joe said, sipping water from his glass.

"I think Jenson was kidnapped by a foreign power," Chet declared.

"Maybe he *worked* for a foreign power and left on his own," Joe put in.

"You mean as a spy?" Chet asked.

Joe nodded. "Perhaps he developed the Firebird Rocket and sold the secret to someone else."

Frank shook his head. "But why would he wait until the United States finished building the missile? I think he would have given away the secret earlier and stolen the plans in order to prevent us from completing the project."

Chet nodded. "I'm with Frank. The spy angle doesn't seem to fit in this case. Jenson was probably kidnapped."

"So where do we start with our work?" Joe wanted to know.

"We interview all the people at the lab," Frank said. "Let's hope somebody there will be able to give us a line on that bearded creep."

The boys discussed their strategy during dinner, and after they had dessert, Chet suggested that they go for a walk to clear their heads.

"I have a better idea," Joe said. "I noticed a sign saying that there's dancing after dinner. Why don't we listen to the music for a while?"

"Oh, good," Chet said. "I'm all for it."

A combo was playing in the lounge, and couples edged onto the dance floor. The boys sat down and before long Joe noticed three attractive girls standing nearby.

"Hey, what say we meet those young ladies over there?" he said.

"Sounds great," Frank agreed. "I'll invite them to our table." He got up and soon returned with the girls in tow.

"Hi," said the pretty blond right behind Frank. "I'm Hedy Hollweg. My friends are Pat Morrison and Jane Linski."

The boys introduced themselves and asked the girls to dance. Frank paired off with Hedy, Joe with Pat, and Chet asked Jane. After a while, they went back to the table, and animated conversation followed.

"We're freshmen at Princeton," Hedy said, "and are studying American literature. What are you doing here? I haven't noticed you on campus."

"Detective work!" Chet boomed. "I've solved a lot of cases with the help of the Hardys!"

Frank and Joe grinned. They were used to having Chet brag a little, especially in front of girls.

The coeds were intrigued. They bombarded the boys with questions about crime investigation.

"You must be here on an important case," Jane surmised.

Chet opened his mouth but Frank kicked his foot under the table as a signal to keep quiet about

Dr. Jenson. Joe changed the subject. "How do you girls like Princeton?"

"It's great!" Hedy said. "I'm glad they let coeds in."

Pat nodded vigorously. "This is one thing Women's Lib did for us. Princeton used to be for men only. But no more!"

"Personally, I wouldn't want to go to a school that excludes girls," Chet said, eying Jane appreciatively. He smiled at her. "Would you like to dance?"

The young people had a fun-filled evening, and when they finally said good-by to each other, the Bayporters thanked the girls for their pleasant company. Then Hedy, Pat, and Jane went to their dorm while the Hardys and Chet walked up to their room. Soon they were fast asleep.

A sudden noise woke Joe in the middle of the night. It came from the alley below their room. Throwing off his blanket, he got out of bed and padded silently to the window.

A pebble landed squarely on the pane. Joe peered over the sill into the darkness. He could barely see a figure on the ground below, throwing another pebble, and another.

Joe pushed the window open. "Hey, what do you want?" he whispered loudly.

"Joe! It's me, Smoky. I've got something for you!" was the reply.

"Okay, come up the fire escape," Joe said.

As Smoky climbed up the rungs of the ladder, Joe roused Frank and Chet. "We have a visitor," he told them. "It's Smoky."

"At this time of night?" mumbled Chet, who was still foggy with sleep.

"Strange time for a visit, all right," Joe agreed.

Smoky clambered in through the open window.

"What's wrong with the front door?" Frank grumbled.

"They lock the place up at night," Smoky explained, "and I didn't want to cause a disturbance."

"There's also the telephone," Chet pointed out.

"I know. But I didn't want to call because I have something to show you. I———"

"How did you know this was our room?" Frank interrupted.

"It was the only vacant one before you came," Smoky answered. "There was no other place for them to put you in."

"Smoky, I think you're crazy. Do you know what time it is?" Joe asked.

"Hey, don't get mad. I'm trying to help you!"

"Why couldn't it wait till morning?"

"Because I've got to get some sleep. I've worked in the lab till now and I have an exam at noon. By the time I would be able to call you, you'd be gone."

"All right. What have you got?" Frank asked.

Smoky withdrew a sheet from his pocket and

held it up for them to read. "Look at this!" he said.

A row of words had been cut out of a magazine and glued onto the paper, just as in the threatening note Professor Young had received. It read: *The Firebird will never fly!*

Frank, Joe, and Chet were flabbergasted by the message, which seemed to leap at them from the paper.

"Where did you get this?" Frank asked Smoky.

"It was under the blotter on Dr. Jenson's desk," the boy replied. "He keeps memos there. As I told you, I worked late on the reactor, and I needed to clear up a problem about the power transmission. I thought Dr. Jenson might have left a memo on it, since we talked about it recently. So I looked under the blotter and found this paper instead."

"Any idea how it got there?" Frank inquired.

"None. But I know that Dr. Jenson's missing and figured you're investigating. I couldn't help hearing that much when you thought I was eavesdropping in the corridor. I decided I'd better get this message to you pronto. I'll let Professor Young know about it in the morning."

"Thanks for your trouble," said Frank. "This could be important."

"Professor Young told us Jenson's desk was searched for clues when he disappeared," Joe said. "How come it didn't turn up then?"

"Must've been put under his blotter after that,"

"Strange time for a visit," Joe said.

Frank guessed. He shot a questioning glance at their visitor, waiting to hear his comment.

Smoky shrugged. "It could easily have been overlooked, because it was between a couple of memos. Well, I'd better be going. I have to get some rest or I'll flunk my exam tomorrow."

The boy jumped on the windowsill and swiveled his legs onto the fire escape. He climbed down into the alley and seconds later vanished behind the buildings.

Frank placed the puzzling message on the table under the light of the lamp and the boys studied the warning.

"What do you make of it?" Frank asked his two companions.

"The way it reads," Chet declared, "this could be a threat or just a straight message."

"Why cut out words to send someone a message?" Frank objected. "Why not just write it?"

"To avoid having your own writing recognized."

"Sure, but *whose* own writing?" said Frank. "Are you saying Jenson himself is a phony or a traitor?"

"Well, he must be," Chet argued, "if this is his work."

"Yeah. If! That's the question," said Joe.

"There's no way to tell. If you ask me, our first problem is, How did this get under Jenson's blotter after he disappeared?"

Frank glanced at his brother. "You think Smoky's lying?"

"Let's just say we have no reason to trust him so far."

"Maybe not. On the other hand, the message could have been overlooked, as he says."

"That's right," Chet added. "Jenson may have put it under his blotter and forgotten about it. Perhaps he didn't take the warning seriously."

"Boy, the situation looks serious now," Chet said. "If NASA goes ahead with the Firebird launching, it may be curtains for both Young and Jenson."

"For all we know," Joe warned, "it may have been curtains for Dr. Jenson already!"

CHAPTER VI

A Ghostly Hand

CHET gulped. There was silence for a moment.

Then Frank said, "We don't have much time to solve this case. Professor Young said the Firebird will be launched in a couple of weeks."

"From the Space Flight Center," Joe added. "Maybe Dad's onto something down there. Let's call him in the morning and find out."

The boys went back to sleep and were up bright and early. After breakfast they found the maid cleaning their room, which prevented them from using the phone. They decided to use the club phone in the basement.

Frank and Joe squeezed into the booth and shut the door, while Chet stood guard outside in case any suspicious character tried to listen in. Joe dialed SFC-1234, the hot-line number Mr. Hardy had given them for top-secret phone calls.

A woman's voice answered. "This is Space

Flight Center Control," she said crisply. "Please identify yourself and the party you wish to speak to."

"Frank and Joe Hardy," Joe said. "We'd like to speak to Fenton Hardy."

"Oh, yes. I've been alerted that you have clearance. But Mr. Hardy isn't here."

"Can you tell us when he'll be back?" Joe asked.

"Sorry, but I don't know. Mr. Hardy wasn't in yesterday, either, and he hasn't phoned. Would you like to leave a message for him?"

"Yes. Please tell him to call us at the Aerospace Lab or at the Nassau Club in Princeton as soon as possible."

Leaving the phone booth, the Hardys told Chet they had failed to reach Mr. Hardy.

"Where do you suppose he's gone?" said Chet.

Frank shrugged. "He may be following up an outside clue or keeping someone under surveillance. Maybe that's why he hasn't had a chance to phone."

"So what do we do now?" Chet asked.

"Let's go over to the lab and start talking to people," Joe said.

"Okay, but how about stopping at the library on the way?" Frank suggested. "I'd like to bone up a little on Australia. When Professor Young was telling us about Woomera yesterday, I realized how little I know about that whole continent."

"Same here," said Joe. "I guess we could all do with a quick fill-in on the scene down under. Who knows, it might even suggest another angle on the case to us!"

The three set out across the campus, passing students and professors on the way.

The university library was a stone building, three stories high. At the desk inside, Frank asked where they could find books about Australia. "On C Floor," an assistant told him. "Three stories down. You can take the stairs or the elevator."

"I don't know about you," Chet declared, "but I'll ride."

The Hardys followed him into the elevator, and Frank pressed the button. The doors closed, and they descended to the bottom floor, where a wall chart guided them to the left. Following the numbers that marked the shelves, they came to the section on Australia.

Each of the boys grabbed an armful of books, which he carried to a large circular table. They sat down and began to turn the pages, flipping through to the chapters and illustrations that interested them. Frank concentrated on geography and history, Joe and Chet on the people.

"I'm going to see if I can find something specific on Woomera," Joe said finally and stood up. He returned his stack of books to their places. Then he scanned those on the shelf beneath. As he reached for one, a ghostly hand appeared from the opposite side! It clamped around Joe's wrist and held tight!

Startled, the younger Hardy boy pushed a big volume out of the way with his free hand and looked through the opening. A young man grinned at him.

"Smoky Rinaldo!" Joe exploded.

"I couldn't resist it," Smoky said. "I'm a great practical joker, you know."

"Some joke," Joe grumbled. "You scared me half to death."

"I didn't mean to," Smoky said. "Sorry."

"What are you doing here anyway?" Joe asked. "I thought you wanted to get enough sleep to be fresh for your exam?"

"I woke up early so I came here to do some research. By the way, you're being watched."

"What?"

Smoky jerked a thumb in the direction behind Joe, who whirled around in time to spot an indistinct figure sneaking furtively between the stacks.

"I didn't get a good look at him," Smoky said, "but he seemed to be eavesdropping on you before, when you all sat at the table."

"I'm going after him!" Joe decided. "Want to come?"

"Sure thing."

Smoky and Joe met at the end of the stack. There was no time to alert Frank and Chet, since the man was hastening toward the exit.

Joe saw a ray of light reflected by tinted glasses. It was the man who had been shadowing them at the lab! He darted into the elevator and pushed the button. Joe and Smoky ran after him. He glowered savagely as they drew near, and then the elevator doors closed in their faces. The boys ran around to the stairs and took two steps at a time to the main floor, where they almost bumped into Professor Young!

"It's lucky you're here, professor," Joe blurted, and quickly described their pursuit of the bearded man with the tinted glasses.

"I saw him!" Young declared. "He got out of the elevator and went up to the next floor. You may be able to catch him!"

The boys rushed up, found no one on the second floor, and continued to the top. There was no sign of the man anywhere! Joe and Smoky asked a group of students if they had seen him. No one had.

"He must have gone down the back stairs," said a girl.

The boys returned to the ground floor. Young was still there and told them he had been watching the main staircase. "I was ready to call for help if the man appeared, but he didn't."

"He probably took the back staircase," Joe said.

"Too bad," Young said. "Well, I hope you catch him next time. I'll keep an eye open and have him arrested if he shows up at the lab again.

By the way, he apparently got in yesterday by flashing someone else's pass. An employee reported that his was stolen. But now that everyone's alerted, the fellow won't be able to pull the same trick twice."

Young walked off to work in the card-index file, and Smoky said he had to get going, too. He returned to the bookstack he had been examining before, while Joe went to question the attendant at the door.

"A man with tinted glasses and a beard?" the fellow said. "Yes, he walked out a few minutes ago."

"Thank you," Joe said. Disappointed, he joined Frank and Chet and told them about his unsuccessful pursuit.

"Don't worry. I'm sure we'll see our shadow again," Frank muttered. "Meanwhile we looked at all the books, including the one you pulled halfway off the shelf. We didn't find anything interesting on Woomera, so let's get over to the lab and start working."

The trio spent the rest of the week questioning employees and students at the lab, searching files and records, and investigating Dr. Jenson's background and family. Not a single clue turned up.

As they were painstakingly searching the scientist's desk, Frank noticed a lightning bolt engraved on one side. He asked Professor Young about it.

"That's Adrian's unofficial trademark," Young

told them. "The staff claims he solves problems with lightning speed, and one of the fellows marked his desk one day after Adrian helped him out on a critical project."

On Sunday night the phone rang as the boys were getting ready for bed. Frank lifted the receiver. "It's Dad," he called out. Joe and Chet joined him at the instrument and filled the elder Hardy in on what they had done in Princeton.

"I'm still investigating people at the Space Flight Center," Fenton Hardy said. "Director Henry Mason is afraid that an attempt may be made to destroy the rocket on its pad. I joined the work crew in disguise and spent two days at the launch site. However, so far I'm up against a stone wall."

"Will you stay there until the launching?" Frank asked.

"Yes, I think so. It will take a lot more leg work to uncover a lead. Also, I'm setting up a brand-new security system for the launching. It's of vital importance that nothing go wrong."

"What do you suggest we do?" Frank asked. "We've talked to everyone in the lab and nothing has turned up."

His father was thoughtful for a moment, then said, "I think your best bet is to go to Australia!"

CHAPTER VII

Radioactive Evidence

"AUSTRALIA!" Frank exclaimed.

"Yes. Tell Professor Young I want you to try to pick up Jenson's trail in Sydney. A room was booked for him at the Australian Arms Hotel, but apparently he never checked in."

"Okay, Dad. We'll go as soon as we can."

"And another thing. Try to shake your shadow. He worries me. He obviously knows you're investigating the case and follows you wherever you go."

"We'll get rid of him on the way home," Frank promised and hung up.

"Do you think Young will let me go along?" Chet asked apprehensively.

"We'll ask him," Frank said and called the professor's home. He told Young about the conversation with his father and the detective's suggestion.

"That's a good idea," Young agreed. "Your father is right. You're being watched here. So far I haven't been able to find out anything about your shadow, and it's probably best if you leave Princeton without returning to the lab. Take a roundabout route and make sure you're not being tailed."

"Will do," Frank said. "If I can't get plane reservations for tomorrow or Tuesday, I'll call you back. Can we take Chet with us?"

Young hesitated. "I'm responsible for the expenses in this case, Frank. I can't really make a requisition for three people without a pressing reason."

"I understand," Frank said, disappointed.

Chet, who had overheard the conversation, looked crestfallen. After Frank hung up, he patted his friend on the back. "Don't feel bad, Chet. We might be back sooner than you think."

"Feel bad!" Chet said. "I feel worse! I would love to see the kangaroos and the Great Barrier Reef. Just think of skin diving in the coral reef, more than a thousand miles of it! And fish in all colors of the rainbow——"

"Listen, we're not going sightseeing. We have a mystery to solve," Joe put in. "Now I'd better call the airline and make reservations."

Frank and Joe booked a flight to Sydney on Tuesday. Early Monday morning the boys left the Nassau Club and drove home, making sure they were not followed.

"The coast is clear," Joe reported. "No one is behind us."

They were not far out of Princeton, however, when Chet noticed a black limousine that seemed to keep them in sight. When Frank stepped on the gas, the driver of the limousine followed suit.

"You'll have to get off this road to lose him," Joe said to his brother. But before Frank had a chance to do this, the limousine pulled nearly abreast of them. The driver honked his horn and motioned for them to pull to the side.

"Make a run for it!" Joe advised and Frank pressed the accelerator to the floor.

Another car drove between the limousine and the Hardys. Their pursuer swerved to the left, increased the speed of his powerful V-8 engine, and passed the second vehicle. He inched up to the Hardys and proceeded to cut them off!

Frank noticed the legend on the limousine's side: PRINCETON AEROSPACE LABORATORY, as he wrenched the wheel desperately to avoid a crash. With split-second timing he turned to the right, past the front fender of the limousine, careened off the highway into a rest area, and skidded halfway around before coming to a stop in a cloud of dust.

The limousine jolted after him and its driver braked to a halt. He bent his head and seemed to be searching for something in the seat beside him. Neither Frank nor Joe got a good look at him, but they wasted no time. They leaped from their car and wrenched open the door of the limousine. In a split second they collared the man and wrestled him out.

"Hey, fellows, wait a minute!" the driver pleaded. *He was Smoky Rinaldo!*

Frank dropped Smoky's arm. "You nearly caused a crack-up!" he said angrily.

"Is this another one of your practical jokes?" Joe almost shouted.

"Of course not," Smoky said. "But I had to catch you, and you ignored the horn when I tried to flag you down. You wouldn't stop, so I had to make you!"

"We thought you were the guy who followed us all over Princeton," Joe said, his anger cooling.

"I assumed you'd recognize me."

"With that goofy cap pulled down over your face?"

"Anyway, I didn't mean to cause an accident," Smoky went on. "I thought I could detour you into the rest area by cutting you off."

"What did you want to stop us for?" asked Chet, who had joined the boys.

Smoky held up his hand and revealed a metal flask with Dr. Jenson's name on it. "Here, look at this!"

"What about it?" Frank asked.

"It's radioactive!" Smoky asserted.

Chet retreated hurriedly. "It might explode!"

"Radioactive material doesn't just explode," Frank calmed him. "It takes a triggering device to start a chain reaction."

Smoky swung his flask by its heavy top. "No fear of that. It's not even radioactive enough to kill a cockroach."

Frank was getting irritated. "Did you chase us all the way from Princeton to tell us that?"

"No. I wanted you to know that I think Dr. Jenson was up to something."

"Why?"

"Because I found this flask in one of the file cabinets. I was digging in some records and ran across the flask in the back of the bottom drawer. It's against regulations for anyone to take anything radioactive out of the lab."

Smoky explained that the steel flasks were used to hold nuclear materials during experiments. When the experiment ended, the scientist conducting it was supposed to send his flasks to a storeroom lined with lead, where they would be decontaminated.

"Dr. Jenson took this one and hid it in the file," Smoky concluded. "He shouldn't have done that."

"Did he ever break the rules before?" Joe asked.

"I have no idea."

"Did you tell Professor Young about it?"

"Sure. Right away."

"What did he say?"

"He found it very odd and called you at the

Nassau Club. He was informed that you had just left. Since he didn't know what arrangements you had made and whether you would go home before you left for Australia, he asked me to try to catch up with you. He also gave me a photo of Jenson for you. So I drove in the direction of Bayport. I figured I'd go down the highway for a while, and sure enough, I saw your car."

Frank was thoughtful. "This is odd. I'm glad you caught us, Smoky."

"One thing bothers me," Joe said. "We searched all the files in his office and the flask was not there then."

"It wasn't in his office. It was in the record room." Smoky said. "In one of the general files that a number of people use. But it was Jenson's flask, all right, none of the others have any occasion to handle radioactive materials." He looked at the three boys. "Now you're not mad any more that I cut you off?"

"Of course not. You had no choice," Frank told him.

"Okay. I'll head back then. And good luck to you. I hope you find Dr. Jenson!" Smoky got into the limousine and drove off.

Frank, Joe, and Chet resumed their trip to Bayport and discussed the latest development.

"How about that!" Chet said. "I wonder why Jenson hid that radioactive flask in the general file?"

"Maybe he was going to smuggle it out of the lab," Joe suggested, "to hand it over to someone on the outside. The more I think about it, the more I'm convinced that he wasn't kidnapped by foreign agents after all. He made a deal with them!"

Frank was doubtful. "What could anybody do with a radioactive flask?"

"I don't know. They might analyze the atomic formula from the stuff in the flask," Joe guessed.

"Okay," Frank gave in. "But where does that leave the warning message Smoky found under the blotter on Jenson's desk?"

"Jenson himself might have planted it there to throw people off his trail," Chet said.

"I don't know," Frank mused. "Suppose his kidnappers did it to mislead us after they grabbed him? And, frankly, I have my doubts about Smoky. He found the note and the bottle. Yet, Young assured us that Jenson's desk was searched. How do we know that Smoky didn't plant the stuff?"

"Aw, Frank," Chet said impulsively, "Smoky's a nice guy. He wouldn't do anything like that."

"Frank's right," Joe said. "We can't take anything for granted, not even that Smoky is a nice guy."

Chet sighed. "I don't know what to think any more. I give up."

"Let's call Dad before we leave and ask him to

check out Smoky," Joe said. "And we'll call Professor Young to make sure he sent Smoky after us."

Some time later the trio rolled into Bayport. The Hardys dropped Chet at the Morton farm on the outskirts of town, then continued to their house, where they were welcomed by their mother and aunt.

"I'm so glad you're back!" Mrs. Hardy said, giving them each a hug.

"Not for long," Frank told her.

"What do you mean?"

"We're leaving for Australia tomorrow!"

"Australia? Hmph, next thing you'll be taking off for Mars," Aunt Gertrude grumbled. "Now tell us what this is all about."

The boys did, and Gertrude Hardy frowned. "Do you suppose this missing scientist could have been captured by headhunters?"

"I doubt it," said Frank, keeping a straight face. "The Australian abos aren't headhunters, Aunty, and they don't run wild in Sydney."

"I know that," Miss Hardy snapped. "You didn't say he disappeared in Sydney."

"Well, that's where his trail ends, anyhow." Frank grinned and turned to his brother. "I'm going to call Professor Young."

"Good idea," Joe said. "I'll come with you."

They called Princeton, and the professor verified what Smoky had told them. "We didn't check that file because Dr. Jenson seldom used it," he said. "I'm sure it was his flask, though, because he wrote his name on it, and I know his handwriting. When are you leaving?"

"Tomorrow," Frank said. "We'll get in touch with you when we find a lead."

When Frank put the receiver back into the cradle, Joe said, "While you're at it, would you call Mr. Ponsley? We'll have to tell him that we can't work for him."

"Sure." Frank dialed the man's number. "This is Frank Hardy," he said a few seconds later. "I'm sorry we can't take the Moran assignment, but we're involved in our father's case and have to leave the country."

Ponsley was unhappy. "That is disappointing news. I was counting on you to locate Michael," he said. "Well, I'll have to get another detective. I need one now more than ever, because I have a new clue!"

CHAPTER VIII

Danger in the Surf

FRANK started to ask what the new clue was, but a loud click at the other end of the line told him that the man had hung up.

"Mr. Ponsley says he has a new lead on Mike Moran," Frank said to Joe.

"What is it?"

"Don't know. He didn't tell me. Anyhow, it doesn't matter. We're tied up with the Jenson investigation. Somebody else will have to find Mike, wherever he is."

Early next morning the boys packed their bags and were just about ready to depart for the airport, when Chet arrived in his jalopy.

"Guess what!" he called out, bubbling over with excitement.

"What?" Frank asked.

"I won first prize in my category of the science competition, fifteen hundred dollars in cash!"

"Wow, that's great, Chet!" Joe exclaimed. "Have you decided what to do with it yet?"

"Sure! I'll go to Australia with you guys, of course!" Chet said. "I already called the airline. They had a vacant seat on your plane, so I packed my bags and came over here pronto!"

"That's terrific!" Frank said. "I'm glad you can come with us."

"So am I," Joe added. "And now we'd better leave so we don't miss our flight."

The boys said good-by to Mrs. Hardy and Aunt Gertrude and drove to the Bayport airfield, where they parked their car in an overnight lot. They took a plane to New York and transferred at Kennedy Airport to a jumbo jet for Sydney, Australia.

Soon they had settled into their seats at the rear of the plane. Chet sat at the window, Frank in the middle, and Joe on the aisle. Frank took a map of the Pacific from a folder provided by the airline and began to plot their route.

"We'll touch down at Los Angeles and Honolulu," he informed his companions. "From there it's nonstop to Sydney."

The plane took off. Suddenly a flash of red caught Joe's eye. A stout man was napping on the other side of the aisle, a few rows in front of the boys. The color came from a large ruby ring he wore.

Joe stood up to see better. "That's Ponsley!" he exclaimed.

Frank picked up the map spread across his knees and got up, too. He looked where his brother was pointing. "It sure is, Joe. What's he doing here?"

"Maybe he's tailing us," Chet guessed.

"Well, if he is, he's not very good at it," Joe replied. "He's asleep, and that giant ruby is a dead giveaway. Let's wake him up."

"Not me," Chet said hastily. "I'll stay in this seat until we land!"

Leaving their friend, Frank and Joe walked up the aisle. Joe nudged their portly acquaintance with his elbow.

Ponsley stirred, yawned, opened his eyes, and stared at the Hardys. He looked startled as he recognized them.

"Are you following us?" Joe demanded.

"Of course not," Ponsley replied.

"How come you're on this plane, then?" Frank asked.

"Senator Moran had a tip from a friend who just returned from abroad," Ponsley explained. "The man said he recognized Michael in a newspaper photograph of a soccer game in Sydney. The senator didn't give me time to find another detective. He told me to go to Australia myself, so I caught this plane and here I am."

"Quite a coincidence," Frank commented.

"That's right," Ponsley challenged. "What are *you* doing on this plane?"

"I told you we had to leave the country," Frank pointed out. "Our investigation led us to Sydney."

Ponsley beamed and gestured with his hand, causing his ruby ring to throw off rays of deep red. "Wonderful!" he exclaimed. "Both investigations will take place in Sydney. You can work on them at the same time!"

The Hardys talked it over and concurred that they might handle the two cases while they were in Australia.

"That's okay," Frank told Ponsley, "but our assignment comes first. We can't let the search for Mike Moran get in the way of that."

"All right," Ponsley said. "I'm glad you'll help me. After all, I really am not a detective!"

The Hardys returned to their seats and informed Chet about their conversation with Ponsley. Then they settled back for the rest of the flight to Los Angeles, where some passengers got off, others got on, and the jet became airborne again. The boys napped as it crossed the California coastline and headed out over the Pacific. Finally the Hawaiian Islands came into view, and soon they landed in Honolulu.

The captain's voice came over the intercom. "Please disembark. There will be a delay because of a technical problem."

Everybody went down the steps and into the terminal, where a stewardess informed them that the delay would last overnight. "A bus is ready to take you all to a hotel on Waikiki Beach," she said. "We'll continue the flight in the morning."

The boys and Ponsley boarded the bus with the other passengers and an hour later they had checked in at a luxurious hotel. From their window, the three Bayporters could see the broad band of white sand where the waters of the Pacific lapped ashore. White foam formed where the breakers rolled in. Surfboard riders tried to keep their footing on huge swells that carried them forward at express-train speeds, and most fell into the water. The rest glided triumphantly to the beach.

"What say we try it, too?" Joe asked.

"Affirmative," Frank replied.

"I'll show you how to ride a surfboard!" Chet boasted. "Lead me to it!"

They called Ponsley and asked him if he wanted to join them.

"No thanks," he replied. "I'll take a walk instead."

Leaving him in the hotel, the boys went to the bathhouse, rented swim trunks, and toted surfboards into the water. They pushed through the shallow waves and reached the point far out where breakers began to form.

"Last one in gets the booby prize!" Chet shouted gleefully, as he climbed up and balanced himself with his arms stretched out. A breaker caught hold of his board and sent it flying toward the beach.

Frank and Joe followed on either side. The

three made long curves up and down over the ocean swells, and they leaned to one side or the other to compensate for the tilt of their boards. Sunlight gleamed off the water and the wind blew spray into their faces.

Chet had a lead at the start, but Frank and Joe skillfully maneuvered over the turbulent breakers until they were zooming along just behind him.

Then a wave cutting across the breakers at an angle struck Chet's surfboard, knocking it around. The heavy impact caused him to lose his footing and he tumbled into the water. His crazily floating board whacked him on the side of the head and he sank out of sight!

Frank dived from his own board into the water in Chet's direction, and Joe came headlong after him. They groped underwater as long as they could hold their breaths. Forced to surface, the Hardys gulped air and looked around frantically. Chet's head bobbed up near Joe. His eyes were closed, and his body limp. Presently he slipped below the surface again!

"He's out cold!" Frank yelled. "Grab him before he disappears!"

Joe did a seal flip that took him arching from the surface down into the depths, where he spotted Chet being dragged toward the open sea by a strong undertow. Using the breaststroke and kicking his feet hard, Joe reached his friend and pushed him to the surface. Frank splashed over, crooked an elbow under Chet's chin, and swam on his back in the direction of the shore. Joe, who surfaced beside them, gave Frank a hand with his burden. As they touched the sand in the shallow water, Chet came to. The three stumbled onto the beach and sat down, gasping for breath.

A lifeguard jogged across the sand. "That was a great rescue," he complimented the Hardys. "I didn't come in because I could see you had the situation under control." He turned to Chet. "How do you feel?"

Chet rubbed his head. "Okay, I guess," he mumbled. "But I sure have a powerful headache. I'm going back to the hotel. Besides, I'm nauseated from swallowing half the Pacific."

He got to his feet and walked off. Frank and Joe went with him. They insisted that he see the hotel doctor, whose prognosis was that Chet would be fit again after a night's sleep. The diagnosis was correct. Chet woke up in the morning with nothing more than tenderness on the side of his head.

After breakfast the bus took all the passengers back to the airport, and soon they were on their way again. They flew southwest across what seemed to be an endless expanse of ocean before Samoa came into view. The boys talked to Ponsley for a while, then went back to their seats to read.

They stopped when the stewardess served their meals. Chet ravenously dug into everything that was put in front of him, looking blissful.

"Chet, there's nothing like chow to bring you back to normal," Frank declared.

"Lucky the airline doesn't have to feed you every day," Joe needled him. "It would go broke."

Chet downed the last mouthful of cherry pie. "That'll hold me for a while," he predicted.

The stewardess removed the trays and the boys dozed off until the plane ran into turbulence and began to wobble.

Chet opened his eyes, slumped in his seat, and placed a hand on his belt buckle. "I don't feel so good," he confessed.

As the turbulence increased, the plane bounced up and down. Chet turned pale. His freckles stood out and his eyes bulged. "What's happening?" he muttered fearfully.

"We're in the jetstream, that's all," Frank reassured him. "We'll soon be out of it."

Suddenly the plane flew into a downdraft and dropped a number of feet.

"We're gonna crash!" Chet cried. Desperately he clawed the life jacket from under his seat, slipped it on, and pulled the strings, triggering the inflation mechanism. The life jacket ballooned out, pinning Chet between the seats.

A stewardess rushed up. "Sir, what are you doing?" she demanded.

Chet closed his eyes and gasped. "If we survive the crash, we'll all drown!"

CHAPTER IX

The Porter's Clue

"NONSENSE!" the stewardess retorted sternly. "We are not going to crash!"

Chet opened one eye. "We aren't?"

"Certainly not. Turbulence in the air is routine! You are disturbing the other passengers."

Frank hastily assured her that he and Joe would take care of the situation. The stewardess thanked him and moved toward the cockpit. By now the jet was flying steadily on course. Frank let the air out of the life jacket, helped Chet wriggle out of it, and stowed it under the seat.

Chet swallowed hard and looked remorseful. "I thought we'd crash for sure," he said.

"Forget it," Joe said. "No harm done."

"Get ready for Australia, Chet," Frank advised.

The freckle-faced youth regained his composure. His broad grin returned. "Kangaroos! Boomerangs! I can't wait!"

Finally they could see the coastline of Australia as the plane thundered down over Port Jackson, a large bay with long watery indentations into the land. Sydney Harbor came into view, spanned by a long suspension bridge.

"When we were reading up on Australia," Joe said, "I remember one of the books said the people in Sydney call that bridge 'the coathanger.'"

The boys could see big ocean-going ships tied up at the docks, and clusters of tall buildings. The city and its suburbs lay spread out below them in a pattern of streets, squares, and parks, illuminated by the evening sun.

The plane landed at the airport. After getting through customs, the boys and Ponsley took a taxi to their hotel. They had booked rooms at the Australian Arms, where Dr. Jenson had also made a reservation before he disappeared.

"May as well start our detective work right now," Frank decided.

As they got out of their taxi, he showed the hotel porter photos of Dr. Jenson and Mike Moran.

"Recognize these people?" Frank queried.

The porter studied the faces and shook his head. "I've never seen either of them," he declared.

They made the same inquiry at the hotel desk, but to no avail. During dinner, they discussed how they should proceed.

"We ought to check with police headquarters

first thing in the morning," Frank decided. "By now they may have some news on Dr. Jenson, and they may know something about Mike Moran, too."

"I'm going with you," Ponsley declared.

"Good. We'll meet for breakfast at eight," Frank said; then they retired for the night.

The following morning the Hardys got up bright and early. Chet did not feel well and decided to sleep a little longer.

"We'll see you when we come back," Joe told him, then he and Frank met Ponsley in the cafeteria. They had a quick breakfast and an hour later took a taxi to police headquarters. Here they explained their mission to a sergeant on duty.

"You'll have to talk to Inspector Morell," the sergeant replied. "He's in charge of the search for that missing Yank scientist. But he's not here right now. Should be back in half an hour."

"Okay, we'll talk to him later." Frank added that they were also trying to trace another missing American, named Michael Moran, whose face had been spotted in a Sydney newspaper photo.

"Hmm." The sergeant rubbed his jaw thoughtfully. "We don't keep tabs on all the tourists who come here—unless they get in trouble, of course. Let me just check with our Criminal Records Office."

He picked up the phone, dialed, and conversed for a few minutes. Then he hung up with a grin.

"You're in luck, mates. Our computer turned up his name straightaway. He's listed as a witness to an auto accident about a month ago. Gave his address as Flynn's Guesthouse on St. James Road."

The boys and Ponsley thanked the sergeant and took another cab to the guesthouse on St. James Road. They were disappointed, however, when the owner informed them that Mike Moran had departed about three weeks before, saying only that he was leaving town.

"So Moran's trail ends right here," Joe said glumly.

"And we haven't even picked up Jenson's yet," Frank added.

"What'll we do now, go around with the photographs?" Ponsley asked.

"Right. Let's start here," Joe said. He showed the owner Jenson's picture, but the man told them he had never seen the American before. Then the group walked out into the street. The boys returned to police headquarters while Ponsley took a taxi to their hotel.

After the Hardys had introduced themselves to Inspector Morell, he said, "I was just about to call Professor Young at the Aerospace Lab. We have traced Dr. Jenson to a shabby place on Sixteen Wallaby Drive. There was a fire there recently in the lobby that destroyed the hotel register and forced the owner to close for a while. That's why it took so long to track Jenson down."

The boys noted the address and thanked Inspector Morell. Then they took a taxi to Wallaby Drive. It was in a rundown section of town and number 16 looked like a decrepit apartment building. Only a small faded sign over the door indicated that it was a hotel. The blackened woodwork around the doors and windows showed signs of a recent blaze.

"I wonder if that fire the inspector mentioned was an arson job," Frank mused.

"That's an idea," Joe said. "Maybe someone was trying to keep the police from finding out Jenson stayed there."

The boys went inside. Two men stood behind the desk in the empty hallway that now served as a lobby. One was the manager, the other had "porter" stitched on the breast pocket of his threadbare jacket.

When Frank inquired about Jenson, the manager looked annoyed. "I've already told the police all I know," he said curtly. "Dr. Jenson left with two Americans the day after he checked in and I never heard from him again."

"Did he pay his bill?" Joe inquired.

"The men did."

"Why not Dr. Jenson himself?"

"How do I know?" the manager asked gruffly.

There was a brief silence before Frank said, "Were you afraid of trouble if you told the police too much about Jenson?"

The man's face turned sullen. "Whatever gave you that idea?"

"You had a fire here, for one thing. And maybe you received some threats."

"I dunno what you're talking about."

Frank flashed a twenty dollar bill. "Try to remember. Was there anything even the slightest bit unusual about Jenson's departure?"

The manager hesitated, obviously tempted. He glanced furtively around, then took the money and quickly put it in his wallet. "Well, Jenson seemed drunk," he told the boys. "He was sort of slumped between these two blokes. They paid and led him outside, then pushed him into a car and drove off."

"Do you think he was forced to go with them?"

"I dunno. I think he was drunk."

"Can we look in his room for a clue?" Joe asked. "We must find him!"

"Go ahead. I haven't rented it since." The manager gave him the key and the boys went into Jenson's room.

Joe looked into the closet while Frank went through the bureau drawers. They turned the wastebasket upside down, and lifted the mattress from the bed.

"Nothing here," said Joe, standing in the middle of the room and gazing around. His eyes fell on the door, which was covered with scratches and graffiti. Joe went over and bent down, staring at the bottom panel.

"Hey Frank, come here a minute!"

Frank looked at the initials and sentences

scribbled on the lower part of the door. "Graffiti," he said. "Courtesy of the hotel's high-class clientele."

"Look close," Joe advised. "See this sign?"

"A bolt of lightning!" Frank exclaimed. "The same as we saw on Dr. Jenson's desk!"

"Correct. And after it are the letters Al S. What do you think that means?"

"Maybe those are the initials of Dr. Jenson's kidnapper!" Frank said, excited. "Could be his name is Albert Smith."

"Or Alfred Scott, or a million other combinations," Joe commented.

Their enthusiasm diminished as they realized the number of possibilities. "There are too many names with those initials," Frank concluded. "We'll have to find Jenson to find out whom he meant."

"Let's think about it as we go back to our hotel," Joe suggested. "What say we walk instead of taking a cab?"

"Suits me," Frank agreed.

Before leaving, they wrote down their room number at the Australian Arms and asked the manager to call them if he remembered any other details. Then they walked toward the center of the city, which was not far, and found that Sydney was built on a number of hills. Rows of houses painted in bright colors lined the streets, and cars whizzed back and forth through narrow thoroughfares.

"Why do you think Jenson checked into that crummy hotel?" Joe asked his brother.

"Maybe he suspected he was being followed and wanted to hide," Frank replied.

"Or, if he's not on the level, perhaps he wanted to disappear and obscure his tracks," Joe concluded.

"I think he was kidnapped. I don't believe he was drunk when those guys took him out of the place," Frank said.

"You're probably right. Boy, these streets are all uphill or downhill," Joe said. "I'm getting tired!"

"Cheer up. We're coming close to level ground," Frank told him. He referred to Macquarie Street, where they saw the law courts before cutting over to George Street, the site of the magnificent Town Hall and St. Andrew's Cathedral.

They stepped off the curb and began to cross over to the cathedral, when a car swished around the corner and barreled straight at them at top speed!

Instinctively Frank and Joe whirled to leap back onto the sidewalk. The car followed them, heading them off. Again they raced into the street, hoping to make it to the other side. The car careened after them. It was a wild chase until Frank slipped and fell. The car hurtled straight at him!

Joe barely had time to shove his brother out of

the way. There was no chance to escape himself. He took a death-defying leap at the car, sprawling across the hood to avoid being run down!

The car zoomed past Frank, missing him by inches, and jolted over a patch of grass bordering the sidewalk. Joe was blocking the driver's view, but a sharp twist of the wheel sent the youth sliding off. He rolled over and over. Only the cushion of grass saved him from serious injury.

As Joe lay half-stunned, he caught a parting glimpse of the bearded driver, scowling at him through the open window as the car roared away. The man was wearing tinted glasses!

He continued up the street, rounded the corner, and vanished. Frank and Joe got to their feet, shaking their heads at their narrow escape. The few pedestrians ran to help, but nobody had caught the car's license number.

"Thanks for saving me, Joe," Frank puffed. "Are you okay?"

"Yeah, except that fall rattled my eyeteeth." The younger Hardy waited till they were alone again before adding, "Did you get a look at the driver?"

"No. Who was he?"

"The guy who shadowed us in Princeton!"

Frank gave a long whistle. "He followed us to Australia! How did he know we'd be here?"

"He didn't follow us to Bayport," Joe said. "And I watched on the way to the airport. No one was behind us."

Joe took a death-defying leap at the car.

"Maybe he overheard our telephone conversation with Professor Young," Frank said. "Or he could have overheard Young and Smoky talking when the professor told Smoky to catch us before we left for Australia."

"Or Smoky could have told him!" Joe added.

"Right. Once he knew we were coming here, all he had to do was check with the airlines and take an earlier flight or even get on the same plane with us in disguise!"

"This is getting serious," Joe said. "The guy's out to kill us. If we don't crack this case soon, he may succeed!"

Taking various detours, the boys returned to the Australian Arms Hotel. When they arrived in their room, Chet was still sleeping. Frank woke him up and told him what had happened. He was just about finished when the telephone rang. Joe picked it up.

He heard a muffled voice say, "If you want information on Dr. Jenson, be at the Botany Bay Coffeehouse in King's Cross in one hour!"

CHAPTER X

A Spy in the Crowd

"Who are you and how will we know you?" Joe asked.

"I'll know you, and that's all that matters." The phone went dead. Joe relayed the message to Frank and Chet.

"Sounds like a trap," he added. "Probably another one of our shadow's tricks."

"I think we should chance it," Frank said. "We don't have any other leads in the case."

There was a knock on the door. Frank walked over to it and asked, "Who is it?"

"Ponsley." It was their friend's familiar voice. Frank let him in and brought him up-to-date on the latest news.

"Suppose," Ponsley said, "I go along and trail behind you. If the crooks gang up on you, I'll call for help."

"Great idea!" Joe said. "How about you, Chet?"

Chet was awake by now, and felt better. "Of course, I'm coming, too," he said.

"Wait a minute," Frank objected. "I think it will be better if we split forces. You stay here, Chet, and if we're not back in an hour, alert the police. If you come along, they might get all of us and no one would know we're missing."

"Okay," Chet agreed readily. The thought of being caught did not appeal to him at all. Ponsley looked a bit doubtful, too, but did not retract his offer.

The three left, and just before the hour was up, the Hardys entered the Botany Bay Coffeehouse, a popular gathering place for Australians of all types from Sydney businessmen to shop girls, office workers, and people in the arts. Like most Aussies, they seemed to have a sun-tanned breezy look about them that the boys liked. Over coffee and tea, a babble of cheerful voices could be heard.

Frank and Joe sat down at a table in a corner and ordered coffee. They surveyed the room without spotting a familiar face until Ponsley walked in. He took a table on the opposite side of the room, winked to indicate that he was keeping them under surveillance, and told a waitress to bring him a pot of tea.

"You're right on time," a voice said at Frank's elbow. "You must be interested."

It was the porter from the hotel Dr. Jenson had stayed in!

The man sat down and accepted a cup of coffee. "Look, mates," he said in a low tone, "I know about Dr. Jenson. I opened the door for him and the two blokes who were with him. I could tell from the look in his eyes that he was drugged. When they pushed him into the car, he began to struggle. I went out to see what was going on, and I heard him mutter something."

"What was it?" Frank asked eagerly.

"He said 'Alice Springs' just before they slammed the door and drove off!"

"Why didn't you mention this before?" Joe inquired.

"I told the manager. He said he didn't want any trouble, and that I might have made a mistake. That's why I couldn't tell you at the hotel that I recognized Jenson's photo. After thinking it over, I thought you should know that he wasn't drunk. He was drugged!"

The porter drained his coffee cup and, after accepting some money from Frank in payment for his information, he rose to his feet. He was due back at the hotel and strode off. The Hardys stared at each other in consternation.

Joe broke the silence. "Now we know what Al S stands for. Alice Springs! She must be the leader of the kidnap gang. Maybe she's holding Jenson a prisoner right now here in Sydney!"

"Joe, Alice Springs isn't a person. It's a place— a town way off in the Outback in the middle of the country. Jenson left a message saying that he was taken to Alice Springs!" Frank said.

Joe jumped up from his chair. "This is a hot clue, Frank! We'll have to go to Alice Springs!"

"That's the way I see it. We'd better get out there in a hurry."

Ponsley left his table and joined them. "Who was that fellow and what did he say?"

Frank told him and repeated the conversation.

"Where is Alice Springs?" Ponsley asked.

"Let's find out," Frank suggested and pulled a map of Sydney from his pocket that showed all of Australia on the reverse side. He spread it flat on the table, running a fingertip from Sydney west across New South Wales into South Australia, and then up into the Northern Territory. His finger stopped almost exactly in the center of the continent, where the words "Alice Springs" were printed in black letters.

They could tell from the relief coloring that the town nestled in the foothills of the Macdonnell Ranges, at a point where a number of streams converged. The illustrations indicated that all around Alice Springs there were homesteads, mines, and cattle ranches.

Ponsley was aghast. "Impossible!" he cried, thumping the table with his fist until the ruby on his finger seemed to be a streak of red in the air. "That town is over a thousand miles from here!"

"A long trip," Joe agreed.

"Too long!" Ponsley snapped. "You have to stay in Sydney and continue the search for Mike Moran!"

Frank shook his head. "Mike will have to wait," he said firmly. "Jenson comes first. Besides, Mike said he was leaving town. Chances are he's not in Sydney anyway."

Ponsley groused and grumbled, but finally gave in. "I'll go with you," he decided. "I'm not the detective around here. I need you boys to solve my mystery. I'd better stay with you so I can be sure you start looking for Mike the minute you find Jenson."

"Fair enough," Frank said and paid the bill. He asked the waitress about the nearest travel bureau, which happened to be around the corner.

The boys were unable to book a scheduled flight for the next day, but the clerk referred them to the pilot of a small private plane, who had just come in to pick up possible fares.

"I belong to the Royal Flying Doctor Service," the pilot told them. "The RFDS flies doctors, nurses, and medicine over the Outback wherever someone is ill or injured. Planes are the only way to get around quickly in that area."

"You must be like the bush pilots in Alaska," Joe surmised. "They cover a lot of territory."

"Quite similar," the pilot agreed. "Well, I operate out of Alice Springs and will be flying back there tomorrow morning. I'll be glad to take you."

"We'll need four seats," Frank said. "A friend of ours is coming, too."

"That's okay. I have enough room."

The boys thanked the man and left the travel agency. "What say we call Chet to tell him the latest news, and then see a few more of the sights on the way back to the hotel?" Frank suggested.

"Good idea," Joe and Ponsley agreed. They called from a public phone booth, then strolled along the Elizabeth Street shopping area, glancing at items in store windows and enjoying the bustle of the city. They paused at a fishmonger's barrow.

"Anything on the menu from the Great Barrier Reef?" Frank inquired.

"Too far away, mate," the man laughed. "My fish come from Ulladulla, down south of here. How about some tasty snapper or John Dory? Blimey, you'll find 'em delicious!"

"Okay, you've convinced us." Joe chuckled.

They all bought fish sandwiches and munched them hungrily. Then they deposited their paper napkins in a trash bin and walked on.

Suddenly Frank spotted someone watching them from the opposite side of the street. The older Hardy boy recognized the man with the beard and the tinted glasses!

"Our shadow from Princeton!" he told his companions.

"The guy who tried to run us down!" Joe exploded. "Let's get him!"

The boys turned and hastened to the corner to cross Elizabeth Street. Ponsley brought up the rear as fast as he could. But the light turned red just as they arrived at the intersection and the flow of traffic compelled them to wait. By the time they got across, they could barely glimpse their quarry almost a block away.

"He's heading toward the waterfront!" Frank cried.

The Hardys and Ponsley ran after him. A sign, HARBOUR BRIDGE, pointed the way to the busy eight-lane steel span connecting Sydney to the North Shore.

Presently they came to the dock area, where ocean liners and tramp freighters were tied up at the piers to disgorge and take on passengers and cargo. Across the waters of Sydney Cove on their right could be seen the dazzling new opera house, looking like a cluster of pointed white concrete sails.

As the boys slowed to get their bearings, they almost bumped into a sailor who was hurrying in the opposite direction.

"Sorry, mates! I didn't see you coming," he apologized.

"Did you happen to pass a bearded man with dark glasses?" Frank asked him.

The sailor shoved back his cap and scratched

his head. "Don't recall noticing anyone like that," he replied, "but if you want to come back to me ship for a minute, I'll find out if anyone saw him."

"That's mighty kind of you, but weren't you going the other way? We don't want to hold you up."

"That's all right, cobber. I was just going on shore leave. Nothing that urgent."

Ponsley sat down on a wooden bollard to catch his breath. "I need a breather after all that running," he said. "You two go on. I'll wait here."

The boys accompanied the sailor to his freighter, which was moored nearby. On its stern was the name *Sydney Cove*.

The sailor grinned. "Recognize that name?"

Frank and Joe shook their heads. "Should we?" the younger Hardy boy asked.

"Maybe not, seeing as 'ow you're Yanks. But there once was a ship called *Sydney Cove* that sank. Only three 'ands survived to tell the tale. So now some say every ship with that name is jinxed."

Frank laughed. "We don't believe in jinxes."

The sailor grinned. "Then you got nothin' to fear. Come on aboard. You can call me Salty, by the way. Everyone else does."

He led the way up the gangplank to the well deck, where the captain was giving orders to his bosun and deck hands. One of the men was attaching a huge bale to a cargo boom near the open hold.

"What're you doing back aboard, Salty?" the officer bellowed.

"Just 'elpin' out these two Yanks, sir. They're lookin' for a bearded man with dark glasses. Anyone see 'im go by?"

The skipper and crewmen, who had stopped work, shook their heads. The boys thanked them and left the ship. They saw Ponsley coming toward them across the dock.

"I've seen enough of Sydney," he declared. "I'm going back to the hotel. Want to share a taxi with me?"

"May as well," Frank answered. "Looks like we've lost that creep we were chasing."

As they turned to go, the freighter's cargo boom swung out over the side with a heavy bale in its cargo net. The net opened just above the three and the bale hurtled down on them!

CHAPTER XI

Chet's Clever Plan

FRANK caught a glimpse of the bale as it tumbled out of the cargo net. "Watch out!" he shouted.

Frank and Joe lunged into Ponsley, pushing him out of the way and knocking him over backwards. The three went down in a tangle of arms and legs as the heavy cargo slammed into the dock a few feet away from them!

The Hardys got up but Ponsley lay still. Joe leaned over and shook him by the shoulders. "Mr. Ponsley, are you all right?" he asked, worried.

Ponsley groaned and stirred feebly.

"He's stunned," Frank judged. "He'll come around in a minute."

Salty hurried down the ship's gangplank to join them. "Blimey, I'm sorry!" he panted. "Someone swung the ruddy boom too far out. The net's not supposed to open till the operator presses the button. I don't know what 'appened. That bale might've 'urt you somethin' terrible!"

"It would have squashed us like beetles," Frank said. "But we're okay."

Ponsley sat up and opened his eyes. "Speak for yourself!" he cried. "I can hardly see! Good heavens, I think I'm going blind!"

Joe noticed that Ponsley's spectacles had been knocked off when he fell. The younger Hardy picked up the gold pince-nez, made sure the lenses had not been broken, and placed them back on Ponsley's nose.

"How's that?" he asked.

Ponsley adjusted the glasses with his thumb and forefinger. "Why, I can see again!" he said, relieved.

"We're not hurt, Salty," Frank told the sailor. "But I don't want to be in the way the next time your cargo net goes haywire."

Salty nodded and went back to the ship. Since Ponsley was more determined than ever to return to the hotel, they took a taxi to the Australian Arms.

When they stepped into the Hardys' room, they found it empty!

"Where's Chet?" Joe wondered.

"We'd better find out—fast," Frank replied tensely as he called the hotel desk. The clerk denied any knowledge of Chet's whereabouts. "Perhaps he went out for a newspaper," the man suggested.

The Hardys and Ponsley waited for an hour to see if Chet would come back, but there was no sign of him. Finally Frank jumped to his feet. "Joe, what if Chet has been kidnapped?"

"A dreadful thought!" Ponsley interjected.

As they considered what to do next, a key scraped in the lock. Somebody was trying to get in without being heard!

"It may be Chet's kidnapper!" Frank whispered.

The Hardys tiptoed across the room and stationed themselves on each side of the door, waiting for it to open.

The knob turned and the door swung inward. The mysterious visitor stealthily entered the room.

"Chet!" Frank and Joe cried in unison.

Their rotund friend closed the door quietly. Placing a finger on his lips, he jerked his head in the direction of the window, and led them over to it. He motioned them to stand back so as not to be seen and pointed to a department store across the street.

Two men were standing in front of it, watching the hotel. Another joined them and pointed at the boys' window. He had a black beard and wore tinted glasses! When a policeman came along, the men pretended to look at the display of clothes behind the glass panels. When he had passed, they resumed their vigil.

Chet tugged Frank's sleeve and drew his friends away from the window. "I noticed them right after you left," he reported.

"Obviously they stayed here while Tinted Glasses shadowed us through Sydney," Joe said.

"Maybe we should call the police," Chet suggested.

Frank shook his head. "They can't arrest these guys just because they're standing down there watching us. Besides, Tinted-Glasses and his partners might not know where Jenson is. Their only job may be to keep us from finding him. If we get tied up in a hassle between these guys and the law, that may be just what they want. It'll keep us from looking for Jenson."

Turning to Chet, Frank explained the clue they had just received, which pointed to Alice Springs as the next focus of their search.

"Gosh, stop to think of it," Chet said, "those lookouts may even be trying to find Jenson themselves—by shadowing *us*!"

"That's possible." Frank agreed. "Either way, I think our best bet is to give 'em the slip."

"How?" asked Joe.

His brother turned back to their chubby pal. "Does the hotel have a rear door?"

"I checked that," Chet replied. "Two more guys are out there in the alley. They look like they're ready to jump us if we leave."

"The roof!" Joe said. "Maybe we can try that."

Chet shook his head. "I went up there. There's a lookout on the opposite building. He's watching the fire escape. And there's no other exit."

"Then we're trapped!" Ponsley exclaimed.

"We are," Chet agreed. "But I've worked out an escape route!"

"How?" Frank asked.

"Just grab an overnight bag with a change of clothes and come with me," Chet said mysteriously. "Hurry up!"

Ponsley went to his room and was back shortly. The boys had each packed a small bag and were ready. Chet motioned them out of the room and locked the door carefully. Then he led the way to the freight elevator. They took it down to the basement, and followed Chet to a storeroom.

A tradesman was lifting empty crates into a truck backed up to the exit.

"These are the friends I told you about," Chet addressed him. "Since we left our belongings in our room, you know we're not trying to gyp the hotel. We're coming back."

"Righto," the man replied. "You paid me. Now I'll carry out my part of the bargain. Get into the truck, all of you, and lie low."

Chet climbed into the vehicle and edged his way toward the cab. Ponsley came next, then Frank and Joe. They crouched down behind the load of empty crates and the driver slammed the tailgate up. Then he went around to the cab, started the engine, and slowly moved the truck away from the hotel.

Through a crack in the tailgate Frank could see the two men in the alley watching the back door of the hotel.

"We outsmarted them after all!" he said with a chuckle. "They'll be standing there forever!"

The driver took them to George Street, where he stopped and let them off. "This is as far as you go," he said. "Good-by and good luck!"

The boys jumped out and thanked the man, then the truck sped away.

"I saw the truck coming up to the back door when I was in the basement," Chet revealed. "I figured the driver might make a deal with me, and he did."

"Good thinking, Chet," Joe complimented him.

Chet looked pleased. "What next?" he asked.

After a council of war, they decided to go to the airport and spend the night at a motel. From there, they phoned Inspector Morell and asked him to have the bearded man and his cohorts picked up for questioning. But an hour later Morell called back to report failure. Apparently the crooks had discovered that the Hardy boys and their friends had gotten away, and had abandoned their stakeout of the hotel.

Early next morning, the Hardys, Chet, and Ponsley took off for Alice Springs. The green areas around Sydney disappeared, and they found themselves flying deep into the Outback, where sand and huge stones extended to the horizon on all sides. Clusters of rocks ballooned from the desert floor into fantastic shapes.

"If we were in the States," Frank said, "I'd guess we were over Death Valley."

"Or the Dakota Badlands," Joe added.

"Well, it's hot and dusty here, too," the pilot pointed out. "There aren't any rattlesnakes down below, but there are Australian brown snakes, which are nearly as deadly."

"You are not going to land, are you?" Ponsley asked, frightened.

The pilot laughed. "Don't worry. Landing in this part of the Outback is the last thing I want to do."

The plane crossed rivers where good farmland spread along the banks. Big cattle ranches occupied hundreds of square miles beyond the Macdonnell Ranges in Australia's Northern Territory. Finally they landed at Alice Springs, and the four Americans got out. They stretched their muscles, cramped after the long flight, paid the pilot, and took a bus into town.

They found Alice Springs crisscrossed by rows of hardy trees that managed to stay alive in the arid soil. The buildings were mostly small and roofed with tin. On Anzac Hill, a shining monument commemorated the Australians and New Zealanders who fell in two world wars.

The boys stopped at police headquarters and asked about Jenson and Mike Moran. The officer on duty could supply no information on either, but gave the boys a list of hotels and guest houses where they could inquire.

"Good thing this town isn't big," Frank said.

"We won't have too much trouble checking these out."

"Are they all within walking distance?" Chet asked.

Frank had obtained a map of Alice Springs at the airport and looked at it. "I don't know. Let's start here and work toward the periphery of the town."

Checking with various hotels on the way, the four walked through Gorey's Arcade, the shopping center of Alice Springs. They went along the streets past bars and hamburger joints, and noticed that many men wore cowboy hats, shirts, trousers, and boots. Some of the men were dark-skinned "abos."

"Those guys look like they came from Tombstone with Wyatt Earp after the gunfight at the O.K. Corral!" Chet commented.

"Except that none of them carry six-shooters," Frank added with a grin.

They came to a fenced-in enclosure where a competition was being held. Cowboys lined the rails, waiting for their turn to rope steer and ride bucking broncos. Three judges on a raised platform judged the performances and awarded prizes.

"A rodeo!" Joe exclaimed. "How about that!"

"Let's spread out and keep our eyes open," Frank suggested. "There's always an outside chance of spotting Mike or Dr. Jenson in the crowd. While we're at it, we can chat with people, too, and find out if anybody has noticed an American answering either description. We'll meet here in half an hour."

"Good idea," Joe said, and the four separated and began buttonholing cowboys and spectators for information on the two missing men. None of the Australians had heard of them.

They were on the way to their meeting place again when the main event of the rodeo began. A rider came out of a chute, like a streak of lightning, on a coal-black horse that leaped and twisted in a savage effort to throw the man off its back.

Chet was fascinated by the violence of horse and rider contending to see who would win.

"I could get a better view from that fence post over there," he thought and climbed up. Carefully he positioned himself on the small post. But he got so involved in the show that at one point he lost his balance and dropped into the enclosure.

Frank, who saw the incident from a short distance away, muttered something about Chet and his ideas. Then the bronco threw its rider and charged full-tilt at Chet, who had just gotten to his feet.

"Watch out!" Frank yelled.

CHAPTER XII

Kangaroo Confrontation

CHET froze as the black horse, glaring and snorting, galloped toward him with pounding hooves!

Frank moved like lightning. He snatched a lasso that had been used in the steer-roping competition and hurled the noose in a long flying arc.

As it settled over the horse's neck, he fastened the other end of the lariat to a fence post. The enraged animal was about to trample Chet when the rope tightened and brought it to a rearing halt in a cloud of dust!

Chet scrambled over the fence and fought for breath. "Frank," he puffed, "you're better than those TV cowboys any day!"

There were loud cheers and a round of applause for Frank's rescue. One of the contestants came up and spoke to him admiringly. "Good-oh, cobber! Your China would've ended up a proper mess if you hadn't come through with that rope trick!"

"China?" Frank looked puzzled. "Is that a word you cowboys use down under?"

The Aussie laughed. "It's good old cockney rhyming slang—'China plate' for 'mate.' And we're not cowboys down here, Yank. We're stockmen. My name's John Harris."

Shaking hands, Frank introduced himself and his companions. Together they watched the rest of the rodeo, and Harris captured first prize for broncobusting. He invited them to join in the horseback ride around the ring. Ponsley quickly refused, saying he would rather wait on the viewing stand. He climbed up the few steps and sat down in a chair vacated by one of the rodeo judges.

Harris brought up three mounts. Frank, Joe, and Chet climbed into the saddles and trotted in the procession around the enclosure. The Hardys, who had ridden horseback many times, guided their mounts with practiced skill.

Chet clutched the reins with one hand, waved the other, and shouted, "This is for me!" His horse, feeling the tug of the bridle, thought it was time to rear up on its hind legs. The movement alarmed Chet, who slackened his grip and let the horse have its head.

Finally the ride ended, the rodeo broke up, and the boys joined Ponsley for a walk back toward the center. They checked two more hotels without luck, then stopped at a luncheonette and ordered hamburgers.

Chet pitched into his enthusiastically. "Nothing like a horseback ride to set you up for chow."

Frank laughed. "Chet, who was in charge, you or the horse?"

"Maybe you'd like an encore," Joe needled him. "We can go back if you like."

"No, thanks," Chet said. "I showed the rodeo what I can do. That's enough for me."

Ponsley was becoming annoyed. "This trip has not been a success," he argued. "I'm sure Dr. Jenson isn't here, and neither is Mike Moran."

Frank munched a pickle. "We only have a few more places to check, and we never give up prematurely."

Just then John Harris walked into the luncheonette, recognized the Americans, and came to their table.

"Mind if I join you?" he asked.

"Of course not," Frank said, inviting him to sit down. Harris ordered a hamburger. While he ate, Frank told him they were looking for two missing Americans. "Got any suggestions?"

Harris looked thoughtful. "I overheard a Yank talking to someone right here in this luncheonette not too long ago. He mentioned Cutler Ranch, a cattle station up north, owned by Americans."

Frank showed him the photographs. "Was it either of these two men?"

Harris shrugged. "He had his back turned to me. I just remember the accent, since it's rare in these parts."

Frank exchanged glances with his brother.

"Worth a try," Joe agreed.

"It's a long ride up north, beyond McGrath Creek and the Sandover River." Harris warned. "So pick a car that gets a lot of miles to the gallon. You won't pass any petrol pumps on the way."

Finishing his hamburger, he said good-by and left. Joe seemed to be watching someone. Presently he got up and muttered, "Let's go!"

Frank and the others paid their bill and followed Joe outside. But they had gone scarcely a block when Joe suddenly whirled around. His three companions saw him grab a seedy stranger in a battered, greasy-looking felt hat, who had been walking several paces behind them.

"Why are you following us, mister?" the younger Hardy demanded angrily.

The stranger cringed when he saw the fighting look on Joe's face. "You've got me all wrong, mate," he mumbled. "I wasn't following nobody."

"Don't give me that! You were eavesdropping on everything we said back there in the restaurant."

"Well. . . ." The stranger hesitated nervously, then blurted, "I expect I did listen closer'n I should've done. But I was worried about what that stockman was telling you. Didn't know if I ought to warn you or not."

Joe frowned. "Warn us about what?"

"The Cutlers."

"What about them?" Frank demanded.

"They're strange blokes. From what I hear, they don't welcome visitors—especially visitors who ask questions."

"How come?" Joe pressed.

The seedy stranger shrugged. "All I know is what I've heard some of the abos hereabouts say."

"What do they say?"

"That they've seen nosy swagmen ride up to the Cutlers' cattle station, but they've never seen none of them ride away again!"

The four Americans stared at the seedy stranger uneasily. Before they could cross-examine him, he wriggled free of Joe's grasp and hurried off down the street.

"What did he mean by 'swagmen'?" Chet asked with a worried, wide-eyed look.

"Traveling cowhands, carrying their 'swag' or personal belongings in a blanket roll," Frank explained. "I remember that much from what I read about the Outback."

"They may be traveling cowhands," said Pons-ley, "but if what we just heard means anything, once they go nosing around the Cutlers' place, their travels come to a sudden end!"

Chet felt cold chills. "You really think the Cutlers polish off trespassers?"

"Suppose that guy was just trying to scare us off?" Joe suggested. "Suppose he doesn't want us to see something out there? Maybe Jenson is a prisoner at the Cutler Ranch and they don't want us to rescue him?"

Frank stood up. "It's still daylight. Let's go!"

Ponsley was against it. "I believe this will be another wild-goose chase," he protested.

"Mr. Ponsley, we can't stop now," Frank urged. "We know Americans took Jenson to Alice Springs. The Cutlers are Americans, and someone's trying to keep us away from their place. We have to see what's going on at the Cutler Ranch!"

"You can stay here until we get back," Joe proposed.

"No, no!" Ponsley objected. "I don't want to stay alone. I'll go with you!"

The group went to the only car-rental agency in town and selected a compact that gave them good mileage to the gallon.

"You're lucky," the agent told them. "We were all out of cars, but someone returned this one sooner than expected."

"Good," Frank said and paid for the rental. Then they drove north from Alice Springs with Joe at the wheel. The fertile region gave way to desert, after which signs of agriculture reappeared around McGrath Creek. They could see farmhouses with tall windmills pumping water from underground.

Soon the desert began again, and they were traveling a dusty road through desolate country marked by the bleached skeletons of horses and cows that had succumbed in the waterless waste.

"I believe we should pause for a rest," Ponsley finally said. "Let's stop here."

Joe pulled over to the side of the road, where a strange formation of huge rocks rose above the desert. They noticed that one of the rocks was covered with painted figures. A serpent wound its way in long sinuous coils up from the base of the cliff. On the left, an owl perched in a flutter of feathers, as if terrified by the snake. On the right, a kangaroo hopped fearfully out of the way. Above these animals, a medicine man wielded a magic wand to ward off the serpent's poison.

Chet scratched his head. "How did this guy and his pets get here?"

"The Aborigines painted them," Frank replied. "I read about their rock paintings when we were in Princeton. These could be hundreds of years old."

Ponsley nodded. "Terrific technique," he declared. "Compares favorably with modern art."

The four marveled at the figures done in white, black, brown, and dark red. At last, the boys sat down with their backs against the cliff. Ponsley, who complained about his stiff back, wandered away into the desert. A moment later he shouted frantically.

The boys scrambled to their feet and raced toward him, but stopped halfway, jarred by what they saw.

Their portly friend was confronted by a large kangaroo!

The animal stood on its hind legs with its heavy tail extended on the sand. Its fur was gray, shading to white underneath, and the tip of the tail was black. It held its small front paws up in the air and stared at Ponsley, who raised his hand in a frantic effort to frighten it off. His ruby ring glittered in the sun.

Suddenly the kangaroo began to hop toward him! The more Ponsley waved, the faster it bounded forward, its eyes fixed on his hand.

Frank recalled that kangaroos are attracted by bright objects. Obviously this one was after Ponsley's ruby ring!

"Stop waving!" the boy yelled, but Ponsley did not seem to hear him. He backed away from the kangaroo, turned frantically, and ran as fast as he could. The kangaroo also increased its speed, caught up with, and sprang at him in a high bound!

Ponsley's feet became entangled with one another, and he fell headlong into the sand. The kangaroo leaped clear over him! The boys yelled at the top of their lungs to frighten the creature, and, after landing on its strong hind legs, it hopped rapidly away into the distance.

The Hardys helped Ponsley up and brushed the sand off his suit. He was indignant about the kangaroo confrontation, and for the rest of the drive he kept insisting that they should never have ventured into the Outback.

They crossed the Sandover River and continued north until Frank spotted a large warning sign: CUTLER RANCH—KEEP OUT!

"Maybe we shouldn't drive in there," Chet advised.

"Hey, we've come all the way from Alice Springs to check this place out," Joe reminded him. "Besides, it's almost dark already and no one will see us." He switched off the headlights and turned up a rutted drive leading to the property. He drove slowly till they reached a wire fence with a gate. Beyond it stood the ranch house.

Joe stopped the car and the boys strained to look at the building. Suddenly a light snapped on in one window.

"I don't think it would be wise to barge up to the front door and knock," Frank commented.

"Right," Joe agreed. "We'll have to sneak in."

Ponsley shook his head. "You do as you please. I'll stay here."

"That's okay," Frank told him. "Joe, why don't you park behind that pile of rocks over there so the car will be out of sight."

Joe did and the boys got out, leaving Ponsley huddled in the back seat. The three youths headed for a point well to the right of the gateway. The fence was made up of five taut wire strands.

When they reached the gate, Frank and Joe got

down on their hands and knees and crawled under the lowest strand. Chet followed, but the wire caught him in the back. "I can't move!" he muttered to his friends.

"We'll get you loose," Frank whispered. "Just a minute!" Bracing himself with his feet, he lifted the taut wire as far as he could. Joe took hold of Chet's collar and tugged it. The wire released the boy, who shot forward on his face into the sandy soil on the opposite side of the fence.

"Okay, let's go!" Frank said.

"Wait. I lost a shoe!" Chet pleaded.

Joe slapped his forehead. "What a time to pick!" He felt around in the darkness, found the shoe, and pushed it into Chet's hand. "Tie it right this time," he warned. "You'll run like a lame duck with one shoe on and one off.

Chet did and the boys slipped from the fence across the yard to the lighted window, which was open halfway. Carefully stationing themselves in the darkness to one side of the light, they peered into the room.

A sofa stood against the wall, facing a big sideboard holding a number of decanters. In one corner a roll-top desk was open, revealing a series of pigeonholes filled with documents.

Six men sat around a table. Frank craned his head to get a better look at them. Then he whispered excitedly, "There's Tinted Glasses!"

"And Salty, the friendly sailor who almost killed

us with his cargo!" Joe added. "And there's the guy who tried to scare us away from Cutler Ranch!"

One of the men spoke, addressing Tinted Glasses. "I've got to hand it to you, Stiller. Everything's worked out just as you said it would."

Stiller nodded. "Sure, Bruno. But it would be better if Salty had picked the Hardys off on the dock!"

"I 'ad them set up," Salty declared. "They were lucky to get out of the way when I dropped that bale on them!"

"Well, make sure you carry out your assignments without any slip-ups in the future!"

"Sure I will," Salty said sullenly. "It's my neck as well as yours, you know."

"The next job is the most important of all," Stiller continued. "It's the last one. And everything's riding on it."

"I'll be glad when it's over," Bruno declared. "I want to get back to Wisconsin."

Stiller nodded. "I feel the same way. I'm tired of trailing the Hardys halfway around the world."

Salty chuckled. "Me, I'm luckier than you Yanks. Australia's 'ome to me."

Stiller frowned. "Your captain doesn't suspect you, does he?"

"No danger, mate. When I led the 'ardys down to the docks and tipped me the wink, I just slipped ashore long enough to get 'em off your back and set 'em up for the kill. All the skipper knows is, I'm an able seaman what knows 'ow to off-load cargo."

The door from the hall opened and a man and woman came in. The man was burly with long arms and large hands. The woman was short and dark with an intense expression. Both looked pleased as they shut the door.

Stiller addressed the man, "Well, Cutler, have you got the final marching orders for us?"

"I sure have," Cutler grinned. "I've just been on the phone to Sydney. We're to finish the job tonight!"

CHAPTER XIII

Daring Escape

"You finally got clearance to dump him in the Outback?" Bruno said. "Good. The desert will take care of him."

Stiller gave a wolfish grin. "That's right," he chortled. "It's as lethal as Death Valley back home in California."

"Dr. Jenson will never see the Firebird fly," Mrs. Cutler smirked.

"Right. The boss will come here to extract the missing information, then we'll dump him out among the snakes and lizards and leave the sun to finish the job."

The seedy man from Alice Springs shook his head doubtfully. "I'm not so sure that we'll be home free after the job," he spoke up. "I don't like the idea of the Hardys being in Alice Springs. I tried to scare them off when they started to get nosy, but we can't be sure it worked."

Cutler frowned. "Too bad this cowboy had to open his mouth about the ranch," he muttered.

"Well, they can't come out here to tonight," the seedy man went on. "I called the car rental agency and they were all out of transportation. But the Hardys just might show up here in a day or two and snoop around."

"By that time we'll be rid of Jenson," Stiller assured him. "And we'll destroy any incriminating evidence before tomorrow morning. I agree. We can't be careful enough. These guys are pretty smart. I still don't know how they got out of the Australian Arms Hotel without our seeing them!"

"And what gave them the idea to come to Alice Springs?" Bruno asked. "I know Jenson had no chance to leave word when Jim and I took him out of that fleabag hotel on Wallaby Drive. He was so doped he couldn't have written his own name, even if he had had a piece of paper."

"Maybe they just guessed," Bruno suggested.

"I don't know," Cutler said. "I have a bad feeling about this. Stiller, you'd better burn the lists of clients. The stuff about our previous kidnappings and the smuggling job could send us all up for life. Also, for as long as we're still here, we'll post a guard down at the road."

The Hardys listened outside the window with bated breath. Chet felt a cramp in one of his legs. He turned to place his weight on the other leg, stepped on a twig, and made a slight rustling noise.

Those inside looked in the direction of the sound. "What's going on?" Cutler snarled.

"Maybe someone's outside the window!" Mrs. Cutler cried. "Somebody might be spying on us!"

She rushed across the room to the window, while the boys ducked around the corner in the nick of time. Mrs. Cutler lifted the lamp and thrust it through the opening. Leaning out, she surveyed the area for a minute or two. Finally she pulled her head in, put the lamp down, and said, "Nobody's there. It must have been the wind blowing through the bushes."

The boys tiptoed back to the window as Cutler turned toward the gang. "What about our new man—the one guarding Jenson?"

"He's okay," Bruno declared. "I recruited him myself."

The boys felt their hearts pounding with fear as they listened to the criminals. Frank plucked Joe's and Chet's sleeves and motioned to them to move back from the window. They stopped near the fence where they had sneaked in.

"We've got to help Dr. Jenson!" Frank urged.

"How?" Chet queried. "We don't know where they're holding him. Could be anywhere in the farmhouse from the basement to the attic."

"We'll have to climb into the house and search it," Joe suggested.

Frank agreed. "Let's case the place and see if there's a way in. I tell you what. I'll scout the fence and see if there's an escape route. You two circle the ranch house in opposite directions and check the windows and doors. We'll meet here in a few minutes and compare notes."

"Right," Joe said. "Come on, Chet."

The pair went off into the darkness while Frank walked up to the fence and began following the strands of wire to guide himself around the perimeter of the yard. About every twenty-five feet he came to a post, but there was no break in the fence until he reached the gate in front. It was fastened by a chain and a padlock, but no guard was at the gate as yet.

"They must think no one but the gang will ever get out here," he thought. He continued around the fence to the place where they had sneaked in.

Joe, meanwhile, had gone to the left of the house. His path took him to a cellar door, a sloping wooden oblong obviously covering a small flight of stairs to the basement. Taking hold of the metal handle, Joe strove to lift the door. It was locked!

Farther on he passed a pickup truck and a station wagon. Noting that the keys were in both, he reflected, "These guys must really feel safe. Wouldn't it be something if the crooks' cars were stolen!"

Chet circled the house around the right side. He tried the dark lower windows only to find that they would not move. Then he stepped back for a view of the upper windows, which were inaccessible from the ground. "Not even a corner drainpipe to climb," he thought, disappointed.

Moving on, he met Joe sneaking toward him. Consulting in whispers, they decided to join Frank at the fence.

"If we can get Jenson out," Frank reported, "we'd better make a run for it down the road. Otherwise we could get lost in the desert."

"We may not be able to get him out," Chet said. "The ranch is buttoned up."

"I think the cellar door is our best bet," Joe stated. "Maybe we can spring the lock while they're all in the front room."

Frank nodded. "And then we'll have to jump the guy guarding Jenson before he can alert the gang. Let's hope it works!"

The three crept stealthily back to the house, edged around to the cellar door, and tried to wedge it open. Suddenly an uncanny scream made their hair stand on end!

"What's that?" Chet gasped.

A cat raced past, pursued by another. Noisily they vanished into the bushes and the boys breathed in relief.

"Wow!" Frank whispered. "They nearly gave me heart failure!"

The boys started to work on the cellar door once again. Joe took out a small set of pocket tools he carried for such emergencies, slipped the end of a tiny chisel between the edge of the door and the jamb, and levered skillfully until the spring of the lock snapped back. Elated, he began to lift the door.

A sound came from the rear of the ranch house, and Joe immediately eased the cellar door down into place again. The boys sprang up, pressed themselves flat against the wall, and froze as the back door opened.

Cutler came out on the patio. He held a flashlight in his hand and played it over the yard from the fence to the house. Foot by foot the light advanced across the ground to the cellar door. The boys stood stock-still, not daring to move a muscle! Now the beam shone inches from Chet's shoes, moving toward him!

At the last moment it wavered to one side because Mrs. Cutler emerged from the house and joined her husband on the patio. "What was that screeching sound?" she demanded.

"That's what I'm trying to find out," Cutler replied. He flipped the beam from the ground to the bushes, barely missing Chet's belt buckle.

Suddenly two pairs of eyes gleamed through the bushes and one of the cats began to growl.

"Only a couple of cats," Cutler informed his wife. "Nothing to worry about." He snapped the flashlight off and they went back inside.

Chet let out a sigh of relief. "Boy, that was a close call. I thought we were goners for sure!"

"What was that screeching sound?"
Mrs. Cutler demanded.

"If he'd aimed that flashlight a little higher," Joe whispered back, "he could have taken our pictures."

"There's no time to lose," Frank warned. "Let's make sure they're all in the front room. If one of them is prowling around, we're in trouble."

He led the way to the lighted window, where they could see that the Cutlers and gang members were assembled.

"Good," Frank declared. "We can go in——"

Wham! A window slammed over their heads and two men leaped down toward them from the darkness above. Instinctively the boys flattened themselves out against the wall. The men hurdled clear over them, hit the ground, jumped to their feet, and ran to the station wagon.

The Hardys got a good look at one man's face in the light from the window and recognized him from his photo. He was Dr. Jenson!

They could not see the other man's face, but as he jumped his hand caught the light from the room and sparkling red rays were reflected from a large ring on his finger.

"That must be Mike Moran!" Frank gasped.

CHAPTER XIV

Frank Foils the Gang

A TUMULT of furious screaming and shouting broke out in the ranch house.

"The room is empty!" Cutler yelled at the top of his voice. "They're gone—both of 'em!"

"Catch them!" Mrs. Cutler screeched savagely. "Don't let them get away!"

"We'll head 'em off!" Stiller shouted. "Put on the searchlight so we can see 'em!"

A moment later a beam of yellow light from a lookout post on the roof cut through the darkness. It picked up Jenson and Moran as they jumped into the station wagon. Moran started the car. The engine turned over—and died!

Shots rang out and bullets flew toward the station wagon, clanging off fenders and hub caps. One shattered the rear window as the men rushed out with Stiller in the lead. They pounded across the yard toward the fugitives.

Moran desperately turned the key in the starter

again. This time the engine came to life. He shifted gears, and the vehicle moved off just as Stiller grabbed the door handle on the driver's side. He glared angrily at the two men inside. He reached for the steering wheel and struggled with Moran for control, but Moran held on with an iron grip.

Stiller was dragged for about ten yards before losing his hold and falling off. He somersaulted in the dust and landed flat on his back. Cursing furiously, he got to his feet. The gang rushed up. Those who carried guns opened fire, but the station wagon was far ahead, moving quickly toward the gate.

"They'll have to stop!" Stiller snarled. "The gate's chained!"

The criminals ran as fast as they could, while the searchlight focused on the speeding station wagon. Moran stepped on the gas and smashed into the gate, causing it to splinter under the impact. The vehicle plowed through, carrying broken boards with it, and disappeared down the road.

Frank, Joe, and Chet observed the escape after sneaking to a corner of the ranch house from which they had a view of the gate. They felt like cheering when they saw the station wagon vanish into the darkness.

"They got away!" Chet chortled.

Joe shook his head. "Those guys'll go after them in the pickup unless we act fast!" He ran to the truck, followed by Frank and Chet, leaned in, and snatched the keys from the dashboard. "That'll stop 'em!" He grinned.

"They may have another set of keys," Frank said. "Better let the air out of this tire." He tried to unscrew the valve cap, but it refused to budge.

Taking out his penknife, Frank gouged its point into the rubber and began carving a small slit in the tire sidewall until air leaked out with a low hissing sound.

"Look out!" Joe warned. "They're coming!"

The boys melted into the darkness and hid behind tall shrubs.

"We'll take the pickup and go after Jenson and Moran," Stiller ordered. "Don't stand there! Get in. I'll drive!"

As his henchmen obeyed, he squeezed behind the wheel and reached for the keys. His fingers hit an empty keyhole on the dashboard.

"My keys are gone!" he exploded. "Who took 'em? Which of you guys has been fooling around this heap? Fork the key over!"

Each one denied knowing anything about the key. Finally Bruno fished his own key from his pocket and gave it to Stiller.

"No use arguing about it, boss," he said. "They got a head start on us. We'll have to move if we want to catch up."

Muttering to himself, Stiller turned on the ignition and the pickup took off with a roar. But by this time the leaking tire had gone completely flat. The rapidly whirling wheel bumped and clattered loudly over the rough ground, throwing the flattened tire casing halfway off the rim.

The truck lurched and jounced crazily from side to side while Stiller fought to bring it under control. One jolt broke the catch on the back gate, which dropped, and one of the men tumbled out. Finally Stiller brought the pickup to a stop.

"We've got a flat!" he fumed. "Salty, I thought you were gonna put new tires on so we could take Jenson for his ride!"

"I did, boss," Salty said defensively. "Look for yourself if you don't believe me."

"Don't worry. I will," Stiller retorted. He got out along with the others. The man who had fallen joined them, rubbing his shoulder.

"I'm okay," he said, "but those guys won't be when we nab 'em." He waved his fist.

"If you ask me, the tire was slashed!" fumed Bruno. "I'll bet Moran did it!"

"That's right," Stiller said. "He came out earlier to stretch his legs—or so he said. No doubt he punctured the tire while we weren't looking. He's the only one who could have. But he won't get away with it. We'll track him down."

"What I want to know," Salty interjected, "is 'ow Moran became a member of our group."

Bruno shrugged. "My fault. I met him at a soccer game in Sydney and he told me he wanted a job in the Outback because the law was after him. I fell for his story."

"You stupid jughead!" Stiller granted harshly. "We never should have listened to you."

"What do we do now?" Cutler asked.

"Change the tire. What else?" Stiller hissed. "Get busy, you guys!"

"The jack's in the station wagon," Bruno said sheepishly.

"What! You've got to be kidding!" Stiller screamed furiously. A shouting match followed until Salty brought it to an end. "Mates, I've got it!" he yelled.

"Got what?" Stiller demanded.

"The station wagon's low on petrol. I forgot to top 'er up yesterday. They'll get stuck somewhere between 'ere and Alice Springs!"

Stiller was thoughtful for a moment. "That's right. And all they can do is hide in the Outback, close to the road. We can get in touch with Bartel in the morning, and——"

"We won't have any trouble finding them, boss," Bruno added. "Don't worry about that."

"All right. But I don't want any more slip-ups. Let's set up guards for the rest of the night. We can't be sure that these snoopy boys won't show up sooner or later! Go inside and get some more ammunition. Then position yourselves around the property. We'll do two shifts."

The men agreed and everyone went inside. Frank pulled Joe and Chet by their jackets. "Let's get out of here, quick!"

CHAPTER XV

A Deadly Snake

THE boys raced through the darkness and wriggled through the fence. Then they ran around the rocks to the car. It appeared deserted as they approached.

"Where's Mr. Ponsley?" Chet puffed. "Do you think he got scared and ran off?"

"We'll have to stay and look for him," Joe said. "We can't just drive away and leave him behind!"

A loud noise interrupted him.

"No need to look for Mr. Ponsley," Frank observed. "He's here all right."

The boys peered through the window. Ponsley was sitting in the back seat with his hands crossed on his vest. His head was bent forward and his chin touched the enormous tie he wore. His mouth was open; and with every breath he snored.

Relieved to find he was still in the car, Frank, Joe, and Chet piled into the compact, then Frank took the wheel as they moved off. He drove carefully, not daring to use his lights until they were around the rocks and well down the road.

"We're safe now," Frank said, snapping on the headlights and stepping on the gas.

"As long as our car doesn't conk out," Chet stated. "I'll give three cheers when we get to Alice Springs."

"First we've got to find Jenson and Moran," Frank reminded him.

They came to a rough part of the road and jounced up and down over rocks and deep potholes. Frank shifted into low gear to maneuver past the worst spots. The jolting ride brought Ponsley awake with a start. He raised his head and looked around. "Where are we?" he demanded irritably.

"On the Cutler road," Frank replied.

Ponsley became peevish. "Well, you are driving this car as if you were riding a bronco at the rodeo."

"Can't help it," Frank said. "The Cutlers never built a paved highway for visitors to drive to their ranch."

Joe turned around and addressed their companion. "Mr. Ponsley, did you notice anything after we left you in the car?"

Ponsley covered a yawn with his hand. "What do you mean?" he asked.

"The station wagon. Did it keep on going down the road past the rocks?"

"What station wagon?" Ponsley inquired. "I know nothing about a station wagon."

Frank was incredulous. "You mean a station wagon crashed through a board fence only a few yards from where you were and you didn't hear anything?"

"I don't recall a thing between the time you left and just now, when you woke me up."

Frank increased speed as they reached a better stretch of the road. "Unbelievable!" He chuckled.

"Why are you going so fast?" Ponsley complained.

Joe explained that they had to get safely away from the gang of crooks at the Cutler Ranch.

Ponsley became cross. "I should think we are far enough away to slow down. I don't like being in an automobile at high speeds."

Frank turned onto the main road and increased his speed. "We have another reason for making time, Mr. Ponsley," he declared.

"Oh, what's that?"

"We're trying to catch Dr. Jenson and Mike Moran!"

Ponsley's mouth dropped open as the meaning of the statement sank in. The boys took turns describing events at the Cutler Ranch leading up to the climax, when Jenson and Moran leaped from the window of the house and fled in the station wagon.

"How did you know the man with Jenson was Michael?" he spluttered.

"He was wearing a ring with a red stone," Joe said. "It reflected in the light from the house."

Ponsley became excited. "Then it must be Michael! Frank, speed up! Catch the station wagon!"

Frank kept the gas pedal flat on the floor as the car raced forward. But trouble was in store. Several miles farther on, the car suddenly stalled. Lacking proper tools and light to work by, the boys puttered over the engine a long time before discovering that the distributor cap had sprung loose.

Later, after resuming their journey, they sighted distant figures silhouetted on the skyline. Ponsley insisted that they stop and investigate. The figures turned out to be wild aborigines hunting at night. Returning wearily to the car, they continued southward to Alice Springs.

Dawn began to break. Shafts of sunlight glanced from the desert in shimmering rays. Near the Sandover River, a group of kangaroos bounded away, and a rabbit scooted across the road, seeking safety in scrub vegetation.

Then something caught Joe's eye up ahead. "The station wagon!" he exclaimed.

Frank hit the brakes and brought the car to a stop behind the vehicle they had been chasing. Rocks and gullies extended on both sides of the road.

"Salty was right," Frank said. "They must have run out of gas."

Ponsley got out of the car as fast as he could. "Michael, Michael!" he called out.

There was no reply. Ponsley groaned. "They're gone!"

"The keys are still here," Joe pointed out.

Chet squeezed into the front seat, turned on the ignition, and glanced at the dashboard dials. "The gas needle's down to empty," he confirmed.

"Then they must be somewhere near here," Ponsley said hopefully. "But where?"

"Let's see if we can find their footprints and follow them," Frank suggested.

The four walked around the station wagon, but the terrain was too rocky for footprints.

"It's no use," Joe finally said. "We can't tell which way they went."

The boys shaded their eyes with their hands and scanned the horizon. Ponsley sat down on a boulder. Not a sound broke the silence of the desert, and not a movement could be seen among the rocks.

Joe was about to say something when he looked in Ponsley's direction and stopped short. Their friend was staring down toward his left hand, which was hidden by the boulder on which he sat. He looked deathly pale, his eyes bulged with fear, and a trickle of sweat rolled down his face. He seemed to have stopped breathing.

Joe stepped slowly around to see what was wrong. He noticed an Australian brown snake, about five feet long, coiled behind the boulder!

The snake's neck arched in the air. Flashing wicked fangs only inches from Ponsley's hand, the serpent swayed menacingly back and forth, hissing ferociously.

Ponsley was mesmerized by the venomous creature. He sat as if turned to stone, too terrified to move.

Cautiously, to avoid startling the snake and causing it to strike at Ponsley's hand, Joe gave a danger signal to Frank and Chet. Responding, they moved up, and were horrified when they realized that Ponsley was in danger.

Chet picked up a dried branch, evidently blown from a far-off straggle of gum trees, made a wide circle, came up behind the snake, and brushed the sand with the stick. With blinding speed, the snake whirled and sank its fangs into the wood!

Frank and Joe instantly grabbed Ponsley and pulled him away from the boulder. He trembled and gasped for breath. Chet stepped back, dragging the snake, which maintained its grip on the stick.

"Look!" Joe cried suddenly.

Between the serpent's coils gleamed a piece of metal. When the snake released the stick and slithered off among the rocks, Joe retrieved the object, a key chain with the initial M on it.

"That's probably Michael's!" Ponsley exclaimed. "He must have dropped it here!"

"Most likely on the way up this gully," Frank observed. "So that's where we go."

The gully led to a point where the rocks were taller and more spread out, with defiles leading in several directions. They halted, not knowing which way to take.

Frank cupped his hands around his mouth. "Mike Moran!" he shouted. "Come on out! We're friends!"

His words echoed among the rocks and then silence fell again.

Joe called, "Dr. Jenson! Dr. Jenson!"

Again silence. A small stone tumbled from one of the tall rocks. Looking up, the boys saw a figure vanish over the top.

"There they are!" Chet cried out.

The four climbed over a pile of rocks and reached the top just in time to see the figure jump down on the other side and run into a defile.

"They think we're Stiller and company," Joe said. "They won't come out."

"You follow them," Frank replied. "I'll cut them off."

Noting that the defile curved around in a semicircle, he scrambled down the pile of rocks, turned left, and met Moran and Jenson running through toward him!

Jenson was a slight, scholarly-looking man. Moran appeared to be the outdoor type, and he assumed a boxer's stance as soon as he saw Frank.

"Relax, Mike," Frank told him. "We're not in

league with the Cutlers. Those crooks are a long way from here."

Just then the others came up. Ponsley hastened forward and cried, "Michael! Michael!"

Moran stared at him in utter astonishment. "Mr. Ponsley, what are you doing here?"

"And who are these boys?" Jenson put in.

"Friends!" Ponsley said. Then he explained how they happened to be searching for Moran and Jenson.

When Ponsley mentioned that Michael had been accused of tipping off two bank robbers about the Mid-County Bank's alarm system, Moran shook his head in disbelief. "Dad needn't have worried about that. The alarm system they've got now is totally different from the one in use when I worked there. I know nothing about the present system."

"Can you prove that?" Joe asked.

"Sure. The old system had a number of flaws. I know because I checked it out. The manager called in a security engineering firm to install a new one. The job hadn't been finished when I left. The records will back me up on that."

"So the two men who were arrested must have been trying to frame you to cover up for someone else," Frank reasoned.

"You bet they were!" said Mike.

Ponsley heaved a sigh of relief now that he knew the senator's son could be cleared. The conversation reminded Frank of something. "You spoke about a bank employee named Thurbow, who helped to throw suspicion on Mike," he said to Ponsley. "What's his job there?"

"Security guard, I believe."

"Any idea what he looks like?"

"I have," Mike broke in. "He's a stocky, red-haired guy with a broken nose. I never did like him."

Frank turned to his brother. "Remember the man who was in the chemistry shop talking to Mr. Oakes when we ordered that methyl yellow?"

Joe's eyes widened and he snapped his fingers. "Holy smoke, you're right! It was a chunky red-head! I remember wondering if he might be a pro boxer with that broken nose. That must have been Thurbow."

"Check! Mr. Oakes told us he was talking to a security guard when the mistake occurred. I'll bet Thurbow switched the methyl yellow with his own bottle of liquid gas."

"Probably because he heard at the bank that Senator Moran planned to call us in on the case."

The two boys told their listeners about their accident with the tear gas.

Later Ponsley inquired reproachfully, "Michael, why did you leave your home like that?"

"I wanted to see the world without my father's help. I decided to stop being Senator Moran's son for a while and try to make it on my own."

"How did you get involved with the Stiller gang?" Frank asked.

"I met Bruno at a soccer match in Sydney. He said he was from a ranch in the Outback and when I told him I was looking for a job, he hired me. I didn't know anything about the illegal operations till I got to Cutler Ranch."

Frank remembered that Bruno said Moran had claimed the police were after him, but decided not to mention it at this point.

"Mike was already there when they dragged me out of the hotel in Sydney," Jenson took up the story. "They drugged me to make it easier, but I heard them mention Alice Springs and wrote the letters AL S on the door. Did you read my message?"

"Sure did," Frank said. "But tell me, why did you pick that fleabag hotel in the first place?"

"I had a feeling I was being followed. I had reservations at the Australian Arms, but I took a taxi at the airport and told the driver to take me to the opposite part of town. Unfortunately, it didn't help. They found me anyway."

"So after that you two met at the Cutler Ranch," Joe said to Mike.

"Right. That's where Bruno took me. He told me to guard Dr. Jenson when they brought him in. Bruno handed me a rifle and ordered me to see that Dr. Jenson stayed put in the upstairs room until his fate had been decided. When it seemed that they were going to drop him in the Outback, we escaped through the window. We didn't see you fellows. It was too dark. I had been in the yard, and I knew the keys were in the station wagon. That's why we used it for our breakout. We drove till the gas ran out."

"Then we hid in the rocks," Jenson continued. "When you came along and stopped behind the station wagon, we thought you were Stiller and his henchmen."

"That's why we hid even deeper," Moran said. "By the way, how did you know which way we had gone?"

"We found this at the head of the gully," Joe replied. He handed the key chain to Mike Moran.

Moran took it and put it in his pocket. "I must have dropped it after we got out of the car. Good thing you found it!"

"Thank the deadly snake, Mike," Joe quipped.

"What's that again?"

Joe described the incident of the hissing serpent.

Moran became solemn. "I'm sorry you were in so much danger, Mr. Ponsley."

The latter held up his hand. "Think nothing of it, Michael. I have found you, and nothing else concerns me at this point."

Frank turned to Jenson. "Do you have any idea why the gang kidnapped you?"

"None at all. It's a mystery to me."

"Could they be agents of a foreign government?"

"They might," Jenson confessed. "Professor Young and I received several messages warning us not to test the Firebird Rocket. Certainly a foreign power might be involved. It might be a plot to hold up our space program."

A loud clatter broke out overhead and a helicopter zoomed through the sky. It was painted white, and bore no markings. The pilot made a wide circle around the two cars parked by the side of the road. Obviously interested in them, he returned for a second look.

"Chopper!" Chet cried. "If we can attract the pilot's attention, maybe he'll pick us up. Come on, we'll send him an SOS before he flies off!"

The rotund youth ran down the gully and out into the open. The others followed on his heels. Chet began to wave his arms frantically.

"Chet, be careful!" Frank warned. "It could be Stiller and his gang!"

Chet ignored the warning. Exultantly he realized that the pilot had spotted the group. "He saw us and is coming down for us!"

The chopper swung low toward them. Then machine guns chattered! Bullets kicked up puffs of sand on the desert floor!

CHAPTER XVI

Helicopter Hunt

"RUN BEHIND the rocks!" Joe shouted. "We're clay pigeons out here in the open!"

He raced back up the gully, followed by the others. The helicopter pursued them, its machine guns spraying bullets at their heels. They circled around the rocks until they found sanctuary under an overhanging ledge. Baffled by this obstruction, the chopper pilot hovered in the sky like a hawk waiting for its prey to emerge from a hole in the ground.

The six fugitives crept into a large cave at the end of the ledge. Ponsley sank down and mopped his brow with his handkerchief. Jenson sat down beside him. The Hardys, Chet, and Moran peered through the mouth of the cave at their enemy overhead.

"We're safe for the moment," Frank said. "But the helicopter will keep hunting us."

Ponsley turned pale and gasped, "Then why are we staying in here? We'll be trapped!"

"We can't get back to the car while the chopper's in the air," Frank replied. "Let's wait until the pilot lands."

As if in response to his words, the whirlybird began to circle lower and lower, finally settling on the desert in a cloud of dust. The door opened and Stiller jumped out, followed by Bruno and another man. They both carried machine guns.

"Run before they find us!" Frank called out to his companions. "Now!"

He was first out of the cave. Chet, Moran, Jenson, and Ponsley came after, with Joe at the end of the line to make sure no one was left behind. They took the reverse direction along the overhanging ledge, just making it around the rocks before a volley of shots rang out as the gang spotted them.

Quickly they ran down the gully to the car and piled into it. The gang pounded after them.

Frank took the wheel, and the car roared off amid a hail of bullets fired by Stiller and his henchmen.

"Anybody get hit?" Joe asked anxiously.

He felt relieved when everyone reassured him that he had not. Peering through the back window, he saw the gang turn and run up the gully.

"They're going back to the chopper!" he said grimly. "That means they'll be after us again."

"Oh, no!" Ponsley protested. He was squeezed into one corner of the car with his elbows pressed tightly against his sides. "It's bad enough riding like this! I can't breathe!"

"It'll get worse in a minute," Joe predicted.

He was right. The helicopter appeared in the sky and thundered after the car. One of the machine guns opened up again, kicking up sand behind the rear wheels of the speeding vehicle.

Frank swerved sharply from one side of the road to the other, presenting a moving target to the gunner. Reaching a row of hills, he dodged into them. He sped in and out among them, rocking the car violently as he took sharp corners on two wheels. The brakes squealed.

"We'll never get out of this alive!" Ponsley lamented. "We're done for!"

"Not yet!" Frank vowed. "We'll give them a run for their money!"

The hills ended, and the car was forced back onto the road through the Outback. The chopper resumed the chase, throwing a moving shadow on the earth like that of a giant prehistoric bird flapping through the early morning sunlight.

Frank raced down the road. "How long can that guy keep missing us with his burp gun?" he wondered.

"They're trying to draw a bead on us," Joe warned. "Here they come. Everybody duck!"

"Duck?" Ponsley quavered. "I can't even move!"

"What's that?" Chet cried, pointing down the road to a speck on the horizon that was growing larger by the second.

"It's a car!" Frank exclaimed.

The two vehicles raced toward one another. Frank blinked his headlights on and off as a signal to the other driver that he was in trouble.

"I hope he can help us!" Chet said.

"He sure will!" Frank replied. "That's a police car!"

The helicopter pilot, recognizing the police insignia, veered off and clattered away, vanishing in the distance. Frank drew to a stop, and so did the patrol car. Two officers got out.

"Boy, are we glad to see you!" Frank exclaimed.

"What's the matter?" asked one of the officers.

Frank introduced himself and his companions, then explained that the helicopter had been chasing and firing at them.

"Why were the men in the chopper after you?"

Joe and Chet took turns describing what had occurred since they arrived at the Cutler Ranch. Moran and Jenson added their testimony, and told how they happened to be at the ranch.

The policemen listened in amazement. "We saw the copter and heard the gunfire quite a distance away, but we couldn't figure out what was going on," said one officer.

His partner added, "We'll call for reinforcements and drive to the Cutler homestead immediately."

"But the chopper will get there before you," Frank pointed out.

"True. But it's too small to fly out that many people. We should be able to nab at least some of the gang."

The two officers got into their patrol car and started up the road through the Outback, while Frank and the others continued to Alice Springs. They drove straight to the rental agency and returned the car.

Ponsley was so stiff that he had to be pulled out of the back seat by Chet and the Hardys. "Oh, my aching back!" he complained. "Mike, why did you ever have to come to a place like this?"

"I like this country," Mike said with a grin. "What do we do next?"

"Fly back to America at once!" Ponsley declared. "Michael, your father can't wait to see you."

Moran nodded. "And I can't wait to see him and Mom."

"I'd better fly to Sydney to check in with the Australian authorities and confirm my clearance at Woomera," Dr. Jenson said.

Frank said, "And I think we should go with you in case the gang tries to kidnap you again. Until they're behind bars, I know Dad would want us to act as your bodyguards, Dr. Jenson."

The scientist smiled. "I'll be happy to have you. It makes me feel a lot safer."

On the plane to Sydney, Mike Moran told them about some of his experiences and how he had run out of money and accepted the job Bruno offered him.

"Did you tell him the police were after you?" Frank asked bluntly.

Mike stared at him for a moment. "No. Why do you ask?"

"Bruno said you did."

"You spoke to him?"

"No. We overheard him saying it."

"Well, it's not true."

Frank had doubts but changed the subject. "Now you can help your father in his political campaign," he suggested.

"I'll be glad to," Mike said. "After my experiences down under, politics will be a tame game. But that's all right. I don't want to get involved with any more criminals."

At the Sydney airport, Ponsley and Moran said good-by and went to catch a plane for the United States. The boys accompanied Dr. Jenson to police headquarters and then returned with him to the airport to await a flight to Adelaide, where they would transfer to another plane for the Woomera rocket station.

While they were sitting in the terminal, a voice announced over the loudspeaker: "Call for Joe Hardy! Call for Joe Hardy!"

"Who can that be?" Joe wondered.

"You'll find out when you answer," Chet said.

After checking with the information desk, Joe went to the designated phone booth and picked up the receiver. "Joe Hardy speaking."

"Listen, punk," growled a disguised voice, "you and your brother better get out of Australia! And take your fat friend with you—or all three of you will wind up in the hospital! Or in coffins!"

CHAPTER XVII

Woomera Welcome

JOE started to ask who the speaker was but the phone clicked off at the other end. Replacing the receiver, the boy returned to the others and quickly described the warning call.

"The helicopter gang knew we were with Dr. Jenson," Chet said. "They could have called ahead of us to alert another member. He may follow us, so we'd better be on our guard."

Frank nodded thoughtfully. "But do you know what this means? Unless they called their accomplice while they were still in the air, they escaped the police!"

"I'm going to get in touch with the Alice Springs police right away," Joe said and hurried off to a phone booth. He managed to reach the officer in charge. "Did you capture the Stiller gang?" he asked.

"No such luck. We found the Cutler station abandoned. Obviously other gang members arrived with cars to help evacuate everyone. So far we haven't traced the helicopter or its crew."

Joe groaned in disappointment. "Any clues in the house?"

"Nothing. It was cleaned out except for some fingerprints. There were a lot of ashes in the fireplace and bits of paper, but nothing conclusive. They obviously burned anything incriminating."

"And no hint to where they might have gone?"

"None. But we're working on the case and will find out sooner or later."

Joe thanked the officer and hung up. When he joined his brother and the others, they could tell from the expression on his face that something had gone wrong.

"The Cutler gang escaped?" Frank asked.

"Without a trace. They burned all the evidence and were gone when the police arrived."

"They must have been prepared even before the helicopter went off to chase us," Frank muttered.

"Do you think they'll make another attempt to kidnap Dr. Jenson?" Chet asked.

"It's possible. We have to be very careful."

The scientist turned pale when he heard that his captors were still at large. "I'm glad you fellows are with me," he said. "And I'll feel better yet once we get to Woomera. The security there is so tight, I doubt that any of the gang could get in."

His companions nodded, and they kept a sharp

eye out for anyone who might be following them. They boarded the plane without noticing anything suspicious.

The plane flew over the desolate terrain of Southern Australia, then made a big circle to the coast over Gulf St. Vincent and into Adelaide for a landing at the airport. There, a message was waiting for Dr. Jenson.

"Professor David Hopkins is here to meet me," he declared after reading the note.

"Dr. Jenson, who is this professor?" Frank asked. "Do you know him?"

"We can't take chances with strangers," Joe added.

Jenson laughed. "I've never met him, but I know he's a famous scientist. He's one of the experts I came to Australia to meet. Hopkins works out the astronomical tables for interplanetary probes and will help track the Firebird."

"The man who is meeting us here could be a phony," Frank objected.

"Don't worry," Dr. Jenson assured him. "I know what Hopkins looks like. I've seen several pictures of him."

"Good," Frank said. "I'd hate to walk into a trap."

Jenson led the way to the waiting room, looked around, then waved to a man sitting on a bench. It was obviously Hopkins. Frank was relieved by the gesture.

The scientist was a short-sighted individual

wearing steel-rimmed glasses. He came forward and introduced himself.

"Dr. Jenson, the Sydney police informed us that you were coming," he said. "I couldn't wait to see you, so I flew down to Adelaide. We're all so glad to hear that you survived your ordeal unharmed!"

"So am I," Jenson said with a smile. He shook Hopkins' hand, introduced the Hardys and Chet, and gave Hopkins a brief rundown on his escape from the Cutler Ranch. "The boys came along as my bodyguards," he concluded.

"That's a splendid idea in view of the danger," Hopkins declared emphatically. "Now then. We'll fly to Woomera in an official plane. The station's in the desert, where the rockets can be safely tested."

The plane was a medium-sized, propeller-driven craft, just large enough for them to squeeze in behind the pilot. After taking off, they headed northwest over Spencer Gulf and Port Augusta into a region of lakes that broke up the arid, sun-bitten terrain of western Australia.

After their long, cramped flight drew to an end, Hopkins pointed out the window and said, "This is the Woomera prohibited area. It's a very large tract of land, absolutely barred to visitors who don't have official permission to enter."

"I know why," Chet boasted. "Your rockets are top secret! Space probes! Spy-in-the-sky! All that hardware!"

Hopkins smiled. "You seem to know about this."

Chet puffed his chest out. "I built a rocket myself and won the high school science competition!"

The Australian smiled again. "Perhaps some day you'll be working here as a scientist."

Chet looked pleased. "I would——"

"We're about to land," the pilot interjected. He maneuvered the plane in line with the runway, set down the wheels, and taxied to the terminal. Hopkins oversaw his companions' clearance by the Woomera security staff, then took them in his car to their hotel.

"This town sprang up overnight," he said as they drove along. "Even the trees you see were planted. Now we have homes, apartments, swimming pools—everything from a post office to a hospital. We'll go out to the rocket range in the morning," he added upon drawing up to the curb to let his passengers out.

It was decided that Dr. Jenson would share his room with Chet for security reasons, and the Hardys asked for adjoining quarters. However, the night passed without an incident, and Hopkins picked them up, as promised, early next day.

They drove to the central installation and saw rockets of all sizes at launch sites. Some stood upright, ready to fly into orbit. Others were canted at an angle that would keep them from reaching outer space.

Hopkins took the boys into a building and led them to its main room, which contained rows of sensitive instruments. Scientists and technicians were seated at consoles, checking the readings. "This is the control room," he said, "and these instruments monitor our rockets."

A man in a white coat was bending over a telemetry computer. When he heard Hopkins' voice, he straightened up and looked around. The Hardys stared in surprise. He was Professor Young!

"Adrian!" Young exclaimed, stepping over and shaking Jenson's hand. "I'm so glad the Hardys found you! Good job!"

Frank and Joe smiled and Chet looked a little disappointed because he had not been mentioned.

"Well, I want to welcome all of you to Woomera," Young went on. "I came here to follow the Firebird flight because I was afraid you wouldn't make it!"

"I almost didn't," Jenson said, and told Young about his experiences since he was last heard from.

Young looked grim. "NASA will do everything to see that your kidnappers are brought to justice. Please give me all the details of your capture."

He questioned Jenson and the boys very closely for an hour. At the end, he said, "Adrian, I take it you still have no idea why the Stiller gang kidnapped you."

Jenson shook his head. "I wish I could tell you. But I can't."

"When Cutler and his men are found, they may talk," Frank suggested.

"Let's hope so!" Young declared fervently. He

invited Jenson to come into his office for a briefing about the Firebird. Then he turned to the boys. "While Dr. Jenson and I are talking, I'll bet I know what you fellows would like to do."

"I'd like to see a rocket launching!" Chet said.

"I figured that," Young said with a smile. "You're in luck. There will be one in about five minutes. Come along with me."

He escorted the boys to a special observation window through which they could see a huge missile poised on its launch pad. Then the two men disappeared while the Hardys and Chet waited expectantly, their eyes glued to the rocket.

The nose cone was painted dark green and the booster was white with the name *Wallaby* on it. A supporting gantry moved back, leaving the rocket standing by itself on the launch pad.

An Australian scientist came up to watch. "You're Americans, aren't you?" he asked.

Frank said they were.

"I thought so from hearing you speak. That rocket is named for a small kangaroo, the wallaby. It will put a weather satellite into orbit." He stood near them while preparations for the launching continued. At last everything was ready.

"Here we go!" Chet cried. "The countdown!"

A voice intoned the numbers: "Ten, nine, eight, seven, six, five, four, three, two, one, zero! Lift off!"

Exhaust gases poured out onto the launch pad in a dense white cloud. The rocket started straight up, slowly at first, then gathered momentum, and increased its speed. Soon it was hurtling through the sky high above the earth.

The scientists and technicians in the control room cheered loudly and the boys joined in.

"That's a beauty!" Joe said enthusiastically. "I hope she makes it into orbit!"

"So far, so good," reported Frank, who was following the flight through a pair of binoculars offered him by the Australian. "It looks like a perfect flight."

"I'll show you how perfect," the Australian said when the rocket had disappeared from view. He took them to a battery of instruments to check the moment the booster rocket fell away and the nose cone continued into orbit.

Young's voice sounded behind them. "Everything is going as planned. The flight is A-okay."

He and Jenson had come up without being noticed, and stood looking at the instruments over Frank's shoulder.

"It's an important flight for us," Jenson said. "The data it sends back will be used to plot the flight of the Firebird."

Everyone in the control room relaxed. They began to discuss the Firebird, its revolutionary nuclear engine, and the path it would take deep into space. Young showed the boys around, introducing them to Australians and Americans responsible for space programs conducted jointly by the two nations.

The rocket slowly started straight up.

Chet eagerly asked as many questions as he could think of and the scientists cooperated good-naturedly with the boy. Finally, in the late afternoon, the young detectives escorted Dr. Jenson back to their hotel. They had a pleasant dinner, then retired to their rooms. Before going to bed, Frank telephoned Alice Springs again.

"Any clues yet?" he asked the officer in charge.

"We found the helicopter abandoned in the Outback," was the reply. "It was registered in the name of Bartel. At this point we haven't been able to establish yet whether that's a fictitious name or not. But there's no trace of the gang."

"I was afraid of that," Frank said. Slowly he hung up and told Joe what the officer had reported.

"I just hope that dodging the police will take up all the gang's time and attention," Joe commented. "This way they won't be able to follow us."

Joe's hopes, however, were dashed the following morning when a loud knock sounded on the door. Dr. Jenson and Chet burst in. The scientist looked pale and shaken, and his hand trembled slightly as he held out a piece of paper to show the boys.

"This was slipped under the door of our room," he exclaimed. "They're going to kill me!"

CHAPTER XVIII

The Trap

FRANK and Joe stared at the message. It was pieced together with letters cut out of a newspaper, a method the crooks had used before, and read: THE FIREBIRD WILL DIE, AND SO WILL YOU!

"They haven't given up," Joe stormed. "And they know where we are. It looks as if security isn't tight enough, even here at Woomera!"

"Maybe Arthur can help," Jenson said. Suddenly he sounded tired and depressed.

"Look," Frank told him, "don't worry about the gang. That's what we're here for."

Jenson smiled wanly. "Okay, I'll let you worry. Do you think it's safe to go downstairs and have some coffee?"

The group went into the cafeteria, and less than an hour later the official limousine picked them up. They were driven to the rocket range, where they met Young in the laboratory.

He was agitated when he saw the note. "This is unbelievable!" he exploded. "But they won't get away with this. I won't let them!"

"You didn't get a note like this?" Frank inquired.

"No," Young said, and he turned pale. "Not yet."

"What are you doing for your own safety?" Joe added.

"I traveled with the two men who guarded me in Princeton," Young replied, "and we're sharing a room. That, of course, may not discourage the gang from coming after me, too."

"What are we going to do?" Jenson asked.

"I'll talk to the security people here and arrange for a hideout where the four of you can stay until the gang is captured," Young replied. "I'll figure out a way we can communicate with each other, and also request closer protection for myself. Just wait here while I make a few phone calls."

Young disappeared into his office and returned a short time later. "All set," he declared. "The private pilot who flew me here will take you to a safe place down in Port Augusta. No one will suspect you're there, and the local police will keep an eye on it. Please don't leave until I contact you."

Soon Jenson and the boys took off, and less than an hour later they landed at the Port Augusta airfield, where a car was waiting. The pilot himself drove them to a hotel on the outskirts of town. He pulled into the rear and backed up closely to the door.

The boys had noticed a large sign out front that read: CAPTAIN COOK'S FLAGSHIP. The ancient three-story building needed a coat of paint, the windows needed washing, and the lawn needed mowing.

"This is not exactly a first-class joint," Chet commented.

"Why did Professor Young send us to a place like this?" Joe wondered.

"Obviously he thinks no one would look here for an eminent scientist," Frank suggested.

They went in and found a surly clerk at the desk. He glowered at them as they signed the register, and told them their room was on the third floor.

"The only phone in the hotel is this one on the desk," he snapped. "You can have sandwiches from the kitchen. Water and ice are in the basement. Take the stairs up, and don't ask me if there's a lift. There isn't."

"He's about as friendly as that brown snake Ponsley met in the Outback," Frank said sarcastically as they climbed the stairs. Finding their door number, they entered a dusty room with four cots, and a window that was stuck. Joe and Chet had to force it up by pushing together.

Jenson looked around and sighed. "I hope we don't have to stay here very long."

"Stiller and his friends might be rounded up at

any time." Frank reassured him. "Then we can leave."

Joe punched one cot with his fist. "This'll be like camping out in the Bayport Woods," he grumbled.

Chet clicked his teeth. "I'm thirsty. I'll go get some ice water in the basement."

He went out, carrying a cracked jug that had been sitting on a small table. Joe locked the door and put the key on the bureau. Frank and Jenson sat down on two cots and discussed the situation, wondering what would come next. Suddenly the floorboards in the hall creaked and footsteps approached.

"I didn't think Chet would be back that fast," Joe said.

The steps came closer and stopped outside their door. However, the caller did not knock.

"Whoever's out there must be eavesdropping on us!" Jenson whispered nervously.

"Shhh!" Joe warned, putting his finger to his lips. He and Frank tiptoed over to the door. Joe stationed himself flat against the wall next to it, while Frank turned the knob quickly and flung the door open.

Outside stood the desk clerk!

"What's the idea of eavesdropping on us?" Frank demanded.

"Who's eavesdropping? I came up to tell you there's a phone call for Frank and Joe Hardy. You can take it at the desk."

"Then why didn't you knock?"

"I wanted to make sure no one was around. I was told to be cautious and not to draw attention to this room."

"That sounds reasonable," Jenson spoke up. "Arthur doesn't want anyone to know we're here. He's being careful."

"It's possible," Joe commented.

The desk clerk glared at them. "I delivered the message," he grated. "Now I've got other things to do." He walked out and disappeared down the hall. The Hardys followed him after warning Jenson to lock the door and not to open it for anyone except Chet until they returned.

"This call must be from Professor Young," Joe said as they descended the stairs. "Maybe the police caught the gang!"

They took the lower stairs two at a time and ran to the desk. The clerk was not in sight and the phone lay on its side off the hook.

Frank lifted the instrument to his ear and Joe stood close enough to listen in. "Hello?" Frank said.

A disguised voice replied, "Listen, Hardy! You and that stupid brother of yours don't seem to have sense enough to save yourselves, much less protect Jenson!"

"Who is this?" Frank demanded.

"The same person who called Joe Hardy at the Sydney airport."

"What are you calling about now?"

"You all disregarded my warning," the man retorted. "I gave you a chance to save your necks and you didn't take it. You decided to stay in Australia. All right, now you'll stay permanently. Six feet under!"

The man continued his threats. Frank put his hand over the mouthpiece and whispered, "Joe, do you recognize his voice?"

"It's disguised," Joe replied. "I don't know him from Adam."

Frank removed his hand from the telephone and said, "Who's going to make us stay permanently?"

The man hung up without answering and the Hardys stared at one another in puzzlement.

"This means we can't stay here either," Frank said. "We'd better phone Professor Young!"

Joe called and described the threat. Young was disturbed. "Good heavens!" he exclaimed. "I'll phone my pilot to go back for you right away. He's still in Port Augusta. All of you had better go to the airfield with him before the gang gets to the hotel!"

"Will do, professor," Joe said. "See you later." He and Frank hurried upstairs and knocked on the door of their room. There was no answer. Joe tried the knob and found the door was locked.

"Dr. Jenson!" the Hardys called in unison.

Frank looked grim. "Something's happened. We'll have to break in!"

He kicked the door until a panel splintered under the impact. Reaching through, he turned the key in the lock and pushed the door open. The room was empty!"

Footsteps in the hall made them whirl around. Chet came in, carrying his jug. "The ice water comes out in a trickle," he complained. "Say, what have you done to the door?"

"Dr. Jenson is gone!" Frank said. "Did you see him downstairs?"

"Or anybody else?" Joe added.

Chet shook his head. "I was all by my lonesome."

"There's only one other way out," Frank said. "Through the window!"

The Hardys rushed over and saw that a sheet had been torn into strips and knotted together to form a rope. One end was tied to a radiator. The other dangled over the windowsill to the ground.

"Dr. Jenson got out through the window!" Frank exclaimed. "We've got to catch him!"

"But why would he do that?" Chet asked.

"I have no idea. All I know is that we must get him!" Frank said. He left a bill on the dresser for the damage to the door, then gripped the improvised rope, and shinned to the ground with the celerity of a squirrel. Joe followed at the same speed, then looked up.

Chet was hesitating.

"Hurry up or stay behind!" Joe urged.

Faced with the choice, Chet climbed down. He got hold of the torn sheet, and squeezed through the window, shutting his eyes tight. He dangled over empty space. "It's a three-story drop," he quavered.

"Slide down! Let gravity take over," Joe advised. "You'll make it in no time."

Chet had almost reached the bottom when one end of the torn sheet snapped. He plummeted down with a loud yell. Frank grabbed his shoulders and Joe caught his legs, and the three ended in a tangle on the ground.

"Good show!" said a familiar voice behind them as they struggled to their feet. The boys froze. It was Stiller! He and his gang had them surrounded! In the background, Salty was guarding Jenson, whose hands were tied.

"We laid a trap," Stiller smirked, "and the smart Hardys walked right into it!"

Frank realized what had happened. "You guys must have sneaked in the back way before we ever got that call. And somehow you fooled Dr. Jenson into opening the door while your confederate kept us talking down at the hotel desk."

"That's right." Stiller gloated. "We pounded on the door and pretended you two had had an accident. When Jenson opened, we grabbed him and left that knotted sheet dangling out the window before we ducked down the back stairs again. One of my men actually climbed down the sheet so he could lock the door from the inside. You fools fell for the trick and plopped right into our arms!"

Jenson and the young detectives were taken to two parked cars. At the wheel of one was the hotel desk clerk!

"So you're in the gang, too," Frank accused him.

The clerk grinned. "I am now," he said as the captives were pushed into the cars. "It pays well."

"Where are you taking us?" Frank asked Bruno, who sat next to him.

"Shut up!" his guard answered and jabbed him viciously in the side with his elbow.

Frank winced in pain and asked no more questions. The cars were driven to an abandoned warehouse several blocks away. It was a five-story building. Most of the windows were broken or boarded up.

The gang marched the captives inside and up a flight of dark stairs to the loft at the top. One man was posted to guard them while his companions left. About an hour later, the other crooks returned with a new prisoner. The boys gasped as they recognized him.

"Professor Young!" they cried out in disbelief.

Dr. Jenson stared at his partner. "Arthur! So they've got you too! How on earth did it happen?"

"A fake phone call right after I talked to Joe," Young replied. "The caller pretended to be with the Port Augusta police. He said they had a line on the gang and were ready to close in. He wanted me to fly here immediately to help identify them as soon as they were captured. But the person who met me at the airfield when I landed turned out to be my kidnapper."

"We tricked you as easily as we tricked your friends here," Stiller sneered at him.

"What are you going to do with us?" Chet asked.

"Finish you off, what else!"

CHAPTER XIX

The Rope Trick

FRANK and Joe looked at each other. Both realized that they would have to fight their way out. Frank counted the gang members that were in the room with them. Stiller, Salty, Bruno, the hotel clerk, and another man that Stiller had called Bartel. "The owner of the helicopter, no doubt," Frank thought and wondered vaguely where the Cutlers were.

The Hardys knew they had a chance to subdue their adversaries if Young helped. Jenson was handcuffed. With a yell to Joe and Chet, Frank threw himself on the man nearest him. Joe did the same, and Chet, who caught on immediately, flattened Salty with a blow to the chin.

The next few minutes were bedlam. Stiller attacked Frank, while Joe took Cutler with a flying tackle. Young seemed frozen and stood stock-still as Chet seized Bruno in a tight headlock. Even Dr.

Jenson got into the fray and tripped a couple of men who were about to attack the Hardys.

Just then Mr. and Mrs. Cutler arrived. Cutler threw himself into the fight, turning the odds heavily against the young detectives. One by one the boys were overpowered. Jenson was lying on the floor, and Young stood frozen, as if in shock.

"Let's tie 'em up," Cutler panted, and his wife went to get a supply of rope. Soon the boys and the two scientists had their hands bound behind their backs and their ankles tied. Then the gang filed out of the room.

"They won't be here long," Stiller muttered to Salty on the way out. "And I'll be glad when we're rid of them for good!"

The door slammed shut, a key turned in the lock, and the men went downstairs. Slowly their footsteps died away.

"Work on the ties," Frank advised his companions. "If we slide up to one another, we can try to use our fingers to loosen each other's ropes. Here, watch me." He rolled up to Joe and wriggled until the two lay next to each other, facing opposite directions. Then, with great patience, he worked on his brother's bonds. Jenson and Young followed suit, while Chet waited until Frank had untied Joe and was able to help him. A half hour later everyone was free. Dr. Jenson sat down in a corner with his head in his hands. He had gone through so much already that he had lost all hope.

Young, however, had overcome his panic and

tried to encourage his partner. "Adrian, don't give up yet. Perhaps we'll all be saved, and the Firebird will be launched on schedule. Let's go over those final calculations again so we'll be prepared."

"You really think there's a chance?" Jenson asked, wanting to believe there was.

"There always is," Young assured him. "Here, I have some paper in my pocket. Let's write down the equations."

Frank, Joe, and Chet, meanwhile, looked around the huge bare dusty room, seeking some means of escape. Aside from the door, which had been locked, the only other way out seemed to be through a single unboarded window. Its pane was cracked and the frame broken, but Chet managed to open the sash far enough to peer out.

"We can't climb down," he informed his friends. "Too high up."

Frank and Joe joined him and saw that the wall descended five stories without offering a toehold anywhere along the way. Nor was there any possibility of climbing to the roof, ten feet above.

"Are you sure?" Young called out, interrupting his discussion with Dr. Jenson.

"Positive," Chet confirmed. He craned out as far as possible, surveying the wall to the left and right.

"Maybe if we tied all the ropes together," Young suggested, getting up to see for himself.

As he approached the window, he suddenly

stumbled and fell heavily against Chet. The chubby youth lost his balance and, with a yell, started to plunge over the sill!

Desperately Joe leaped forward and grabbed Chet's pants leg. He managed to hold on long enough for Frank to seize their friend's arm and clutch his shirt. Together the Hardys pulled him back into the loft.

Chet was as white as chalk and Joe's hands were shaking.

"I'm sorry!" Young said, staring at the boys. "I didn't mean to—it was an accident—I——"

Chet gulped. "That's okay, professor. It's just that I'm not built for flying." He tried a brave smile, and Young turned around in embarrassment to sit with Dr. Jenson.

The boys stood without talking for a while. Finally Frank said, "There's only one possibility and that is to clear the boarded-up windows. Maybe we can escape through one of them and climb down one of the other walls."

The young detectives wrenched the boards loose from each window, but were disappointed. The ground and the roof remained inaccessible.

"There goes our last chance," Joe said, discouraged. "We can't climb up or down, and the only stairs are guarded!"

Suddenly Frank had an idea. "Do you have a pencil?" he asked his brother and Chet.

"Yes, here," Joe said. "Why?"

Frank pulled a piece of paper out of his pocket and scribbled a hurried message. *"Help. We are being held prisoners in the warehouse!"* Then he leaned through the window and tossed the paper out. It drifted down onto the deserted street.

"Do you have any more paper?" Joe asked, excited.

"No. Do you?"

"No."

Chet did not have any either, and Frank said, "Let's ask the others."

The two scientists were involved in a serious conversation. Dr. Young had scribbled a number of equations on a piece of scrap. He looked up in surprise when the boys approached him. "This is all I had," he declared. "What do you need it for?"

They explained, and he said, "Forget it. This place is obviously so deserted that no one would find it anyway."

"It was a good try," Chet said. "And we have nothing to lose, right?"

"I suppose so," Young muttered, but he did not seem convinced.

They sat in silence for a while, overwhelmed by the hopelessness of their situation. Joe stared out the small window, his mind desperately trying to find a solution. Suddenly he sat up straight.

"Hey, did you see that?"

"See what?" Frank asked.

"The rope! In front of the window!"

"What?" Everyone looked in the direction of the opening, at the same time noticing a scuffling of feet on the roof.

"Someone's up there!" Frank exploded, as the rope came into view again, swinging back and forth wildly in the empty space.

"He's climbing down!" Joe shouted.

Young and Jenson stood up. They were about to rush to the window when a man shinnied down the rope, braced his foot against the wall, pushed back, and swung forward in a wide arc through the opening into the loft.

Everyone stared in amazement as the newcomer landed and bounced in an upright position. He looked at them with a big smile.

Jenson and Young hastened over, and Frank cried out, "Dad!"

"Mr. Hardy?" Chet mumbled, his mouth agape. "Is it really you?"

"Mr. Hardy!" Young stammered. "Are—are you here alone?"

"Yes," the detective replied, looking intensely at the scientist.

"Dad, how did you get here?" Joe asked. "We thought you were still in Florida at the Space Flight Center!"

"I discovered a clue that led me to Australia. Then I got a line on the gang ringleader. I followed him till I came to this place."

"Why did you post yourself on the roof?" Joe wanted to know.

"I knew the gang was using the warehouse as a hideout, and I had reason to expect them to bring you here. When they left this morning, I followed them but lost them. So I came back and decided to wait. I climbed up to the roof, tied a rope around the big weathervane, and eventually saw the gang taking you up to the loft."

"You think we'll get out of here safely?" Jenson asked anxiously.

Fenton Hardy nodded. "We will, except for the one rocket scientist who's at the bottom of this mystery."

Jenson turned pale. "I don't understand. Are you accusing me?"

"Not you, Dr. Jenson."

"Then what do you mean?"

Fenton Hardy looked straight at Young. "Professor, you're facing criminal charges in Australia and the United States!"

CHAPTER XX

Surprise in Port Augusta

As THE boys and Jenson stared in utter astonishment, Fenton Hardy pointed a finger at the professor. "You were behind the whole thing!"

"Prove it!" Young sneered.

"I will, and you'll spend time in prison! You're under arrest!"

"That's what you think, Hardy!" Young snapped viciously. "This is your last case. We've got you outnumbered. You're finished!" Pulling a whistle from his pocket, he blew a shrill blast that echoed through the whole building.

Bruno's voice responded from the landing at the top of the stairs. "Okay, chief," he said and turned the massive key in the lock. He pushed the door open and entered, covering the group with a revolver while Young moved over to join him.

Footsteps pounded up the stairs. Led by Stiller, the rest of the gang came in. The Cutlers brought up the rear with puzzled looks on their faces. "What's going on?" Cutler asked.

"We caught a real big fish this time," Young chuckled. He pointed to the Bayport detective and asked Stiller, "Do you know who this is?"

Stiller grinned. "Sure. That's the gumshoe Fenton Hardy, who sent me to jail ten years ago. I've been itching ever since to get even!"

"You were guilty," Mr. Hardy reminded him. "You got what you deserved."

Stiller scowled. "I'd have got away with it except for you. Now I'll take care of you and your punk sons, too."

"This is your chance for revenge," Young said. "Get them out of here. I don't want to see any of them again, ever!"

"It'll be a pleasure!" Stiller snarled.

He and his gang moved forward. Frank doubled his fists. "We may as well go down swinging!"

Joe assumed a karate stance with upraised palms and challenged the gang, "You won't take us without a fight!"

Stiller looked at Cutler. "Shall we finish them off here?" he asked roughly.

Cutler shook his head. "I had to rent this dump. Any evidence of a crime committed here might be traced to me. We'll take them to the woods out in back. There'll be plenty of cover out there."

Cutler glanced at Young. "Sure you've got all the dope you need from Jenson?"

Young nodded impatiently. "Don't worry about that. He's given me the final equations. Come on —let's finish this job so I can get back to Woomera."

The gang began to circle the boys and Mr. Hardy held up a hand. "Don't resist," he told the boys.

The advice surprised the three so much that the gang members were able to break through and overpower them after a brief struggle.

"Tie 'em up again and do a better job this time," Mrs. Cutler commanded as Bruno picked up the ropes and handcuffed the prisoners.

"Dad!" Frank cried out. "Why did you tell us not to fight?"

"There's no need to resist," Mr. Hardy said. "Didn't you hear tires screech down below?"

The gang froze in dismay, then Cutler dashed to the open window and looked down. "It's the cops!" he cried. "Let's get out of here!"

He and Mrs. Cutler ran from the loft and down the stairs, followed by other members of the gang. But the police already had the building surrounded. A detective sergeant and several uniformed constables arrested and disarmed the crooks as they tried to escape. The prisoners were herded back upstairs, and the captives were untied.

"You're right on time, sergeant." Fenton Hardy grinned.

"No trouble, sir. Mr. Moran alerted us a couple of hours ago."

"Mr. Moran?" Frank asked incredulously.

"That's correct," Mr. Hardy replied. "Here he comes." He pointed to Michael, who had followed the police to the loft.

Chet's mouth dropped open. "Mike! Wh-what are you doing here?"

"It's a long story," Mike said with a smile as the criminals were handcuffed and taken downstairs by the officers.

Professor Young stared at the newcomer. "You double-crossing rat!" he fumed. "You were supposed to be working for *us!*"

"Sorry, professor." Mike grinned coldly. "I happen to be working for the U.S. government. And it was my assignment to investigate the Cutler-Stiller gang for a series of international kidnappings and other offenses. I didn't know then they were behind the Jenson disappearance."

"Fantastic!" Frank exclaimed. "So you got a job with them—saying the law was after you?"

Mike grinned. "I'm sorry I couldn't tell you the truth, Frank. Now I can because my assignment is over and I'm a free agent again."

"What about Mr. Ponsley?" Chet asked.

"I had to let him know because I wasn't going with him."

"But how did you meet with Dad?" Joe inquired.

"After I left Ponsley at the airport, I phoned my superior at the U.S. Consulate," Mike went on. "He instructed me to assist Mr. Hardy in the Jenson case and the rounding up of the gang. So I met your father in Sydney and told him all I'd learned. We combined forces and flew into Port Augusta yesterday evening. By pooling all we knew, we were able to trace Stiller's mob to this warehouse—but we still didn't have the evidence to convict Young."

"You've got it now," said Chet. "Boy, what a case! So that's why you couldn't let your dad know what you were doing or where you were."

Mike nodded. "But it's all over now." He glanced at the two Hardy boys. "By the way, your deductions about that bank security guard were correct. Thurbow has confessed that he was the one who tipped off the robbers about the alarm system, and that he switched those chemicals in the hope of putting the Hardys out of action."

By now all the crooks had been taken downstairs except for Young. When a constable approached him with a pair of handcuffs, the scientist made a sudden break for the window. He squirmed through, grabbed the rope still dangling outside, and in seconds had shinnied down to the ground.

The constable leaned out the window and took aim with his gun.

"Don't shoot!" Mr. Hardy warned. "We want him alive!"

Frank edged past them and went down the rope after the fugitive. Young headed for the woods behind the warehouse, and Frank followed at top speed. Joe, meanwhile, flew down the stairs, hoping to head Young off. The others followed.

The prisoners were being loaded into police cars in front of the warehouse. The constable paused to explain the latest turn of events to the sergeant, while Mr. Hardy and Chet followed Joe around to the rear of the building, just in time to see Frank disappear into the woods.

"Young must be ahead of him!" Joe said as they hurried after the young detective.

Frank lost sight of Young among the trees, but a path led him through the underbrush and he went forward until he came to a fork, where he had to guess which way Young had gone. He decided to take the left branch. A hundred yards in he caught sight of the fugitive.

Young, glancing over his shoulder, noticed Frank. Puffing from exertion, he darted from the path into the underbrush. He stumbled and tripped in the thick shrubbery, but he refused to slow down because he could hear his pursuer forcing his way through after him.

Young reached the right-hand path, looked around, and then ran back toward the fork, hoping to confuse Frank.

Joe, meanwhile, had taken the right-hand path, his father and Chet the left. The boy ran until he reached a towering tree, where he paused to get his bearings. He heard a rustling sound and looked up.

Young leaped down on him!

The rocket scientist hit the younger Hardy between the shoulders, and the pair went down amid leaves, vines, and plants. Stunned by the collision, Joe felt Young's hand closing around his throat and choking off his breath. Grimly he struggled to break the hold. The man had a strategic advantage over him, and Joe gasped convulsively. The branches of the tree above him seemed to swing wildly as if whipped about by a heavy storm; then everything darkened and Joe went limp.

Suddenly he felt a hand pull him by the shoulder. He seized a wrist with his last bit of strength.

"Hold it," Frank said. "It's me!"

"Where's Young?" Joe croaked.

"He ran off when he saw me coming—back toward the warehouse. We've got to get him. Think you'll make it?"

"Sure, now that I can breathe again!" Joe rubbed his throat and the boys raced up the path. They reached the open space behind the warehouse and spotted Young jumping into the gang's pickup. Two policemen hurried around the corner, but Young got the truck going and roared straight at them, forcing them to spring out of the way.

The man powered toward a side road near where the Hardys emerged from the woods.

"Don't get in front of him!" Frank warned his brother. "He'll run you down!"

"I won't," Joe replied, "but this will! Give me a hand, Frank!"

Together, they levered up a fallen log from the ground and hurled it under the front wheels of the speeding truck. The vehicle struck the log with a thump, careened wildly to one side, and jolted to a halt in the underbrush.

The Hardys pounced on Young and dragged him out of the driver's seat. Realizing he could not escape again, he surrendered without a struggle. He too was loaded into one of the police cars in front of the warehouse, where Frank and Joe rejoined their father and Chet.

The Australian police detective complimented the Hardy boys on their quick thinking and fast action. "Now we have the whole gang," he added with satisfaction.

Young gave Fenton Hardy a venomous stare. "What made you suspect me?" he rasped.

"Frank and Joe asked me to check out Smoky Rinaldo. He'd found all the clues at the Aerospace Lab that seemed to incriminate Dr. Jenson, and he could easily have planted them himself. But he turned out to be clean, as far as I could tell. Then I realized you could have planted the clues just as easily. What's more, you were the only person who could have kept the gang tipped off about Frank and Joe's moves. For that matter, you were probably the one who stole that pass Stiller used to get into the Aerospace Lab."

"So Stiller followed us around the lab," Frank commented. "And, on orders from Young, he shadowed us at the Nassau Club."

Joe looked at Young. "You put on an act at the Princeton Library! You told me Stiller got out of the elevator and ran upstairs. Instead, you probably warned him to leave through the front door while you sent us on a wild-goose chase!"

Young glared at him but said nothing.

Frank spoke up. "And you told Stiller that we would be flying to Sydney so he could resume his job in Australia. By the way, was it you who phoned us at Sydney Airport and threatened us after we'd returned there with Mike Moran and Dr. Jenson?"

"What do *you* think?" Young snapped.

"I think he's right," Chet broke in. "I also think it was you who made that phone call to the hotel here in Port Augusta to keep Frank and Joe busy while your gang kidnapped Dr. Jenson from our room."

"Right," said Joe. "By that time, his private pilot was probably already flying back to Woomera to pick him up and bring him here."

"And later," Chet said to Young, "you tried to push me out of the warehouse window. If you weren't handcuffed, I'd punch you right in the nose!"

Dr. Jenson spoke up with indignation. "Arthur, why did you go through that miserable play acting up in the warehouse loft just now?"

"Because I needed the last Firebird equations you'd been working on. That's why. So I pumped you for the information in order to handle the project on my own."

"But I don't understand. Why was that so important to you?"

"I can answer that," Mr. Hardy said. "In case you didn't realize it, Young's been working for a foreign power. When their intelligence agents picked up news of the Firebird's development, they approached Young and paid him to eliminate you, Dr. Jenson, so *he* would be the one controlling the project. He was then to devise a scheme to foul up the launching in such a way that it would take NASA a long time to find out what went wrong. Young was supposed to turn over all our plans to this power so they could build a Firebird rocket of their own before we could recover from the foul-up and thus be ahead of us in this area of our space program."

Frank shook his head in disgust. "It's a good thing we prevented him from going through with his scheme," he said. Frank was proud that he had had a part in solving the case, but also felt the familiar emptiness he always experienced when a case was finished. Would there ever be another mystery for the Hardy boys? Frank did not realize at this moment that their help would soon be needed in *The Sting of the Scorpion*.

"Well, Dr. Jenson," Joe said, "now the tables are turned. You'll be in charge of the rocket launching."

"And it'll be right on schedule!" Chet added enthusiastically. "I'm sure it'll be a great success!"

Frank nudged his friend and grinned. "Not like yours at Bayport Meadow, Chet!"

Order Form
Own the original 56 thrilling
NANCY DREW MYSTERY STORIES®

In *hardcover* at your local bookseller OR
simply mail in this handy order coupon and start your collection today!

Please send me the following Nancy Drew titles I've checked below.
All Books Priced @ $5.99

AVOID DELAYS   Please Print Order Form Clearly

☐	1 Secret of the Old Clock	448-09501-7	☐ 30 Clue of the Velvet Mask	448-09530-0
☐	2 Hidden Staircase	448-09502-5	☐ 31 Ringmaster's Secret	448-09531-9
☐	3 Bungalow Mystery	448-09503-3	☐ 32 Scarlet Slipper Mystery	448-09532-7
☐	4 Mystery at Lilac Inn	448-09504-1	☐ 33 Witch Tree Symbol	448-09533-5
☐	5 Secret of Shadow Ranch	448-09505-X	☐ 34 Hidden Window Mystery	448-09534-3
☐	6 Secret of Red Gate Farm	448-09506-8	☐ 35 Haunted Showboat	448-09535-1
☐	7 Clue in the Diary	448-09507-6	☐ 36 Secret of the Golden Pavilion	448-09536-X
☐	8 Nancy's Mysterious Letter	448-09508-4	☐ 37 Clue in the Old Stagecoach	448-09537-8
☐	9 The Sign of the Twisted Candles	448-09509-2	☐ 38 Mystery of the Fire Dragon	448-09538-6
☐	10 Password to Larkspur Lane	448-09510-6	☐ 39 Clue of the Dancing Puppet	448-09539-4
☐	11 Clue of the Broken Locket	448-09511-4	☐ 40 Moonstone Castle Mystery	448-09540-8
☐	12 The Message in the Hollow Oak	448-09512-2	☐ 41 Clue of the Whistling Bagpipes	448-09541-6
☐	13 Mystery of the Ivory Charm	448-09513-0	☐ 42 Phantom of Pine Hill	448-09542-4
☐	14 The Whispering Statue	448-09514-9	☐ 43 Mystery of the 99 Steps	448-09543-2
☐	15 Haunted Bridge	448-09515-7	☐ 44 Clue in the Crossword Cipher	448-09544-0
☐	16 Clue of the Tapping Heels	448-09516-5	☐ 45 Spider Sapphire Mystery	448-09545-9
☐	17 Mystery of the Brass-Bound Trunk	448-09517-3	☐ 46 The Invisible Intruder	448-09546-7
☐	18 Mystery at Moss-Covered Mansion	448-09518-1	☐ 47 The Mysterious Mannequin	448-09547-5
☐	19 Quest of the Missing Map	448-09519-X	☐ 48 The Crooked Banister	448-09548-3
☐	20 Clue in the Jewel Box	448-09520-3	☐ 49 The Secret of Mirror Bay	448-09549-1
☐	21 The Secret in the Old Attic	448-09521-1	☐ 50 The Double Jinx Mystery	448-09550-5
☐	22 Clue in the Crumbling Wall	448-09522-X	☐ 51 Mystery of the Glowing Eye	448-09551-3
☐	23 Mystery of the Tolling Bell	448-09523-8	☐ 52 The Secret of the Forgotten City	448-09552-1
☐	24 Clue in the Old Album	448-09524-6	☐ 53 The Sky Phantom	448-09553-X
☐	25 Ghost of Blackwood Hall	448-09525-4	☐ 54 The Strange Message	
☐	26 Clue of the Leaning Chimney	448-09526-2	in the Parchment	448-09554-8
☐	27 Secret of the Wooden Lady	448-09527-0	☐ 55 Mystery of Crocodile Island	448-09555-6
☐	28 The Clue of the Black Keys	448-09528-9	☐ 56 The Thirteenth Pearl	448-09556-4
☐	29 Mystery at the Ski Jump	448-09529-7		

VISIT PENGUIN PUTNAM BOOKS FOR YOUNG READERS ONLINE:
http://www.penguinputnam.com/yreaders/index.htm

Payable in US funds only. Postage & handling: US/Can. $2.75 for one book, $1.00 for each add'l book not to exceed $6.75; Int'l $5.00 for one book, $1.00 for each add'l. We accept Visa, MC, AMEX ($10.00 min.), checks ($15.00 fee for returned checks), and money orders. No Cash/COD. Call (800) 788-6262 or (201) 933-9292, fax (201) 896-8569, or mail your orders to:

Penguin Putnam Inc.
PO Box 12289 Dept. B
Newark, NJ 07101-5289

Bill my
credit card # _____exp._____
___ Visa ___ MC ___ AMEX
Signature: _____

Bill to: _____
Address _____
City _____ ST _____ ZIP_____
Daytime phone #_____

Ship to:_____
Address_____
City _____ ST _____ ZIP_____

Book Total $_____
Applicable sales tax $_____
Postage & Handling $_____
Total amount due $_____

Please allow 4–6 weeks for US delivery. Can./Int'l orders please allow 6–8 weeks.
This offer is subject to change without notice.   Ad # _____

Surviving Death

Surviving Death

A Journalist Investigates
Evidence for an Afterlife

LESLIE KEAN

Crown Archetype
New York

Library of Congress Cataloging-in-Publication Data is available upon request.

ISBN 978-0-553-41961-0
Ebook ISBN 978-0-553-41962-7

Printed in the United States of America

Jacket design by Alane Gianetti
Jacket photograph by Anthony Harvie/Digital Vision/Getty Images

3   5   7   9   10   8   6   4   2

First Edition

For my father,
Hamilton Fish Kean
1925–2016

Contents

Introduction

While exploring the evidence for an afterlife, I witnessed some unbelievable things that are not supposed to be possible in our material world. Yet they were unavoidably and undeniably real. Despite my initial doubt, I came to realize that there are still aspects of Nature that are neither understood nor accepted, even though their reality has profound implications for understanding the true breadth of the human psyche and its possible continuity after death.

I was directly exposed to people capable of perception that seemed to transcend the limitations of the physical brain; unexplainable forces, acting with apparent intelligence, able to move objects; and the delivery of obscure and accurate details by possible discarnate beings communicating through people unknown to them. I also studied numerous published papers, including those by medical doctors, describing clinically dead patients with no brain function who reported journeys to a sublime afterlife dimension.

My explorations of these and other remarkable phenomena gave rise to many questions. How can it be that an apparition returns a wave from a human observer? Or that people watch their own resuscitation from the ceiling in the operating room, aware that they have left their bodies? How about a human hand materialized by a declared disembodied survivor of death, on multiple occasions? And how could a two-year-old boy seem to remember numerous specific facts about a previous life, unknown to anyone in the family, that are later verified as accurate?

As documented within the scientific literature for over a hundred years, these and other manifestations have one aspect in common: they suggest that consciousness—or some aspect of ourself—may survive physical death. In these pages I will take you on a journey into this world.

An investigation of such evidence has rarely been systematically consolidated and subjected to in-depth, rigorous scrutiny by a journalist. This task has been left primarily to a few courageous scientists, philosophers, medical doctors, psychiatrists, and other investigators usually writing about one specific area of research. My intention is to present some of the most interesting evidence from diverse sources and show how it interconnects, making it accessible for the intelligent and curious reader encountering the material for the first time. Strict journalistic protocols can be applied to any topic for which there is data, no matter how unusual or even indeterminate.

Yet, this book is far from a catalog of evidence for the survival of bodily death. It is also a very personal story for me. My narrative would have remained one-dimensional and abstract without the experiences and "personal experiments" that are part of it. In this sense, I have taken a step inside this investigation in a new way—through experience and first-hand examination, and not just from the perspective of a detached observer who studies data and peers into a strange world from the outside. It may be professionally risky to expose these very personal events, but I feel it is my obligation to do so. It would be dishonest to omit elements that had an impact on my thinking and my effort to come to terms with many remarkable phenomena, elements that drew me even more deeply into the material. However, I was also careful to step back from them afterward, remaining as analytical and discriminating as I was with everything else. The tricky aspect lies in the interpretation of the extraordinary events, not in their reporting.

As a journalist, I have been interested in the question of whether there is evidence for survival past death for over ten years. In 2007 I became an associate producer for a documentary film on this topic, which offered me exposure to some of the best cases and experts in the United States and abroad. I traveled to Glasgow, Scotland, to meet with the family of a small boy named Cameron who had talked about a past life that haunted his early years. The memories had generated much emotion and longing for his previous family. His mother and psychiatrist Jim Tucker, an expert on child reincarnation cases, eventually took Cameron to his "previous house" on an island called Barra, where they were able to document the accuracy of his memories. Although very sad and subdued while walking through the home, Cameron seemed to be healed after that; his memories faded away and he was able to live a normal life in the present.

Was all of this just wishful thinking on the part of a mother with a disturbed little boy? Strange as it might seem, was three-year-old Cameron using some kind of psychic mental power to retrieve information about this location to which he had no known connection? Or, was he actually remembering a life lived before this one, as seemed indisputable to him and eventually to his mom?

I also assisted with interviews of two physical mediums—those who facilitate the manifestation of extraordinary physical phenomena while in a trance state that they say is generated by forces coming from the "spirit world." In this case, these included moving lights, levitated objects, materialized hands, unusual images on factory-sealed photographic film, and detailed information provided from deceased relatives. These manifestations were witnessed by hundreds of people between 1993 and 1998 in the village of Scole, England, and in six other countries. The stated purpose of the Scole experiments, as the more than five hundred sessions were called, was to demonstrate the reality of life after death. The sessions were scrutinized for three years by three qualified outside investigators, who often conducted and controlled the experiments themselves, and who documented the events as genuine in a lengthy, scholarly report. Others who studied the data after attending only a few sessions questioned whether enough controls were in place, especially since most of the experiments were conducted in darkness. I was determined to experience these astonishing phenomena myself someday, which I finally did with a different physical medium while researching this book.

During this time I was also exploring another tantalizing question: whether we are alone in the universe. In 1999 I began an indepth investigation into evidence for unidentified aerial phenomena, popularly known as UFOs, reviewing decades of official case reports, government documents, and interviewing pilots, military personnel, and government officials. Over many years, I learned that there is solid evidence for the existence of remarkable unknown physical objects in our skies, but we have not yet determined what they are, why they are here, or where they come from. My work culminated in the publication of *UFOs: Generals, Pilots, and Government Officials Go on the Record* in 2010. Understandably, this phenomenon is difficult to study for a host of reasons, and more hard data is needed. But it is unfortunate that the extensive documentation on UFOs has been marginalized or dismissed by scientists searching for more conventional signs of extraterrestrial life. Similarly, the "paranormal" events covered in this book have been considered a fringe topic by the scientific establishment for a long time, even though in reality they are worthy of serious academic and scientific attention.

Curiosity about the physical universe is one thing, but the universal question of the state of consciousness or "spirit" after bodily death, pondered by human beings since the beginning of time, has a particular urgency on our home planet. People foment hatred and even kill one another over ideological differences, and distortions in faith can be used to justify the most horrendous human activity. What if we could develop a broad unified view of what could be the reality of life after death, *based on facts*, and thereby diminish the potency of competing, rigid belief systems? Perhaps a more rational understanding could bring consolation to many people at the end of their lives, while also motivating us to be more ethical and compassionate throughout life. Greater understanding of the nature of consciousness and its possible survival beyond death could have far-reaching, enlightening effects on humanity.

It must be clear by now that this book has nothing to do with dogma, whether we're talking about the dogma of an immaterial God through various religions, or the dogma of materialist science that holds that matter is all that exists and that all phenomena, including consciousness, are reducible to physical processes. This does not mean that one's personal or religious beliefs need be in conflict with the material presented here. I fully respect all perspectives and hope that evidence suggestive of survival might enrich and support anyone's search for more objective answers, regardless of their background. My intention is to provide clarity and not to create conflict. I hope you will agree that it would be interesting to look at what actually *is* when dealing with such an important question.

Regardless of our individual perspective, we must all face our own impending death and the tragedy of losing those we love. In the last four years, while working on this book, I lost my father, younger brother, and dearest uncle. In 2011 I was present the moment a close friend with cancer took his last breath. Some people rely on religious or mystical belief systems to cope with the incomprehensible, shocking, and often surreal finality of death. But for many others, this simply doesn't work. Like these others, who may be agnostics, I want to understand what this momentous end to life actually means, to the extent that this is possible. Are we only the body left lying there, physical matter with a brain that has shut down all human functioning and every element of our consciousness, leaving only empty matter no different from a lump of clay? Or, does something essential and conscious leave our physical body at the time of death and transition to another existence in a nonmaterial realm? Even if it may be impossible to prove, we can be comforted by the ample objective evidence suggesting that those we have lost survive in another form and may even be able to communicate to us from "the next world."

Most people are probably not aware that a "survival hypothesis" has been formulated and debated within many disciplines for a long time. Usually hidden away in obscure volumes, scientific papers, and diverse areas of research, it has a strong academic and scientific foundation. To enhance my narrative, I invited ten leading experts and important witnesses, offering astonishing and groundbreaking stories, to contribute exclusive chapters so the reader could hear from them directly, in their own words.

The American contributors are a child psychiatrist from the University of Virginia studying children with past-life memories; a parapsychologist who is an expert on apparitions; a leading researcher studying mental mediumship under strict controls; a medical social worker with personal involvement in a veridical out-of-body case; and a parent of a young boy with dozens of past-life memories that were later found to be accurate. From the UK, you will hear from a neuropsychiatrist specializing in end-of-life experiences; a retired psychologist from the University of Nottingham on investigations into trance mediumship; and a well-established, genuine physical medium. A Dutch cardiologist and expert on near-death experiences has also contributed a chapter, as well as a psychologist from the University of Iceland with evidence for survival after death provided by a young Icelandic physical medium. Many others have been willing to be interviewed and provide case material and witness accounts for this book.

I want to cover a few basic points, and then we will begin this journey. By the end of the book, I think you will conclude that the nature of consciousness is more vast and complex than anyone understands; that belief in survival past death is rational and supported by the facts; and that this body of information deserves further investigation by the scientific community since it deals with one of the most fundamental questions ever addressed by human beings.

First, it is important that I make clear what I mean by "survival." This concept does *not* refer to an impersonal merging into pure awareness or becoming one with universal consciousness as envisioned by many who meditate or are influenced by Eastern religions. If this were all that happened, we would lose our individuality. The question here concerns *personal* survival—a postmortem existence in which distinct traits, memories, and emotions are sustained at least by some of us for an unknown period of time. It refers to a psychological continuity after death, which makes it possible for the disembodied personality to be recognizable by those left behind when communication is received. The survival hypothesis is proposing this kind of personal survival as an unproven but rational theory explaining much compelling data. In other words, without meaning anything religious, this represents survival of the individual essence, spirit, or soul.

Within this context, we must also understand that human beings have extraordinary mental abilities that science cannot explain. They may be controversial, but they have been documented by legitimate scientists for many years; I have also personally witnessed them in operation. We call these abilities "psi," or psychic functioning, interchangeable with "extrasensory perception" (ESP). They refer to that force that is used for the acquisition of information through the mind without the use of any of the currently accepted five senses (sight, taste, touch, hearing, and smell). This is why some refer to it as a "sixth sense."

In order to study the survival hypothesis, we must understand the various forms of psi. Telepathy occurs when one mind influences or "reads" another, such as when one perceives someone else's thoughts. Clairvoyance involves the perception of objects or physical events at a distance, such as knowing the location of something missing or what a faraway document says. Psychokinesis (PK) is the active influence of the mind on matter, causing observable physical effects like the movement of objects. Precognition involves an awareness of future events before they happen. The results of all of these perceptive abilities can be documented and verified.

If communications occur between the living and discarnate beings in a nonphysical realm, these psychic abilities are often the tools required on one or both sides to make that possible. The discarnate consciousness no longer can communicate through bodily senses and must rely on psi to reach from "beyond the veil" into the physical world. Some living people have the ability to act like a telephone operator with a "psychic antenna" into this other realm, using their psi to receive specific information from the discarnate, like invisible fiber optics.

Your red flag may have just jumped up. Certainly fraud abounds when discussing this topic. Many so-called psychics and mediums have taken advantage of gullible and earnest people for a long time. But in certain instances, extraordinary abilities have been exhibited by people with decades of experience, and they have been studied under controlled conditions. Believe it or not, after over a hundred years of research, and even though mainstream science may not accept it, this repeated documentation has established that these abilities are real.

We don't understand how telepathy or clairvoyance might work, but this is not a reason to dismiss them. We also don't understand how gravity works, yet no one denies its reality. And then there is something scientists call "dark energy," which makes up about three-quarters of our universe. It weighs more than all the energy of the stars and galaxies combined. Even so, standard models of the universe, established by physics, did not predict its existence, and scientists don't have a clue about what it is. "No theory can explain dark energy, although experimental evidence for it is staring us in the face," says Michio Kaku, the well-known theoretical physicist and bestselling author. University of Chicago cosmologist Michael S. Turner ranks dark energy as "the most profound mystery in all of science."

And within our interior universe, science does not understand the nature of consciousness either. "Consciousness poses the most baffling problems in the science of the mind," says David Chalmers, philosophy professor at New York University and the Australian National University. "There's nothing that we know more intimately than conscious experience, but there is nothing that is harder to explain." Cognitive scientist and philosopher Daniel Dennett says we at least know how to think about the unanswered questions within cosmology, particle physics, and other areas of science. "With consciousness, however, we are still in a terrible muddle," he writes. "Consciousness stands alone today as a topic that often leaves even the most sophisticated thinkers tongue-tied and confused."

Psychic abilities, or psi, are one very puzzling subset of this consciousness muddle, making the study of consciousness even worse for those who don't like to stray far from the status quo. It seems many scientists simply want to run away from the whole unexplainable mess and find ways to avoid dealing with the evidence for psi and related phenomena.

One exception to that is Dean Radin, perhaps the leading authority on the scientific study of psychic phenomena in relationship to consciousness. With a doctorate in educational psychology, he is Chief Scientist at the Institute of Noetic Sciences in Petaluma, California, and has held appointments at Princeton University. He also worked within a classified program now known as Star Gate, investigating psychic phenomena for the US government. He writes:

> The reality of psychic phenomena is now no longer based solely
> upon faith, or wishful thinking, or absorbing anecdotes. It is
> not even based upon the results of a few scientific experiments.
> Instead, we know that these phenomena exist because of new
> ways of evaluating massive amounts of scientific evidence
> collected over a century by scores of researchers.

British psychologist David Fontana studied the evidence for psi for over thirty years. "Psychic abilities are a matter of fact, not of belief," he writes. "What they are and they mean for our view of reality is another matter, but one cannot dismiss them as fiction and yet retain credibility as an unbiased observer." The reader will encounter the reality of the most refined psychic functioning throughout this book, and by the end will have no questions as to its existence.

Proponents of survival, often called "survivalists," believe that the hypothesis of personal survival provides the best explanation for the kind of evidence you will find in these pages. (And this book provides only a small portion of that evidence.) However, Michael Sudduth, an Oxford-educated professor of philosophy and religion at San Francisco State University and prolific writer in the area of postmortem survival, points out that survivalists are confused, or even disingenuous, in their deployment of the survival hypothesis. Their version of this hypothesis carries certain "auxiliary assumptions" along with it that they take for granted without acknowledging them to be the unprovable and untestable premises that they are. In other words, certain beliefs about what survival would look like, which cannot be proven, are built into what survivalists call their "hypothesis." They assume that at least some discarnate persons (those who have died and passed into the afterlife) have memories and personal identifying characteristics; these discarnates have the intention of communicating with the living; they have the psychic powers necessary to communicate with the living; and they have knowledge of what is happening in our world, allowing them to find someone through whom they can communicate.

Without these suppositions being part of the survival equation, it would be impossible for us to know what counts as evidence either for or against the hypothesis. Yet how do we know if these suppositions are true? They are assumed to be so in order to allow the survival hypothesis to fit the data. These characteristics of the afterlife realm and of the survived consciousness must be assumed to be true in order for the survival hypothesis to have explanatory power.

This may seem abstract, but it represents an ideological problem that we can't ignore. We are assuming that the nature of consciousness "on the other side of death" would have characteristics and motivations similar to ours when alive. "We do not know how the experience of death might alter consciousness or the mental states or causal powers of immaterial persons," Sudduth states. Think of it this way: We know the quantum world—the infinitesimal components of matter imbued with life—is governed by different principles and realities from the ones we know in our everyday lives. How different and unimaginable to us might be a world where consciousness exists post-death?

Fortunately, Sudduth offers what he calls a "strengthened" or "robust" survival hypothesis: one in which we can attach the assumptions previously listed, as long as we are aware that we're doing so, so that we have something to work with. This is the one examined in these pages. If we accept those assumptions about the nature of this existence, which survivalists believe to be true but can't prove, then indeed the evidence is compelling. And you will see why they believe in these characteristics of existence in the afterlife when you discover the case studies and personal accounts presented here. Numerous theorists have made the argument that survival after death is the most logical explanation for the data; scholarly volumes and research studies have been published making this point.

So this brings us to the obvious question: Is there another way of interpreting the extensive evidence, other than survival, that makes sense and could explain it? (I recognize that the reader has not yet perused the evidence, but these concepts are the background needed to make a proper assessment.)

There is one competing hypothesis that has generated much discussion and consternation within the research community. It claims that the evidence can be explained as psychic functioning *solely among the living* rather than through communication with the deceased. This would mean that mediums who receive verifiable communications, which they interpret as coming from discarnates, for example, are actually using their highly developed telepathy to read the minds of those connected to the deceased person, where the information can also be found. The human sources can be physically far away; that has no bearing on telepathy. Or, gifted people able to locate a hidden will unknown to anyone living could be using their own clairvoyance rather than relying on the now disembodied author of that will to convey its hiding place. People with highly developed psi abilities might unconsciously misinterpret this information as coming from a disembodied consciousness external to themselves. But in reality, the hypothesis proposes, all the information is acquired through their own telepathy and clairvoyance solely from earthly sources, no matter how refined the ability is.

This counter explanation is known as the "living-agent psi (LAP) hypothesis" as opposed to the survival hypothesis, which proposes that the source for the information is a discarnate. Sometimes the more extreme examples of human psychic ability have been called "super-psi" since they go way beyond what can be demonstrated in the laboratory, but LAP includes the full range. In other words, it's only the source of that psi that is up for debate, not the psi itself.

The validity of the living-agent psi hypothesis has been argued and dissected in detail by philosopher Stephen Braude, professor emeritus of the University of Maryland, in his brilliant and sophisticated work *Immortal Remains: The Evidence for Life After Death* (2003). This meticulous treatment has served as an indispensable reference for my research because of its rigor. Along with Michael Sudduth, Braude is among the toughest and most fastidious of any contemporary critical analyst of this evidence.

However, like the survival hypothesis, the LAP hypothesis depends on its own auxiliary assumptions, or built-in theoretical beliefs, to sustain itself. The central assumption is that human psychic abilities can be virtually unlimited in reach and scope, based on evidence of extraordinary psychic functioning. "No scientific theory renders any form of psi improbable," Braude states. With this assumption, virtually anything that could be interpreted as evidence for survival can also be theoretically interpreted as a product of unlimited human psi. Some analysts can't accept that human beings are capable of producing the psi required in the most extreme cases we have on record, which you will soon encounter, so they postulate that these manifestations must come from somewhere other than the human mind. But, there is a catch here. Is it logical to argue that these extreme psychic abilities are more acceptable when attributed to a deceased person than to a living one? Braude also makes the point that we have no clear scale or standard for what counts as super or extraordinary. Maybe the amount of psi required by LAP is not so extreme—it's just better than what we tend to see in the lab.

Regardless of the source of psi, the displays of psychic functioning that you will shortly encounter are truly magnificent. I introduce the "LAP vs. survival" debate to set a framework so we can examine it periodically throughout the book.

Braude's primary objective in writing *Immortal Remains* was to determine whether a survivalist interpretation of the evidence is reasonable, while also looking at the role living-agent psi might play.

"Overall, I'd say that the evidence most strongly supports the view that some aspects of our personality and personal consciousness, some significant chunk of our distinctive psychology, can survive the death of our bodies, at least for a time," he states. Sudduth concludes that how much of the phenomena either hypothesis can explain depends on what auxiliaries you enlist and what sort of explanatory criteria you use. On this theoretical level, the conclusion is a matter of personal opinion. "Braude and I are critiquing arguments for survival, not the hypothesis of survival itself," he told me.

Another expert commentator who will be given a voice in this book is British psychologist David Fontana, mentioned earlier, who is the author of the classic tome *Is There an Afterlife?* (2005). Fontana died in 2010. He wrote more than two dozen books on psychology translated into twenty-six languages, and was also a psychical researcher for many decades, serving as president of the well-known Society for Psychical Research in London. Fontana is a survivalist, and a knowledgeable one, with whom Braude does not always agree. Fontana recognized that some of the evidence for survival could also be explained as living-agent psi, "but to argue that such abilities explain all or even most of it stretches the hypothesis way beyond the breaking point," he wrote.

One final note: In the cases presented here, we can rule out the obvious—what Braude calls "The Usual Suspects"—such as fraud, errors in observation, misreporting, or any kind of dishonesty or deception. These are always the first considerations, and if they were in question, the cases would not appear in this book. Braude's "Unusual Suspects," defined as "abnormal or rare processes" such as dissociative pathologies, unprecedented forms of savantism, or latent creative abilities, are harder to rule out in some cases, but these are more obscure angles that are unlikely to explain the phenomena included here.

The reader must understand that for each case or witness report I present, there are many others. I chose to offer fewer cases in more detail rather than a survey of many cases with a superficial treatment of each. Although I have tried to select those cases that are most evidential, the reader will find much more to ponder in the literature.

The endnotes will help open the door to further reading and video watching.

So, let the journey begin. Going forward, we must remember the famous words of William James: "If you wish to upset the law that all crows are black, you mustn't seek to show that all crows are black; it is enough if you prove one single crow to be white." Maybe you will find your white crow in the following pages, upsetting the law that death is final. In any case, I hope you enjoy the ride.

PART ONE

Is There "Life" Before Birth?

After your death, you will be what you were before your birth.
—ARTHUR SCHOPENHAUER

Chapter 1

"Airplane Crash on Fire!"

Over many decades, investigators have documented cases of children, often as young as two, reporting memories they say are from a previous life. In some cases, the children provide enough specific details—such as names, locations, and mode of death from this previous life—to "solve" the case. This means that records and family members from that claimed previous life are located, and the facts provided by the child are shown to be accurate to the life of one specific person. Nightmares about the previous death, behaviors and knowledge related to a previous career, longing for past family members, and phobias related to the past life are often part of the child's world along with the memories. Most published cases have occurred in Asian countries, but recently some have been well documented in the United States.

Needless to say, these confusing events can be very troubling for the parents of such a child, especially when the culture and religion of the family do not support a belief in rebirth. For these families, such as the ones you are about to meet, the undeniable accuracy of their child's memories has to take precedence over any resistance they might feel. Such cases provide strong evidence for the possibility that we can be born again, and thus survive death.

Bruce and Andrea Leininger—two attractive, well-educated, middle-class American parents from Lafayette, Louisiana—had no idea what awaited them in the year 2000, when their young son James began to talk. Andrea, once an accomplished ballerina with the San Francisco Ballet and American Ballet Theatre, now teaches ballet with a local dance company. Bruce is the director of human resources for the Lafayette Parish School System. After many conversations with me, he provided original excerpts for this chapter describing his emotional and spiritual transformation throughout the ordeal.

When James Leininger was not quite two years old, his father, Bruce, took him to the Cavanaugh Flight Museum while they were visiting family in Dallas. For some reason, when they were outside on the tarmac, James shrieked with delight when he saw the F-104 Thunderchief parked there. Once inside, the well-adjusted and happy toddler stood still by the World War II planes, fixated as if drawn by a magnet. Nothing separated him from the parked fighter planes except a single rope barrier, and he kept trying to get closer. Whenever his dad took his hand and tried to steer him to another exhibit, James resisted with desperate, piercing screams. Bruce was perplexed; it felt eerie to him. After three hours, he lured James away only by promising a trip to an airfield to watch actual flying planes take off.

The following month, James's mother, Andrea, was pushing him in a stroller when she passed a hobby shop with a bin of plastic toys outside. She picked up a plastic propeller-driven model of an airplane and handed it to James, pointing out to him that it even had a bomb attached on its underside. James studied it for a moment, looked up and informed her: "That's not a bomb, Mommy, it's a 'dwop' tank."

Andrea didn't know what a drop tank was. Bruce later told her it was an extra gas tank carried by airplanes traveling long distances. Neither one could explain how James, who could barely talk, had ever heard of anything remotely like a drop tank.

James was the Leiningers' only child, and they adored him. At the time, Bruce had just begun working for Oil Fields Services Corporation of America and Andrea was a full-time mom. Bruce was raised a Methodist, going to church every Sunday throughout his childhood, and he found comfort and safety there. As he matured, he became part of the Evangelical Christian movement, and met with the Full Gospel Business Men's Fellowship biweekly for Bible study and discussion. He considered himself to be "a developed Christian on a continuous path of spiritual growth." But in a short time, Bruce felt all of that threatened by something that shook his faith and his very identity to its core.

In May, a month after James turned two, Bruce took him back to the Dallas flight museum, where he photographed the boy ecstatically mesmerized by a World War II aircraft. Since the last visit, Bruce and Andrea had watched their son become fascinated with toy airplanes, playing with nothing else. His obsession was not just with any toy planes, but with World War II airplanes in particular; he had an uncanny familiarity with them, a consuming attachment to them, and even knowledge about them that seemed to come from nowhere.

And then, the nightmares began. Actually, these were worse than your average nightmares. James was in terror, thrashing violently in a deep sleep while uncontrollable bloodcurdling screams issued from his crib. They plagued the family up to five times a week. The nightmares were so disturbing that Andrea took James to the pediatrician to find out if something was wrong with him. The doctor could offer nothing, and the repetitive dreams continued relentlessly, destroying the equanimity at home.

Then, after a few months, a turning point came when one night words suddenly accompanied the raw screams. Andrea called for Bruce to come. As he describes it:

I stood in my son's doorway. James was lying on his back, kicking and clawing the covers in his crib, like he was trying to break his way out of a coffin. He flung his head back and forth and screamed over and over: "Airplane crash on fire! Little man can't get out!"

James had just turned two and was beginning to learn to talk in sentences, yet his words seemed so unchildlike in their desperation. "Airplane crash on fire! Little man can't get out!" My concern was to protect him, but I felt frightened and paralyzed. What was happening to my son?

The dreams and the same words repeated themselves over and over again, for months more. Then James started to say the same words when awake. Once, when in the car while Andrea was dropping off Bruce at the airport for a business trip, James turned to his parents as his dad got out of the car. "Daddy's airplane crash! Big fire!" he told them. He crashed his toy planes with propellers headfirst into the coffee table so many times that the propellers broke off, damaging the table. And at night it seemed like he was reliving something all too real. It made absolutely no sense to his troubled parents.

One evening before bed, Andrea was reading Dr. Seuss to James. In a very relaxed state, James spontaneously started talking about the dream, and reenacted the crash with his little body while fully awake. His mother, trembling, asked him who the "little man" was. James said, "Me." Bruce came to the room, asked him again, "Who is the little man?" and he repeated, "Me." Bruce describes the conversation:

> "Son, what happened to your plane?"
> James replied, "It crashed on fire."
> "Why did your airplane crash?"
> "It got shot."
> "Who shot your plane?"
> James cocked his head and looked at me like the answer was obvious. It seemed to strike him as so inane that he rolled his eyes.

"The Japanese," he said with disdain, like an impatient teen-ager.

He was only just two. It felt as if the air had been sucked out of the room.

On another occasion, James got even more specific. He told them the little man's name was James. His parents assumed he was simply repeating his own name, as any two-year-old would, playing out some kind of scenario in his mind involving a pilot. But when they asked him more about the plane, James said that the "little man" flew a type of airplane called a Corsair. He also said that his plane took off from a boat. His dad asked him for the name of that boat, and he replied, *"Natoma."* Bruce commented that the name sounded Japanese, but James assured his parents that it was American, once again with an annoyed look as if they were idiots. Bruce writes:

I flinched, as if I'd been punched. He knew the plane. How could James know the name of a World War II fighter aircraft, much less with certainty that it was the aircraft in the dream? And how the hell did James know they were launched from aircraft carriers? Nothing that he had ever seen or read or heard could have influenced him to have this memory.

I was convinced that I somehow had to trap James to find the cracks or flaws in his story. I wanted something hard, on paper, providing proof that this was some kind of fantasy. I dismissed the Japanese, the Corsair, and even the boat, as some sort of strange story in his head. But then I went onto the Internet. After reading several pages of hits on the word "Natoma," I stared at a black-and-white picture of the *Natoma Bay*, a small United States aircraft carrier that fought in the Pacific in World War II. Andrea came in and I showed her as we stood there stiffly, frozen, as the hairs stood up on the back of our necks.

In a funny way, this made me mad. He wasn't even potty trained, and he was telling me something that shook my world. I was venturing into truly unknown territory. I began to panic, quietly. My wife and her family wondered about a possible "past life." I told them, "Never, not in my house!" I needed to be right about this. My spiritual side was ruled by the Christian faith, which did not accept reincarnation, and that was the end of that story. And the world was a rational place controlled by the scientific method. There had to be a logical explanation!

Bruce printed out information on the *Natoma Bay* from a website, which remains in the case file with the date of 08/27/2000 on the page. This is important, because it provides a time-stamped record of when Bruce conducted the search, in response to James's statement, making it clear that the statements were made before anything was known about the person James might have been describing from a "past life." The Corsair was an American fighter aircraft that was used primarily by the marines, but also the US Navy, in World War II. It's important to note that there was no Corsair at the flight museum that James visited, and he had not been exposed to anything to do with that aircraft.

By this time, a number of family members had visited and witnessed the chilling spectacle of the nightmares. In October, when he was two and a half, James explained one evening that he could not remember the last name of the "little man" James from his nightmares. But he said that this James had a best friend. When asked for his name, James said, "Jack Larsen, and he was a pilot too." The specificity of the name changed everything. And another important detail surfaced as well. James told his parents that his plane was shot in the engine, in front, where the propeller was. Strangely enough, all of his single engine toy airplanes had the propellers broken off their front ends from James's continued reenactments of the crash.

And finally, James provided another piece of the puzzle, out of the blue, on Thanksgiving weekend. He was waiting for cartoons to come on, and when he became impatient, his dad asked him to come sit on his lap. They started looking through the book *The Battle for Iwo Jima,* which Bruce had ordered as a Christmas present for his father, a former marine. (James's grandfather lived fourteen hundred miles away in Pennsylvania and was only at the house once during these events.) When they turned to a page with a photo of Iwo Jima, James pointed to it and said, "Daddy, that's when my plane was shot down and crashed." He used the word "when" rather than "where" while pointing to a photo of Iwo Jima and an accompanying diagram, never mentioning the island by name.

Each time a new clue was revealed, Bruce became more deeply unnerved. "The more I learned from James, the stronger my mission became to prove that the nightmares and everything else were simply the coincidental rants of a child," he writes. "I was hardened into a committed skeptic. Now that I had the name Jack Larsen, I could find out about him and this would make my point, I reasoned. I had to represent the voice of reason within the family."

At this point, Bruce assumed that the person in the dream, who died in the crash, was Jack Larsen. When Bruce asked James for the name of the "little man" in his dream, he always said James, which was simply his own name. Since Bruce didn't accept that James was dreaming about a past life, he concluded that therefore Jack Larsen was the important name, and that Larsen was likely the subject of the dream. (In retrospect this reasoning seems odd, but it made sense to Bruce at the time as he struggled to deny what was happening.) So, if Larsen was the person crashing in the dream, he was now dead. Bruce began to search for records. He found the American Battle Monuments Commission (ABMC) website, which listed US soldiers who were either missing in action or buried abroad. On that list, there were 170 Larsons or Larsens killed in World War II, but only ten of them had a first name of Jack, James, or John.

Bruce then spent many months diligently researching anything he could find to help explain what James was saying. He found that the USS *Natoma Bay* had been commissioned by the navy in October 1943, so the Jack (or John) Larson (or Larsen) crash would have to have been between then and the end of the war in August 1945. The Corsair did not enter naval carrier service until 1944. And he discovered that the *Natoma Bay* had been at Iwo Jima to support the invasion by US Marines there in March 1945.

Sometime later, Bruce searched "World War II War Veteran Reunions" and dozens of websites popped up. One of them, Escort Carriers Sailors and Airmen Association, contained a reference to a *Natoma Bay* Association reunion. Over a period of weeks, Bruce attempted to call people listed there, saying he was researching a book about the *Natoma Bay*. He finally reached Leo Pyatt, who said he flew thirty-six combat missions off the aircraft carrier, in the VC-81 squadron, during the battle for Iwo Jima. Bruce printed out information during this search dated from the year 2000, which remains in the case file.

Bruce asked Pyatt if he knew a Jack Larsen, and Pyatt didn't even pause. He said yes, he knew a Jack Larsen who "flew off one day and we never saw him again." He also told Bruce that he didn't know of any Corsairs being flown off the *Natoma Bay*. Bruce was both relieved and disturbed:

> The fact that James got something wrong—the Corsairs—made
> me feel reassured in a strange sort of way. The Corsairs were cru-
> cial to my skepticism. James insisted that he flew a Corsair, but
> this wasn't consistent with the facts. It was my one strong grip on
> reality. After all, it was only a dream.
>
> But Leo knew the name Jack Larsen. How could James have
> dreamed up the name of a real member of the squadron? It was
> a revelation that made me shiver and go quiet. This conversation
> with Leo lit a fire in me that consumed my soul. I was scared,
> bewildered and angry. But for sure one thing rose up in me. I
> would not stop searching until I found the answers.

Acting on the advice of counselor Carol Bowman, who had researched and written about such cases, Andrea started to explain to James that his nightmare memories happened to him in the past, but that now he was here and he was safe. Gradually the frequency of the nightmares decreased to once about every other week. Andrea's elaborate bedtime rituals, taking the scary out of his head and "putting the good dreams in," might have helped. But James's obsession with many varieties of World War II airplanes continued—he turned his Halloween pumpkin into an F-16 Thunderbird.

And in the spring of 2001, James began to furiously draw pictures of his memories, scores of them. They showed battle scenes usually including the violent descent of a plane in flames with bombs dropping around it. Barely able to write, he managed to sign them "James 3," which his parents assumed was because he'd turned three in April of that year. But when they asked him why, he replied, "Because I'm the third James." And he continued doing hundreds of drawings and signing many of them "James 3."

University of Virginia child psychiatrist Jim Tucker, an expert in such cases (who has contributed a future chapter), was not a stranger to this sort of behavior. "This kind of compulsive repetition is a phenomenon often seen in children who have survived or witnessed a major trauma; post-traumatic play, it's called," he states. "Since the drawing occurred along with repeated nightmares about the same kind of scene, they suggest a child trying to work through a traumatic event." In addition, Tucker, who met with the Leiningers when James was twelve and interviewed Bruce and Andrea extensively, reports that James had created a play cockpit in a closet, sitting in an old car seat. He would play pilot and then fall out the door as if parachuting down after being hit. Since his dream and his drawings depicted a man trapped in the plane and not able to push his way out to escape the fire, it seems likely that James's reenactments with this positive outcome could have represented an attempt to resolve the previous trauma—to act out his escape from the burning plane by evacuating it.

As far as we know, nothing had happened to James in his short life to explain the potential trauma that dominated his mind and emotions both day and night. One can only imagine how disturbing this was for his family. Fortunately, time would pass and things would be smooth for a while, with James playing, conversing, and growing up like any other ordinary child. Yet Bruce and Andrea never knew what else might surface, or for how long this would go on.

Through Carol Bowman, the Leiningers were invited to appear on a pilot for a new television show called *Strange Mysteries* produced by ABC. Although hesitant at first, they thought the resources brought to bear by the production company might help provide more answers. They agreed to it, but would not use any last names or state where they lived. During the preparations for the show, host Shari Belafonte searched for a navy pilot named Jack Larsen who had died in World War II, and this is documented in her correspondence with Bruce.

The show was filmed in the summer of 2002, when James was four. As often happens when pilot episodes are made for potential shows, it never aired, but now important footage exists that provides a record of statements made by James before the case was resolved. This provides confirmation that nothing was added to the story later, after the fact; James's statements were on the record before it was known if they made any sense or if answers to them would ever be found.

When the ABC producer for the segment, Shalini Sharma, met James, he unexpectedly told her more about the Corsair while showing her a picture of the plane in a book. "They used to get flat tires all the time. And they always wanted to turn left when they took off," he said. When she looked up Corsairs later, she discovered this was true. These were not the only details James provided about various airplanes when he was three and four; there were many such statements.

In September 2002, Bruce finally took the step of attending a *Natoma Bay* reunion in San Diego, California, expecting to find some answers there. If they supported James's statements, then he would be forced to confront this head-on and would no longer be able to live in denial. It was like jumping off the cliff and testing his faith even further. What happened there marked the point of no return.

When he arrived at the reunion, Bruce asked the *Natoma* historian John DeWitt about a *Natoma Bay* pilot named Jack Larsen. DeWitt pulled out the current association roster, and there was his name. Incredible! He was alive! Bruce had spent two years searching for a dead Jack Larsen who did not exist, and now here he was suddenly, fully alive and living in Arkansas.

Bruce also obtained a list of all twenty-one casualties from the *Natoma Bay,* twenty of them from three squadrons and one from the ship's company. At that moment, he saw something powerful that would permanently change his life. On the list was the name "James M. Huston Jr." Huston was killed on March 3, 1945, during the Battle of Iwo Jima, while attacking the island of Chichi-Jima about a hundred and fifty miles from Iwo Jima. In fact, although the details of the deaths were not provided, James Huston had been the *only* airman killed during the Battle of Iwo Jima, the location that his son James had pointed to in the book. Bruce says his mind froze and at first he couldn't grasp the meaning of it.

He called Andrea. She almost screamed on the other end of the phone. "Junior" meant that the downed airman was the second James Huston. This explained why their James called himself James 3—if he was James Huston reborn, he would be the third James. This was intensely difficult for Bruce to accept. He says it felt like "spiritual warfare"—"I felt I was getting closer and closer to something dangerous," he says. "It was like putting my hand in a fire, but I had no choice but to continue on."

But he still had a way out. The veterans told him that no Corsairs had ever flown off the *Natoma Bay*. James Huston had been flying an FM-2 Wildcat when he was killed. Happily, Bruce fixated on this—no Corsair! And no one saw the plane go down, so there was no way of knowing why he crashed, or how. Bruce pored over records and documents and brought many more home, but still these remaining questions lingered on.

A few weeks later, he visited Jack Larsen and his wife, Dorothy, at their home in Springdale, Arkansas. Jack pulled out his flight logbook and showed Bruce that he had been on a mission to strike Chichi-Jima on March 3, 1945. It was only when he returned that he learned James Huston was missing. No one saw him go down because he was at the tail end of the fighter formation. It was a terrifying battle for these young men, flying solo in small, vulnerable planes roaring through dense antiaircraft fire and thick clouds of black smoke. "Some men screamed all the way through the attack; some lost bladder control; some squeezed the joystick so hard that they almost broke it off in their hand. And some died," Jack told him.

The next morning Bruce told the Larsens over breakfast that his four-year-old son somehow had knowledge about aircraft from that time period. "He can even distinguish between a Corsair and an Avenger, and he can identify the Japanese Betty and the Zero," Bruce told them. Jack went out to his garage, and came back with an old canvas bag that he said was for James. Inside was the flight helmet, goggles, and oxygen mask he wore on that very day, when he flew just ahead of James Huston at the moment he was killed.

Bruce took the helmet and its gear home and gave them to James. Even though they did not belong to James Huston, they were likely identical to what Huston wore. James now had something powerful to connect him to his memories. According to Bruce:

> He went through a kind of grim ceremony when he first got into
> the helmet. He put it on firmly, professionally, slapping on the
> air bubbles, shaping the fit, as if he were setting out to work.
> James wore it when he went into his closet cockpit which he had
> constructed. He wore it while flying his flight simulator and
> while watching tapes of the Blue Angels. He and that helmet
> were inseparable.

And there was something else linking James to his memories, which Bruce and Andrea only understood on their next Christmas a few months later. When James was three, he had been given two G.I. Joe dolls, which he named "Billy" and "Leon." He was very attached to them, playing endless combat games with them and sleeping with them every night. Billy had brown hair and Leon was blond. That Christmas, when he was four, he received a third G.I. Joe, this time with red hair, and named him "Walter."

His parents were puzzled by the names, since their family did not know any Walters or Leons. After Walter joined the others that Christmas, Bruce asked James why he named them Billy, Leon, and Walter. James looked up from his play and answered matter-of-factly, "Because that's who met me when I got to heaven," and continued on with his activity.

Bruce went into his office and found his list of the names of the men killed who served on the *Natoma Bay*. On the list with James Huston were Billie Peeler, Leon Conner, and Walter Devlin, and they were all in Huston's VC-81 squadron. Checking further, he saw that they were all killed in late 1944, so they were already dead when James Huston also became a casualty. They would have gone to "heaven" first.

The Leiningers contacted the families of those three men and found out that the hair colors of all three men matched those of the G.I. Joe dolls that had their names. How could it be possible that James would name his dolls the same first names as those dead pilots, all of whom had died before James Huston? As a four-year-old, he had not read the list of the twenty-one casualties and had no way of knowing their names, let alone their hair color.

Bruce continued to learn more. Historian John DeWitt sent him the official war diary of VC-81, James Huston's squadron. On March 3, 1945, it described three attacks at nearby Chichi-Jima, saying that on the first one, "James M. Huston Jr. was apparently hit by antiaircraft fire. The plane went into a 45-degree dive and crashed into the water just inside the harbor. It exploded on impact and there was no survivor or wreckage afloat." It then went on to praise the fallen airman who was "quiet and unassuming, always alert."

Still, there was no eyewitness to the crash. And the discrepancy about the Corsair remained. Bruce became as obsessed about finding answers to these lingering ambiguities as his son was with his drawings. As an example, he spent three weeks at the library copying nine rolls of microfilm of *Natoma Bay* records—five thousand pages—sent to him by DeWitt. "I was crazy to get answers—and the answers made me crazy—because they only verified what he was saying," Bruce told me. "In every instance, when I found facts, which were scores upon scores of things, they never wavered from what he said or did."

Through census records for Pennsylvania, Bruce learned that James Huston Jr. had two sisters, Ruth and Anne. (This corresponded to what James had told them.) Huston's parents died in the mid-1970s, and Ruth had also died, but Anne Huston Barron, eighty-four at the time, lived in Los Gatos, California. Andrea called her initially, followed by Bruce, who told her he was writing a book; she was very sweet, the concerned father said, and promised to send a package of photos. They arrived on February 24, 2003. First was a photo of the whole squadron with a plane behind it. The next one showed James Huston standing alone in front of an airplane. It showed everything: the fuselage, the gull wings, the high cockpit. And Bruce recognized the plane immediately: it was a Corsair.

Huston's military service records showed that before joining his squadron aboard the *Natoma Bay*, he had been part of an elite squadron of pilots assigned to learn how to fly the Corsair, the navy's premier fighter at the time. Once he completed his service with that squadron, Huston joined the VC-81 squadron on the *Natoma Bay* about four months before he was killed. He was not flying a Corsair when he was shot down, but the veterans told Bruce that the Corsair was a very special plane and a privilege to fly, and therefore flying it was a memorable experience, unlike the FM-2 Wildcat, which was nothing special by comparison.

The only remaining hole in the case now was the absence of an eyewitness, to verify whether the plane was hit on the engine on the front and then caught fire, like James had said. Finally, Bruce found a diagram in an official *Aircraft Action Report* of the squadron showing the spot where Huston's plane crashed, and learned more details about the crash. Most important, he discovered that the Avenger torpedo bombers that also took part in the attack were from a different squadron, VC-83, which took off from the USS *Sargent Bay*—not the *Natoma Bay*. This meant the eyewitness could have been from that squadron!

Just after James turned five, a veteran from the *Sargent Bay* squadron, Jack Durham, called Bruce in response to a post he had made on a website months earlier. Durham had been part of the attack on Chichi-Jima. He said he had seen Huston's plane when it went down, and then minutes later he was also hit. He had written up the event in his own informal memoir, and he also had the logbook record showing that this was his mission on March 3, 1945. "One of the fighters from our escort squadron was close to us and took a direct hit on the nose," he had recorded in the diary. "All I could see were pieces falling into the bay." The important revelation here was the phrase "on the nose."

Other witnesses eventually surfaced. One of them, John Richardson from Texas, described the black smoke that surrounded his plane while it was smothered in flak. He noticed a plane off to his left wing. The pilot in that plane was firing his machine guns, and then turned and looked at Richardson from only about thirty yards away. "I caught his eyes and we connected with each other. No sooner had we connected than his plane was hit in the engine by what seemed to be a fairly large shell. There was an instantaneous flash of flames that engulfed the plane." It disappeared below him. Richardson recognized Huston from the photographs Bruce brought. "I have lived with that pilot's face as his eyes fixated on me every day since it happened," he told Bruce, his voice trembling. "I never knew who he was. I was the last person he saw before he was killed."

Another witness later told Bruce that the shell took the propeller off Huston's plane, and another confirmed once again that the plane was hit in the engine and caught on fire immediately. This was exactly what James had remembered.

Bruce finally surrendered. He took the risk of telling the veterans about James and his memories, his knowledge of World War II airplanes, and his dreams of the plane on fire. He dropped the charade of researching a book—although by this time he had become an expert on each of the twenty-one casualties from the *Natoma Bay*. The veterans were receptive, and many shared their own "paranormal" stories involving premonitions and after-death communications. Suddenly Bruce didn't quite understand why he had fought against this for so long. "James's experience was not actually contrary to my belief. God gives us spirit. It lives forever. James Huston's spirit had come back to us. Why? I'll never know. There are things that are unexplainable and unknowable."

By this time James's nightmares had stopped. In April 2004, the week James turned six, the ABC show *Primetime* covered the case, in a segment taped the prior October. And the following September, Bruce took James and Andrea to the *Natoma Bay* reunion. James, with his innocent maturity, was a captivating presence there, enjoying himself immensely. According to his parents, he recognized the voice of one of the veterans the first time he saw him, providing the man's full name. James also met Jack Larsen, and listened closely to war stories as he shared meals with the men, even though, he told his mother, it made him sad because they were so old. But he dazzled them with his knowledge of the *Natoma Bay,* provided spontaneously during a tour of the nearby museum.

And, Anne Barron, James Huston's sister, also came to the reunion. James was shy when he first met her—she had been only twenty-four when her brother James died—and now she was a very elderly lady. Anne felt he was studying her, trying to figure this out, and eventually they bonded, but quietly. Her age was clearly perplexing to the young James. "James called her 'Annie' and approached her with a tender familiarity," Bruce told me. "Anne said only her brother had ever called her 'Annie.'"

Before he met her, five-year-old James had told eighty-six-year-old Annie (as Huston always called her) on the telephone many details of their childhood, including family secrets, that he couldn't possibly have known. Anne sent James mementos from her brother's childhood, such as a painting their mother, an accomplished artist, had made of him. "Where's the one of you?" James asked when he received it. According to Anne, no one else but she knew that their mother had painted one of her as well. She was stunned by this. It was in her attic and she sent that to James also. "The child was so convincing, coming up with all these things that there's no way in the world he could know, unless there is a spiritual thing," she said in the 2004 *Primetime* show.

As time passed, James was more at peace and he seemed like any other kid. "But there was still something lingering within him," Bruce says.

In 2006, when he was eight, James and his family were invited by a Japanese production company to go to Chichi-Jima, where Huston's plane was shot down. The producers wanted to tell the story in a one-hour special for Fuji Television, and they offered to host a ceremonial healing event on the water, in the exact spot of the crash. The Leiningers visited the island after a twenty-six-hour boat ride taking them 650 miles across the Pacific from Tokyo. As they had seen in the VC-81 action report diagram and in many photos, Welcome Rock greeted them at the edge of the harbor, like a gigantic marker noting the spot where James Huston Jr. died in his burning plane.

They walked the hills of Chichi-Jima surrounding Futami-ko, the harbor's name, which were dotted with rusted cannons covering every angle of attack. On a cliff, James recognized the view. "This is where the planes flew in when James Huston was killed," he told his dad.

Carrying flowers, they took a small fishing boat out to the spot where Huston's plane went down, and, as captured on the family video, James seemed like any other happy eight-year-old, enjoying the ride and the sights on the way out. But when they reached the location where Huston fell so violently under the water and died, something changed. The captain cut the engines and they sat quietly. Bruce read the name of each of the twenty-one *Natoma Bay* heroes who died at Iwo Jima, and James tossed a piece of coral into the water for each one, symbolically joining them at Huston's resting place. At first it seemed James was trying to contain his emotions. But his mom, who was herself emotional, drew him close and told him that James Huston would always be part of who he is, but that now it was time to say goodbye. Bruce recalls what happened:

> James put his head down in his mother's lap and broke into
> tears. It was a deep, heart-wrenching sob, as if he was unleashing
> all the pent-up emotion that had boiled inside his child's body
> for the past six years. He sobbed and wept for fifteen minutes.
> Everyone else on the boat was silent and awestruck by the sight
> of a little boy in such deep grief. He seemed to be weeping for
> himself and for James Huston.

Then, James took the bouquet and tossed it into the choppy waters, and with a face streaked with tears, he said goodbye to James Huston. "I'll never forget you," he said, as he stood up straight and saluted. Still in tears, he returned to his mother's lap.

The resolution for James at Chichi-Jima was healing. He went to the place where it all began. He came full circle. The result was palpable and moving. He mourned death and grabbed life in the same moment. And this finally gave James closure.

All of this was captured on video in the family's possession; short scenes from it are in a few TV pieces on YouTube.

After that, James's memories faded away, and today they are gone. As of this writing, James is an accomplished eighteen-year-old high school graduate. He was an honor roll student, an Eagle Scout, and in 2015 was selected from twenty-five hundred students in his high school to attend a national leadership conference in Washington, D.C. Following my extensive communications with Bruce, I finally had the good fortune of meeting James and his parents when they visited New York in April 2016. James was handsome, stalwart, and serious; quiet at first, but then he spoke at length about his future plans. Since second grade, James has said he wanted to be a soldier when he grew up, and he has never wavered from that. He told me he will be pursuing a career in the navy, and I was impressed by the knowledge he had of the rigorous training and future programs he would undertake. I asked him, why not the air force? "Not this time," he replied.

And Bruce found his own spiritual resolution, as he wrote to me after we met:

This journey was a struggle to reconcile my faith with something that scared the daylights out of me. James confronted me with the possibility that souls can pierce the veil from beyond and return. I closely watched for the fruit the tree would bear, and it has been good. My faith is deeper and I relate to what the doubting Apostle Thomas must have felt when Jesus revealed Himself after returning from the grave. In James's case a spirit returned; my effort provided proof of that. My epiphany: God *does* give us eternal life—nothing new there! James's experience is but one demonstration of how eternal life is manifest in our lives. Every day I try to live with that realization.

Chapter 2

The Case of James 3

How can one explain a two-year-old boy providing specific details about someone unknown to him or his family who died fifty-three years before he was born? James insisted he *was* that person and never had any doubt about that. And it turned out that all his memories matched the life of one person: James Huston Jr., a committed World War II pilot who loved to fly and who died in Japan in 1945. There was absolutely no connection between the two families.

The James Leininger case is one of a handful of solved American cases on file at the leading research institute for this subject, the Division of Perceptual Studies (DOPS) at the University of Virginia. Researchers there have investigated cases of young children who report memories of previous lives for over fifty years. Psychiatrist Ian Stevenson, the pioneer of this work, published numerous scholarly articles and lengthy books about cases from all over the world.

Over 2,500 cases have been documented of young children with memories they say are of a previous life, and 1,400 cases, like that of

James Leininger, have resulted in the identification of what Stevenson called the "previous personality," based on facts provided by the child. In 350 of these solved cases, the previous personality was a complete stranger to the child's family, just as Huston was for the Leiningers. Most of them have occurred among families in Thailand, Burma, India, and Sri Lanka, some of them many decades ago, where the cultures accept the notion of rebirth and are more likely to make the cases known. It is somewhat of an irony that one of our strongest cases on record happens to be in America.

After working with Stevenson for several years, Jim Tucker took over his research when Stevenson retired in 2002. (Stevenson died in 2007.) A board-certified child psychiatrist, Tucker is an associate professor of psychiatry and neurobehavioral sciences at the University of Virginia. He is the director of DOPS and has published two books on children with past-life memories, and numerous papers in scientific journals. Along with his research, he also sees patients and supervises care at the University Child and Family Psychiatry Clinic.

In 2014 I made a trip to Charlottesville, Virginia, to meet with Jim Tucker and review selected case files housed at DOPS, some going back many decades. Jim is a soft-spoken, gentle person from North Carolina, with the kind of soothing voice that you could imagine would be perfect in sessions with children because they would feel instantly safe with him. He is devoted to this work, and always responsive to parents who contact him about their children with perplexing memories.

I arrived with a list of the cases I was most interested in after studying Stevenson's papers and books, and Jim graciously pulled the thick files from their drawers and left me with a formidable pile on the library conference table. Most of Stevenson's hard copy files contained extensive handwritten notes from interviews, original letters, notes and lists of memories made by family members, old newspaper clippings, and photographs of the current and previous families. (They are therefore confidential documents, and I agreed to keep them confidential, as Jim requested.) Stevenson was meticulous and detailed in his investigations. Going to the source for the cases I had read about was eye-opening and highly educational, and gave me new appreciation for the difficulty of investigating these cases, especially within non-English-speaking families.

In 2015, I accompanied Jim to Columbus, Ohio, to interview the family of Luke Ruehlman, a young boy who said he remembered being an African American woman named Pam who had died after jumping out of a burning building in Chicago. I was able to observe the thoroughness of Jim's work and the ease he had in relating to both anxious parents and lively children while conducting these informal interviews in the family's home. The case looked promising, with some other details provided by Luke and a potential previous personality located through research on the Internet. After the meeting, I contacted the son of this possible "Pam"—whose last name I am withholding out of respect for her family—and information he provided about his mother's death did not match what Luke remembered. There is no way to determine what was correct, and since we could not acquire any further data, the investigation did not pan out. This is not unusual—it is rare that a case of the caliber of the Leiningers' is documented and then later solved.

Crucial to the importance of the Leininger case is the fact that there was a record of James's statements made long before the identity of Huston was discovered. This is always important because it shows that no memories were altered or adjusted after the fact to make them fit the life of the discovered previous personality—they were all on the record before that person was located. (There were many additional details and comments, some witnessed by relatives, veterans, and Huston's sister Anne, that were not dated and recorded.) Equally important were the intense emotions connected to the memories, especially those manifesting in repetitive, terrifying nightmares so vivid it was as if the small boy were reliving the crash. The acting out of the memories in play, and the display of inexplicable knowledge about World War II aircraft, also add to the strength of the case. "The children in our cases often show behaviors that appear connected to their reports of past-life memories, which relate to the occupation or skills of the previous person," Jim says. Examples in James's case include the "cockpit" he created in the closet of Bruce's home office in an old car seat, the scores of aircraft drawings he made, and his knowledge of obscure details such as a missing antenna on a model airplane and a Japanese Zero plane being miscalled a "Tony" as it shot across a television screen.

Even though no one conducted psychological assessments of Bruce and Andrea, there is no evidence that anything external to James, such as trauma or psychological disturbances in the family, contributed to the memories that were surfacing in his mind. James's parents did not appear to have an undue influence on the unfolding of the memories and have stated that they only asked James about them when he brought them up. "We have found no evidence that parental influence causes the cases to become exaggerated," Jim Tucker states. "The initial attitude that each parent has toward the past-life claims shows no correlation with the number of accurate statements the child is eventually credited with making or with the overall strength of the case. Rather than enlarging the claims, many of the parents actively discourage their children's talk about a previous life." Despite Andrea's openness to belief in past-life memories, Bruce was determined to *disprove* the case, not to prove it. Regardless, the differing beliefs of James's parents regarding the source of his information would not, and did not, change the precision of the details James provided. Both parents were primarily concerned for James's well-being above all else.

Although James provided many more statements overall, those relevant for research are the memories recorded and written prior to the resolution of the case. These could then be checked against the life of James Huston Jr. discovered later. It is this group of primary statements, dated by Bruce's printed documents, emails, and the ABC video footage, which I will focus on now. Twelve were well established by the time James was three years old. They were:

1. He was a pilot.
2. He was trapped in an airplane on fire.
3. The plane was shot by the Japanese.

4. The plane was hit in the engine in front.

5. The plane crashed into the ocean and he died.

6. He flew a Corsair.

7. Corsairs got flat tires all the time.

8. The plane took off from a boat.

9. The boat was named *"Natoma."*

10. His pilot friend was "Jack Larsen."

11. His plane crash was near Iwo Jima.

12. He was "James 3."

We must consider that perhaps these are not memories at all. Could they be explained as information obtained through the living-agent psi of James and his parents? Perhaps James was picking up information about Huston through highly developed ESP (as described in the Introduction). Could the use of telepathy and clairvoyance be a simpler explanation for his knowledge of the life of James Huston Jr.? First, if this were some unusual psychic ability that linked James to information about Huston rather than an actual memory of a past life, why would that ability appear only in connection to one person who died more than half a century earlier? "James's parents denied that he showed any other psychic abilities, which would suggest that for a paranormal transfer of information to occur, there would need to be something distinct either about Huston's memories or about the connection between Huston and James," Tucker writes in a 2016 journal paper. "There is no evidence to indicate the latter." Would James have such vivid, disturbing memories and exhibit obsessive behavior if the information being retrieved by him was a psychic perception of the life of someone unrelated to him in any way?

To explain such a case in terms of psi only, "we may need to posit either implausibly successful ESP links between the subject and multiple sources, or even more incredible psi on the part of the parents, involving both information gathering and telepathic influence over the subject," says Stephen Braude, the expert investigator I described in the Introduction. It is worth remembering the numerous sources and multiple people that Bruce needed to access to research James's

clues and eventually confirm his memories. So if James was to somehow be receiving the information through ESP rather than memory,
beginning before he turned two, how many sources would he have
needed to draw from to acquire the information that would lead him
to believe he was once James Huston? And for what reason? Is such
clairvoyance possible before one learns to read? As implausible as it
may sound, the evidence points toward James actually remembering
and reliving a previous existence.

James conveyed a sense of having *been* the previous person, not
knowing *about* the other person. He was always clear that he understood the source of the memories: they were a life he lived before.
The emotions were just as powerful as the memories, and he seemed
to be reliving experiences, acting them out as if they carried great
meaning for him and remained unresolved. The trauma that elicited
the torment of his nightmares, in which he thrashed and screamed
night after night, seemed to be the visceral memory of something that
actually happened, and his perceptions about that plane crash were
accurate to the death of James Huston in every detail. I also wonder if
the intensely emotional experience James had when he was eight, on
the boat at the location where Huston's plane went down, would have
been likely if his perceptions of Huston were not part of his inner reality due to a connection with real events rather than a psychic link to
something external to himself.

Stephen Braude also points out the importance of ruling out psychological disorders such as dissociative pathologies or possession in
such cases. Clearly, child psychiatrist Jim Tucker, who spent time investigating this case and interviewing the family, has ruled these out.
Braude concludes that the most impressive cases, which would include this one, "tilt the scales toward the survivalist," even if we can't
demonstrate conclusively that the living-agent psi hypothesis does not
apply. And when we look at the totality of these strong cases of children with accurate past-life memories, he says their "cumulative force"
makes "the survivalist position seem stronger still."

But there are other valid questions. Could James have absorbed the
details of his memories from people or material in his environment?

"He could not have learned from the people around him, because they knew nothing about either the ship or Huston when he began talking about them," Tucker points out. "James had made all of the documented statements by the time he was four years old, so he could not have read about them. Regardless, no published materials about James Huston are known to exist. No television programs focusing on *Natoma Bay* or James Huston appear to have been made either." Bruce and Andrea were aware of everyone who came in contact with James, and no one provided him with information about the life of James Huston. Also, the statements were unpredictable. "There was no linear schedule to the past-life tidbits he casually dropped on us, and no way to prepare for his statements," Bruce explains. Fraud and fantasy can clearly be ruled out.

The years of work involved in Bruce's search for answers illustrates how hard it can be to solve such cases. How many parents would show such perseverance and determination, and spend as much time at it as Bruce did? To the contrary, most American parents would dismiss something like this as fantasy, and not take the child's memories seriously. "The nightmares and post-traumatic play that James experienced, which are typical of the behaviors many of these children display, demonstrate how difficult apparent past-life memories can be for children to have," Tucker notes in his paper. Understanding the story of James Leininger should help parents to recognize when such a situation may be arising with their child.

"The documentation in James's case provides evidence that he had a connection with a life from the past," Tucker concludes. "On the face of it, the most obvious explanation for this connection is that he experienced a life as James Huston Jr. before having his current one. The facts in the case indicate that this explanation warrants serious consideration." I have to agree. Cases such as that of James Leininger provide some of the strongest evidence suggesting a continuity of consciousness—before life, during life, and after life.

Chapter 3

Investigating Cases of Children with Past-Life Memories

By Jim B. Tucker, MD

Jim contributed the following original chapter to give the reader a taste of some of the more extraordinary cases discovered by Dr. Ian Stevenson, and also to share some of his own research.

James Leininger is only one example among many of children who have described memories of a past life. Reports of such cases appeared sporadically in the first half of the twentieth century. The cases became the subject of systematic research when Ian Stevenson, then the chairman of the Department of Psychiatry at the University of Virginia, began studying them in the 1960s.

Though quite accomplished, with dozens of publications to his credit and an appointment as chairman of the department while still in his thirties, Stevenson was a bit of an iconoclast. He stated in an article called "The Uncomfortable Facts About Extrasensory Perception" that the mounting evidence for ESP was increasingly hard to ignore or explain away. And in an essay entitled "Scientists with

Half-closed Minds," he discussed how a surprising number of scientists were scared of new ideas. He was definitely not one of them.

For a number of years, Stevenson had collected published reports of individuals who claimed to remember past lives, finding these stories in various places such as books, magazines, and newspapers. He then wrote a two-part paper summarizing a group of forty-four such cases in 1960. The most impressive ones tended to involve children who were under the age of ten when they began reporting the memories, with a number being age three or even younger. Stevenson was struck by how children from different parts of the world made very similar statements about remembering a past life.

After his paper was published, Stevenson started hearing about new cases, and he accepted a small grant to go study one in India. By the time of his trip, he had learned about four or five additional cases there. He went for four weeks and ended up seeing twenty-five, meeting the children and their families and piecing together the details of what had happened in each case. He had a similar experience in Sri Lanka. Upon returning to Virginia, Stevenson got a call about a case in Alaska; he discovered a number of cases among the Tlingit tribes there in the area around Juneau.

It was clear at that point that this phenomenon of young children reporting memories of past lives was more common than people, in the West at least, had known before. Stevenson was intrigued. As he had written in his paper, the cases could be especially important in addressing the question of life after death. He thought it might be easier to judge in this situation whether someone who was clearly living had once died than it was in studies of mediums to assess whether someone clearly dead still lived.

Stevenson began devoting more and more time to the cases and eventually stepped down as chairman of the department to focus all his energies on his research. He established a small unit in 1967 at the University of Virginia, now known as the Division of Perceptual Studies, to conduct studies in parapsychology, including research into the question of life after death.

Thus began what became forty years of work by Stevenson. He

logged thousands of miles of travel, going wherever he could to investigate cases. They were easiest to find in cultures with a belief in reincarnation. Stevenson focused on Asia, but traveled elsewhere as well, and cases have now been documented on every continent except Antarctica. He was able to interest a small number of other researchers in studying cases—psychologists Erlendur Haraldsson, Jürgen Keil, and Satwant Pasricha, anthropologist Antonia Mills, and later me as a child psychiatrist—and all of us have now published numerous papers in scientific journals as well. Together, we have studied over twenty-five hundred cases, and in two-thirds of them, a previous person has been identified whose life matches, to a greater or lesser degree, the statements the child made.

A Case in India

An example is a little girl in India named Kumkum Verma. When Stevenson investigated her case, he learned that she had begun talking about a past life when she was three and a half. Though her family lived in a village, she recalled being a woman in Darbhanga, a city of two hundred thousand people that was twenty-five miles away. Not only did she name the city, she also gave the section of the city where she said she had lived. It was an area made up of artisans, craftsmen, and small business owners, and Kumkum's father, an educated landowner and author, did not know anyone there.

Kumkum made many statements about the past life. Her aunt wrote down some of them six months before anyone searched for a previous person. Stevenson was able to get a partial copy of her notes, which included eighteen of Kumkum's statements. Eventually, Kumkum's father talked to a friend about what his daughter was saying. The friend had an employee from the section of Darbhanga Kumkum had named, and he was able to identify a deceased woman whose life fit the details Kumkum had given. All eighteen of the recorded statements matched, including the city section, the name of the woman's son and the fact that he worked with a hammer, her grandson's name, the town where the woman's father had lived, the location of his home near mango orchards, and the presence of a pond at her house. The notes included other small personal details as well. Kumkum had recalled having an iron safe at her home, keeping a sword hanging near the cot where she slept, and even feeding milk to a pet snake she had near the safe. These were all true for the deceased woman, who died five years before Kumkum was born.

Kumkum said that in her previous life she died during a family disagreement and that her stepson's wife had poisoned her. No autopsy was performed on the previous woman, but she had died unexpectedly as she was preparing to be a witness for her son in his suit against her second husband. Her son believed that her second husband, his stepfather, had mishandled his deceased father's money.

Kumkum's family said she spoke with an accent different from theirs, one they associated with the lower classes of Darbhanga. They didn't know the previous woman or her family, and the two families had little in common. Neither had visited the area where the other family lived, and no shared friends could be identified. Kumkum's father was apparently not proud that his daughter seemed to recall a past life as a blacksmith's wife, and even after the woman was identified, the two families had little contact with each other.

These children typically start talking about a past life very early, as Kumkum did, with the average age being thirty-five months. This happens not through hypnosis, but spontaneously, as the children begin recounting events they say they experienced in another life. Though they may talk about a past life many times and with great intensity, they tend to stop making such statements around the age of six, the same time when children typically lose memories of early childhood and also when they begin school, getting more involved in the greater world outside of their families. Most children in these cases seem to lose the apparent past-life memories, though Haraldsson found in follow-up studies that a surprising number reported as adults that they still remembered some details of a past life.

Most of the children describe only one past life. Their memories usually focus on people and events from near the end of that life, and three-quarters of them relate how they died. They very rarely report being anyone famous. Instead, they recall a largely nondescript life of a person who typically lived fairly close by, almost always in the same country. The one part of the life that is often out of the ordinary is how the previous person died. Around 70 percent of the children describe a life that ended in an unnatural death, such as murder, suicide, accident, or combat. Though there are exceptions, the life also tends to be quite recent. The average interval between lives is four and a half years, while the median interval—meaning half are shorter and half are longer—is only seventeen months.

The interval in James's case was much longer, of course. Though it is unclear why the interval can vary so much, cases with a longer time between lives do offer one advantage. We can be quite certain that little James was not exposed to information in his environment about the pilot Huston's life, due to the simple fact that no easily accessible information about him still existed. Had James been born in 1948 instead of 1998, one could conjecture that various returning servicemen and servicewomen would talk about their experiences and that James might have overheard one discussing details about Huston's crash from the USS *Natoma Bay*. That seems extremely implausible, however, fifty years later.

Behavioral Memories

Along with talking about a past life, many of the children show behaviors that seem connected to their statements. A lot of them display great emotion when they discuss events from that life. They do not dispassionately list a number of facts, but instead they cry that they miss people or beg to be taken to them. A little girl in India named Sukla Gupta was under the age of two when she began cradling a block of wood or a pillow and calling it "Minu." She gave a number of details about a past life, such as the name and section of a village eleven miles away. A woman there, the mother of an infant named Minu, had died six years before Sukla was born. When Sukla was five and Minu eleven, she met Minu and cried. Sukla acted maternal toward the older girl, and when Minu later fell ill, Sukla became distraught upon hearing the news and demanded to be taken to her.

Some children have repeated nightmares about events from a past life, as James Leininger did. Others show phobias related to how the previous person died. In cases involving an unnatural death, 35 percent of the children have an intense fear about the mode of that death. For reasons we don't understand, such fears are particularly common when the previous person drowned. In the fifty-two solved cases of drowning we have on file, forty-three of the children were scared of water. A girl in Sri Lanka named Shamlinie Prema hated being put in water from the time she was born, and it would take three adults to hold her down for a bath. At about six months, Shamlinie also began displaying a great fear of buses. When she became old enough to talk, she described the life of a girl in a nearby village who died a year and a half before Shamlinie was born. The girl in the previous life had been walking along a narrow road when a bus came by. As she tried to get out of its way, she fell into a flooded paddy field next to the road and drowned.

The phobias often fade as the memories do, and sometimes before. Shamlinie got over her fear of water by the time she was four, while her fear of buses lasted until she was five and a half. Though not typical, some of the children continue to show a phobia even after their memories have apparently faded.

Themes from the past life often appear in the children's play activities as well. Parmod Sharma, a boy in India, spent much of his time from ages four to seven pretending to be a shopkeeper of biscuits and soda water, the occupation of the previous person. This caused him to neglect his work when he started school, and his mother felt he was never able to fully catch up.

A few children have repeatedly acted out how the previous person died. James's habit of saying "Airplane crash on fire" and slamming his toy planes nose first into the family's coffee table might be seen as an example of this. Maung Myint Soe in Myanmar recalled being a man who drowned in a ferryboat, and he would sometimes act out a scene of trying to escape from a sinking boat. Ramez Shams in Lebanon reenacted the suicide of the previous person by repeatedly putting a stick under his chin and pretending it was a rifle, behavior that must have been unsettling to his parents.

The various behaviors the children display indicate that if there is in fact carryover from previous lives, it involves more than just memories, but an emotional component as well. Stevenson argued that in addition to genetics and environment, previous lives might be a third factor that contributes to the development of human personality.

Birthmarks and Birth Defects

Along with statements and behaviors, many of the cases include physically tangible signs of a connection to a past life. Some of the children have birthmarks that match wounds, usually the fatal wounds, on the body of the previous person. They are often unusual in some way, in shape or size or by being puckered or raised rather than flat.

An example is Chanai Choomalaiwong, a boy in Thailand who was born with two marks, a small round one on the back of his head and a larger, more irregular one toward the front. When he was three, he began saying he had been a schoolteacher named Bua Kai and that one day he had been shot and killed on his way to school. He gave the names of his parents from that life, as well as his wife's name and those of two of his children. He begged to be taken to a town he named, saying he had lived there as Bua Kai.

Eventually, when Chanai was still three years old, he and his grandmother took a bus to a town near the place Chanai had named. Chanai then led the way to a house where he said he had lived. His grandmother discovered that it was owned by an elderly couple whose son, Bua Kai Lawnak, had been a teacher. He was murdered five years before Chanai was born, shot in the head as he rode his bicycle to school. Bua Kai's parents tested Chanai, and he was able to pick out

Bua Kai's belongings from others. He recognized one of Bua Kai's daughters and asked for the other one by name. He insisted that Bua Kai's daughters call him "Father" and refused to respond to them if they did not.

Stevenson was unable to obtain an autopsy report for Bua Kai, but he talked with several of the man's family members about his injuries. His widow remembered that the doctor who examined Bua Kai's body said he must have been shot from behind, because he had a wound on the back of his head that was much smaller than one he had on his forehead. This is the typical pattern in wounds of gunshot victims—a small, round entrance wound and a larger, more irregular exit wound—and it matched the pattern of Chanai's birthmarks.

Chanai's is not the only such case. Stevenson listed eighteen that involved double birthmarks, ones matching both the entrance and exit wound on the body of a gunshot victim. In most of them, one birthmark was larger than the other, and the smaller one tended to be round while the larger one was more irregularly shaped.

Instead of birthmarks, some of the cases involve dramatic birth defects, such as missing limbs or deformed skulls. Lekh Pal Jatav in India talked about the life of a boy in a nearby village who had lost the fingers of his right hand in a fodder-chopping machine. Lekh Pal was born with a completely normal left hand but only stubs for fingers on his right. Semih Tutuşmuş of Turkey had memories of being a man who was killed by a shotgun blast to the right side of his head, and Semih was born with an underdeveloped right side of his face and only a linear stump for his right ear.

Overall, we have four hundred cases in which the child had a birthmark or birth defect that corresponded to a fatal wound the previous person suffered, along with two hundred in which the mark or defect corresponded to a nonfatal wound. Such cases intrigued Stevenson, who had a long-standing interest in psychosomatic medicine before beginning this work. He devoted many years to studying birthmark/birth defect cases, before eventually writing *Reincarnation and Biology*, a two-volume, twenty-two-hundred-page collection of over two hundred such cases. These cases suggest that children may have physical sequelae from a traumatic death in a past life, just as the phobias and nightmares in some cases indicate psychological wounds. As Stevenson discussed in *Reincarnation and Biology,* mental images can sometimes produce very specific effects on the body. If some part of the consciousness has in fact continued from the previous person to the child, it would follow that mental images, particularly ones from a traumatic death, might affect the new fetus as it develops.

Past-Life Recognitions

Some of the children appear to recognize people from the previous life, as Chanai did with Bua Kai's family. These recognitions sometimes occur spontaneously—a child may pass a stranger on the street and tell his mother he knew that person in his past life. At other times, meetings are arranged to see if the child can recognize people. These tests can be suspect, as a crowd often gathers around the child and may inadvertently give clues about, for example, who among the assembled women was the previous mother. Other cases can be more impressive, with the child giving specific details, including the name, of a previous family member or friend upon meeting that person.

Gnanatilleka Baddewithana was a little girl in Sri Lanka who made numerous statements about a past life in another town. After investigators identified a deceased teenage boy as the likely previous person, they set up recognition tests in which people the boy had known came in one by one for Gnanatilleka to identify. She not only gave the correct relationship that the previous person had with each individual; she also gave other details that she could not have deduced from their appearance alone. She said for example that one woman had been her sister and that the family had gone to her house to sew clothes. When individuals the previous person had not known were also presented to Gnanatilleka to test her, she correctly denied knowing them.

The recognitions can sometimes involve photographs. As you will read in the next chapter, a little boy named Ryan Hammons pointed to a figure in a picture from the 1930s and said he had been that man in his past life. We eventually identified him and verified that over fifty of the details Ryan had given were accurate for his life. Another American boy named Sam talked of being his own paternal grandfather. When his mother showed him a class picture from his grandfather's elementary school days, Sam was able to pick him out of a group of twenty-seven children, including sixteen boys.

American Cases

When Stevenson started his research, he focused on Asia, for the simple reason that it was where cases were being reported. When a child talked about a past life in a place such as India or Thailand, word would often spread, sometimes through a newspaper story, and one of Stevenson's associates would learn about it. The reactions that people in the West have when children describe past-life memories can be quite different. Most of the American parents who contact us say they had no belief in past lives before their children started reporting memories. They often don't know what to make of their children's claims and may be embarrassed by them. Word about the children does not tend to spread, since the parents do not want people to know what they are saying. Even the grandparents are often kept in the dark about the children's statements.

This is one reason—and perhaps the primary reason—why cases have been harder to find here. But they certainly do exist. Once Stevenson started publishing his case reports, he began to hear occasionally from American parents who learned about his work. The children had often talked about a past life years before their parents contacted Stevenson. Even so, he published a paper on seventy-nine American cases in 1983. He reported that most of the children had not made statements about a past life that were verifiable, and those who had almost always talked about being a deceased family member. He noted, however, that in many ways, the American cases were very much like ones in India: the children talked about a past life at an early age, the content of their statements was similar, and they often showed behaviors such as phobias that appeared linked to their purported memories.

We have continued to work on American cases. This includes one study that involved psychological testing of a number of the children. What we saw was that they were not dissociating or showing any psychological disturbance. Instead, the one outstanding finding of the testing was that the children tended to be very intelligent and very verbal.

When I became involved in this work, I initially took several trips to Asia but then decided to focus on the American cases. Though they can be harder to find, and though many of them include few verifiable details, they offer the advantage of occurring away from any cultural influences that could impact them. Happening here in Christian families like the Leiningers and the Hammonses, they demonstrate that children's past-life memories are not something that only occurs to people practicing Eastern religions in faraway countries. They can also take place in families living down the street. As the Internet has made it easy for people to learn about our work, we now hear from American parents all the time. They describe the same kinds of statements and behaviors and sometimes even birthmarks and recognitions that families in other places began reporting to Stevenson over fifty years ago.

I wrote about a number of American cases, including those of James and Ryan, in my latest book, *Return to Life*. Adding them to the strongest ones from around the world that Stevenson and other researchers have studied, I am now ready to say we have good evidence that some young children have memories of a life from the past. Precisely what this says about survival after death and the ultimate nature of our existence is less clear to me. The various areas of research described in the pages of this book appear to provide significant insights into these issues, and I hope future efforts in these fields will lead to a more definitive picture. Progress will only be made with a continued attitude of scientific inquiry. That means approaching Ryan's case in the next chapter—and indeed all the cases—with a critical eye, yes, but also with an open mind, not the half-closed minds Stevenson described in his early paper. We may all discover that children who report memories of previous lives have much to teach us.

Chapter 4

"The Old Me"

By Cyndi Hammons

Following is the story of another extraordinary American case, which had the advantage of Jim Tucker's involvement from the beginning. Ryan Hammons was five when he started talking about his past life—significantly older and thus more verbal than James—articulating dozens of memories in great detail. He also identified with the previous personality for a greater portion of his waking time than James did, as if the memories had a more continuous grip on his consciousness. He too had nightmares.

Ryan's mother, Cyndi Hammons, kept careful records of everything Ryan said as a way of coping with this overwhelming situation, and delivered them incrementally to Jim Tucker before any search for the previous personality began. This meant that Jim could go back to these files from Cyndi months later to see if Ryan's statements were accurate for the life of the previous personality, once they found him.

The struggle with the impact of these unsettling events and the many sleepless nights took a toll on the family, as it did with the Leiningers. I met with the Hammons family in early 2015 at their home. After talking extensively with Cyndi, I thought there was no better person to tell Ryan's story than she. For the first time, she has provided an inside, firsthand account of what happened to her son and the resolution of the case.

Cyndi is a deputy county clerk with the Muskogee County Clerk's office and her husband, Kevin, is a lieutenant with the Muskogee Police Department, in Warner, Oklahoma, where they live. Ryan was born in 2004, and their story begins in the fall of 2009.

I was afraid to tell my husband, Kevin, about our five-year-old's memories, which seemed to be the reason for his nightmares. Kevin is a police officer, and often was out until early morning on his shift, leaving me to take care of Ryan. By this time, he was getting tired of coming home and finding me exhausted and Ryan in our bed. Some nights I was up half the night with Ryan. I had been trying to learn more about what Ryan called his memories, which he talked about a great deal, before telling Kevin about something I knew he wouldn't want to hear.

Early one morning, Kevin came home and, as usual, removed his bulletproof vest and unsnapped the straps of his gun belt. I told him that I thought I had figured out the cause of Ryan's nightmares. To help him understand, I showed him a book about cases of children having past-life memories and asked him to read two chapters. He did, but then the book went flying across the bed.

"Dammit, Cyndi! Reincarnation? We don't have a child that's had another life before this one. Where the hell did you come up with this stuff? We have a regular little boy that doesn't want to sleep in his bed and you just give in to him and let him sleep in here. He's a kid and kids have nightmares and I don't want to hear any more of this new age bull." Kevin and I had both grown up in Christian homes where the notion of rebirth had not been part of our teachings or belief systems.

All of a sudden we both turned to the doorway and saw Ryan standing there in his little Spider-Man pajamas with his teddy bear. He burst into tears. Kevin knelt down and wrapped his son in his arms. "Hey, buddy, it's okay. You can tell me anything. Maybe Mommy just didn't explain it right. Maybe you can tell me."

"Really, Daddy? Wow. Wait, hold Bear. I'll get my book."

Ryan left for a moment and came back carrying a big book about Hollywood. He crawled up beside Kevin and thumbed through the thick pages until he found the picture that he was so excited to show his daddy. "See, Daddy, Mommy got this book. She found me. That's me and that's George and we did a picture together," he said, pointing at two men in a photo of six. The "me" was on the far right, in a bowler hat, and George was second from the left. The photo caption was on the far edge of the opposite page, saying the still was from a 1932 movie called *Night After Night* starring George Raft, whom Ryan had pointed to. It was Mae West's first movie.

Kevin was speechless. His face was full of questions. Ryan talked for a few minutes and said that he loved us both and was glad that he could finally tell us both about "the old me." He then asked if he could go into the living room and watch cartoons.

So I explained everything to Kevin that I had been holding back for months. Ryan had told me one night that he had a secret and he was pretty sure that it was a secret that he wasn't supposed to tell. He knew that he used to be somebody else. He was once another person who was a movie star and lived in Hollywood. He was rich, and had lived in a big house with a large swimming pool in the yard. It was a house that had been full of children. In fact, he had had three boys. He didn't think that they were his boys but he gave them his name because nobody else could. He had been in movies and had driven a green car. He went to fancy parties, with the cowboy man—the guy who had the horse that did tricks. This man was his buddy and was also in the movie. The cowboy had also done all of those cigarette commercials.

There had been many stories and I had started to research online about children who believed that they had had a past life. I learned that if you could find books or photos from the places from the child's past life, then that would sometimes help the child to remember more details. So I began to get books about Hollywood from everywhere I could think of and I would bring them home at night, sometimes five or six at a time.

I had never imagined finding a picture of a man that Ryan would say was him. That never even occurred to me. But it happened, just as he had shown Kevin that night. Ryan had pointed to the same photo a few weeks ago, saying the same thing: "You found me, Momma! You found me! That's me and that's George and we did a picture together."

The nights that Ryan and I looked at the books were the nights that he seemed happy and he seemed to sleep better. That's why I kept getting the books. With each passing week he provided new details. He told more stories. He knew small things, which seemed like the kind of things that only people who really know another person would know. Things like "I hated cats." Or "I used to travel on the big boats because that's how you see the world, on a big boat."

The little things he remembered seemed to bring comfort, but the big things really haunted him. He seemed to know the intricate details of another man's life but he didn't know that man's name. Most nights his main concern seemed to be, what happened to the children? What was his other mother's name? He could remember her. She had short, dark, curly hair. What became of his sister?

I sat there that night and told Kevin story after story. I told him about the odd details that Ryan revealed during the times he awoke crying and screaming in the middle of the night, even though he did not know what the dreams were about. I told him about the unusual behaviors and grown-up vocabulary that Ryan would use when he seemed lost in this other man's world—a world that he said was from long ago, before hardly anyone had a TV.

Kevin had seen the nightmares, which were so frightening to both of us. Sometimes Ryan would get up and say his chest hurt, and he would gasp for air. I was often in tears when this happened, and was constantly worried and sleep deprived.

Kevin then asked me how much I knew about the photo in the book that Ryan pointed to. There wasn't much that I could tell him. There were very few actors listed in the movie credits that you could actually find pictures of or any detailed information about. I had already tried, and had crossed the few actors off that did not match the man in the picture. The other names seemed to have almost nothing to go on; maybe dates of their births and deaths.

Kevin suggested we look for clips of *Night After Night* on YouTube. Even though it was such an old movie, he was able to find the whole thing. We went into the kitchen and pulled up two chairs in front of the computer and began to watch. When it came to the brief portion with the man from Ryan's photo, we stared at it in silence. The actor in question never spoke a word. Kevin then called Ryan into the kitchen and had him watch some of it for the first time. We came to the part that showed the men opening up a closet stocked with guns. Ryan had remembered this earlier. He had already told me that while making the movie, they had all helped to carry in the guns and load them into the closet. Ryan then went on to tell Kevin very excitedly about the closet being full from top to bottom. His little face was completely animated because now he knew that it was okay to tell Daddy about everything.

Kevin and I watched the rest, and the actor whom Ryan pointed to was only in one other short scene, also without any lines. This meant he was just an extra, meaning that none of the names mentioned in the credits—and there weren't that many—belonged to him. So we had no idea who he was.

I wanted to get some help. I suggested that we contact Dr. Jim Tucker from the University of Virginia, who had written the book, *Life Before Life*, that had so upset Kevin earlier. On February 10, 2010, I wrote my initial letter to Dr. Tucker listing some of the statements that Ryan had made and enclosing a copy of the photo from the movie. It seemed to me that Ryan didn't have anyone's name or any of the specific facts that you would need for research. His details were personal and seemed unverifiable. The story of why he didn't allow anybody to drive his green car. How the Chinese restaurant was his favorite. How he had worked at what he called "the agency" as an agent. He spoke at length about his agent wardrobe and extensive sunglass collection.

My mind told me that it could all just be a child's fantasy, but my heart told me something very different. He cried over the people whom he said he had loved and so desperately missed. Kevin suggested that I begin to record every detail, narrative, comment, and behavior exactly as Ryan provided it. He said this would help him believe it and understand it, and then maybe it would help us figure out what to do.

Often it was like working a jigsaw puzzle. Sometimes there would be full stories about dancing on the stages of New York with his buddies. How the little man who ran the Chinese restaurant had become his friend and had taught him how to meditate. What it was like to have what sounded like an endless supply of money and to be able to travel the world. He said he knew Rita Hayworth, whom he saw in a photo, and that she made "ice drinks." Other times they were just fragmented statements. But it helped me feel more in control somehow to write them down, even though I wasn't. It gave me a way of focusing, and I called this my journal.

Although he often talked like a grown-up, we must remember that Ryan was only five years old. He came up with all of this spontaneously. I never asked him anything unless he brought it up. Instead, I hoped to avoid it if possible, so he could just be Ryan. But he had so much to say. Ryan was only a small vulnerable boy, even if at times he behaved like someone tough from Hollywood.

Bath time before bed became the new dreaded part of the end of the day, because the relaxation this provided for Ryan often led to more memories. Afterward he would turn into what seemed to be a completely different person. There were nights when he was very funny and I really enjoyed hearing his stories. Then on other nights he just seemed to be mad at the world. Why couldn't I just fly him to Hollywood and let him eat at his favorite place? Sometimes our house would be too small in his opinion and he would rant about how he couldn't believe that he was being expected to live in these conditions. His old room had been large and grand and he had his own swimming pool. Why couldn't we have servants? Do you know how much easier your life is with hired help? He even wanted to pay me for cleaning up his room.

I spent my lunch hours at the public library poring over books, hoping to find the man in the picture. I spent every extra minute I had researching old Hollywood movies on many websites, and at night I stayed up late watching old movies on the classic-movie channels. At the same time, I prayed that this would all go away and it wouldn't matter anymore if we never found out who the man in the picture was. What mattered to me was that my child find some form of peace.

Dr. Tucker responded and asked if we would consider an in-home visit from him and if he could speak with Ryan. I really didn't think that Ryan would say much to a complete stranger, but Dr. Tucker was so kind to reassure me that most of the young children didn't usually have a whole lot to say in the interviews.

Before our meeting, I would send almost daily emails to Dr. Tucker documenting what Ryan said, while adding the information to my journal. One time I wrote, "He thinks he lived somewhere with the word 'mount' or 'rock' in it." He had said this had been part of an address of the place in Hollywood that he had lived. And when Ryan spoke about the agency and working as an agent, Dr. Tucker and I both assumed that meant that he had done some type of detective work. So I started researching the different agencies that he could have worked for at that time. I would also occasionally send emails to old-movie enthusiasts and historians on Mae West movies, who could tell me all kinds of information about George Raft. But nobody seemed to have a clue as to who that actor was who never spoke in the movie.

Ryan didn't only talk about his memories, but he lived through them spontaneously and naturally in our daily lives. Some days when I picked him up from school he talked about being an agent, and when I asked what he did at school, he would say, "You know, agent stuff." He also played that he was making movies. When he was four, I remember taking him to a birthday party where he assembled all the children there to direct them for his movie. He yelled at the adults that he needed help because it was hard to act and direct a major production. We all just laughed it off.

He used to hum show tunes and dance like he was tap-dancing.

He would want to dance with me and tell me he couldn't wait until he was big again and got to go on dates on the big boats and dance with the pretty ladies. One time he began doing a tap-dance routine in the middle of the floor, saying "Tip tap tip tap" as if he was keeping a beat for himself. He said he remembered how to do it, and asked if I would get him some tap shoes. "I heard some music today on a cartoon and it made me remember how to dance because it reminded me of one of the songs we used to use," he explained.

He also would cry for me to buy him "agent clothes"—ties, suits, dress shirts, and clothes that were not appropriate everyday dress for little boys. He wanted black-rimmed "agent glasses." He took a pair of kids' 3-D movie glasses and popped the lenses out and wore them everywhere.

Some days he was just Ryan, and it was wonderful. One day in March we went to the park and he told me he was through talking to me about Hollywood. "Mommy, I don't want to be an actor and I don't want to go back there. Hollywood is scary and I just want to be Ryan." But later that night, he cried for thirty minutes before going to sleep, telling me over and over that he was homesick.

Sometimes Kevin was home at night, and he would stay up with Ryan or help him when the nightmares came. Over time, he became convinced that Ryan was telling the truth. In his more than fifteen years as a police officer, he had interviewed many people suspected of crimes, from stealing all the way to murder. He had learned to recognize when someone was lying. And it wasn't just because Ryan was his son. Kevin would have said if he didn't believe him.

One evening I was getting Ryan ready for bed, and he said something to me that I will never forget. I told him, "Ryan, you do know that you are not that man in the picture anymore. We just want you to be Ryan." And he said to me, "Mom, you still don't get it, do you? I am not the same as the man in the picture on the outside, but on the inside I am still that man. You just can't see on the inside what I see." Kevin and I were often struck by how much Ryan talked like an adult, although we were used to it by now. He seemed to have wisdom that was sometimes uncanny for his age.

A few weeks later, I had one of the more important conversations with Ryan. When we went to visit my brother's grave at the local cemetery, Ryan told me that he had been in a graveyard before, because he and his buddy had to go to the graveyard to see Senator Five. I asked, "Ryan, who's Senator Five?"

"He was the meanest villain that you would ever want to meet. When me and my buddy worked for the agency they were investigating him. He was one dirty, mean guy."

"Ryan, was this while you were in Hollywood?"

"Mom, I don't think you really want to hear about Senator Five. I'm not talking about one of my films. This happened, but the graveyard wasn't in Hollywood; it was somewhere else."

We had been home about two hours when Ryan asked to see a map of the United States. He then pointed to New York. "Mom, that's where we went to meet Senator Five. We went to New York. I wonder if they ever got him. We never did. The agency wanted him, the police wanted him, but we never got him."

Ryan said he saw Senator Five's face at night when he was asleep, and at that moment I knew exactly what it was that was haunting my child's dreams. Ryan seemed to always be looking over his shoulder. Somehow he was frightened of Senator Five, whoever he was, whether real or fantasy.

On April 17 we had our meeting with Dr. Tucker, who was just as pleasant as I imagined he would be. During the interview, he asked me if I believed that the agency could have been all make-believe. I told him that the agency was the one thing Ryan was certain of. He had been an agent, with an agency that had been involved in changing people's names.

A television show called *The Unexplained,* which was covering Dr. Tucker's work, was interested in Ryan's case. They thought they knew who the man in the bowler hat was, but when they showed us a photo of him, Ryan thought it was the wrong man. Dr. Tucker wasn't convinced either, but when they offered to take Ryan to Hollywood, Ryan was intensely excited, so we decided to go. It was a disaster, because Ryan didn't react to any of the locations they took him to, except for that of his cowboy friend from the movie whom we had identified as Wild Bill Elliott. They did not treat us well and we returned emotionally drained, feeling we had wasted our time looking for the wrong man. Ryan seemed to fall into a depression and I was worried about him.

A few months later I received a call from Russ Stratton, a very excited executive producer for *The Unexplained*, who said that they had had a breakthrough on Ryan's case. He had hired a Hollywood historian to go to the archives at the Academy of Motion Pictures Arts and Sciences Library in order to identify the man in the picture. He had already contacted Dr. Tucker and they were interested in visiting us with a different camera crew. He couldn't disclose much information because he didn't want to taint the investigation process, and neither did Dr. Tucker. "Cyndi, I have been producing television shows for ten years and this is the most extraordinary thing that I have ever seen," he told me.

When the team arrived the following week, Ryan warmed up to Russ and instantly liked him. As part of the process, with the cameras rolling, Dr. Tucker laid out four black-and-white pictures on our table. All of them were pretty women and the pictures looked similar to one another. He then asked Ryan if any of them looked familiar to him. Ryan instantly pointed to one of the unmarked photos and stated, "That one, she looks familiar." I saw Dr. Tucker's smile widen and I asked nervously, "Who is she?" Dr. Tucker replied, "She was his wife." Ryan grinned and shook his head with gratification.

Ryan then picked out a picture of his previous family. He (the man in the bowler hat) was not in the photo, but it showed his wife, two stepdaughters, the three adopted sons, an insert of the biological daughter. But the most shocking was when Dr. Tucker laid out another group of pictures, all of older men in suits. Ryan didn't need any time with these, despite Dr. Tucker's instructions to take his time and think about them. He quickly pointed to one and said, "That's Senator Five!" Dr. Tucker then asked him if he was sure. Ryan never hesitated: "I'm sure."

Dr. Tucker went on to explain that the man's name was Senator

Ives and that he had been a New York senator during that time; to Dr. Tucker the names "Senator Ives" and "Senator Five" would sound a lot alike to a child. Ryan was furious as he said, "I missed his name by one stupid letter."

Next, Ryan was presented with four photos of a young man in tennis clothes, three of them holding a racket. He pointed to one and said it was familiar. It was the man in the bowler hat at a young age. Then, finally, Dr. Tucker asked Kevin to read four names out loud, and asked Ryan to choose one. He read them slowly: John Johnson, Willy Wilson, Marty Martyn, Robert Robertson. Ryan shook his head no for the first two and the fourth, but did not respond at all to Marty Martyn. At the end, he said this name was the one. Dr. Tucker told us he was right; this was the name of the man in the photo. He proceeded to go over many of the memories Ryan had, which he had written down and had in front of him, and told us they were correct for the life of this man. Marty had indeed been an agent—he ran the Marty Martyn talent agency, representing some of Hollywood's leading stars, most of whom had changed their names.

Marty had died on Christmas Day in 1964, when he was sixty-one, in the hospital. I was stunned. I remembered that Ryan had said one day that he didn't know why God would let you get to sixty-one and then make you come back again as a baby. This was written on April second in my journal. A few days before, when we were in the hospital when I had some tests done, he had said that you go to a room with numbers on the door before you die. At the time, I had no idea what that meant, but now it was clear that Marty's hospital door would have had a number on it.

When the film crew left, Ryan and I sat alone in what became a very private time for both of us. They had left the pictures for him to keep. In fact, Russ had made Ryan a complete book filled with photos and even an old sheet that contained vital statistic records that verified that he had indeed changed his name just as he had said, and that there had been two sisters. Their ages were scrawled out along with their names in a early handwritten 1900s census form. The sister he had loved so much was in some of the photos with him, dancing on the stages of New York. In fact, she had lived in Paris, dancing there at a young age, and there were photos of Marty in front of Paris landmarks when he had visited her. There were even photos of the big fancy boats that he took to get there. Seeing the photo of the oldest stepdaughter gave Ryan a headache. He became furious as he said, "She had no respect, no respect." He was quick to let me know that he had no desire to see her again, ever, at all.

The photos were powerful for Ryan. He loved the ones that showed Marty as young and handsome. He wasn't pleased at all to see the ones that showed him older and bald. He would say, "Let's go back to the ones before." He then told me that he hoped that he didn't lose his hair this time around like he had last time.

The producer told us that they had contacted Marty Martyn's one biological child, and she had agreed to meet with us at a neutral spot. She was only eight years old when her father had died, so we really were not sure just how much she would be able to tell us. But we all felt it would be worthwhile, even though I suspected it would be hard for Ryan to see his previous young daughter now old enough to be his grandmother. The trip was planned for August, a month past Ryan's sixth birthday.

Ryan was very shy when we were with Marty Martyn's daughter. He didn't want to talk much to her and stayed out of the room most of the time. Now in her fifties, she was very agreeable and tried to be helpful. She was able to confirm many of the details that Ryan had provided and that I had written down in my journal for Dr. Tucker's files. They were the small personal things, like he did drive a green car and nobody else was allowed to drive it but him. Ryan had claimed that his address had the word "rock" or "mount" in it, and they lived on Roxbury Drive. Her father hated cats and never had allowed her to have one as a child, but instead he had bought her a dog, and she admitted that she had hated the dog, just as Ryan had told me previously. Marty had had an extensive collection of sunglasses. And there was more. She answered all of the questions as best she could, at least the ones that she could remember.

When we went to Marty's home, it had been partially torn down and was in the process of renovation. But the swimming pool was still there and Ryan smiled during the whole trip. He seemed so relieved that he finally had proof that he hadn't just made it all up.

The most amazing part was when we went back to the building where the Marty Martyn talent agency had been. It was a beautiful old building in downtown Beverly Hills, with a chandelier in the entryway. The offices were locked but we were still able to walk around inside. The ceilings were some of the most beautiful that I had ever seen. Ryan ran up the stairs so that he could show his dad how you could sit out on the roof and smoke. At one point he sat on the windowsill and just smiled, taking it all in. He would have sat there all day if we had let him. He didn't say much, but his face said everything.

We returned home with a different outlook. Marty's daughter sent us many photos, which we had seen when we were there, of her father, mother, herself, and their home. Some showed Marty at the beach, or in Paris, or holding his daughter when she was about two years old. We also had pictures of the Rolls-Royce that was part black, which his wife drove, the piano in the house, and her with the dog Marty gave her since he hated cats.

Ryan was relieved of a lot of uncertainty, and seemed better able to live in the present as Ryan. He had been able to prove that he was right and that there really had been an "old me" who matched his stories. For the most part, he was content to believe that now he could leave the past behind and just enjoy his new life. He seemed more peaceful. He still talked about his memories somewhat, but less and less over time. I felt as if we had finished. We now had an ending.

The day that I walked through the agency building with Ryan forever changed my life. I saw a small boy act as if he were truly returning home after a long journey. The sadness was gone and his whole face was lit up with joy. I didn't know what to make of it, but it made me feel as if anything was possible.

Chapter 5

Fifty-five Verified Memories

When I went to Warner, Oklahoma, to meet the Hammons family, Ryan was ten years old. He was a subdued and polite, intelligent boy who seemed older than his years, as if he had a lot going on inside but was good at not revealing it. In that sense, it was sometimes hard to "read" Ryan, as one usually can a ten-year-old boy, but he was happy to tell me about his favorite video games, movies, and friends at school, and we got along well. He seemed more adult and sophisticated in his language than I would assume his friends were. It was clear to me that Cyndi and her son were very close.

Thankfully Ryan is no longer unresolved or haunted by his past life. He sleeps well, does well in school, and has the normal interests of a boy his age. But although he is distant from it, Ryan has not completely forgotten about the past life, as is usually the case by the time children with memories turn ten.

After I arrived at their home and spent some time chatting with

Ryan, Cyndi and I sat together at her kitchen table, which opens to the living room, going over material about the case while Ryan was within earshot playing video games. I felt a little uncomfortable with this proximity, but then Ryan addressed this problem. "I just want you to know I can hear everything you're saying," he said, turning away from the computer to face us. I asked him if it was okay with him that we were talking about all this, and he said yes, and Cyndi assured me this was nothing he had not heard before.

I went out to dinner with the family, and spent a few days getting to know them. Just before I left, Ryan and Cyndi stopped by my hotel. With a big smile, Ryan handed me a *Downton Abbey* calendar as a gift, because I had been talking with his mom about how much I loved the PBS series. As we were saying goodbye, I asked Ryan if he could remember a particular detail about the case that I had on my mind. He said, "I don't think about this very much anymore." I was actually glad, and I told him this was a good thing.

Cyndi and Kevin are a very responsible, caring set of parents who went through quite an ordeal but are now relieved to be able to put Ryan's past life behind them. After Cyndi and I spent a day on our own, I felt privileged to receive a copy of her journal—the same documentation that she had sent to Jim Tucker as the case progressed. This was the all-important written record, beginning in the fall of 2009, that showed none of the points were made up or embellished after the case was solved, proving that Ryan had actually said what he said on the date he said it. If this record had not been kept so diligently, and sent to Jim as soon as each entry was written, I think it would have been hard for almost anyone to believe that Ryan could have made so many statements that turned out later to be accurate. As things unfolded, Cyndi was in regular communication with Jim, who was a lifeline for her. He was a source of solace and support, as well as strength and understanding, and she expressed much gratitude and respect for his stabilizing presence when we met.

Jim Tucker was also crucial to the case from a research perspective; having a competent and informed child psychiatrist involved made such a difference. Jim brought Russ Stratton to the case, who engaged the film archival experts to try and identify the all-important man in the photo. Without the professional perseverance of Jim and Russ, I think it's fair to say that the case never would have been solved. Since Bruce Leininger worked on his own, and felt he had to keep his motives secret from those he contacted in the process, it took him years to find James Huston Jr.

After taking my copy of Cyndi's journal back to New York, I went through it meticulously, noting down all of Ryan's specific points beginning with Cyndi's first letter to Jim Tucker in February 2010. Other statements made by Ryan were recorded by Jim during interviews with Ryan or documented by the film crew; some came from the July meeting with the film crew when the family first learned about Marty Martyn; and, finally, from the August trip to L.A. in which they met Marty's daughter, Marisa Martyn Rosenblatt. I have since been in touch with Marisa, and she has been gracious and helpful with some of my questions about her father. I asked her about the meeting with Ryan and his family. "The experience of meeting Ryan was strange. The first thing he said to me was that I was so old!" she replied, acknowledging that this makes sense since she was only eight years old when her father died. Along with the information Marisa provided to the family, I was able to confirm a source to verify each of Ryan's key statements from public records at the national archives, newspapers, obituaries, census reports, death certificates, travel documents, and photographs. I made a list of these memories, leaving off the more general statements that would be obvious from the time period or would logically follow from something he already stated (such as "I lived in a house full of children," when he had already stated more specifically that there were three boys there, a daughter and a stepdaughter). Many other memories recorded in Cyndi's journal were unverifiable, and remain so to this day.

James Leininger had twelve verified memories, which are of high value because they contained specific names of people, the ship *Natoma,* and locations. It's the sheer *number* of accurate memories, more than making up for the lack of specificity, that makes Ryan's case so extraordinary.

Some of Ryan's initial memories, provided shortly after he pointed to the photo in the book and said "That's me," were verified privately by Cyndi on her own, before Jim became involved. She sent them to Jim in her earliest correspondence, complete with the answers she found through the movie credits and looking up what she could find online. For research purposes, these memories are in a different category from those that remained unsolved until archival records and Marty's daughter Marisa were located. These earliest memories involved Ryan's recognizing "George" in the photo with him and memories about his cowboy friend who made cigarette commercials and had a horse that did tricks. Cyndi was easily able to verify the actor George Raft and to find out that the cowboy was Gordon Nance, aka Wild Bill Elliott, and that Ryan's memories about him were accurate. Ryan also told his mom things about the movie (like "It had a closet full of guns in it") that Cyndi and Kevin were able to verify when they watched it online.

The following statements were all made by Ryan before anything was known about Marty Martyn, and were not verified by anyone until *after* the identity of the man in the photo was established. (This list does not include those verified initially by Cyndi.) They are all accurate for the life of Marty Martyn.

1. He is the man in the photograph from the movie *Night After Night*.
2. He lived in Hollywood.
3. He lived somewhere with the word "rock" or "mount" in it; a street address.
4. He was very rich.
5. His house was big.
6. There was a brick wall at the house.
7. There were three boys.
8. He didn't think the boys were his but he gave them his name.

9. He had a daughter.
10. He brought coloring books home.
11. He had trouble with his oldest stepdaughter—she wouldn't listen; didn't respect him.
12. He had a large swimming pool.
13. His mother had curly brown hair.
14. He had a younger sister.
15. He bought his daughter a dog when she was about six.
16. She didn't like the dog.
17. He hated cats.
18. He knew Senator Ives (Five).
19. He used to see Senator Ives in New York (found on a map).
20. He had a green car.
21. He didn't let anyone else drive the green car.
22. He had many wives.
23. His wife drove a nice black car.
24. He was an agent; he ran an agency.
25. The agency changed people's names.
26. He tap-danced on the stage.
27. The stage was in New York City.
28. He saw the world on big boats where he danced with pretty ladies.
29. He ate in Chinatown a lot; his favorite restaurant was there.
30. He got "skin burns" in Hollywood.
31. He went to Paris; saw the Eiffel Tower.
32. He took his girlfriends to the ocean.
33. He played the piano; owned one.
34. He had an African American maid.
35. He knew Rita Hayworth—she made "ice drinks" (photo recognition).
36. He knew that Mary lady—you couldn't get close to talk to her (photo recognition, Marilyn Monroe).
37. Bread was his favorite food.
38. He had a sunglasses collection.

39. He was a smoker.

40. He had many girlfriends and affairs—never had problems getting the ladies.

41. He liked to watch surfers on the beach.

42. He owned guns.

43. He didn't have a TV when he was a little boy; they had radio first.

44. He hated FDR.

45. You go to a room with numbers on the door before dying.

46. "I'm not 5; I'm closer to 105 from when I was here before" (would have been 106).

47. He died at age sixty-one.

When you add the eight original statements verified by Cyndi, there are a total of fifty-five accurate statements. "Ryan holds the record with just a few others in our collection at the University of Virginia for the most past-life statements, in part because of the contact Cyndi and I have had over a long period of time," Jim told me.

Marty had a career as a dancer in New York and was very close to his sister, Florence Maslow, an internationally known dancer in the 1920s and 1930s who appeared in the "Ziegfeld Follies" and worked with Josephine Baker. He then went on to run the Marty Martyn talent agency. He changed his name—his birth name was Kolinsky. Marisa—Marty's only biological child—said she remembered seeing a photograph of her father with Senator Ives, and confirmed their friendship. Marty had four wives and many girlfriends. Many of the statements were already explained in the previous chapter, and as I already stated, every statement on this list was discovered to be accurate. Ryan also made some statements that were wrong, although not many. He said his (Marty's) father died when he was a boy, which was not the case (Marty's father died six years before he did). Ryan had said he was cremated, but Marty's death certificate says he was buried. Many more statements are impossible to verify.

Ryan had not seen *Night After Night* when he said, "That's me and that's George and we did a picture together." Having a photo recognition by a child first—before anything else is known about the previous personality—is unprecedented, according to Jim Tucker. Usually a photo of the previous personality is not found until the end of the investigation, if the search team is lucky. "In most of our cases, people have tried to see if a deceased person could be identified whose life matched the statements the child had made," Tucker explains. "Here there was only one guy that Ryan could have been talking about, because he had pointed to him in a picture. We weren't trying to see if there was anyone whose life matched Ryan's statements; we were looking to see if Marty Martyn's did."

And that task could not have been accomplished without professional assistance. Russ Stratton hired a professional footage researcher, Kate Coe, who was stymied by the fact that she only had one photo of an unnamed extra from a 1932 movie. Coe then took the image to the Academy of Motion Picture Arts and Sciences library and film archive, the single largest film research library in the world, occupying forty thousand square feet in Los Angeles. Searching many files, she finally found one for *Night After Night*. Flipping through the 8 x 10 glossies from the film, she was shocked to find a close-up of what looked just like the man in the bowler hat; he was wearing the same hat and spouting a large cigar. She turned it over, and there on the back was: "Marty Martyn playing a racketeer in Paramount's *NIGHT AFTER NIGHT*." It was clear that the two photos showed the same man. This happened right before Jim went to the Hammonses' home for the second time and did the photo recognition tests with Ryan.

Was there any way that the Hammonses could have found out themselves? When Cyndi and Kevin first watched the movie, Marty Martyn was listed in the credits as "Malloy." However, as it was for many of the actors in the film, all one could find in the Internet Movie Database was Martyn's incorrect date of birth and his death date. Jim remembers that even in 2010, there was nothing else online about Martyn. Now that has changed—but only because of the Hammons case drawing attention to Marty Martyn's history.

In April 2010, Cyndi wrote to a producer from *The Unexplained* before the first crew came to the house, and one paragraph confirms the fact that she had no idea who the man in the photo was at that time, and assumed that his name was not even listed:

> There are only two guys in the cast list of *Night After Night* that I haven't been able to identify. They are a man named James Gillis and another man named Marty Martyn. I have spent hours working on this. I have had the picture since probably January or February. I really do not think he was ever listed in the cast list since it was such a small part.

And her motivation for allowing the filming was clearly spelled out in the same letter:

> We would appreciate any help that we can get. Dr. Tucker has been so kind to me and has answered many questions for me. I know that Ryan is special. I do not know if who he claims to be and the man in the picture will even match. I want you to know we are not ashamed of what Ryan is going through . . .
>
> I do think this show could help other people who have children like Ryan. If you do find out who he is will you please tell me. Sometimes I go days with only a few hours of sleep because I am up and down with Ryan so much. I think if we could just answer his questions we could get back to some kind of normalcy.

The twenty-two-minute piece that Stratton produced on the Ryan case was filmed in 2010, when Ryan was five and six, and aired in April 2011 on The Biography Channel. Thanks to Russ, I was able to see the piece, which includes footage of Ryan during the photo lineup when he identified Senator Ives and others. (Unfortunately it is not available for public viewing.) In most child reincarnation cases, memories begin to surface years earlier than they did with Ryan, especially if there seems to be trauma associated with them. In Ryan's case, his "previous death" was not sudden, violent, or at a young age as it was with James, which is less typical. But Ryan had speech difficulties, and early in life he suffered multiple ear infections that filled his ears with fluid and limited his hearing. According to Cyndi, he was quiet as a toddler. He had his adenoids removed before he turned four, and that allowed him to become more verbal, but he still required speech therapy following the surgery, which continued during first grade. When Jim Tucker met Ryan, he had a good vocabulary but was not as verbal as his peers and sometimes was hard to understand. Ryan told his mother that he did remember his past life when he was much younger. "When you are a baby and you remember being bad, you can't tell anyone because you can't talk," he told Cyndi, who dutifully wrote the statement down in her journal.

Like James, Ryan had painful nightmares. Ryan's were not repetitive of one scene, and often his parents did not know what they were about. But he did say that sometimes he dreamed about Senator Five, and had many dreams related to how he (Marty) died. He cried a lot at night even when awake, saying he was homesick and wanted to see his other family, the one he had when he was big. And like James with his airplanes, Ryan liked to play movie director and agent, as if those skills still lived within him. Also similar to James, the interwoven emotions, nightmares, and related behaviors suggest that Ryan was actually reliving something that was deeply internalized and real for him.

In fact, Ryan sometimes seemed to have difficulty separating his past life from his present one to an extent that seems especially extreme compared to other cases. There were times when he and Marty were so merged that he could not distinguish one from the other. These did not appear to be simple memories that popped in and out, and then left him alone to be in the present for long periods until the next memory surfaced, as is usually the case with younger children such as James Leininger. Ryan sometimes seemed confused as to what was then and what was now, and what were reasonable expectations now as opposed to then. He thought he should pay his mom for cleaning his room because before he had a maid who came in every day to clean his house. He expected to see his buddies when he went to

Hollywood, and said he might stay with them for a while and come home after his parents.

Ryan also seemed aware beyond his years, and this was sometimes conflicting for him. "Mommy, you know how there are kind of two people on the inside of me? There is Ryan and there is Marty," he said just after turning six. "I know about things Marty knows about." Perhaps the unusual intensity of this intertwining of the two personalities—the presence of Marty so vividly and continuously in his interior world—attributed to the flood of memories he had and the large number of accurate ones.

Unlike James (at least as far as James's parents could tell), Ryan seemed to have psychic abilities. He could sometimes predict things that were about to happen, or know things through some kind of extrasensory awareness, usually involving his extended family. Since most of Ryan's memories about Marty occurred after he saw the picture in the book, could he have picked up the details of Marty's life psychically through the photograph? The emotional turmoil of his longing for the past, his nightmares, and his play related to the previous life suggested that this connection was living within him. It did not seem like a reaction to information gleaned psychically from a photograph that had no personal meaning and was something separate from himself. Many of Ryan's memories were repeated at different times and in different locations, some numerous times, which suggests that they were actually memories that were triggered and surfaced in his mind. Nonetheless, no matter how unlikely, we can never rule out completely the possibility of some unusual psychic mechanism playing a role in Ryan's case.

Like the Leiningers, Cyndi and Kevin did not appear to have any psychological reason for facilitating the surfacing of the memories, which wreaked havoc on the family. Neither one came from a religion or belief system that supported the idea of reincarnation. Cyndi was raised going to a Baptist church and Kevin's father was a Church of Christ minister. They lived in a small town where this might not have been looked at with kind eyes, and were concerned about the reactions of coworkers and family members. Yet the Hammonses were intelligent and sensitive enough to allow Ryan to express himself without denying the legitimacy of his memories. Their love for Ryan emanates from the pages of Cyndi's journal, as she is forced to endure the trauma along with him. Her primary goal was to find peace for Ryan.

Also in Ryan's favor is the fact that he was taken initially to Hollywood when the film crew had the wrong man—an actor named Ralf Harolde—who resembled the man in the bowler hat. Even though Ryan said this was not the man in the photo, there was some uncertainty and Ryan wanted the opportunity to visit L.A. The family kept an open mind. When they took Ryan to Harolde's house, he had no reaction; in contrast, he did react at the house of Bill Elliott, Marty's cowboy friend. Later he recognized the location of Marty Martyn's house, which was under construction but had the swimming pool intact. And when he went to the building where Marty's agency was housed, he was elated and clearly was totally at home there.

The photo lineup was interesting, but a tricky process. Most important was Ryan's immediate recognition of Senator "Five" and secondly that of the previous wife. Recognizing himself as a younger man may not have been difficult since he had stared at the photo of Marty in the book so often. And it's possible that he had heard his mom mention the name "Marty Martyn" before, since it was listed in the movie credits. Also, it would have been ideal to have had an outsider who was not informed about the identity of anyone in the photos be the one to present them to Ryan. But Ryan would likely have felt uncomfortable and shy having someone there whom he didn't know; he was bonded to Jim Tucker and trusted him, so he would have been more responsive to Jim than he would have been to a stranger. Still, this was a context conducive to both on-the-spot psi, since Tucker knew the correct answers, and also an unconscious reaction by Ryan to subtle nonverbal cues that might have been present.

Could Ryan's parents have researched this and hoaxed the whole thing, by feeding Ryan information? The answer is no, because the information about Marty was not available on the Internet at the time.

There was nothing linking this name to the name of the man with the bowler hat whom Ryan pointed to, and one would logically assume, as Cyndi did, that an extra with no lines would not be listed in the credits along with the stars and the speaking parts. And, even if somehow Cyndi and Kevin had guessed that the man was Marty, and then influenced Ryan, most of the facts Ryan provided could be found only through extensive archival research and through the memories of Marty's daughter, whom they met for the first time after the film archivist identified Marty. It was very difficult even for the professionals to identify Marty, and it is inconceivable that the Hammonses could have done so from Warner, Oklahoma.

Cyndi and Kevin have never benefited from any of the publicity about the case—quite the opposite. Reading the many pages of Cyndi's emotional, painful, and very sincere journal—which she never expected anyone but Jim Tucker would ever read—it seems inconceivable that all of it was made up on an almost daily basis with her police officer husband as a coconspirator. Ryan would have had to learn his lines well for his interviews with Jim and the film crew. As far as I am concerned, it barely needs mentioning that the case cannot be explained as a hoax.

Some of the information Ryan remembered was obscure. The birth date of 1905 was on Marty's death certificate, so Jim and the others initially assumed this was when he was born. This would have made him fifty-nine when he died in 1964. But Ryan stated that he was sixty-one when he died. ("Why would God let you get to be sixty-one and then make you come back again?") Well, newly acquired documents revealed that Ryan was right, despite what everyone else had thought. Census reports from 1910, 1920, and 1940 show Marty's birth year as 1903. The California marriage index, 1949–1959, lists Marty's age as fifty-two in 1955 when he married Margaret Skouras, which would make him sixty-one in 1964. And a 1929 New York passenger list from the boat *Minnesota* arriving in New York from France has Marty Kolinsky's birth date clearly typed as May 19, 1903. Nobody had been able to change Ryan's mind that he had been sixty-one when he died, despite their convictions—and for good reason. In

2016, I acquired a photo of Marty's grave for the first time, with the dates 1903–1964.

Those involved most closely with the Leininger and Hammons cases believe that the continuity of personal consciousness from one life to the next provides the best explanation for the statements and behaviors of the two boys. If this is so, these cases and hundreds of others suggest that the consciousness or "mind" of a person—which retains memories, knowledge, and emotions—survives death and is then reborn. Within this scenario, this consciousness must persist somehow during the nonsomatic period and must not be dependent on the brain for its survival, like the human body is. "I think these cases contribute to the body of evidence that consciousness—at least, in certain circumstances—can survive the death of the body; that life after death isn't necessarily just a fantasy or something to be considered on faith, but it can also be approached in an analytic way, and the idea can be judged on its merits," Jim said in 2014.

But how can consciousness exist without a brain? Some studies support the possibility of there being a separation between the "mind" and the body, at least temporarily. The cases explored in the next section reinforce the concept that consciousness may not depend on the human brain and therefore could conceivably have continuity from one life to the next.

PART TWO

To Death and Back Again

The boundaries which divide Life from Death are at best shadowy and vague. Who shall say where the one ends, and where the other begins?
—EDGAR ALLAN POE

Chapter 6

The Shoe on the Ledge

By Kimberly Clark Sharp, MSW

Kimberly Clark Sharp had a long career as a medical social worker. She was a pioneer in the fields of critical care and coronary care social work during her ten years at Harborview Medical Center in Seattle, Washington, and in 1985 founded the Department of Social Work at Fred Hutchinson Cancer Research Center, the world's first bone marrow transplant center. She was also a practicum instructor for University of Washington social work graduate students and retired from her position as clinical assistant professor of social work at the University of Washington after teaching for twenty years about death and dying at the School of Medicine. Sharp is the founder and president of the Seattle International Association for Near-Death Studies, the world's oldest and largest support group for near-death experiencers.

In 1977, I was a young social worker employed at Harborview Medical Center in Seattle, a large trauma center with a busy coronary care unit and medical intensive care unit. My particular job was crisis intervention and related psychosocial issues in those units.

My life was forever changed that April by a middle-aged Mexican migrant worker named Maria. She had come to Seattle to visit friends, but upon arrival suffered a massive heart attack, and was admitted through the Harborview emergency room to the coronary care unit. I met with her the following day for the purpose of completing a psychosocial workup, finding next of kin and referring her to sources of financial assistance. Maria knew a bit of English and I knew a bit of Spanish, so, in the absence of a translator and with added pantomime, we forged a simple but adequate form of communication, and I stopped in to see her regularly during her stay.

One day, when I was working on medical records in the coronary care unit, a loud piercing alarm suddenly sounded. I could see through a window into the nurses' station where the bank of cardiac monitors blinked and beeped. The alarm meant that a particular patient was "coding"—in other words, she was in cardiac arrest—and that patient was Maria.

I stepped the short distance to the door of her room as a dozen healthcare providers jogged past me in response to the emergency. This was not unusual—there would be the attending physician, residents, interns, nurses, respiratory therapists, students, and perhaps observing healthcare visitors. It sounds like chaos, but it wasn't. Cardiac arrest codes were a common occurrence and the response team was a well-oiled machine, with everyone knowing where to go and what to do. I watched as the team manually thumped and massaged Maria's chest, and saw a tube go down her throat to bring air to her lungs. Maria was hooked up to a portable electrocardiogram machine in order to measure her heart activity, and I watched as paddles were positioned on her chest to shock her heart into beating again. But mainly I watched the screen of the portable monitor showing she was flatlining—no heartbeat, no breath. She was what we call clinically dead.

Fortunately, this turned out to be a relatively easy resuscitation and after a couple of applications of the paddles, Maria, though still unconscious and on a ventilator, was deemed in stable condition. Several hours later she had awakened and was breathing on her own. But then a coronary care nurse paged me asking me to come and assess a very agitated Maria. She was so rattled that they were quite concerned she would revert to cardiac arrest again because of the stress. As a social worker, I was asked to go in and solve this problem.

As I entered her hospital room, Maria was partly elevated in bed waving her arms around and speaking Spanish too fast for me to comprehend. Our forged pidgin language was not about to work at that speed, but I could tell she had something important to tell me. My efforts to help her settle down seemed only to upset her more and she burst into tears of frustration. Eventually she calmed down, and we returned to our usual means of small words and pantomime and she proceeded to explain her agitation, which to my surprise had not come from fear or anger, but from tremendous excitement.

Maria pointed to a corner of the ceiling in her room and told me that she had left her body and had been up there, watching her resuscitation from that place. She accurately told me who had been in the room, where they had stood, what they had said, and what they had done. She also described the placement of the machinery that had been used, particularly the electrocardiogram machine that had continuously spit out volumes of wide white paper, which, when it reached the floor, had been kicked under the bed by a staff person to get the paper out of the way. Then, by snapping her fingers to show how quickly her view changed, she said she found herself above the doors of the first-floor emergency room. Again, with accuracy, Maria described the curvature of the driveway, the vehicles all pointed in one direction, and the automatic doors opening when people entered and exited.

My professional, rational mind did not allow me to believe her, even though the descriptions she provided were accurate. The people she identified in the room had, indeed, been present. And the placement of the machinery was correct. But I knew that Maria had been well educated as to what would happen if she had a cardiac crisis. And she knew who was on duty that day and would be able to recognize their voices in the room. I knew that hearing is believed to be the last sense to go before death.

However, Maria had observed paper being kicked under the bed, something she could never have anticipated. My skeptical mind could not get around her accurate description of this particular detail. There is absolutely no way that she would have known about the paper. It was not taught, it was not discussed, it is never shown in television and movies depicting cardiac arrest. And she was lying on her back on the bed and thus could not have seen staff kick the paper because it was below the level of the bed. She could have known this detail only through observation. But how? Her eyes were definitely shut; I observed this firsthand.

In terms of Maria describing the scene at the entrance to the ER, she had been admitted at night and had not been privy to any outside scenes because the edges of her oxygen mask and the looming presence of medics over her head would have blocked her view. Her eyes were reportedly closed because she was writhing in terrible pain. Furthermore, emotions run high when one is rushed to a hospital in an emergency, making it very unlikely that a patient would be interested in the outside environment. Even if she had seen the doors opening, she would not have had access to windows in the car that would have revealed the curved driveway with all the cars driving one way only. She did not have a view of this from her hospital window either, because a large overhanging roof designed to protect incoming ambulance patients from the rainy weather blocked the view.

I had no more time to linger with my thoughts, because Maria had something even more important to tell me. She said that while she was out of her body she was distracted by something in another part of the hospital. By gesturing with the same quick snap of her fingers, she described somehow finding herself three or four stories above the ground staring very closely at an odd object sitting outside on a window ledge: a single tennis shoe.

From an extremely close perspective, Maria described the single shoe as large like a man's shoe, dark blue with a scuffed side next to where the little toe would go, with a white shoelace tucked under the heel. And then Maria explained why she was upset: she very much wanted someone to go get the shoe, not to prove to herself that the shoe was there—she knew it was—but to prove to others that while "dead" she was quite lucid and able to float inside and outside the hospital walls. And then she looked at me expectantly, with an expression of hope that I would be the one to retrieve the shoe.

I thought such a search would be futile. Maria had no idea where outside of the vast building the shoe might be, just that it was a few floors above the ground. But in order to show my caring, and to prevent getting her upset and potentially in cardiac danger again, I agreed to go on this quest.

I began with the logical conclusion that if I went outside and walked around the hospital, I would be able to spot any object, particularly a blue tennis shoe, from the ground. But as I followed the sidewalk that hugged the building, I couldn't see the full width of any of the window edges. I completely circled the building without seeing a thing, including a bird that flew to an upper floor ledge and disappeared from sight. I was just too close to the building, which was on a cliff, and at that time there were only two places—the driveway and a parking garage—that allowed one to step back from the sidewalk. To do so required crossing through unsafe, high-traffic areas, and since the shoe could have been on a ledge anywhere on four steep sides of this humongous building (and I didn't expect to find it anyway), I didn't take that risk.

So I went back into the building and up to the third floor, randomly searching the windows on the east side of the building. I went into the patient rooms, walked to the window and looked down. Some sections had screened windows and other sections had different window configurations, depending on which area within the huge complex I was exploring. In many rooms things were stacked up against the lower part of the windows, and I had to walk up to closed glass to look down upon the ledge. My hunt of the east-side windows yielded nothing. I moved through all the windows on the north side—nothing. Then the west side. I searched several windows there and went into the next room expecting nothing. But when I pressed my face against yet one more windowpane, peered down on one more ledge, I felt my heart jump. There it was.

Out on the narrow ledge was a man's dark blue tennis shoe. It had the end of one lace tucked under the heel, just as Maria had described it; the lace emerged from under the heel on the side near the window, but I couldn't see the continuum of where it came out on the other side facing the outside of the ledge. The area of the little toe, which Maria had said was scuffed, was also outside my field of view, since it was facing away from the window.

I was shocked. Time stopped. For that first moment I could not support my own body weight and slumped against the glass, hitting it with my forehead. This was impossible.

My mind raced to find an explanation, and I thought of four possibilities. In the distance, I could see one lone downtown edifice, Smith Tower, about a half mile away. Before her heart attack, perhaps Maria had somehow gained access to an upper floor of Smith Tower and with binoculars or a telescope had spied the shoe on the ledge. But she had never been to Seattle before being admitted to Harborview and most likely did not have binoculars or a telescope. Secondly, maybe Maria had managed to unhook herself from her IVs and monitor leads, wander unobserved to the opposite side of the third floor, walk into a room with two patient beds, and look down at the window ledge to see the shoe. Inconceivable; it would have been noticed immediately if she left her bed.

Another option: someone planted the shoe on the ledge and convinced Maria to conspire in a hoax, telling her in detail what to say. This was far-fetched, to say the least. Maria had no outside visitors on the day of her resuscitation. I knew this because I was paged to Maria's bedside right after she regained consciousness, and that was when she told me about the shoe. What about the hospital staff? I could not imagine a busy doctor or nurse engaging in such odd and unprofessional behavior, risking that someone would find out. And why would Maria agree to this deception? None of the staff spoke Spanish anyway, so no one could have communicated with Maria about something convoluted like this.

This left me with my the fourth option: While unconscious with her eyes closed, with no heartbeat or respiratory activity and a roomful of medical professionals working frantically to resuscitate her, Maria somehow had visual and auditory awareness of distant locations. While I watched her body being thumped and jolted, she was somewhere else. While her consciousness journeyed around the premises outside of her body, one stop was the outside of a window ledge in another part of the hospital where she observed this tennis shoe, and it was something she remembered. None of these conclusions made sense, but I felt I had no choice but to believe the fourth scenario. But how could that be?

Gathering myself, I opened the window and picked up the shoe. It was in my hand, it had weight and dimension. When I turned the shoe around, I noticed the defining detail: it had a scuffed part where the little toe would be.

When I returned to Maria's room, I held the shoe behind my back so I could ask one more question, which was my final way of seeking validation. Through gestures and my minimal Spanish, I asked if she could tell me about the inside of the shoe, because if her perspective was, as she called it, "eyeball to shoelace," she would not be able to tell me what the inside of the shoe looked like. If she did, then I could say, *aha,* she was making it all up. But she communicated to me that she couldn't see inside the shoe. Her view had been eye level with the side of the shoe facing away from the building. From my perspective at the window, I was looking down on it, so I could see the inside.

This reinforced the fact that the perspective she described would only be possible from midair, three stories above the ground. And what really shocked me was to realize that the detail of the scuffed side where the little toe would be could not be seen from *anywhere*—not from inside the hospital, from the ground, or from any other building, because there weren't any structures close enough on that side. Yet she described seeing that scuffed area from a point in empty space, while her body was under cardiac arrest in another part of the hospital.

With that, and with a dramatic flourish befitting the occasion, I produced the shoe from behind my back. What ensued was a lot of excited Spanish language, strong emotions, and a nurse who was very concerned about Maria's heart monitor going crazy. We joyfully hugged each other. We showed the shoe to the nurse and explained the whole story.

In the days to come a parade of nurses and doctors visited Maria to behold the shoe, which she kept on a side table in her room. Everybody wanted to see it. They saw, they touched, they paid their respects to the humble shoe, and they left. The reaction of the staff was astonishing. None of us had heard of anything like this before. We were mystified by it. My joke for a long time was that the shoe became the Shroud of Turin of Harborview.

No one disputed her account, at least not around me or the members of her resuscitation team. They knew the seriousness of her condition, and that it would have been impossible for her to have foreknowledge of the shoe. It was clear to me that the intensity of the emotions that accompanied both her realization of what had happened to her and her insistence that I find the shoe was genuine.

Maria was discharged after two weeks in the hospital. As we said goodbye, she handed me the tennis shoe as a gift, and asked me to keep it. I never knew how important both Maria and the tennis shoe would become over the years. Veridical out-of-body experiences—those in which the patient under cardiac arrest reports sights or sounds experienced out of the body that can be verified afterward—have since become the focus of serious research. Sadly, I lost touch with Maria after a few years, and the shoe somehow was misplaced in one of my moves. In retrospect, I wish I had remained aware of Maria's whereabouts and kept better track of the shoe.

The story has not changed an iota since day one, even though over the course of time I forgot about a Nike logo on the shoe. Years later, I came across a filmed reenactment of the event shown on television, using the actual tennis shoe. Skeptics have claimed that the shoe never existed, but in fact we do have this filmed documentation. The film shows me as much younger in very dated clothes, thus belying any suggestion that this was a recently filmed piece.

The story of the shoe on the ledge has become well known. It spread to other hospitals, then to other cities and states, primarily by nurses who invited me to their locations and conferences to speak about it. Absolutely no one expressed anything but wonder and feelings of inspiration in response, at least to me.

Many years later the skeptics came on board with their opinions, but they were all people with a prior agenda and none were associated with the case. I had no problem addressing their objections and laying them to rest. More important, finding the shoe on the ledge had a meteoric impact on my life and the lives of others. I actually had had a near-death experience in 1970 when I was young, but given that I had no frame of reference for anything like this, I let it go. The shoe validated that out-of-body experience and emboldened me to tell others about it.

It also awakened a curiosity in me to ask all my patients who had been close to death if they remembered anything while in that state of consciousness. Many people did. I have since devoted much of my professional life to supporting these experiencers, researching their reports, and writing about them. Mainly, I have learned that what we call death may not be the end of our awareness, nor our sense of self, nor our relationship to others. Our consciousness does exist outside of time and space and the confines of our bodies. This knowledge, because of a simple shoe, provides the comfort of a possible continuity not just when near death, but also at our actual death.

Chapter 7

Journeys out of Body

Maria's case is an exceptional example of a veridical out-of-body experience (OBE)—one in which perceived sights or sounds inaccessible by normal means can afterward be corroborated as accurate. Maria described the visual details of the shoe on the ledge from a position of being outside the window, three stories up; the scuffed side of the shoe she reported was not visible from the inside at all. When she "saw" the shoe, her body lay unconscious in another part of the hospital. She described her resuscitation accurately, including the paper being kicked under the bed, which she could not have seen from her prone position. Like many other experiencers, Maria had no doubt that she actually left her body and that in that disembodied state she was able to travel to those locations.

Such cases—and there are others—do not in any way prove survival past death. As Mark B. Woodhouse, associate professor emeritus of philosophy at Georgia State University, has said, "It is a tremendous conceptual jump from, say, a thirty-minute OBE to immortality." But veridical OBEs are a stepping-stone toward that possibility, indicating that our aware minds seem to exist and function independently of the brain and the physical body. Such data also has a bearing on the childhood past-life cases that—if they have occurred as the children perceive them—involve a disembodied, personal consciousness sustaining itself for a much longer time after surviving the irreversible physical death of the body.

But there are other considerations to contemplate. Maria's detached consciousness may have been dependent on her living body for its existence, even if it could make a short excursion into the external world. The effect on consciousness may be different during actual death. "The consciousness associated with a body that *has not yet* lost the potential to live may or may not be the same as the consciousness associated with a body that *has* lost that potential," writes Janice Holden of the University of North Texas, who has studied the veridical OBE extensively.

The psi hypothesis offers another potential explanation. Perhaps Maria's ESP—especially her clairvoyance, which allows for the viewing of objects in distant locations—became active while she lay unconscious, facilitating a sort of vivid dream state. In that unusual state, maybe she *felt* herself to be traveling outside her body but instead she was clairvoyantly perceiving the shoe and the other details from her hospital bed. This would mean she did not actually leave her body to travel outside the window, returning with the knowledge of the shoe. "It's reasonable to interpret OBEs as imagery-rich manifestations of ESP," Stephen Braude points out. Michael Sudduth, the San Francisco State University professor I discussed in the Introduction, agrees that the unusual knowledge could have been acquired through psychic functioning alone, without any "extrasomatic interpretation"—perception from outside the body—involved. Of course, psi was in use no matter what, either by Maria's consciousness floating outside a window or by Maria in some kind of unusual dream state.

OBEs have unique characteristics and experiencers do not associate them with the dream state. If clairvoyance and telepathy were used without any departure from the body, wouldn't at least some experiencers simply wake up and recognize the experience as an unusually vivid dream? This doesn't happen—they describe themselves positioned on the ceiling, sometimes shocked and disoriented at first, taking a while to recognize and accept that they are actually there and that perhaps they have died. They view their own bodies and the machinery being used from the perspective of the ceiling. In fact, they are stunned by how different this is from a dream—they often say it is more real than waking consciousness. Dreams tend to be more chaotic, and we forget them over time, but the OBE remains vivid in the memory as something that actually happened. Most experiencers' lives are forever changed by it as well, and they no longer fear death. The profound transformation that does occur suggests that something very unusual happened—something with more impact than a dream.

The detailed perception of the shoe, acquired while unconscious, was extraordinary in itself, no matter how it occurred. But the only aspect of Maria's experience that has a bearing on the question of survival is whether "she"—or some aspect of her consciousness—was actually external to her body. And even if this were the case, this only demonstrates *compatibility* with the survival hypothesis. But when combined with other evidence such as cases of proved past-life memories and near-death experiences, veridical OBEs strengthen the overall argument for survival by making an independent consciousness something conceivable.

Scientists have not been able to explain these occurrences. In a 2009 paper, "Veridical Perception in Near-Death Experiences," Janice Holden says that apparently nonphysical veridical perception "suggests the ability of consciousness to function independent of the physical body." These perceptions, she contests, are not the result of "normal sensory processes" and therefore challenge the concept fundamental to Western science that our sense of self and all experience is produced by the brain and thus can't exist without it. And, "if consciousness can function apart from the reversibly dead body, perhaps it continues to function beyond irreversible death," she writes. But, as Holden quips, unfortunately we will never be able to find proof, due to "the methodological failure of researchers to find reliable, irreversibly dead people to participate in their studies."

Some extraordinary examples of nonphysical veridical perception involve blind people who report "seeing" for the first time when leaving their bodies with their nonfunctioning physical eyes. Vicki Noratuk was born premature in 1950 at St. Luke Hospital in Pasadena, California. Her optic nerve was destroyed, leaving her permanently blind, due to the use of excess oxygen inside the newly developed air lock incubator. Vicki doesn't see anything—no light perception, shadows, or even black. "It's as if my eyes are dead, even though they're living entities, as it were, in my head, but they don't function at all," she explains. And when she dreams, there is nothing visual, just the same sensations she has when awake, such as touch, sound, taste, and smell.

On February 2, 1973, when she was twenty-two, Vicki almost died when she was thrown from a car and dragged across the pavement in an auto accident caused by a drunk driver. She sustained a skull fracture, concussion, neck injury, back and leg injuries, and an injury to the left side of her face.

In the emergency room at Harborview Medical Center (coincidentally the same place where Maria was four years later), she found herself up near the ceiling. But something was different: she could "see," as she describes it. "It was like a nightmare. It was foreign, it was eerie, it was very scary and I couldn't even translate what it was I was perceiving initially, and I didn't like it," she said. "Eventually, though, I was able to make more sense of everything and to start finding out what it was I was seeing." In a state of shock, she describes witnessing a body below her that the doctors were attempting to resuscitate. She recognized her hair, with blood caked on the skull, partly shaved. And then, from her position above the body, she noticed her wedding ring on the third finger of her left hand and her father's wedding ring on her right hand. "That was when it astounded me and I began to grapple with the fact that I was actually dead or dying," she says.

I was observing everything from up on the ceiling and seeing the male doctor trying to bring me back and he said, "We can't get her back, we can't get her back. There must be some problem here, we can't bring her back" and then he said, "It's a pity, now she could be deaf as well as blind, because there is blood on her left eardrum." And I thought, well, is that me that he's talking about? And the female doctor said, "She could be in a permanent vegetative state if she even survives." I floated down to try to talk to the female doctor and my right hand went through her arm when I tried to touch her.

Vicki's heart had stopped. She was told that she had been "dead" for four minutes, and her awareness of the conversations she heard provides a time anchor to her experiences, which were confirmed after she was revived. Unfortunately, no confirmation could be made of something specific that Vicki perceived visually. "I was able to see things in different brilliances of light, I suppose that would be color," she said. Other blind people have reported varying abilities to "see" when they perceive themselves as being out of their bodies, as documented by Kenneth Ring, professor emeritus of psychology at the University of Connecticut, and psychologist Sharon Cooper, in their book *Mindsight*.

More recently, Dr. Sam Parnia, director of Resuscitation Research at the Stony Brook University School of Medicine, directed the largest clinical, multi-hospital study ever conducted of near-death and out-of-body experiences, known as the AWARE study (AWAreness during REsuscitation). Scientists at the University of Southampton in the UK, where Parnia is an honorary research fellow and critical care physician, spent four years investigating 2,060 cardiac arrest survivors, using a three-stage quantitative and qualitative interview system, at fifteen hospitals in the UK, US, and Austria. A hundred and one patients completed all stages of the process and thus contributed to the research. Out of these, there were nine reports of near-death experiences, two with detailed memories of the physical environment. However, one was too ill for an in-depth interview.

As described by Parnia and thirty colleagues in their published paper, a fifty-seven-year-old social worker from Southampton, who wished to remain anonymous, reported that he left his body and watched his resuscitation from the corner of the room near the ceiling. He described what happened, which included sounds from machines. The correlation of these sounds with real-time events allowed investigators to rule out hallucinations or illusions and also to determine if in fact the patient was actually clinically dead at the moments when the experience occurred. "In this case, consciousness and awareness appeared to occur during a three-minute period when there was no heartbeat," Parnia states. "This is paradoxical, since the brain typically ceases functioning within 20–30 seconds of the heart stopping and doesn't resume again until the heart has been restarted." The patient heard two bleeps from a machine that makes a noise at three-minute intervals "so we could time how long the experience lasted for," Parnia said. The social worker also reported observing, from his elevated position, a bald nurse wearing blue, and hearing an automated voice repeating, "Shock the patient." Both were verified—the instructions came from an automated external defibrillator.

The veridical OBE is what Holden calls "the material aspect" of the near-death experience, involving phenomena in the material world. The experience that has so captured the public imagination, which we call the "near-death experience" or NDE, is the "transmaterial aspect," where the experiencer "perceives phenomena in transcendent dimensions beyond the physical world." During the latter phase, the experiencers still feel themselves as out of their bodies, but they have traveled away from the hospital room to another reality altogether.

Often coming after an OBE, NDEs are described as vivid and clear journeys into another dimension, which most NDErs are certain is the afterlife. They are reported by 10 to 20 percent of people who have come close to death, in diverse cultures throughout the world. Psychiatrist Bruce Greyson, director of the Department of Psychiatry and Neurobehavioral Sciences at the University of Virginia Medical School and one of the world's leading NDE researchers, summed up Western approaches to NDEs in a 2015 paper for *Humanities*. He says that the core near-death phenomenology is invariant across cultures. "That invariance may reflect universal psychological defenses, neurophysiological processes, or actual experience of a transcendent or mystical domain." But no matter what, "the vast majority of near-death experiencers report that during the time that their brains were demonstrably impaired, their thinking, by contrast, was clearer and faster than ever before, as if the mind had been freed from the distractions and limitations of the physical brain."

NDEs involve heightened, vivid sensations sometimes beginning with passing through a tunnel; entering an otherworldly ("heavenly") realm; encountering a brilliant light and seeing deceased relatives or friends; sometimes seeing a deity or spiritual figure; a life review; revelations and life lessons; intense positive emotions or mystical feelings; and a return to the body, often unwillingly. Although more abstract and subjective than the material OBE, sometimes the experiencer meets a deceased person unknown to them, giving the experience more evidential value when it can be confirmed that this person exists and has died. For example, according to Greyson, a patient under cardiac arrest saw a man he didn't know during an NDE. His mother later told the patient that he had been born as a result of an extramarital affair. When he was shown a picture of his biological father, the patient immediately recognized him as the man he had seen during his NDE. In another case, a young girl saw a boy who said he was her brother, but she was an only child. Her father then told her she had had a brother who died before she was born.

"Although these data are not compelling proof of survival, they cannot be dismissed as hallucinations based on expectation," Greyson writes. The information about the father and the brother could have been unconsciously assimilated by the experiencers from the family, or acquired psychically by them during their lives. Perhaps they telepathically perceived that these two people existed from the thoughts of their parent while growing up. Unfortunately we can't know what clues may have been available to them. Still, these accounts are intriguing.

Could NDEs be incorrect memories, or fantasies that are simply imagined? Seven scientists from the University of Liège, Belgium, have studied the characteristics of NDE memories as compared with both real and imagined event memories. In 2013, they found that NDE memories have more characteristics than either, which alludes to NDEs appearing more "real," as experiencers so often report. "The present study showed that NDE memories contained more characteristics than real event memories and coma memories. Thus, this suggests that they cannot be considered as imagined event memories. On the contrary, their physiological origins could lead them to be really perceived although not lived in the reality," the scientists report.

A lengthy 2014 paper in *Frontiers in Human Neuroscience* by nine scientists from the University of Padova, Italy, reports on the use of electroencephalography (EEG) "to investigate the characteristics of NDE memories and their neural markers compared to memories of both real and imagined events." This team reached the same conclusion as the Belgian one. "It is notable that the EEG pattern of correlations for NDE memory recall differed from the pattern for memories of imagined events," they state. "Our findings suggest that at a phenomenological level, NDE memories cannot be considered equivalent to imagined memories and at a neural level, NDE memories are stored as episodic memories of events experienced in a peculiar state of consciousness." These memories were very similar to memories of real events in terms of their richness and strong emotional content.

Something actually happens during an NDE that we have yet to understand. Experiencers have no doubt that they crossed over into a wondrous afterlife realm to which they will someday return, and that death is merely a doorway into another world.

Chapter 8

"Actual-Death" Experiences

P am Reynolds was a classically trained songwriter and orchestrator with three children who lived in Atlanta. In 1991, at age thirty-five, she was diagnosed with an aneurysm (a bulge or ballooning in a blood vessel that can leak or rupture) deeply embedded in her brain stem, and was told she had very little time to live. She tried the one rare procedure that could give her a small chance at life. Dr. Robert Spetzler, director of the Barrow Neurological Institute and the chairman of neurosurgery in Phoenix, Arizona, performed the risky surgery, in which Pam was rendered as reversibly "dead" as one can be.

Spetzler, a world-renowned neurosurgeon who specializes in cerebrovascular disease and skull base tumors, has published more than 300 articles and 180 book chapters in the neuroscience literature. Spetzler explained what happened with Pam in a 2007 interview:

Pam Reynolds had what is called a giant basilar artery aneurysm—an aneurysm at the base of the brain. To get there, you take off part of the skull, including the roof of the eye. By taking away the bone, you can create a space that goes right down along the skull base, and that then gets us to the area we need to expose for the aneurysm. You're going underneath the brain.

We use hypothermic cardiac arrest to treat these very difficult aneurysms. For this technique, you lower the body temperature down to 60.8°F (16°C). You do that by hooking the patient up to a heart machine, which cools the temperature down until you get to that target temperature. The cardiac team inserts a catheter into the groin that goes up the artery and then another catheter which goes up the vein. You have a catheter on either side of the heart, and that takes over the heart function. Then for up to an hour you can shut off that machine and basically drain the blood out of the body. Yet the patient is still resuscitable. Once the aneurysm is clipped, the process is reversed. The pump is started back up and the blood is pushed back into the body. The pump, now, instead of cooling, warms the blood and gradually the body temperature comes back up.

Pam's whole body was extensively monitored and her brain was monitored with EEG, which are brain waves, and with what are called "evoked potentials." These are ways to make the nerves send very small signals to the brain and normally you can average them out and get a strong signal. You can use this on somebody who is as deep with anesthesia as you can get. Now, in hypothermic cardiac arrest, those waves completely disappear. They are gone, they are flat. There is absolutely no brain activity that we can detect.

The surgery was successful, and Pam survived. But she was not unconscious, despite the fact that she had no brain activity. Here to present that story is Pam Reynolds herself. I have excerpted the following informal narrative from a lengthy 2005 interview conducted by two documentary filmmakers, former BBC radio broadcaster Tim Coleman and researcher Daniel Drasin. (They also conducted the 2007 interview with Spetzler.) These colleagues provided me with a transcript, which has never been made public, exclusively for this book. (I edited the excerpt minimally, only when necessary for clarity and to avoid redundancy.) Sadly, Pam died of heart failure in 2010, when she was fifty-three, almost twenty years after her surgery. Here is her story:

> The doctors said that the most they could do for me was to try a surgical process, but they could pretty much guarantee me that it would not be successful, and death would be an imminent outcome. I didn't have much choice. I had three little children, so I had to go through with it.
>
> Doctor Robert F. Spetzler performed the operation, but there were more people in that room than I would have ever guessed to be in an operating room. During the stasis operation, which the doctors who perform it have coined "standstill," they cooled my body down and my heart stopped, my brain waves stopped functioning. They tilted the end of the gurney up and drained my blood, like oil from a car, into a heart lung machine, thereby shrinking the aneurysm. I'm told that's what happened but, understand, I was not there when this was happening.
>
> I had been put to sleep. Dr. Spetzler has since assured me that I was nearly comatose. There is no way that I could have heard or seen anything. My eyes were taped shut and my ears had speakers inserted in them making a loud clicking sound which were used to monitor the response by my brain. Nonetheless, I began to hear a tone. It was guttural, it was unpleasant, I did not like it. It drew my consciousness like water from a well. And having done that, I sort of popped out of my head to see what this horrific noise was.
>
> At first my vantage point was rather like sitting on the shoulder of the surgeon, and in his hand I saw the instrument that was making the offensive noise. I have heard the word "saw" all my life—my father used a saw, my grandfather used a saw, brain surgeons use saws. I had assumed they were going to open the

skull with a saw. But this was no saw. This thing was held more like a pencil, it looked like a drill and actually reminded me of an electric toothbrush. There was an open case very close to it and it had bits in it, and it looked like the case that my father kept his socket wrenches in when I was a small child. And, I noticed that one of these bits was attached to this toothbrush thing. This was the thing that was causing the noise that disturbed my slumber, and it was a very, very, very deep slumber.

The feeling of exiting the body was incredible. I've never weighed five hundred pounds, but it was as if I had and had just lost it. I could move around at will; the thought process took me where I wanted to go. I felt no more pain, no more suffering, no more fear. No more anxiety, even for the sake of my children. All of those things disappeared when I left that body. And I was free to wander around, at will, unobstructed. It's clear to me that while I knew what they were doing, they didn't know what I was doing. They thought I was that thing lying on the table.

It was indescribable. It was beautiful to know that I was no longer part of that thing. And, by the way, I did look at this body like it was just that. This thing. Not me. Not my body. "Me" was outside. Being out of my body put me in a position to be able to observe many things that were happening in the operating room, even as they were conducting surgery on me.

I heard a female voice and the voice was saying that the veins and arteries were too small. I was concerned because they were working in an area around my femoral arteries and I thought that this was brain surgery. I had heard these horror stories about doing surgery on the wrong place or removing the wrong limb. So I tried to communicate to the lady who was communicating to the doctor about my veins and arteries being too small, that that's not where she needed to be at all and it was at that point that I realized she could not hear me.

I began to sense a presence. The feeling was rather like having someone looking over your shoulder and yet there being no one in the room. So, I sort of turned around to look at it and instead of a person, I saw a very tiny pinpoint of light. And as I focused on that light, it started to pull me and the pulling had a physical sensation that went with it. It was like from my tummy, going over a hill real fast and it pulled me and the closer I got to the light the better I discerned figures. The first figure I knew was my grandmother and I heard her voice calling me. But, it wasn't a voice that was made of vocal cords and it wasn't the same kind of hearing we have. It was something different. And, of course, I went immediately to her. There were so many people there, many I knew, many I did not know, but I knew somehow we were connected. Didn't know how. But I knew.

The people were wearing light, they seemed to be made of light. The ones I recognized, it's as if there had never been a separation between us. There was that love, that warmth, that protection and I felt, acutely, that I had been brought to this place to be protected, so that my body could be prepared. And it felt wonderful.

I then saw my uncle, who had passed away at the ripe old age of thirty-nine. He didn't use his mouth to communicate with me. He did it in another way that I remembered from my early childhood. He had the look. He would look at me and I would understand. And, it didn't take long until I understood that everyone communicated in this fashion. They had the look. They'd look at you and you understood. I also describe it as the knowing, because you just know. And all of these people had this ability to just kind of look and know.

The quality of communication was much better than we have here because there it moves with the speed of light. It's rather like being on the other end of a pulsing laser. All you have to do is think it and the thought process is sent out. There's no misunderstanding in what gets said. What gets said is the truth.

I asked my grandmother regarding the nature of the light. My communication was, "Is the light God?" and there was great laughter and she said, "No, sweetheart, the light is not God.

The light is what happens when God breathes." That was the communication.

The landscape, the physical landscape, was nonexistent. It was as if the bodies were floating in midair, there was light and shadow, but it didn't seem to fall on anything. And, that's what convinces me that I probably was not in "heaven." It had colors like you wouldn't believe, but I probably was in an in-between place. I was on some sort of bridge on the way, because, let us not forget, they would not let me into that light.

The sound, however, is an entirely different matter and that really interests me. As a musician, I've been taught from the cradle that if you put two tones that are too close together, what you get is discordance. But, in the place where I was, every being had their own tone and every tone was close to the next and yet, when these tones were put together, when everyone was sounding off, it was beautiful. It was harmonic. It was beyond anything that I could ever compose or direct here, or hope to.

I became concerned as to whether or not I was really there. I looked at my own hands and held them up to my face. I saw something, I knew I was there, I could feel me. The odd thing was, I didn't feel so very different than I feel here. And yet, there was no density in the flesh, but still, I held them up to my face to secure the knowledge that I was there.

There came a time that I knew I had to return to the body. My uncle was going to take me and that was fine, I was okay with that, until I saw the thing and then I was not at all pleased. He told me, "Think about your favorite food . . . Won't you miss your favorite foods? . . . Won't you miss your children?" And I figured the children would be okay. And then he told me, "It's like jumping in a swimming pool, baby. Just jump." I looked down and saw the body jump with the first defibrillation. I definitely did not want to get in the thing then, because, to be honest with you, it looked like what it was—dead. I knew it would hurt. So my response to him—I know it's disrespectful and I'm a Southern girl—but it was: no. So he pushed me.

I hit the body at the second defibrillation of the heart, at the exact time that they achieved sinus rhythm, and there I was alive and somewhat uncomfortable. It's taken me a long time to forgive my uncle for that. Getting back into the body was kind of like jumping into a pool of ice water. It was shocking, literally. I could feel the shock and it was very unpleasant. They used the paddles the first time to try and start my heart, and they didn't work. But, the second time they used them, combined with his pushing me back into the body, they worked.

I opened my eyes and all of a sudden, they were packing things away and everything was done. You're not supposed to wake up until you're in the recovery room. Well, I woke up in the operating room long enough to tell one of Dr. Spetzler's neuroscientist fellows, who is to this day my friend, how extremely insensitive he was under the circumstances and to complain a little bit about being shocked. He laughed at me and told me I needed to sleep more.

Afterward, Dr. Spetzler listened very closely to everything I said to him. On the following day, he very firmly explained to me that, beyond a shadow of a doubt, this was not a hallucination. He told me that what I described had actually occurred. For example, they had to defibrillate me twice. Now not even Dr. Spetzler remembered that until he had my records and went over them, and then he found out, yes, it's true they didn't hit me with it once, they hit me with it twice, which is unusual.

The voice I heard was indeed female, and later my doctors introduced me to her. She was the head of the cardiovascular team and she was doing a "cutdown." This is the methodology by which they drew the blood from the body.

The first photograph that I was shown of what I would come to understand is the Midas Rex bone saw was incorrect, and I called the physician doing research on this and told him it was incorrect. It would be another year before I would again have an opportunity to see a Midas Rex bone saw and this time, it was, indeed, the one that I had seen. It did, from what had been my vantage point, appear to have a groove that went into or around the bit, and it did look like an electric toothbrush.

When I had heard this thing while out of my body, it was humming, gutturally, at a perfect natural D, while in the doctor's hand. I don't know what it would hum if you laid it on the table, but in his hand it was a perfect natural D. I could clearly hear that tone. CBS did a test on the saw and at first they said it didn't make a natural D, but a C, the next lower note on the scale. I have intrinsic perfect pitch. No way! So, I called the producer and asked him what their methodology was for the test and they said that they got some Styrofoam and laid it down on that. I said, no, put it in a living man's hand, put it in Dr. Spetzler's hand. They did, and it came out a perfect natural D.

I was a believer when I left the hospital and I wasn't the only one. There were several staff members there who said I wasn't the only case that they had seen that was unusual in this regard.

I know that consciousness survives the death of the physical body because I've had that experience personally. Beyond that, I cannot, in truth, know anything. In my opinion, what happened to me is evidence of an afterlife. But let us weigh my opinion before we call it a fact. What it is for me could be totally different than what it is for you. My arrogance extends as far as my musicianship, but when it comes to science and philosophy, I completely lose my sense of arrogance.

Having had this NDE, I no longer fear death. I fear separation. I thought at first that I wouldn't even fear separation, but there is no experience that makes the separation okay when you lose someone. But when my time comes, I will embrace death. In fact, I know people who are dying right now and I envy them their journey. It's a wonderful, wonderful place to go. But, I just don't like being left behind. I don't think any of us do.

I find it extremely interesting that NDErs from all over the planet, regardless of culture, religious bias, or political lean, defy coincidence by reporting the same basic elements within the structure of their NDE. I think that's more the work for a mathematician than it is for a simple musician, like me. So, if you have a question, see your local mathematician or physicist. It sounds like that's where that kind of question needs to go.

It is rare that a doctor performing surgery during which an NDE occurs is willing to discuss the circumstances and comment on the patient's experience. Yet he or she is in the unique position of being able to correlate the timing of the sights and sounds reported by the experiencer with the status of the patient's brain activity. How "dead" was Pam Reynolds when she heard conversations, saw specific tools, and watched the defibrillation of her heart? Also from the 2007 interview, Spetzler answered this question:

> Through all the stages of coma, through all the stages of deep anesthesia, the lower we get, the less function there is, and you need brain function in order to stimulate a thought. You need blood flow in order to give you the nutrients to fire the neurons. So, if I look at it purely as a scientist, I would say that during hypothermic cardiac arrest, it is inconceivable to me that there is any brain function going on that requires metabolic activity. There was absolutely no question that Pam Reynolds was clinically dead. Her EEG was completely flat, and her evoked potential too was completely gone.
>
> I believe that Pam recalled things that were remarkably accurate. I do not understand from a physiological perspective how that could possibly have happened. I hope not to be arrogant enough to say it can't happen, but from a scientific perspective, there is no acceptable explanation to me. I have absolutely no reason to question Pam's sincerity or not to believe that that's what she heard.
>
> If somebody asked me to describe what the Midas Rex drill looked like, I might very well use the term "like an electric toothbrush." It has the same general shape. It obviously makes a noise like a drill makes a noise, so I think that's a very good description of the tool. Pam's description of the interchangeable bits

for the drill and her description of them as if they were a socket wrench set, I think were very accurate.

And, I don't think that the observations she made were based on what she experienced as she went into the operating room theater. The drill and those things were all covered up. They were not visible, and were still inside their packages. You don't begin to open them until the patient is completely asleep in order to maintain a sterile environment. Hallucination cannot be the explanation because hallucination requires metabolic activity and a functioning brain. It may not function normally, it may give you aberrations that you normally wouldn't have, but it's still very much a product of a functioning active brain. A hypothermic brain has no activity whatsoever.

When Pam told me what she had experienced, I thought it was novel. I thought it was of interest. As a neurosurgeon, I have encountered so many things that I didn't have an explanation for. You keep it in the back of your mind and if in your lifetime you come up with another explanation, then you can recall it and say, "Aha, this is how it works." In Pam's case, I'm far, far from that.

Some skeptics have argued that Pam woke up during the process, and through "anesthesia awareness" was able to hear what was going on in the room so she could extrapolate enough to paint a visual picture afterward. They attribute all elements of Pam's experiences to physiological processes. Yet, in order to help monitor her brain, Pam had speakers inserted into each ear that emitted continuous loud clicks at a rate of 11 to 33 clicks per second at 90 to 100 decibels. That sound was as loud as a lawn mower or a passing subway train. "Nobody can observe or hear in that state," Spetzler said. "I find it inconceivable that your normal senses such as hearing, let alone the fact that she had clicking modules in both ears, that there was any way for her to hear through normal auditory pathways." In addition, Pam's eyes were taped shut.

Pam's brain should not have been capable of generating anything at all. Yet she was conscious, and she reported that her conscious awareness was located *outside* the body and was in no way dependent on her brain. She then took a journey into what she said was an afterlife realm. Like many other NDErs, she did not want to return. And the details she provided had similarities to those of other NDErs around the world. Is it possible Pam and so many others have actually had a taste of life after death?

As mentioned earlier, the point is often made that these "clinically dead" people have not actually died, so maybe their experiences are different from those that occur during irreversible physical death. However, the experiencers are convinced that they journeyed to the same realm that they will return to when they die, and this is why they no longer fear death. David Fontana, author of *Is There an After-life?*, who spent many decades studying evidence for survival as mentioned in my Introduction, raises a bigger question. "It is little use saying that if a person is revived after clinical death this means they were not dead," he wrote in 2005. "It may indeed be that the boundary between life and death can be crossed, albeit briefly, in both directions. Why not? What is to stop us at least accepting this as a working hypothesis, and then studying what people have to tell us about their NDEs in order to learn what they have to tell us about this shadowy boundary between the two states?"

Dr. Sam Parnia, who directed the AWARE study on NDEs and specializes in resuscitation science, has learned more about that shadowy boundary in recent years. Now, with such advanced techniques as cooling down a body, a person who has been dead for hours can be brought back to life because the cells within the body take many hours to die. And we are talking about a motionless, stone-dead corpse—a body with no heartbeat, no respiration, and no brain activity. "Recent scientific advances have produced a seismic shift in our understanding of death. This has challenged our perceptions of death as being absolutely implacable and final," Parnia wrote in 2013.

In June 2011, a thirty-year-old woman died in the forest following an overdose of medications. She had been dead for several hours before the ambulance arrived, so her body temperature had dropped to 68°F (20°C). The ambulance team could not revive her. The emergency doctors went through many procedures to try to revive the woman, and after six hours of treatment, her heart restarted. "Although she had remained physically dead for at least five to ten hours overnight without any treatment, and then for a further six hours while undergoing lifesaving treatment in the hospital, the woman was able to recover and eventually walk out of the hospital without organ and brain damage three weeks later . . . the woman had, in fact, died," Parnia reports.

Two-year-old Gardell Martin fell into an icy Pennsylvania stream in March 2015. By the time the emergency rescuers arrived, he had been dead for at least thirty-five minutes with no heartbeat. He was taken to a hospital and then flown to a medical center, with no one able to revive him. Since he was so young and his body was cold, doctors continued trying to bring him back by continuous chest compression and the infusion of warm fluids into his veins and organs. This went on for an hour and a half. He was "a flaccid, cold corpse showing no signs of life," recalled Richard Lambert, a member of the critical care team. Then, a faint but steady heartbeat was detected. Gardell walked out of the hospital three and a half days later, after having been dead for 101 minutes.

Parnia no longer makes a distinction between the "clinical death" of the person near death who is eventually resuscitated—such as Maria, Pam Reynolds, Gardell Martin, or the woman in the forest— and the patient who dies and does not come back. These people were all in the same state—they were dead. "Death can no longer be considered an absolute moment but rather a process that can be reversed even many hours after it has taken place," Parnia says. He finds the term "near-death experience" unacceptable because he says it's too vague—there is no definition for what "near death" actually means. "I don't study people who are near death. I study people who have objectively and medically died." Therefore, he has renamed the NDE, calling it an "actual-death experience."

"There is a significant period of time after death in which death is fully reversible," he says, which challenges Janice Holden's premise that reversible death and irreversible death may be two distinct states in which consciousness behaves differently. Therefore, the NDE or "actual-death experience" "provides us with an indication of what we're all likely to experience when we go through death."

And that's what is important for the question of survival. Parnia's research suggests that what experiencers call an afterlife realm is encountered when they are dead, not when they are simply near death. They have actually crossed that boundary into death that Fontana refers to—and then returned to tell us about it. This perspective strengthens the argument that what people experience who die and then return to life is what awaits all of us when we make a one-way journey at the end of our lives.

But then why do only 10 to 20 percent of clinically dead people remember such experiences, if this represents what happens to all of us when we die? When one is brought back from death, the brain has been flatlined and all brain reflexes are absent. "We would expect there to be *no* memories whatsoever from anybody," Parnia explains, "because even if you've had experiences, you don't have the apparatus to carry the experience back and allow you to describe it to other people, because that apparatus is completely nonfunctional." He says the pertinent question is why 10 to 20 percent of people *do* somehow, paradoxically, recall these incredibly vivid experiences. Parnia's research suggests that this may have to do with the degree of damage and inflammation occurring in the brain afterward, affecting the memory circuits. This usually lasts for up to three days after the person is resuscitated, and the swelling can erase memories during that time. Those interviewed immediately after waking up remember more; but if they are reinterviewed a few days later, they tend to have forgotten their experiences. (It is difficult to interview patients immediately.) "We think that probably many more people have these experiences, perhaps even everyone, but somehow their memories get wiped," Parnia says.

That is certainly encouraging, but it all remains hard to fathom for those of us who have not had this life-altering experience. The difficulty in assessing the evidential value of these cases has to do with their subjective, anecdotal nature. But the scenarios are intriguingly similar, as reported by millions of people around the world. And certainly these cases strongly suggest that consciousness can operate even when the body is dead, without a functioning brain. That's what is most important.

We must not forget that there is no scientific evidence that our thoughts and feelings, self, psyche, or soul are generated by the brain. Next, Pim van Lommel will address the larger questions about NDEs (reverting back to that terminology) and what they teach us about the nature of consciousness and its survival past death. You may feel your consciousness expanding beyond the boundaries of your brain by the time you finish his chapter.

Chapter 9

The NDE and Nonlocal Consciousness

By Pim van Lommel, MD

Pim van Lommel is a Dutch cardiologist who worked at a teaching hospital in Arnhem in the Netherlands for many years and published several professional papers on cardiology. In 1986, he began studying near-death experiences in patients who survived a cardiac arrest. Dr. van Lommel and colleagues published the results of a breakthrough study in the reputable medical journal The Lancet *in 2001. As the author of the 2007 international bestseller* Endless Consciousness: A Scientific Approach to the Near-Death Experience *(renamed* Consciousness Beyond Life: The Science of the Near-Death Experience *in the U.S. edition), he is now recognized as a world authority on near-death experiences. He has lectured on this topic all over the world.*

Dr. van Lommel has provided the following exclusive chapter, which places evidence from the veridical OBE and NDE in a larger context. The child past-life cases can also be applied to the conclusions he draws about the nature of consciousness and its continuity before and after death.

. . .

After many years of research, it has become clear to me that, beyond a reasonable doubt, there is a continuity of consciousness after the death of our physical body. But at first there were so many questions for me. How was it possible that sometimes patients can report enhanced consciousness when they are unconscious during cardiac arrest or during coma?

My interest in this began in 1969 during my first year of hospital cardiology training. Suddenly an alarm went off at the coronary care unit. A patient with a heart attack had a cardiac arrest (ventricular fibrillation), and was no longer responsive. One nurse started cardiopulmonary resuscitation (CPR), while another administered oxygen. A third nurse rushed over with the defibrillator, fully charged with its paddles covered in gel, and bared the patient's chest. She gave him an electric shock. It had no effect. Heart massage and artificial respiration were resumed and extra medication was injected into the IV drip. Then the patient was defibrillated for the second time. This time his cardiac rhythm was reestablished, and more than a minute later, he regained consciousness, after being unconsciousness for about four minutes. In those days, defibrillation was a new and exciting technique. It was not until 1967 that techniques for resuscitation were available, and before that year all patients with cardiac arrest had died. We on the resuscitation team were of course very happy when this patient revived. But to our surprise, the patient seemed to be very, very disappointed. With great emotion, he told us about going through a tunnel, seeing a light and beautiful colors, and hearing music.

In that time I had never heard of the possibility of having memories from the period of unconsciousness during cardiac arrest. And it was hard for me to accept. I grew up in an academic environment in which I had been taught that there is a reductionist, materialist explanation for everything and that it was obvious that consciousness was a product of a functioning brain. I had learned in my training that such a thing is in fact impossible, because being unconscious meant being unaware, and during cardiac arrest patients are clinically dead. This man, describing being aware, was completely unconscious. I never forgot this event, but I did not do anything with it at the time.

Then in 1986 I read about such experiences in a book by psychiatrist George Ritchie, *Return from Tomorrow,* which relates Ritchie's experience during clinical death in 1943, when he was only twenty years old. While serving in the US Army for basic training, about to enter medical school, he contracted double pneumonia, and essentially passed away. His doctor pronounced him dead twice. A male nurse was so unwilling to accept this, given how young Ritchie was, that he requested that an adrenaline injection be administered directly in Ritchie's heart, despite the diagnosis of death. This kind of injection was quite uncommon in those years. The doctor agreed, to appease the young nurse, and to their surprise, Ritchie's vital signs returned. He had been "dead" for nine minutes. During this time he had an extremely powerful near-death experience, and he remembered seeing his body covered by a sheet when he was returning from his journey. This occurred long before Raymond Moody's famous bestseller *Life After Life* in 1971, in which the term "near-death experience" was first coined.

I wanted to find out more, so I started to interview my patients who had survived a cardiac arrest. It all started for me by scientific curiosity. And to my great surprise, within two years, twelve patients out of fifty survivors told me about their near-death experiences, and I learned much more about them.

As those who return describe it, it is as if you have entered into the beginning of death but then retreated from it. You remember it vividly. It seems clear to these people that this is what death will be like when they fully die, and they lose all fear of it. Like the first NDE patient I knew in 1969, most do not want to return because of the joy and beauty inherent in the experience. In fact, people report that they were more conscious than ever during their NDE.

But how and why does an NDE occur, and how does the content come about? How is it possible that patients can describe veridical details of their own resuscitation or operation? So far we had no answers.

First, what is a near-death experience? I define it as the reported memory of a range of impressions during a special state of consciousness, including a number of universal elements, such as being out of the body, going through a tunnel, seeing a bright light, meeting deceased relatives, having a life review, and making a conscious return into the body. These occur mostly during a critical medical situation like cardiac arrest or in other life-threatening situations, but they can also occur in nonthreatening situations, sometimes even without any obvious reason, where the brain is functional and the person is not near death. The cases occurring during cardiac arrest or deep coma are the most interesting to science.

The NDE is almost always transformational, causing enhanced intuitive sensitivity, profound insights and reevaluations of life, and a loss of a fear of death. There are many wonderful cases that are published and readily accessible, for those who want to familiarize themselves with individual accounts. The content of the NDE and its effects on patients seem similar worldwide, across all cultures and all times. However, the subjective nature and the absence of a frame of reference for this near-ineffable experience has meant that individual cultural and religious factors determine the vocabulary and interpretation of the experience.

While I was hearing from my patients about their personal NDEs, various theories were being proposed. But none explained the experience of an enhanced consciousness, with lucid thoughts, emotions, memories from earliest childhood, visions of the future, and the possibility of perception from a position outside and above the body. We could not explain the fact that the experience appears much more vivid and "real" than everyday waking consciousness, or that it is accompanied by accelerated thought and access to greater-than-ever wisdom. And most important, current scientific knowledge failed to explain how this can be experienced when brain function has been seriously impaired. In fact, there appeared to be an inverse relationship between the clarity of consciousness and the loss of brain function.

A satisfactory theory, one that explains the NDE in all its complexity and does not simply look at each element separately, had not been found. Most theories were based on anecdotal evidence and retrospective studies with self-selected patients and did not include accurate medical data. In order to find more definitive answers, I joined with two psychologists in the Netherlands and in 1988 we launched a comprehensive and scientifically sound prospective study of the frequency, cause, and content of near-death experiences. We wanted to determine whether there could be a physiological, pharmacological, psychological, or demographic explanation for why people experience NDEs. At that point, no large-scale prospective NDE studies had been undertaken anywhere in the world.

The study involved 344 consecutive cardiac arrest survivors in ten Dutch hospitals. Within a few days of their resuscitation, the patients were asked whether they had any memories from the period of their cardiac arrest, during their time of unconsciousness. Their medical and other data were carefully recorded before, during, and after their resuscitation. This design also created a control group of survivors without any memory of their period of unconsciousness. All consecutive cases of cardiac arrest were included in order to provide accurate data. By conducting follow-up interviews with both groups, we were also able to find out whether the transformative aspects of NDEs were due to the NDE or simply to the cardiac arrest itself.

All patients in our study had experienced clinical death. This is defined as a period of unconsciousness caused by anoxia (a lack of oxygen to the brain) due to the arrest of circulation and breathing. The person has no palpable pulse or measurable blood pressure, no body reflexes, and no brain stem reflexes. If CPR is not started within five to ten minutes, irreversible damage of the brain occurs and the patient will die. It is the closest model to the process of dying.

Our results showed 282 patients, or 82 percent, had no recollections at all from their time of unconsciousness while in cardiac arrest. However 62 patients, or 18 percent, had some recollection of an NDE. Of these, 41 (66 percent) had a deep core experience while 21 (34 percent) had a more superficial one. We used a scoring system that allowed us to compare the frequency of the various elements with the depth of the NDE. All the typical elements were reported, such as 50 percent reporting an awareness of being dead, 56 percent positive emotions, 25 percent an out-of-body experience (OBE), 31 percent going through a tunnel, and 23 percent communication with the light.

To study the resulting transformation afterward we interviewed all survivors of cardiac arrest with an NDE two and eight years following their incident, with a matched control group of patients who survived cardiac arrest without NDE. We found a significant difference between those with an NDE and those without it. Experiencers of NDEs had no fear of death anymore, and were convinced of the reality of an afterlife. They had greater intuitive sensitivity and meaning in their lives, coupled with long periods of homesickness, loneliness, and depression caused by the inability to share their impressive and life-changing experience with others. This new insight into life and death took them years to accept and to consolidate.

What distinguished those who reported having NDEs from those who didn't? To our big surprise we found that neither the duration of unconsciousness nor of the cardiac arrest (the severity or gravity of lack of oxygen in the brain), nor any other factors such as medication or a fear of death, had an effect. Nothing seemed to play a role in determining the occurrence, frequency, or quality of an NDE—not gender, foreknowledge of NDEs, religion, or education.

Thus, the first and largest prospective study on NDEs ever could exclude that physiological, psychological, or pharmacological factors caused these experiences during cardiac arrest. If it was purely physiological, such as a lack of oxygen in the brain, most patients who had been clinically dead should report it, but only 18 percent reported an NDE. Why? This is still a big mystery.

But another theory arose from the data. This holds that the NDE could be a changing state of consciousness, based on the theory of continuity, in which memories, identity, and cognition, with emotions, function independently from the unconscious body and retain the possibility of so-called extrasensory perception.

Our Dutch study, published in December 2001 in *The Lancet,* one of the most prestigious medical journals in the world, attracted immediate, widespread attention. It was covered on the front pages of all the major newspapers in Europe, the United States, Canada, Australia, India, China, and Brazil. I never anticipated such huge interest. For a couple of days I had to cancel all appointments to comply with requests for interviews with national and international newspapers, radio, and television. We received hundreds of emails with positive responses from NDErs who felt supported and recognized by this study. Even doctors who had experienced an NDE themselves but had never been able to discuss it with colleagues contacted us.

I did, however, also receive some extremely critical, but rather amusing, comments from certain people. In the Netherlands, Dr. C. Renckens, gynecologist and chair of the Dutch Association Against Quackery, linked our study with "multiple personality disorder, chronic fatigue syndrome, fibromyalgia, and alien abduction syndrome." He described me as "a failed prophet with the personality of a pre-morbid quack." And from Belgium, W. Betz, professor of family medicine and a member of SKEPP (a group for the critical evaluation of pseudoscience and the paranormal), told the Belgian press that "When scientists start spouting nonsense, the public must be warned. Van Lommel belongs to a sect." He associated the research with "astral bodies, the paranormal, and graphology."

But three additional prospective studies with an identical design as our Dutch one followed, and these documented about the same percentage of NDEs during cardiac arrest as ours. We now had four studies involving a total of approximately 562 survivors of cardiac arrest.

Bruce Greyson, MD, at the University of Virginia, authored the American study in 2003, in which out of 116 patients, 15.5 percent had NDEs. He wrote, "No one physiological or psychological model by itself explains all the common features of near-death experiences . . . A clear sensorium and complex perceptual processes during a period of apparent clinical death challenge the concept that consciousness is localized exclusively in the brain."

The four prospective NDE studies by independent groups all reached the same conclusion: there were no physiological or psychological explanations for the NDEs, which took place during cardiac arrest when the patient had complete loss of brain function. Enhanced consciousness, with memories and perception from a position out of and above the lifeless body, can be experienced during a period of unconsciousness, independently of the brain and body. This conclusion was reached on the basis of compelling evidence that the NDE occurs during the period of clinical death and not shortly before or after the cardiac arrest. It was the studies' prospective design, involving complete medical data, that enabled this conclusion. If the cardiac arrest involved an NDE with clear perception of the patient's surroundings, such as doctors' statements or actions with equipment, contents could be verified immediately after the report.

In fact, veridical OBEs, such as that of the well-known case of Maria in Seattle, provide the strongest evidence for the existence of consciousness outside and separate from the body. When we have the medical data in coordination with the report of the patient, we are able to document the timing of the OBE/NDE during the period of unconsciousness. Even people blind from birth have described veridical NDEs in which they "see" in a way that was not possible from their bodies. Color-blind people have perceived colors. People say it's like taking off the body as if it were an old coat, and to their surprise they retain their own identity and emotions. The range of vision can extend to 360 degrees with bird's-eye views.

Dr. Jan Holden of the University of North Texas reports on about 100 OBEs occurring during an NDE, and shows 90 percent were completely accurate, 8 percent contained minor errors, and 2 percent were false. These reports cannot be hallucinations because these correct perceptions during OBE correspond with reality in detail, while hallucinations, such as those caused by psychosis, delusion, or drugs, have no basis in reality. In those cases, the incorrect perceptions are hallucinations or they are illusions, like misapprehended or misleading images. Moreover, one needs a functioning brain to hallucinate, and during cardiac arrest the function of the brain has ceased.

During the pilot phase of our study in one of the hospitals, a coronary-care-unit nurse reported a veridical out-of-body experience of a forty-four-year-old resuscitated patient, found in a meadow by passersby, which I published in *The Lancet*. While the patient was cyanotic and comatose, and still in cardiac arrest, the nurse removed his dentures in order to intubate him, and the CPR continued for more than ninety minutes. Still comatose but with heart rhythm, he was eventually transferred to the intensive care unit. The nurse writes:

Only after more than a week in coma do I meet again with the patient, who is by now back on the cardiac ward. I distribute his medication. The moment he sees me he says: "Oh, that nurse knows where my dentures are." I am very surprised. Then he elucidates: "Yes, you were there when I was brought into hospital and you took my dentures out of my mouth and put them onto that cart, it had all these bottles on it and there was this sliding drawer underneath and there you put my teeth." I was especially amazed because I remembered this happening while the man was in deep coma and in the process of CPR. When I asked further, it appeared the man had seen himself lying in bed, that he had perceived from above how nurses and doctors had been busy with CPR. He was also able to describe correctly and in detail the small room in which he had been resuscitated as well as the appearance of those present like myself. At the time that he observed the situation he had been very much afraid that we would stop CPR and that he would die. And it is true that we had been very negative about the patient's prognosis due to his very poor medical condition when admitted. The patient tells me that he desperately and unsuccessfully tried to make it clear to us that he was still alive and that we should continue CPR. He is deeply impressed by his experience and says he is no longer afraid of death. Four weeks later he left hospital as a healthy man.

Based on these cases of corroborated OBEs, I think that there are good reasons to assume that our consciousness does not always coincide with the functioning of our brain. Who or what is seeing? Not the eye and not the brain. If people are actually outside and above their lifeless bodies and perceiving things, this would show how, under certain circumstances, we don't need a brain or eyes for enhanced perception. It is our consciousness that perceives.

How can it be scientifically explained that people can have clear memories or even verifiable perceptions during a period of obvious unconsciousness? The current view of the relationship between the brain and consciousness held by most physicians, philosophers, and psychologists is too restricted for a proper understanding of this phenomenon. I have come to the inevitable conclusion that most likely the brain has a facilitating or receiving and not a producing function in the experience of consciousness. So under special circumstances our enhanced consciousness would not be localized in our brain nor be limited to the brain.

My conclusions are not always in conformity with the currently widely accepted materialistic paradigm of Western science. This is why scientific research on NDEs still gives rise to many unbelieving and critical questions, especially by physicians and neuroscientists. Materialistic science starts principally from a reality that is only based on physical observable data. But we should be aware that, besides external and so-called objective perception and observation, there are also subjective, not observable and not demonstrable aspects like thoughts, feelings, inspiration, and intuition. We can measure only the electrical, magnetic, chemical activities in the brain by EEG-, MEG-, and PET-scan, and we can measure changes in blood flow in the brain by fMRI, but these are only neural correlates of consciousness. These measurements do not explain anything about the production nor about the content of consciousness. Direct proof about how neurons or neuronal networks could possibly produce the subjective essence of our thoughts and feelings is totally missing. We only measure changing activation. And neural activation is simply neural activation; it only reflects the use of structures. The widely accepted assumption that consciousness and memories are produced by large groups of neurons and are localized in the brain should now be reconsidered, because we have to acknowledge that it seems impossible to reduce all consciousness to neural processes, as is now conceived by contemporary neuroscience.

I also realize that many aspects of consciousness and perception are still a great mystery, and I am motivated by scientific curiosity to understand more through continuing research. So for me it was indeed a scientific challenge to discuss new hypotheses that could explain the possibility of having clear and enhanced consciousness during a transient period of a nonfunctional brain, with memories, with self-identity, with cognition, and with emotion. These hypotheses must explain the reported interconnectedness with the consciousness of other persons and of deceased relatives, and then explain the experience of the conscious return into the body. William James once said, "To study the abnormal is the best way of understanding the normal."

In 2005, the journal *Science* published 125 questions that scientists have so far failed to answer. The most important unanswered question was "What is the universe made of?" That was followed by "What is the biological basis of consciousness?" But I would like to reformulate this second question as follows: "Does consciousness have a biological basis at all?"

Based on the universal reported aspects of consciousness experienced during cardiac arrest, we can surmise that the informational fields of our consciousness, likely consisting of waves, are rooted in an invisible realm beyond time and space (nonlocality), and are always present around and through us, permeating our body. They become accessible, and form our waking consciousness through our functioning brain, in the shape of measurable and changing electromagnetic fields. Our normal, waking consciousness has a biological basis, because our body is an interface for it. But it is one small part of our larger field of consciousness.

Could our brain be compared to the television set, which receives electromagnetic waves and transforms them into image and sound? These waves hold the essence of all information, but are only perceivable by our senses through suitable instruments like the camera and TV. And as soon as the function of the brain has been lost, like turning off the TV, memories and consciousness do still exist, but the reception ability is lost; the connection, or interface, is interrupted. Yet consciousness can be experienced during such a period of a nonfunctioning brain, and this is what we call an NDE. So in my concept, consciousness is not physically rooted.

I refer to this consciousness beyond time and space, which has no material or biological basis, as "nonlocal consciousness." It features an interconnectedness that offers the chance of communication with the thoughts and feelings of others, and with those of deceased friends and relatives. Its roots lie in another invisible, immaterial realm that is always in us and around us.

In trying to understand this concept of the interaction between nonlocal consciousness and the material body, another analogy can be made with modern worldwide communication. At each moment, day and night, we are surrounded by hundreds of thousands of telephone calls, by hundreds of radio and TV programs, and by a billion websites, but we become aware of these electromagnetic informative fields only at the moment we use our mobile telephone or by switching on our radio, TV, or laptop. What we receive is neither inside the instrument, nor in the components, but thanks to the receiver, the information from the electromagnetic fields ("the cloud") becomes observable to our senses and our perception. Internet with more than a billion websites available worldwide is obviously not located inside our laptop nor is it produced by it. Rather, it is stored in "the cloud." But we need a functioning instrument to receive information from "the cloud," which can be compared with nonlocal consciousness.

Nonlocal consciousness can be experienced in many ways, which I explain in my book *Consciousness Beyond Life,* and this concept is not a new one. Scientists and philosophers over the ages have proposed this idea. Aspects of quantum mechanics like nonlocality help us to understand how consciousness actually functions. But the difference is that now we have more data highly suggestive of its reality, such as the NDE, which can be explained in all its elements as an experience of nonlocal consciousness.

The inevitable conclusion that consciousness can be experienced independently of brain function, and what that implies, should induce a huge change in the scientific paradigm in Western medicine. It could have practical implications in actual medical and ethical problems such as the care of comatose or dying patients, euthanasia, abortion, and the removal of organs for transplantation from somebody in the dying process with a beating heart in a warm body but with a diagnosis of brain death. Such understanding also fundamentally changes one's opinion about death, because of the almost unavoidable conclusion that at the time of physical death consciousness will continue to be experienced in another dimension, in an invisible and immaterial world, in which all past, present, and future is enclosed.

After many years of study of many aspects and manifestations of nonlocal consciousness, for which there is scientific evidence, I have come to believe that presumably death, like birth, is a mere passing from one state of consciousness into another. When the brain is turned off, like the TV set or radio, the waves of our consciousness remain. Death is only the end of our physical body. In other words: we have a body, but we are consciousness. It is hard to avoid the conclusion that our essential consciousness existed before our birth and will exist after we die. It has no beginning and no end.

These insights are age-old and timeless, but NDEs have brought them back to the forefront and made it possible for science to explore what lies behind the NDE. It often takes an experience like this for people to realize that consciousness has probably always been and always will be and that death as such does not exist. We do not have irrefutable scientific proof of this conclusion, because people with an NDE did not quite die. But they all were very close to death. Without a body we still can have conscious experiences; we are still conscious beings.

Today science for me means asking questions with an open mind. Science should be the search for explaining new mysteries, rather than sticking with old concepts. We must continue to ask open questions and abandon preconceptions, and not be afraid to challenge the materialistic paradigm. This materialistic worldview has so far not responsibly addressed the challenge provided by research suggestive of the survival of consciousness beyond physical death.

Chapter 10

Intermission Memories: Life Between Lives

Can this nonlocal consciousness, existing in a larger field outside the brain, as van Lommel describes, persist after physical death and then return to life in another body? Any evidence suggestive of this independent existence, with a sense of "self" that retains memories when it returns to physicality, opens the door to the more complex possibility of being reborn. This seems quite hard to imagine—but it is also hard to imagine alternative explanations for the experiences reported by James Leininger, Ryan Hammons, and so many other children around the world.

Particularly relevant to what van Lommel has concluded is that sometimes children with past-life memories also describe their existence "between lives"—between the death of the previous person and their birth in this current life. In cases studied by Stevenson, Tucker, and others, small children spontaneously make reference to their pre-birth state, as if it were natural and simply part of a continuum that is in their memory. Their reports could show what existence might be like after leaving the body and before returning to another one, allowing for comparison between their descriptions and those of NDErs returning from what they say is also an afterlife realm.

About one out of five children who remember past lives recall these "between lives" events, according to the database at the University of Virginia, referred to as "intermission memories" by Jim Tucker and his colleagues. Of course most of them are impossible to verify, although some children have made veridical statements about observations just before they were born, sometimes involving choosing their new parents. In several cases, specific details of their own funerals, observed after death, could be verified, but such confirming evidence is hard to come by.

Interestingly, the intermission memories tend to arise in the stronger reincarnation cases, where more statements were made about the past life that were verified and more specific names were remembered, than in the weaker cases. In other words, if a child has a keener memory of his previous life, he is more likely to remember the intermission stage. Also, when intermission memories are reported, the child's memory of the mode of death from the previous life is more likely to be verified. This supports the possible accuracy of the unusual between-lives memories, since these children have so many other verified memories. "Only an unusually strong memory, and not any other characteristic of the subject or previous personality" distinguishes cases with intermission memories from those without them, report Tucker and Poonam Sharma, a medical student at the University of Virginia School of Medicine, in a 2004 paper. "Their reports of events from the intermission period seem to be part of a pattern of a stronger memory for items preceding their current lives."

Tucker categorizes the intermission memories as referring to three main phases: a "transitional stage" just after death, a "stable stage" for most of the time between the lives, and a "return stage" involving events close to the time of birth. The first stage often involves memories of the funeral and the unstable days following the death, when subjects remain associated with their life and grieving relatives.

Many Burmese subjects recalled this stage, when they described being separate from their bodies. Some can be verified, but most are too general. Ratana Wongsombat, a girl born in Bangkok in 1964, said that after she died, her ashes were scattered rather than buried, against her wishes. This was later confirmed by the daughter of the previous personality. Some describe floating around for several days, or trying to contact family members, or not realizing they were dead.

Children have reported a variety of colorful experiences during the longer stable stage. Some talk about heaven and seeing God, but it's not clear to what extent these concepts were learned as children. Some report meeting deceased relatives or other discarnate personalities, as do many during NDEs. Tucker and colleagues published a case study on Patrick Christenson, born in 1991 in Michigan, who when very young made statements pertaining to his half brother who had died twelve years before he was born. He limped like his brother, which could not be medically explained, and had three birthmarks that corresponded to marks on his brother's body, as shown by medical records viewed by the investigators. During the course of the investigation into Patrick's case, Tucker reports that Patrick told his mother that he had met a relative in heaven—before his current birth to her—who went by the name of Billy the Pirate. He said Billy had been shot by his stepfather in the mountains, and had brown eyes, brown hair, and was tall and thin. Patrick also said that no one talks about this relative, and Billy was upset by that. Patrick's mom knew nothing about any relative named Billy. She called her mother, and it was only then that she learned that her mother's sister (her aunt and Patrick's great-aunt) had a son named Billy.

Tucker explains what happened:

> The details Patrick gave were correct. Billy had been killed by
> his stepfather three years before Lisa [Patrick's mother] was born.
> The murder was never talked about in the family. When Lisa
> asked about the nickname "Billy the Pirate," her mother laughed.
> His wildness had led to the nickname, and Lisa's mother said she
> had not heard it since Billy's death. There seemed to be no way

that Patrick could have ever heard about Billy or his nickname before.

Both James Leininger and Ryan Hammons had return stage transmission memories that were verified by their parents. According to the Leiningers, in 2002 when James was three and a half, he told Bruce that he had picked him to be his father, adding, "When I found you and Mommy, I knew you would be good to me." When Bruce asked for more details, James said he had found them in Hawaii, at a big pink hotel. "I found you on the beach. You were eating dinner at night." Five weeks before Andrea learned she was pregnant, she and Bruce had stayed at the Royal Hawaiian, a landmark hotel that happens to be pink. On their last night there, they had dinner on the beach under the moon. "James had described it perfectly," Bruce says. Neither parent had ever discussed these details with James. And, as described previously, James had said he had met his fellow airmen who had all been killed before him, when he got to heaven. These were the men whose names he gave to his G.I. Joe dolls—he had accurate memories of each of their names matching their hair color.

Ryan also described an incident related to his conception, which Cyndi Hammons recorded early on in her journal and sent to Dr. Tucker. One evening when she was snuggling with Ryan in front of the TV, Ryan asked her, "Mommy, why did you think I was going to be a little girl?" Cyndi asked who had told him that; Ryan replied that no one did. "I saw it from when I was in heaven. This doctor guy did a test and told you that I was a boy. You got mad and said that he was wrong." Ryan told her that this was on his dad's birthday and they both went out to eat, and Cyndi cried for a long time because she was not going to have a girl. This was absolutely accurate. Of course there is no way to know whether Ryan might have acquired this information psychically at some point, but he told his mom he "saw" it before he became part of his new life. In any case, Ryan forgave his mom and she told him she was happy she got a boy "instead of a stinking little girl."

Most significant is the fact that intermission memories often have some similarities to NDEs, which have led researchers to contemplate whether these experiencers might be describing the same after-death reality as the children between lives. In both scenarios, subjects report a recognition of dying; existing in another, unearthly realm; encountering other discarnate friends and relatives; sometimes seeing a mystical being or presence; and returning to earthly life either in a new body (being reborn) or by turning back before death to the same body (NDEs). Children with past-life memories rarely report the feeling of peace and transcendent joy described by NDErs, or the presence of a surrounding, brilliant light that is so common to them. Perhaps the experience of light occurs only at the beginning of a "death experience" and therefore would be harder, if not impossible, for a child to remember. Or perhaps this aspect is unique to those who return from death, rather than to those who actually die. Children have only mentioned fragmented aspects of their time between lives, so we have no way of knowing.

"While the differences in the reports should not be glossed over, the similarities indicate that the intermission reports by children claiming to remember previous lives may need to be considered as part of the same overall phenomenon—reports of the afterlife—that encompasses NDEs," Tucker and Sharma conclude. The children with past-life memories are often so young that they would not be expected to understand the concept of death; this is not something most parents explain to toddlers or to four-year-olds with nightmares. Yet somehow they still describe this reality, and say they were there. "Their reports bear many similarities to NDE reports, thus posing a problem for psychological explanations offered for NDEs. Likewise, the neurophysiological explanations that have been offered cannot explain the similar reports from healthy, young children," the authors state.

It is particularly compelling when different areas of research provide similar results that are mutually supportive in this way. Along with NDEs, which show fascinating similarities to the descriptions of "between life" memories in young children, veridical OBEs provide perhaps the most compelling, concrete evidence for the existence of consciousness independent of the brain. To this package of seemingly interrelated experiences pointing toward a common after-death reality, we can add end-of-life experiences, which are often paranormal and occur at the very edge of irreversible physical death.

Chapter 11

End-of-Life Experiences

By Peter Fenwick, MD

Along with intermission memories, some common end-of-life experiences have similarities to the NDE. Could the transcendent reality that dying people often say they experience sporadically represent the same realm as the one visited during the NDE? And does this also tie in with the dwelling place of consciousness between lives? The end-of-life reports all come from lucid people dealing with their own impending death, or family members and caregivers with their own experiences in connection to the dying person. The similarities between descriptions of NDEs, intermission memories, and end-of-life experiences reinforce the possible reality of another realm or nonphysical dimension where consciousness dwells after death. I believe that these interconnections give weight to the survival hypothesis.

Peter Fenwick is a neuropsychiatrist and fellow of the Royal College of Psychiatrists in the UK. He holds appointments as emeritus consultant neuropsychiatrist at the Maudsley Hospital, the foremost psychiatric teaching hospital in the UK, and the John Radcliffe Hospital in Oxford. He is also an emeritus senior lecturer at the Institute of Psychiatry in London. With over two hundred published papers on brain function, he has been part of the editorial board for a number of journals, including the Journal of

Neurology, Neurosurgery, and Psychiatry, the Journal of Consciousness Studies, and the Journal of Epilepsy and Behavior. Dr. Fenwick has a long-standing interest in the mind/brain interface, the problem of consciousness, and has conducted extensive research into end-of-life phenomena.

Throughout the centuries mankind has wondered what happens after death. In virtually every culture throughout recorded history there are indications of rituals associated with the dead and evidence that they might have been buried with some sense of expectation of an afterlife. Hunter-gatherers believed that the dying would leave their bodies and journey to their ancestors. The concept of "journeying" at death is still central today to the understanding of death in most parts of the world.

The reductionist scientific culture of the West is almost alone in its unshakable belief in the finality of death. The slowly progressing scientific dominance of a materialist view has led us to abandon the concept of the transcendent. It is argued that consciousness is formed entirely by the brain. The idea of the journey after death has almost completely disappeared from the scientific perspective and we are left with a random universe where dying is simply a mechanical process.

However, recent studies of the mental states of the dying suggest that this is too limited a view. I am a neuropsychiatrist, which means that I've been trained in the understanding of the brain and its functioning, as well as in the nature of the mind. So I stand in the zone between mind and brain. I have studied the dying process and written scientific papers in peer-reviewed journals to disseminate a new view of what actually happens when we die, and to ask what the experiences of the dying could contribute to our understanding of consciousness.

A number of studies has suggested that before dying many people will experience deathbed visits from dead relatives, which reassure the dying that the process of death is not as terrifying as they may have believed. The first attempt at a systematic scientific study of these apparitions was made by Sir William Barrett, a physicist whose interest in the topic was aroused when his wife, an obstetrician, told him about a patient of hers who began to see visions as she lay dying. She mentioned seeing not only her dead father, but also her sister. Her sister had indeed died three weeks earlier, but the patient, because of her delicate condition, had not been told. The fact that so far as the patient knew her sister was alive and well, but she had seen her in the company of the father she knew to be dead, so impressed Sir William that he began to collect similar experiences. His book, *Deathbed Visions,* published in 1926, concluded that these experiences were not merely a by-product of a dying brain, but could occur when the dying patient was lucid and rational. He also reported a number of cases in which medical personnel or relatives present shared the dying patient's vision.

I began to study these deathbed visions myself in 2003, after a review of the scientific literature persuaded me that this was an area that had not been properly addressed. My examination has not been limited to deathbed visions but includes many other "end-of-life experiences" (ELEs), such as the dying moving in and out of alternate realities or caregivers witnessing light at the moment of death.

With a group of colleagues, we started the process by looking at accounts of what happens when people die. We drew up a questionnaire asking about these phenomena and gave it to members of a palliative care team in North London, and to medical staff, nurses, care workers, volunteers, and clergy in two hospices and a nursing home in the south of England. In order to control for culture, we also carried out the study in three Dutch hospices. In addition, we collected over fifteen hundred email accounts from the general public, and interviewed doctors, nurses, auxiliary staff, and chaplains, giving us a good idea of the detailed mental states of the dying.

Analysis of this data has provided a comprehensive picture that is far from the mechanical model of death. We found accounts of people having premonitions of their own or another's death, tales of clocks stopping, strange animal behavior, light seen in the rooms of the dying, and shapes seen leaving the body. Did these events actually occur, or were they just fantasies of the dying?

The data have also shown quite conclusively that these ELEs are far more common than has previously been acknowledged—one recent paper suggests that in fact they occur in over 60 percent of those people who die while conscious. The present consensus is that over 50 percent of those dying consciously will have an ELE and are likely to get reassurance and help from the dying process.

Here, we will focus on those ELEs that bear some relationship to the NDE or the survival of consciousness after death. All of them suggest that consciousness is nonlocal, as Pim van Lommel describes—more a field structure than something created by the brain. This is revealed at the approach of death when consciousness begins to separate from the body and enter into an expanded awareness.

Deathbed Visions

Deathbed visions have been largely ignored by the medical profession, though they are well known to, and often reported by, nurses and relatives who care for the dying. They are not dependent on religious belief, though they may be influenced by culture. In strongly Christian societies, for example, angels are often seen, but these are very seldom reported in more secular societies. Often the occurrence of a vision is inferred by those watching because of the way the dying person behaves, rather than anything they say—and often of course by the time they die they are already beyond speech. In this case it may be a change in expression—their face lights up as though they have seen someone they recognize and love—or they may reach out as if toward some invisible presence. So absolutely real do these apparitions seem that the dying person is often witnessed interacting with them, and expecting others to do so too. One of many nurses who has witnessed this told us this story:

> I was attending a patient with a fellow nurse—again around four in the morning. The male patient asked us to stand one on each

side of him because he wanted to thank us for looking after him. He then looked over my shoulder toward the window and said, "Hang on, I will be with you in a minute, I just want to thank these nurses for looking after me." The patient repeated himself a couple of times then died!

A district nurse told us this very typical story of an eighty-year-old lady she used to visit once a week, to help and supervise the family who were giving her care.

She eventually became weaker and was semiconscious, only reacting to painful stimuli. She died and I visited the next day to help. Her daughter said that she was lying peacefully and suddenly sat bolt upright with a beaming smile on her face and said, "Joe, how nice of you to come and see me." (Joe was her deceased husband.) Then she lay back down again and died soon after. The daughter was very sensible and practical and really believed that her father had visited.

What virtually all these experiences had in common was that they were very seldom frightening. The dying are always pleased to see their "visitors" and calm or even joyous after the visit. The visits are also comforting to family members who are told about or witness the positive effect on their relative. In our own studies, the most common visitors were parents (24 percent), spouses (14 percent), and other close relatives (14 percent). This is similar to the NDE, in which dead relatives, friends, and spiritual beings appear about 41 percent of the time. Could both experiences be representing the same other dimensional reality?

The fact that the visitors are occasionally seen by other people automatically removes them from the category of hallucinations; we have to regard them rather as apparitions (to be discussed in a later chapter). Neither can we assume that they come due to expectation: there are accounts of the dying person's surprise when their visitor is someone who they believed to be alive still. This again would suggest an out-of-brain mechanism rather than a within-brain generation.

Using our current science, it is difficult to find any specific brain mechanism that would underpin and explain these wonderful experiences. Perhaps all we can logically do is to recognize their validity for the dying person. We can also accept that these visions carry the message that a mechanistic view of brain function is inadequate to explain these transcendent events, which suggest a wider and greater meaning to both life and death.

With this upsurge of interest in deathbed visions, two further studies have been published. One found a much higher prevalence—about 80 percent—than we found in our own study. The second paper is interesting, as the workers did a study of case notes and found that only 8 percent of case notes reported deathbed visions, although when they talked to the caregivers over 60 percent reported visions.

Transiting to a New Reality

In the days before death some patients say they move in and out of an alternate reality, which they describe as an area full of love, light, and compassion. This alternate reality appears just as real to patients as being in the hospice. In our retrospective survey new realities were reported by 55 percent of the Dutch and 30 to 32 percent of the English caregivers, but in the prospective study they were found by 48 percent of caregivers in each group. In one Swiss study over 50 percent, possibly 60 percent and more, experienced this. Here are three reports:

> Sometimes people seem to oscillate between the two worlds for a bit, sometimes for hours. They seem at some points to be in this world and at others they're not. I think for many people death is not just going through a doorway. You've sort of got a foot on the step and you stick your head in and you have a look . . . I've had people open their eyes and say, "Oh, I'm still here then." (Hospice nurse)

In the last two to three days before she died she was conscious of a dark roof over her head and a bright light. She moved into a waiting place where beings were talking to her, her grandfather among them. They were there to help her. Everything would be okay, it was not a dream. She moved in and out of this area. (Patient's mother)

Suddenly she looked up at the window and seemed to stare intently up at it. This lasted only minutes but it seemed ages. She suddenly turned to me and said, "Please, Pauline, don't ever be afraid of dying. I have seen the most beautiful light and I was going toward it. I wanted to go into that light. It was so peaceful. I really had to fight to come back." Next day when it was time for me to go home I said, "Bye, Mum. See you tomorrow." She looked straight at me and said, "I am not worried about tomorrow, and you mustn't be. Promise me." Sadly she died the next morning . . . I knew she'd seen something that day which gave her comfort and peace when she only had hours to live. (Patient's daughter)

It is very difficult to find a unitary mechanistic cause for these experiences. Caregivers who are familiar with both end-of-life and drug induced experiences are clear that they are quite different in both form and quality. ELEs usually occur in clear consciousness so they cannot be attributed to an organic confusional state. It has been suggested that they could be due to expectation, or the need to comfort oneself in the face of death, but this seems unlikely as they occur irrespective of any previous religion or attitudes toward death, although belief may certainly color the specific aspects of some of them.

These ELEs contain many of the elements described by Pim van Lommel and others in the Western NDE—a beautiful place where they meet dead relatives and spiritual beings to help them, a bright light, and wide transcendent feelings. A "life review" is sometimes reported by the dying, as is the idea of a border to be crossed. As in the NDE, they go into this experience and then come back. The difference is that people who are actually dying don't say that the dead relatives they meet wave them away and tell them to go back. Instead, the relatives promise to come back to collect them, and the spiritual beings they see are there to offer their help in the crossing.

The strong similarities suggest that both could be experiences of the same after-death reality. Within both, the experience includes the knowledge that death is not a finality but a simple crossing to an alternative reality—something very comforting for the dying and their loved ones.

At the Moment of Death

Light is a predominant feature of the NDE and plays a part in the dying process as well. It is seen not only at the time of death but in the days or even weeks before. In both situations, its qualities are described positively, as warm, loving, peaceful, compassionate; and people feel drawn toward it. After an ELE involving the experience of light, the dying person describes it to others, just as the resuscitated person does after an NDE.

Occasionally caregivers or relatives who are sitting with the dying see light at the moment of death, as though they are somehow sharing the same vision. They usually describe the light as bright and white and associated with strong feelings of love that at times permeate the whole room. It is often emanating from or surrounding the body, and it usually lasts over the time of the death process. It can be radiant glowing light or more like "spiritual" globules of light. Three accounts are as follows:

> Suddenly there was the most brilliant light shining from my
> husband's chest and as this light lifted upward there was the
> most beautiful music and singing voices, my own chest seemed
> filled with infinite joy and my heart felt as if it was lifting to join
> this light and music. Suddenly there was a hand on my shoulder
> and a nurse said, "I'm sorry, love. He has just gone." I lost sight

of the light and music, I felt so bereft at being left behind.
(Wife's account)

Sometimes I've seen a light, which is in a corner, like candlelight,
it's a golden light. It's not electric light and it's not one of the
hospice lights. It just appears sometimes. It goes when they die.
They take their last breath and everything settles down and the
light goes out. (Hospice chaplain)

When her mother was dying this amazing light appeared in the
room. The whole room was filled with this amazing light and
her mother died. (Pastoral caregiver in hospice)

One woman described how, as her brother lay dying of cancer,
those around him saw "odd tiny sparks of bright light" emanating
from around the dying body. "Not many, just two or three very brief
instances." She did not mention it to anyone but then her brother's
wife mentioned seeing the same thing.

In addition, the perception of something leaving the body, or seen
in its vicinity, is sometimes reported by professional caregivers and,
most important, by relatives of the dying, though usually only when
they are directly asked about it. I first heard about this phenomenon
from a GP who told me that he had been playing golf one day, when
another player on the course had a heart attack. He went over to see
if he could help and as he approached he saw what he described as a
white form that seemed to rise and separate from the body.

What is seen has been described to us variously as a "smoke," a
"gray mist," a "white mist," a "very wispy white shape," seen leaving
the body, usually from the chest or through the head. Some describe
the air being wavy, like the heat haze of a mirage. It can also be an
almost solid white form.

As he died something which is very hard to describe because it
was so unexpected and because I had seen nothing like it rose
up through his body and out of his head. It resembled distinct

delicate waves/lines of smoke ("smoke" is not the right word but I have not got a comparison) and then disappeared. I was the only one to see it. It left me with such a sense of peace and comfort.

This is how one woman described what she saw immediately after the death of her closest friend:

> . . . Gayle came in to tell us Annick had died and we sat around the bed quietly . . . what I saw then was totally unexpected. Above Annick's body the air was moving—rather like a heat haze you see on the road but swirling slowly around.

Several people told us about a "breeze" or a "rush of air" at the time of death, and this is usually interpreted either as something entering the room, or as the "essence" of the dead person making its final departure.

> I then felt a flapping of air around me and actually physically felt wind moving on my face and arms. It was as if a fan had suddenly been turned on, so I looked around me and up to the ceiling to see if this was the case. There was no fan to be seen. It was just after this experience that my mother died.

Deathbed Coincidences

One of the most interesting and unexpected results of our research were the phenomena often reported by friends or relatives of a dying person. It is remarkably common for a person to have a sudden realization that someone to whom they are connected or emotionally close has died, and to discover later that this recognition happened at the actual time of the death. In our survey these realizations were reported by about half the caregivers and a large proportion of the emails from the general public. A recent analysis of 45 of these events showed that 99 percent occurred within half an hour of death and 96 percent at the actual moment of death. In 48 percent of the cases the person who received the knowledge had no idea that the person was dying. Often the recipients do not even know that the person "contacting" them is ill. Thus expectation cannot be used as an explanation.

An interesting finding is that the type of contact made depends on the mental state of the recipient. If they are asleep, it takes the form of a narrative dream with visual content. If they are awake, then it is usually a strong emotional feeling, and less often a visual apparition of the dead person. Here is one such account of what happened on the day the writer's husband's grandfather died. He had lived with them for three years, and had developed cancer of the esophagus.

> One night my husband, a musician, was out working. I asked Granddad if he would like a cup of tea and he said, "Yes, please," so I went into the kitchen and put the kettle on. As I waited for it to boil, the phone rang and my husband said, "Is Granddad all right?" so I said that, yes, he was all right and I was just making him a cup of tea. He went on to say that he had been playing his guitar at work and a very strong feeling came over him that his granddad was there [suddenly with him at work] and he just had to get off the stage and phone me. I reassured him that Granddad was definitely okay and put the phone down. I made the tea and just as I was about to take it in, my brother in law came out and said, "He's gone." He had just closed his eyes and died.

Telepathy would also be a reasonable explanation for many death-bed coincidences such as this one. Another possibility is that the consciousness of the person who just died persists independently of the brain. There is of course support for this concept in the near-death experiences during cardiac arrest, described previously by Pim van Lommel, when brain function is so severely disrupted that consciousness is not possible, and yet the experiencer reports leaving his body and witnessing his own resuscitation from the ceiling. It is not then unreasonable to argue that the mind in this state has the capacity to travel and interact with other minds to which it is closely linked.

The following account gives an example of the often more explicit contact made during sleep.

> I drifted back to sleep and had the most vivid dream. I saw my twenty-two-year-old son walking toward me, his clothes dripping wet. He was talking to me, telling me that he was dead but that I was not to worry or be upset because he was all right . . . When I woke I was very disturbed and tried to contact my son. I found out later that day that he had been drowned the previous night. I am convinced that he did contact me . . . I have drawn great comfort from his visit to me over the years.

Causation of Physical Phenomena at a Distance

Odd events at the time of death don't always take the form of a vision. Often they are much more prosaic. We've been told of unexplained knocks or raps, doors banging, or telephones ringing at the moment of death with no one on the other end. Many caregivers described inexplicable incidents such as lights going on and off in the room of someone who had recently died or pictures dropping off the wall, and we were told of a bell in the room of someone who had died, which mysteriously continued to ring on the day of his funeral even though no one else was in the room. The most frequently reported phenomenon was clocks—traditionally grandfather clocks with their long slow-swinging pendulums—that stopped at the time of death. It's interesting to see that clocks have moved with the times and even digital ones now seem to show the same behavior.

My father died at 3:15 a.m. At about 8:30 a.m., I went to see my uncle Archie, who'd been close to Dad, rather than phone him, to tell him about losing Dad and bring him back to the house if he wished. As Uncle Archie opened the door it was clear he was distressed and as I began to tell him of Dad's passing away he interrupted me and said he already knew . . . he said no one had telephoned him but told me to look at the clock on the mantel-piece—it was stopped at 3:15, as was indeed his own wristwatch, his bedside clock, and all other clocks in the house. There was even an LED display, I think on a radio, flashing 3:15. I was completely taken aback, but Archie seemed comfortable with the phenomena and was just concerned at losing someone close.

The cause of these phenomena is not understood. However, it is possible to speculate. If one takes a wider view than the simple brain-based theory of consciousness, then consciousness is seen as being not confined to the brain but more widely spread. Its withdrawal from the body might then affect physical objects in its vicinity. That is specula-tion, but what is unarguable is that understanding consciousness as just a brain-based function is not compatible with the phenomena seen at the time of death.

A New Model for Understanding Consciousness

Are these approaching-death experiences "real"? They occur in clear consciousness and thus cannot be due to fever, or to kidney or liver failure, or to an organic process in the brain, all of which would pro-duce a confused state. Neither do they seem to be due to expecta-tion or imagination. There is no doubt that they are comforting. But however hard we try, it is impossible to squeeze the phenomena of the dying process into a brain-generated system. The best we can say is that they are transcendental experiences.

Sir John Eccles, the Nobel Prize–wining neurophysiologist and philosopher, concluded the following:

> The human mystery is incredibly demeaned by scientific reductionism, with its claim in promissory materialism, to account eventually for all of the spiritual world in terms of patterns of neuronal activity. This belief must be classed as a superstition. We have to recognize that we are spiritual beings with souls existing in a spiritual world as well as material beings with bodies and brains existing in a material world.

To explain the phenomena of the dying process, an entirely different model may be needed. But what kind of model should this be? It must be something that can encompass forward views of time, connection at a distance, paranormal local effects such as clocks stopping, access to another reality, and something that raises the possibility of continuation of consciousness in some form.

If we are to ask about the location of the dead relatives, the dying would answer that their location is in the domain of transcendence. So the question now becomes, where is this domain? There are a *number* of theories that postulate that this Newtonian/Einsteinian world we live in is four-dimensional (three of space and one of time) and is not a complete description of reality. It has been suggested by the astrophysicist Bernard Carr, professor of mathematics and astronomy at Queen Mary University of London, that the world is in fact a five-dimensional matrix and that it is within the fifth dimension that these conscious experiences are stored.

Lisa Randall, theoretical physicist from Harvard University, and Raman Sundrum, theoretical particle physicist at the Maryland Center for Fundamental Physics, use a five-dimensional model to explain the phenomena we find in dying. At death, the four-dimensional aspect of reality changes into the fifth dimension. So, as we approach death, the ELE phenomena will be available to the four-dimensional brain on "special occasions" when the fifth dimension can be accessed to some extent, as the structures within the brain weaken and allow it.

This would also explain the NDEs during cardiac arrest. David Lawton, who has made studies of the NDE, has also argued that death is simply the withdrawal of the 4D part (with space-time being the fourth dimension), leaving the 5D intact. (If five dimensions seems difficult to cope with, then remember that the string theory of reality postulates an eleven-dimensional reality.)

There are other features of the dying process that fit neatly into a five-dimensional explanation of reality, such as the alteration of time as shown by premonitions, and in the appearance of a dead relative. Light surrounding the body and shapes seen leaving the body, which do not seem to be physical, would suggest that momentarily at the time of death, these energies can be sensed by others present in the room of the dying. Alteration of space and linking together of minds are shown by deathbed coincidences, in which the dying establish a link to someone they are emotionally close to. It will go some way toward explaining physical phenomena such as mechanical malfunction, or the stopping of clocks.

Robert Lanza is an expert in regenerative medicine and scientific director of Astellas Institute for Regenerative Medicine (formerly Advanced Cell Technology). He recently became involved with physics, quantum mechanics, and astrophysics and developed the new theory of biocentrism, which suggests that life and consciousness are fundamental to the universe. It is consciousness that creates the material universe, not the other way around. The theory implies that death of consciousness simply does not exist.

People often ask me if I believe in life after death. I always say that it is no longer a question of belief. This question must be removed from the field of belief into the field of data. The dying have no doubt about this. Once they have seen their deathbed visitors and have been in the alternate reality, they know that they are going to be picked up, and will be helped to transit into an area of love and light. L. Stafford Betty has described this as "the merging of two worlds":

Whether the dying persons are telling just of the glimpse of the next world, or conversing with people we can't see, we should consider ourselves immensely blessed when it happens. If we don't make the mistake of assuming they are confused, we are likely to feel some of the excitement they convey. For we are witnessing the momentary merging of two worlds that at all other times remain tightly compartmentalized and mutually inaccessible. That merging is what I mean by the spirituality of death.

The great inventor Edison, just hours before his death, emerged from a coma, opened his eyes, looked up, and said: "It's very beautiful over there."

And more recently, the sister of Steve Jobs reported that just before he died, Jobs looked over the shoulders of his family members, right past them, and said, "Oh wow. Oh Wow. OH WOW!!"

PART THREE

Communications from Nonlocal Minds

Sit down before fact as a little child, be prepared to give up every preconceived notion, follow humbly wherever and to whatever abysses nature leads, or you shall learn nothing.

—THOMAS HENRY HUXLEY

Chapter 12

My First "Personal Experiment"

The cases of confirmed past-life intermission memories, veridical OBEs, and experiences of death and dying previously described offer the possibility that some aspect of personal consciousness may survive physical death. These threads, when woven together, paint a compelling picture. Yet, as philosopher Michael Sudduth says, the arguments for survival "can't get off the ground until we have at least a tentative theory of survival informed by a more advanced theory of consciousness, a theory that must be informed in part by future advances in cognitive neuroscience." Pim van Lommel and others have provided what may be the first step in that direction with the theory of nonlocal consciousness, postulating that our deeper consciousness is not generated by the brain. What's important is that the data so far are mutually supportive.

To take the next step into exploring further evidence, let's work with the hypothesis that consciousness is fundamentally independent of a functioning brain and therefore may have the capacity to survive in some way after we die. Is there a way to test this further? If it were true, discarnate personalities would have to "exist" in some unknown dimension, somewhere, as James and Ryan explained experiencing before they were born to their current parents. Van Lommel described nonlocal consciousness as featuring "an interconnectedness that offers the chance of communication with the thoughts and feelings of others, and with those of deceased friends and relatives. Its roots lie in another invisible, immaterial realm that is always in us and around us." From this follows a compelling question: Is there evidence suggesting that a disembodied personality can somehow link into our physical world and communicate with us from that immaterial realm?

Mental mediumship is one practice in which that communication has been put to the test (other "more advanced" forms of mediumship, such as trance or physical mediumship, will be discussed later). In a normal state of consciousness, a mental medium is able to receive messages that she says are coming telepathically from a deceased person. She offers sessions or "readings" for a client, known as the "sitter," and attempts to make contact and receive messages from a departed communicator connected to the sitter. The medium serves as a sort of telephone operator, like an antenna reaching out into nonlocal consciousness, attracting a deceased personality that is drawn in by the sitter's presence. She then deciphers and relays the messages back. The sitter is present to receive the information specific for him or her, and the medium doesn't need to know what the information means, as long as it makes sense to the sitter. Genuine mediums can conduct readings on the phone, with no visual clues at all, knowing nothing at all about the sitter or the deceased person being sought by the sitter during the reading.

Successful readings tend to follow a pattern. First, the medium tells the sitter generally whom she is accessing ("I have a male on your mother's side") and then, knowing this makes sense, she provides numerous specific and sometimes obscure details that can apply to only one person. When the reading is on target, the information is often known only to the immediate family. The sitter does not reveal any-

LEFT: James Leininger at age two with his dad, Bruce, during the period of intense nightmares. *Courtesy of the Leininger family*

BELOW: James at the May 2000 visit to the Dallas flight museum, where he was mesmerized by World War II aircraft. *Courtesy of the Leininger family*

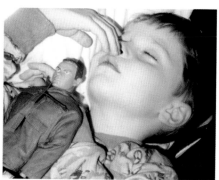

LEFT: In his closet cockpit wearing the helmet given to him by Jack Larsen. *Courtesy of the Leininger family*

ABOVE: Sleeping with his G.I. Joe doll, one of three he correctly named after *Natoma Bay* servicemen killed before James Huston crashed. James said he met them when he got to "heaven." *Courtesy of the Leininger family*

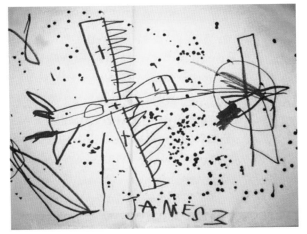

LEFT AND BELOW: James signed his numerous drawings of the plane crash "James 3," saying that he was the third James. Later, his confused parents learned that his "previous personality" was James Huston Jr., which explained the reference. *Courtesy of the Leininger family*

ABOVE LEFT: James Huston Jr. with his sisters Ruth and Anne in 1928. *Courtesy of the Leininger family* ABOVE RIGHT: James met Huston's sister Anne Barron in 2004. Anne said James remembered many accurate details about their childhoods, including family secrets. *Courtesy of the Leininger family*

James Leininger's memories matched the life and death of Huston, who died in 1945. *Courtesy of the Leininger family*

The photo of Huston with a Corsair that Anne sent to Bruce. James had always said Huston flew a Corsair, but this was the first verification of that fact. *Courtesy of the Leininger family*

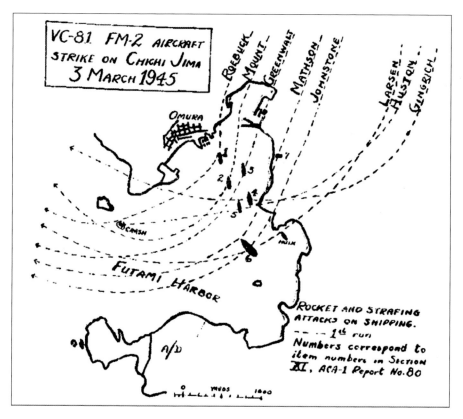

Diagram showing Huston's and Jack Larsen's flight path, and the site where Huston crashed, from the VC-81 *Aircraft Action Report. Courtesy of the Leininger family*

Dr. Ian Stevenson, psychiatrist at the University of Virginia and pioneer of research into cases of children with past-life memories, investigating a case in Burma. *Courtesy of Division of Perceptual Studies (DOPS), University of Virginia*

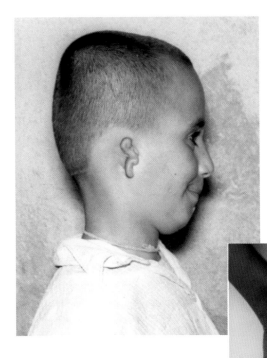

LEFT: The underdeveloped right side of Semih Tutusmus's head showing his defective ear. He had memories of a previous life when he was killed by a shotgun blast to this side of his head. *Courtesy of DOPS* BELOW: Lekh Pal Jatav described having been a boy who had lost the fingers of his right hand in a fodder-chopping machine. He was born with a completely normal left hand but only stubs for fingers on his right. *Courtesy of DOPS*

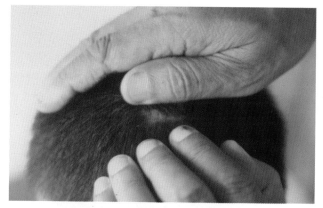

Two birthmarks on the head of Chanai Choomalaiwong, a round smaller one on the back (TOP) and a more irregular one toward the front (BOTTOM). At age three Chanai said he had been shot in a previous life. Along with other details, he gave the name of the previous personality who Stevenson discovered was shot from behind, with a wound on the back of his head that was much smaller than the irregular exit wound on his forehead. *Courtesy of DOPS*

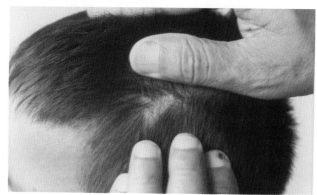

ABOVE LEFT: Ryan Hammons. His memories included being in Hollywood movies and wearing "agent" glasses, roles which he often acted out while playing. *Courtesy of the Hammons family*

ABOVE RIGHT: Ryan Hammons with his dad, Kevin, at the former Marty Martyn Agency building in Los Angeles. Ryan recognized the building along with Marty's home. *Courtesy of the Hammons family*

Five-year-old Ryan pointed to the man on the far right in this picture and said, "Mama, that's me! That's George [George Raft, second from right], and we did a picture together!" *Courtesy of Universal Studios Licensing, LLC*

LEFT: Cyndi Hammons with Ryan during their visit to Hollywood, when Ryan was five. *Courtesy of the Hammons family*

BELOW: A film archivist found this photo of the obscure actor, Marty Martyn, which broke open the case. *Courtesy of Universal Studios Licensing, LLC*

LEFT: Ryan said he remembered dancing on the stage with his sister in his previous life. This photo shows Marty Martyn performing with his sister, Florence Maslow, a professional cabaret dancer. *Courtesy of Marisa Martyn Rosenblatt*

BELOW: As Ryan said, Marty had quite a few wives and girlfriends. *Courtesy of Marisa Martyn Rosenblatt*

LEFT: Marty with his daughter, who was eight when he died. The Hammons family and Dr. Jim Tucker met with her in Los Angeles, and she verified many of Ryan's memories about her father. *Courtesy of Marisa Martyn Rosenblatt*

The Harborview Medical Center in Seattle, Washington, where social worker Kimberly Sharp discovered the tennis shoe on the ledge as requested by her patient Maria. It is so large and inaccessible that it was impossible for Kimberly to see the shoe from the outside. *Courtesy of Kimberly Clark Sharp*

In 1991, Pam Reynolds reported leaving her body during a highly risky procedure to remove a brain aneurysm. With no brain or heart activity, she had a veridical out-of-body and near-death experience, suggesting consciousness can exist independent of the body. *Copyright © Daniel Drasin*

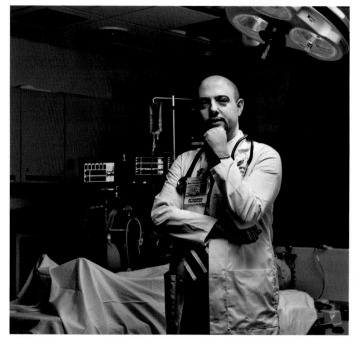

Dr. Sam Parnia, an expert on resuscitation science at Stony Brook University, has determined that people can be revived after many hours of being "dead." He says NDEs provide "an indication of what we're all likely to experience when we go through death." *Copyright © Martin Adolfsson*

thing at all to the medium, but just confirms whether the statements make sense or not. Sometimes personality traits, speech mannerisms, or a sense of humor will manifest from that deceased entity and are recognized by the sitter. Once enough information is provided to establish the identity of that communicator, there are usually personal messages that are passed along.

Many may react to the word "medium" by envisioning the often sentimental readings shown on commercial TV by celebrity mediums like John Edward (his group readings for *Crossing Over with John Edward* were highly edited) or Theresa Caputo of *Long Island Medium*. I am not implying that these two mediums lack abilities or sincerity, but just commenting on the context, which may be all that many people have ever been exposed to.

Some people believe that mental mediumship readings employ what is called "cold reading," and they are correct—many mediums use these techniques, whether consciously or unconsciously. Cold readings involve the use of tricks and psychological manipulation to coax information from the client, which is later fed back and built on so that it appears as something new acquired through psychic powers. These techniques are often used in group sessions. The medium might provide a list of common names and ask who is linked to these "spirits," to start things rolling. He will also use high-probability guesses and build on them; offer general or vague claims that could apply to just about anyone; observe facial expressions, speech patterns, clothing, or rings for subtle clues; ask questions, such as "what does this mean to you?" to acquire information; backtrack if he misses; give generic messages from the deceased; or even study the client ahead of time, if this is possible.

Such techniques can be employed during private, in-person readings also. But obviously, these readings are not what we are interested in here, because they have nothing to do with the question of survival. When strict controls are in place—such as conducting the reading on the phone eliminating all visual cues; making sure the medium knows nothing about the sitter, not even a name; and not revealing any information whatsoever during the reading—we are dealing with something entirely different. In these situations, the medium must provide specific, obscure, and detailed information that is accurate, while the sitter in another location reveals nothing.

Research into mental mediumship shows that a small percentage of mediums do have a genuine ability to access such precise information under controlled conditions. Their results cannot be explained away as fraud, chance, cold reading, or simple guesswork, because under the proper controls, these explanations can be ruled out. These "evidential mediums" even provide accurate facts that are unknown at the time to the sitter, who might say that the information is wrong or doesn't make sense. Later, it is verified through someone else who knew something that the sitter did not.

I was skeptical about mediumship, like many others. But I also recognized that this is something that can be tested. I decided to conduct my own personal "experiments" by seeking out the best possible mediums for a reading.

. To locate them, I checked with two respectable organizations that run certification programs for mediums. Forever Family Foundation (FFF), a volunteer organization based in Long Island, New York, which furthers the understanding of research into the survival of consciousness after death while providing support and healing for people in grief, conducts tests on mediums to establish their competency, which only a small percentage pass. In fact, the website states that the testing process "is designed so that only highly developed mediums will be successful in attaining certification . . . Each medium is exposed to a variety of sitters and a composite scoring system is used to determine the accuracy of the information presented by each medium. The sitter selection is controlled to ensure that none of the mediums has any prior access to the sitter or any information about them. Sitters are pre-instructed on specific scoring procedures to ensure the integrity of the program."

I was interested in finding a medium who was certified by FFF as well as the second organization, the Windbridge Institute in Tucson, Arizona, an independent, scientific research organization founded in 2008 studying "phenomena currently unexplained within traditional scientific disciplines." Each medium seeking certification there is subjected to an intensive eight-step screening and training procedure, which includes extensive interviews, psychological tests, and two blinded phone readings, meaning that the sitter is not even present on the phone during the reading.

Robert Ginsberg, cofounder of FFF with his wife, Phran Ginsberg, explained the certification process and suggested I contact medium Laura Lynne Jackson for my reading. A high school English teacher and mother of three, Laura had passed both the Foundation and Windbridge Institute certification programs. The latter process included so many levels of blinding that any cheating, fraud, cold reading, or even bias in scoring could be ruled out. Laura scored 90 percent accuracy on one reading there and 95 percent on the other, which is unusually high. I was fortunate to get an appointment two months after emailing her, without giving her my last name. I had a friend with an unrelated email conduct all the communications for me.

I knew that the only way I could properly find out if mental mediumship was legitimate was to enter into it on its own terms. A reading is described as being about "energy" and connection. The more harmonious and strong the energy between all involved, the better the connection to the "other side" (the mediumistic version of the dimension where nonlocal consciousness dwells after death). So I started meditating and putting myself in a positive and receptive mindset, to maximize the chances for success. I knew I was not gullible, and could maintain objective awareness of what transpired. And, every word, emotion, and nuance of the reading would be recorded on my own device, so I could step back and examine the results with detachment afterward. But to do a proper reading, I needed to fully let go into the experience.

For the sake of a smooth narrative, I will not keep repeating cumbersome qualifying terms such as "alleged" deceased person or "ostensible" communication or "possible" family member or "supposed" connection and similar phrases. We must recognize that none of this is proven, but I am using the terms that apply within this context; this does not mean that I have lost my objectivity.

In preparing for the reading with Laura, I focused on two people close to me who had recently died—my dear friend Budd Hopkins, an accomplished abstract expressionist painter and UFO researcher, and my brother, Lloyd Garrison Kean. For the days prior to the reading, I had them both on my mind.

Through my friend with the different email address, I sent Laura my phone number so she could call me at the designated time. (She never asked for it, and she would have been just as happy for me to have called her.) Unfortunately, I had not considered the problem this might cause later. A skeptic not willing to accept the legitimacy of the reading could speculate that Laura looked me up on the Internet through this number and learned about my friend Budd Hopkins. I consider this to be entirely implausible, since Laura had been giving evidential readings for over two decades mainly for people whose deceased loved ones are nowhere to be found on the Internet or through any sort of research. Laura had built up her numerous successes and outstanding reputation from these readings, as well as having passed both certification programs, and therefore had no need to snoop into her clients on the rare instances that information was available about them. She did not have my last name and didn't know that I was preparing a book, so why would she bother to search my phone number online? There would have been no reason for her to treat this reading any differently from any other. To me, this is an inconceivable, even preposterous, scenario. Much of the information she provided would not be available on the Internet anyway. Nonetheless, skeptics can use the fact that she had my number as a convenient excuse to reject the reading, and I can't stop them. I bring this up only out of professional obligation; I have since come to know Laura and I have no doubt whatsoever about her integrity.

And she provided an astonishing reading. First, she spent a few minutes "tuning in to me" on the phone, and then began by telling me there was an eager male "busting through," very excited to speak with me. She told me that he was older, maybe by twelve to fifteen years; that he "crossed" two to three years ago, and that we were not married. These all were accurate to Budd Hopkins. To my amazement, she provided me with many additional points about him, our friendship, his family, his death, and even his name. She said, "I see a big 'B'—a 'B' name. It's short, like Bub or Bubba. It's like a nickname; there's another name too." ("Budd" was his middle name, used as a nickname. She had the sound "b" rather than "d.")

But something she said early on, when Budd first "arrived," was so impactful that it gave me chills. "The number one thing he wants to say," she told me, "is 'You were right. You were right!'" I knew what she was referring to instantly, before she said the following: "I feel like it's like you were right about the other side; you were right about this." This had a very specific and private meaning known only to me.

Toward the end of Budd's life, when he was very ill but before he went into hospice with two types of cancer, I thought he might be interested to understand that there is evidence suggesting that death may not be the end. I carefully selected a few books that I thought might appeal to him, one of them being *Old Souls* by *Washington Post* journalist Tom Shroder, who traveled with Ian Stevenson and watched him work. Like Stevenson, Budd was a courageous maverick who had left himself open to ridicule by going against the grain in his UFO research. I assumed because of my interest in this topic, he would at least be curious enough to look through these books.

But when I next saw him, he told me that he didn't want to read them because he didn't believe in any sort of afterlife. This one life was it. The memory of these conversations stayed with me, mainly because I was so surprised; this brush-off seemed out of character to me. Budd was normally an avid reader, interested in just about everything. I was perplexed by his reticence, but I let it go.

When Laura said he burst in and the first thing he said was "You were right," I immediately knew this was what he meant. And then Laura confirmed it. Because this was something very private between Budd and me, it had even more of an impact on me than the many specific facts she continued to convey with remarkable accuracy—that he died from cancer and that I was with him when he died; that he had one child, a daughter; that his third marriage was one of his biggest regrets; that he died toward the end of August (the twenty-fourth, to be exact); that his lungs were filled with fluid (he had severe pneumonia), and much more. Laura said these statements were coming directly from Budd, to establish for me that it was really him. Later in the reading, she corrected her first impression of his name and said it was "Buddy" and that she was also getting an "E" for his name. I found this extraordinary—his full name was Elliott Budd Hopkins. She said that Budd mentioned my sister, saying that she lived in New York and had an "L" name. (This was also correct; Budd knew her.) Suddenly, Laura said, "He's saying Happy Birthday!" It so happened that that very day was my birthday, and Laura didn't know that.

It was uncanny how consistently Budd's personality seemed to be present. He dominated the reading and wanted all the time for himself. Laura said she could perceive a big ego there, to the extent that he did not respect her wishes to step back a bit, and "was not behaving." I was not surprised by this at all and I suspect anyone who knew Budd would understand why. He acted as if "this is all about me! It's a one-man show!" Laura said, and we laughed about it. As I knew Budd, he loved to talk about himself and be the center of attention. He would usually dominate any gathering he attended, often not really listening or responding to what anyone else said, but preferring to be the talker. He had a big, shining, sometimes overpowering personality. This quality permeated the reading, and that was as convincing to me as the facts provided, while also being amusing. All in all, the reading was quite spectacular. It seemed like Budd, the person I once knew, was fully present.

Without telling Laura, I was also thinking about my brother, and eventually I asked her if there was anyone else there. After finally getting Budd to pull back, she said a male on my father's side was there, and then recognized him as a brother. She said he had a "J" or "G" name (the only name my brother went by was Garry), and that his death was unexpected, which it certainly was. She told me about his death (it was very fast, like a popping balloon); it was not an accident but was due to a bodily function; he was alone, at home, and somebody found him; he was not married. There were questions about his sexuality and he had issues with depression and didn't always see things clearly. This was all true, although I didn't know if his death had been fast or not (but it could have been, and this was comforting).

Although irrelevant, I can confirm that all that was available on the Internet about my brother was a three-sentence *New York Times* obituary. It is so short that even if Laura had attempted a search, she would not have found it. When you put "Leslie Kean death," "Kean obituary," or "Leslie Kean brother death" in Google, it does not come up. I never made any reference to my brother on social media.

To continue, Laura provided even more specific details, such as the fact that Garry was the third child in the family and we had a California connection (we lived near each other there in the past). She then said my brother was saying that there was a photograph of him in his pajamas, which he was smiling about. This was a highly obscure detail and took me a moment to understand. I have a photo of my three siblings and me taken on a family vacation when we were children, all of us positioned neatly along a wall posed for the camera, with a gorgeous ocean view behind us. Garry was wearing his pajama top rather than a shirt. I remember our mother being amused by this and commenting on it, and I had a copy of this photo in an envelope along with some others from my brother's childhood.

Then, Laura made the most powerful statement of all, coming from my brother: "He said thank you for keeping his secret." I was taken aback. This involved a private circumstance and related issues involving my brother that no one knows about outside the immediate family except possibly a few intimate friends. For years I had kept this secret from the rest of the family, at his request, until I realized I should no longer do so. This was always a significant and troubling aspect of our relationship throughout our adult lives, but extremely private. At that moment, I have to admit that it felt like this message could be coming only from him.

My brother's reserved and sensitive personality was conveyed through many of the nuances of Laura's description of him, and in the way he expressed himself, which stood in contrast to the assertive, intense energy of Budd, who'd jumped in first. Both personalities seemed to be present in the way that I knew them. It was truly a wondrous and exhilarating experience, because I entered into it openly and it was shockingly accurate.

Later, I made a list of all the points Laura provided, and the correct information *far* outweighed the inaccurate. Laura says that anything that did not make sense was due to her inability to interpret the message properly. "The whole experience for me is like a game of psychic charades," she explained in a follow-up email. "The other side always knows what it wants me to say, but sometimes I don't get it." It can be lost in the translation.

Confirming my own perceptions, Laura told me without my prompting that she experienced a big difference between Budd's and my brother's personalities. "Think of the difference between someone shouting at you clearly and someone whispering . . . that is what the difference can be like. For example, Budd shouted. Your brother— the 'G' sounding name—was more like a whisper I had to strain a bit to hear. He also communicated to me more in feeling impressions than the way Budd chose to communicate—which was more direct thought 'statements.' I don't know how the whole thing works! I find it all pretty interesting!" Her description fit the two very different personalities as I knew them. What was most important was that both had provided at least one very personal detail, among many, many factual details, that Laura couldn't possibly have known. I never expected that a reading with a medium could be anything like this, and I felt expanded and awed by it.

Next, I wanted to set up a second reading with another medium. This time, no phone number or any other potentially identifying information would be provided. I would have to find someone as good as Laura, but the two mediums must not know each other or be part of the same network. That meant this next one would not be certified by any American organization, and would preferably reside in a different part of the world.

Chapter 13

An Almost Perfect Reading

I learned from a colleague about a medium in Ireland, Sandra O'Hara, who came highly recommended. Sandra worked from her home near Belfast and did her readings over Skype, a computer program that allows you the option of seeing the person you're talking to. Unlike a phone, there is no area code—no way to know where on the planet the person is calling from when they ring you.

I adopted a false name, Lesley Lay, and a friend by that last name conducted all the correspondence with Sandra for me on his email address. In those emails, I told Sandra I would prefer to skype her, rather than her skyping me, so I never gave her a Skype address, and instead she sent me hers. I opened up a PayPal account under this assumed name, and made sure that when PayPal notified her of my payment it would not disclose my address. We planned for an April 2014 reading, two months after Laura's.

Like Laura, Sandra had been doing readings for over twenty years. I asked her—all of this as Lesley Lay through this other email address—if I could call her on the phone for the reading, or perhaps turn off the visual part of Skype, thinking it would be more "scientific" and avoid visual cues. She said that would be fine, but that "it is nice to put a face to the voice." Her willingness to use the phone gave me confidence that she did not *need* to see the sitter, so I decided not to disrupt the system she was used to. No facial expression could lead to the level of detail Laura provided, and this is what I was looking for.

Many mediums, including Laura, say that "our loved ones on the other side" can hear our thoughts; that they are with us and can receive mental messages from us. Information brought through in readings often seems to confirm this, because it is responsive to thoughts. I wanted to test these unprovable assumptions . . . or at least play with them. So, for about a week prior to my second reading, I earnestly sent the following thoughts to both Budd and my brother:

> Will you each please come through again with Sandra? And
> will you each say something to Sandra that is *exactly* the same as
> what you said to Laura? If you were really there with Laura, then
> come back and prove it is really you by repeating something you
> said before. Then I will know.

I had nothing specific in mind. I had no idea if these two would come through again at all, let alone repeat something they said before. It seemed extremely unlikely to me, but I thought, why not try, so I mustered up enough conviction to ask for it with fully focused sincerity.

To reiterate: all that Sandra knew was that someone named Lesley Lay was calling her at a certain time. She had no phone number, no email address, no location, or real name that corresponded to me. My friend who was emailing her for me had a common Spanish name. She had no clue about me. Imagine trying to guess very specific information only from a made-up name.

When I called Sandra, we chatted and she seemed down-to-earth, warm, and easygoing, with a great sense of humor. I switched on my audio recorder, and the reading started. She said there were two males. Good, was it them again? But wait . . . next she said there was a female who she thought was my mother (uh-oh, my mother was very much alive . . .) and then someone named William, who praised me for my work (no idea whom that could be . . .), so I started to think this was going nowhere. But then . . . it started to sound familiar. She said there was a male there who was older, died three to four years ago, and it was a relationship, not a family member. Then it all took off.

Sandra's style was different from Laura's, less descriptive but quick and to the point. She stated each message as if it just sort of popped into her mind, making her reading seem like an efficient list of bullet points. Like Laura, she would ask me if the point made sense—I would say simply yes or no, being careful not to reveal anything to her. (She never asked for information.)

Here is what she said was coming from the older man. The text in parentheses explains how it pertains to Budd—but she knew none of that during the reading, of course.

1) He died of cancer.
   (Budd died of complications due to two types of cancer.)
2) He had one other important female in his life.
   (He had one daughter he was close to.)
3) I and another woman important to him were with him when he died.
   (His daughter and I were there at the moment he died.)
4) The word "April" is a reference to something significant.
   (Budd's second wife, his daughter's mother, was named April.)
5) He was an artist—"I see paintings and paintbrush in his hand."
   (Budd was an established painter whose work was in the collections of major museums. This was his main career—the UFO work came later.)
6) Work brought us together—we had a similar passion.
   (I first met Budd at a UFO conference and then in New York to discuss a case of his that interested me. He had been a UFO investigator for two decades, and I had been reporting on UFOs for about four years.)
7) The "star people"—this connects you.

(Budd's focus was on people who claimed to have had encounters with extraterrestrial beings—"star people"—and the work connected us.)

8) From the Spielberg movie *E.T.*, the scene where E.T. points to the boy and says, "Elliott . . . Elliott" in that funny E.T. voice.

(Budd dealt with claims of people contacting ET beings in his work, and here was an ET being. Even more significant was the "Elliott." This was Budd's actual first name, also spelled with two t's. The ET creature is pointing and saying his name. This was a double whammy.)

9) He died shortly after a milestone birthday—one ending with a zero.

(Budd died two months after his eightieth birthday.)

10) He was a New Yorker.

(He had lived in New York since the 1950s.)

11) There was a problem with property after he died and he's unhappy with that.

(His daughter was trying to sell the town house he had lived in for fifty years and was having serious problems with the co-owner who didn't want to sell.)

12) You (Leslie) are behind the camera and in front of it, related to work.

(The month he died, a two-hour documentary based on my UFO book aired on the History Channel, for which I was a field producer—behind the camera. I was also interviewed on camera for the same piece.)

13) A hammer and chisel—he's making something.

(Budd was also a sculptor.)

14) He had more than one lady and was popular—it was more than flirtatious.

(He was married three times and had many affairs.)

15) His biggest connection of all was to me.

(He told me this many times.)

16) He had one child.

(He had a daughter; no stepchildren. This would have been

a good guess, since Sandra already established he had one other important female in his life.)

17) Referring to a name, the song "Amazing Grace" is significant.

(His daughter's name is Grace.)

18) I hear "Bubby."

(The name "Budd.")

19) The painting *Starry Night* by van Gogh.

(Van Gogh was my favorite artist. We used to go to two museums in New York to see this painting and others.)

I could hardly believe it. Where was all of this accurate information coming from? She knew nothing whatsoever about me, not even my name! But here was the grand finale: Sandra told me that Budd said, "You are right. You are right!" He then said, "Proof . . . something tangible is coming." This was it! A repeat of what he said with Laura, which is what I had asked for! The "something tangible coming" I interpreted as my book. I was completely floored by this.

Late in the reading, I asked for the other male who had been present at the beginning to come through. ("Elliott likes to be center stage and take up all the time!" Sandra explained with a laugh, just like Laura had said.) In a few moments, the other male stepped forward and she said:

1) He was a brother.

2) His death was unexpected; there was a shock factor.

(Both are true.)

3) It was very fast—one minute here, the next minute gone.

(Don't know for sure, but Laura said exactly the same thing.)

4) There were two burials or services.

(We scattered his ashes twice in the ocean in two widely separated locations.)

5) He was distressed, shut out in some way.

(This is accurate; he hardly ever saw his family.)

6) "I smell alcohol"—he or someone else was an alcoholic.

(A bull's-eye—he died of alcoholism.)

And then it came. Again, like with Budd . . . She said the word "secrets" came from my brother—a repeat of what he had said with Laura, which I'd asked for. He had said to me through Laura, "Thank you for keeping my secret."

I hope it is clear how impossible it would be to guess these specific points. This reading was above average in its accuracy. There are always some wrong or unclear statements in every reading—the question is, how many, and how specific are the accurate ones? Sandra excelled on both counts. She came up with more than thirty accurate details in our relatively short reading, without even knowing my name. Some points were about family members or me; these were correct too. Using two of many scoring methods employed by the FFF, she was between 85 and 90 percent accurate.

I must reiterate how amazed I was that both "personalities" repeated something they had said through Laura, as I had requested with my thoughts, as if they had received my messages and then delivered. With Laura, Budd said "You were right" twice, with strength and emphasis. Remarkably, with Sandra he also said "You are right" *twice,* again emphatically, in a similar tone. My brother thanked me for keeping his secret, and this time, through Sandra, he provided the word "secrets." In both cases, these two messages were the most obscure and also the most personal and meaningful to me, and the least known by anyone else, among all the many points from Laura's reading. This means that if we want to theorize that they chose something evidential to repeat, *there would be no better choice.* In both cases, the mediums said Budd was assertive and clear, but my brother was withdrawn and harder to read, as if the same two distinct personalities were present in each reading. Both times, Budd appeared first, and did all he could to hog the stage. Echoing Laura, Sandra laughed at his dominating behavior, and said it was quite unusual. "Today was his show," she said. "He was saying, 'I'm here! I have the floor! I'm talking!'" Laura described his behavior in almost exactly the same words. In contrast, my brother was quieter, softer, and had more difficulty communicating, as was true in life, and he came through only at the end of each reading. I think you will agree that these similarities are remarkable. Anyone who has had readings with mental mediums will understand how unusual such accuracy is—especially twice in a row.

Could this mean that the same "nonlocal," once-living entities were present both times? It certainly seemed that way. The similarities were too specific to have been coincidences. Or was Sandra reading my mind, determining what was said at the last reading to fulfill my request for repetition? Perhaps, as the living-agent psi hypothesis stipulates, both mediums were using telepathy to retrieve their information from my mind, and that's why it came out the same—the source was my mind rather than these two discarnate personalities. On the other hand, maybe it makes sense that two superb mediums would come up with the same information if the same two deceased personalities were present both times, regardless of whether I asked for this or not.

I wondered if the reference to a secret could be common in a reading; after all, siblings often share and hold secrets. So I asked Laura if this reference was made often; how many other readings has she done where a thank-you for keeping a secret is provided for the sitter? "Out of all the readings I've done, and they number in the thousands, I would say maybe one or two other times," she replied. "If that. It is not something I normally say during a reading at all."

In August 2015, I was in Northern England for some research. A British medium named Sandy Ingham came to visit at the home of a mutual friend where I was staying. We had never met before, and my host had not told her anything about my having lost a brother. Without any planning, Sandy started spontaneously doing an informal reading for me, sitting on the couch with a few other friends listening in. One switched on a recorder. Sandy initially said there was someone there who was not an old person and had died very quickly; he had been "on drugs or sedated" and had brown eyes, and his name had the letters "O" and "D" in it. All of this applied to my brother and his formal name "Lloyd." As we proceeded, she stated that he shared a name with his grandfather and another family member who had also died, which impressed me. (He actually shared his first and middle name with his grandfather and an uncle who recently died.) But she also provided lengthy messages from him that resonated only somewhat, and there were quite a few other statements that didn't make sense, so I was skeptical. Then, suddenly, Sandy leaned over to me across the couch. She cupped her hands around her mouth and whispered close to my ear, "You kept my secret." I was shocked. I asked her, "He said that I kept his secret?" And she said, "Yes, but this was very private and it was not for anyone else to hear." The secret was something he was ashamed of; indeed, it was not for anyone else to hear.

Three times? From three different mediums who have never spoken to each other, I was given: "Thank you for keeping my secret" . . . the word "secrets" . . . "you kept my secret," all seemingly from the same source. No one can argue with the accuracy of the message. Was my brother there in some capacity each time, honoring my request for repetition yet a third time?

Upon reflection, I see that it is just as likely that all the information could have come from the mediums using their highly developed psi to access information from me telepathically rather than from two discarnate beings. To accept the survival interpretation, we have to make a number of assumptions, as I explained in the Introduction, in order for it to hold. And Stephen Braude says one must discern "the underlying needs and interests which might plausibly motivate living agents to psychically access information that can subsequently be verified normally . . . Whose conscious or unconscious needs would be served by the appearance of evidence suggesting survival?" There is ultimately no scientifically viable way to resolve the LAP vs. survival debate with respect to mental mediumship.

So we come back to the element of impressions and meaning, perhaps too subtle to convey, that are not arguable rationally. I cannot describe adequately how uncanny and exhilarating it is to sit with a total stranger who knows absolutely nothing about you but who delivers a stream of obscure information, personality traits, and meaningful messages that appear to be coming from someone once living. I now understand how helpful this process could be for grieving people. The familiar individuality of these two opposites was easy for me to recognize, and Budd's domination in both readings made complete sense. A list of accurate points can't do justice to the way it feels in the moment; it seems to border on something miraculous—if you are not focused on the LAP interpretation. The readings suggest the possibility of survival past death with an in-your-face, joyful immediacy.

I had readings with two other mediums certified by the two organizations, but they didn't come close to Laura and Sandra. There was quite a bit of wrong or unverifiable information by comparison, and much of the information was too general to be evidential. Robert Ginsberg of Forever Family Foundation says that I was "spoiled" by the outstanding scores that Laura's and Sandra's readings achieved. There are not many mediums capable of performing like this. "Ten years of medium observation leads me to believe that only 10 to 15 percent of all mediums are evidential," Ginsberg told me in an email. "And that percentage is generous."

Chapter 14

Research into Mental Mediumship

By Julie Beischel, PhD

Rigorous controls have been placed on mediums subjecting them-selves to testing by the Windbridge Institute, which is dedicated to conducting research on phenomena currently unexplained within traditional scientific disciplines. Its primary focus is on applied research with the goal of developing and distributing informa-tion, services, and technologies that allow people to reach their full potential. The Windbridge Institute is involved not only with certifying mediums, but also in studying their abilities under the strictest test protocols. I asked Julie Beischel, its cofounder and di-rector of research, to describe the procedures she uses and to explain what they show about mental mediumship and possible communi-cation with discarnates.

Julie received her doctorate in Pharmacology and Toxicology from the University of Arizona in 2003. Following an evidential mediumship reading she had after her mother's suicide, she for-feited a potentially lucrative career in the pharmaceutical industry to pursue scientific research with mediums. She is adjunct faculty in the School of Psychology and Interdisciplinary Inquiry at Say-

brook University and the author of Investigating Mediums: A Windbridge Institute Collection *(2015).*

Although very little mediumship research has taken place since the 1920s, beginning in the early 2000s, a handful of researchers have examined various aspects of mental mediumship phenomena. For example, researchers have investigated (and continue to study) the psychology of mediums and found that they are in good mental health, socially adjusted, and productive. Researchers who have performed experiments providing statistical evidence for mediums' abilities to report accurate and specific information about the deceased under controlled conditions include Tricia Robertson and Archie Roy based in Scotland, Gary Schwartz and colleagues at the University of Arizona, Emily Kelly and Dianne Arcangel from the University of Virginia, and my research team at the Windbridge Institute. To the best of my knowledge, my team is the only one of those four still performing ongoing research with mediums.

Because science is a tool for obtaining new knowledge and not a set of beliefs or facts set in stone, it can be used to examine any phenomenon, and those with the appropriate training in methodological design (like me) can apply it to answer any of a wide range of questions.

I had seen mediums on TV and even had one evidential reading of my own, and I was hearing strong opinions from both camps (from "Mediums are spiritual gifts from God!" to "Mediums are immoral con artists and frauds!"). Thus, I wanted to apply the scientific method to the phenomenon of mental mediumship and come to some kind of objective conclusion. To address the research question at the root of it—can mediums report accurate and specific information about the deceased?—two factors needed to be part of the experimental design: an optimal research environment and maximum controls.

It's important to examine any phenomenon under real-world circumstances or you're not really studying it at all. Unless you can mimic its natural conditions in the laboratory, what you're studying is not actually mediumship. This has repeatedly happened when researchers who think that mediums *should* be able to accomplish a task have tried to test them. Can two mediums both read the same dead person at the same time? Can a medium get the lottery numbers? Can a medium tell you the exact moment when you're going to die?

These questions are not relevant. Regardless of what certain individuals think mediums *should* be able to do, none of those events reflect mediumship as it exists in reality or address claims made by most actual mediums. Again, the purpose of mental mediumship is to convey messages from discarnates to sitters; that's the extent of what most mediums report being able to do. Asking them to do anything beyond that stops being a valid scientific inquiry of the mediumship phenomenon. The analogy I like to use is that a mediumship "study" in which the environment is not optimized for mediumship to happen is akin to placing a seed on a tabletop and then claiming the seed is a fraud when it doesn't sprout. If it can sprout in the soil with water and sunlight, it should be able to sprout on the table. Right?

An optimal research environment also requires the right people. In our research at the Windbridge Institute, medium research participants are prescreened to determine if they are able to report accurate information under regular conditions before they participate in actual controlled studies.

And this research environment can't use experimenters or sitters with a visibly seething hatred for mediums and expect that environment to be conducive to the phenomenon. In a real-world mediumship reading, the people participating want to be there and are open to the possibility that communication can occur. Unless we can prove that open-minded sitters and experimenters are not a factor necessary for mediumship to happen, we have to keep it as part of our experiment. And while we can't directly question the discarnates about their willingness to participate, we can ask their living loved ones (the sitters) if they think the discarnates would want to. Basically, as we design an experiment, we have to carefully select the four kinds of people involved: the experimenters, the mediums, the sitters, and the discarnates.

Similarly, this is an important concept to keep in mind for mediumship readings outside the laboratory in which three kinds of people are involved: the mediums, the sitters, and the discarnates. Thus, if a reading goes well, that implies that the medium did her job well. However, if a reading doesn't go well, factors related to any of the people involved could be responsible. The medium might not be a good medium or she might be a good medium having an off day. Alternatively, the discarnate might not be communicating; the discarnate might be busy that day; the discarnate might not particularly like the medium; the sitter might not be ready to hear from the discarnate; the sitter might have fear about the process, etc. It's important to remember that at least three people might be participating and the medium is only one of them. Making "success" entirely her responsibility just isn't fair. This is especially true if the sitter has unrealistic expectations about how mediumship works based on the heavily edited mediums they've seen on TV.

The second factor important in designing an ideal mediumship study is the use of maximum controls. This usually involves the blinding of the participants and experimenters to various types of information. It is like a double-blind clinical trial in which the patient taking the medication and the doctor checking on her progress are both blinded to whether she has been taking the actual drug or a placebo. As part of our experimental setup, we have to address all the normal, sensory sources of where the medium could be getting her information and other "regular" explanations for positive results in order to rule out fraud, cueing by the experimenter, cold reading, and rater bias (discussed later).

In fact, we use a "more-than-double-blind" protocol with five levels of blinding: the medium, the sitter, and three researchers are all blinded to different pieces of information. Research readings take place over the phone and only an experimenter (me) and a medium who is in a different city are on the line. The associated sitter knows the reading is happening but does not know which medium is performing it and does not hear the reading as it takes place. The medium and I have only the first name of a discarnate, which has been emailed to me by a research assistant, and that I give to the medium at the start of the reading. (I can hear you asking, "How does the medium find the right Jack?" Their experience is that the right Jack finds them. The sitter has requested that Jack participate in the reading and the medium trusts that the person she is experiencing—often before the reading even starts—is the correct one.)

Since first name is all the medium and I know about the discarnate, the sitter, their relationship, etc, this prevents fraud on the part of the medium: she can't google a name or phone number to get any information about the sitter. She doesn't know the sitter's gender, age, or location. This blinding also prevents cueing (intentional or inadvertent) by the experimenter (me). I can't give the medium any information because I don't know anything about the discarnate or the sitter.

This protocol also prevents cold reading as an explanation for positive results. During cold reading an unscrupulous medium will use visual (e.g., tears, pupil dilation, fidgeting) and auditory (e.g., gasps, sobs) cues as well as actual information provided by the sitter to fabricate what seems like a successful reading to the sitter but is actually just good observational skills and reporting back in a different way information the sitter provided. For example, a medium may ask, "Is it a 'J' or 'L' name?" and if the female sitter says, "Yes! My father's name was Louis," the medium can then tailor the reading to include information about father-daughter relationships. To prevent cold reading in regular private mediumship readings, sitters should reply to mediums' questions with only basic responses: yes, no, maybe, sort of, or "I don't know."

Another form of cold reading involves providing information so general it could apply to anyone or that most people will claim about themselves. For example, the medium may say things like "You miss your mother very much," "She says you have a good sense of humor," or "You are actually quite intuitive yourself."

Because the medium doesn't have any access to the sitter during our research readings and as a *proxy sitter* in place of the absent sitter I don't have any information about the discarnate, the medium cannot use cold reading. In addition, we request specific information about the discarnate. After being given the discarnate's first name (and the associated gender if it isn't obvious by the name), the medium then responds to specific questions about the discarnate's personality, physical description, hobbies or interests, cause of death, and any messages he or she has for the absent sitter.

In our research at the Windbridge Institute, each medium performs two readings for two different gender-matched (two female or two male) discarnates, and then each sitter scores each of the two readings in the pair without knowing which is which. For example, say a medium provided one reading for my deceased father and one for your deceased brother. I would be given both readings to score as to how well they applied to my father, and you would be given the same two readings to score as to how well they applied to your brother. Because we didn't hear the readings as they took place, we wouldn't know which one was actually for my father and which was for your brother. By keeping the sitters blinded to the origin of the readings, the protocol addresses *rater bias*. When a sitter scores a reading, if he knows it was a reading for him, he may have a bias to score more items as correct because he wants the items to reflect communication with the deceased person he lost. By blinding the sitters to which reading is for which sitter, rater bias is equalized across readings.

Sitters provide three types of accuracy ratings: each sitter gives each item in the numbered lists of statements a score, gives each reading an overall global score, and chooses which of the two readings he thinks applies to his discarnate.

Sitters are the only people with the extensive and essential knowledge required to appropriately score items describing discarnates and/ or their messages. You could tell me everything you could remember about your discarnate and that still wouldn't allow me to "recognize" him when a medium accurately described him. This is why we don't make transcripts of readings publicly available (which is akin to publishing someone's blood results). A reading is a private conversation between two people, and anyone other than the sitter attempting to determine if the information is "good enough" based on preconceived ideas about how mediumship *should* work is totally unqualified. It would be like someone listening to a phone call between you and your spouse and then claiming to be able to tell how much you loved each other. The purpose of a mediumship reading is to convey messages from a discarnate to a sitter. How could I determine if you experienced communication from your discarnate by reading a list of statements that refer to someone I'd never met?

During analysis, we compare the scores blinded sitters gave their own readings (*target* readings; how you scored your reading and how I scored my reading) to the scores they gave to other sitters' readings (*decoy* readings; how you scored my reading and how I scored your reading). We're not looking for a threshold of success; we just compare the scores for target readings to the scores for decoy readings.

By examining the three types of scores, we can statistically compare target and decoy scores. For example, the reading choice data has a clear probability; there's a fifty-fifty shot a sitter will choose his own reading by chance. Thus, it's easy to test whether more sitters chose their own readings than would be expected by chance (that statistical test is called a binary probability test). Comparing the item scores is a bit more complicated (those analyses include paired comparisons of means) but follows the same principle.

By comparing target and decoy scores, the issue of generality of statements is further addressed. If a medium provided primarily information that could apply to anyone, sitters would score both target and decoy readings similarly and we'd see no statistical difference. Thus, the protocol we use tests the accuracy as well as the specificity of statements made by mediums. However, because people can only be so different from each other, we have found that about 25 percent of the statements in any given reading might be generally applicable.

In March 2015, we published an article in the peer-reviewed *EXPLORE: Journal of Science and Healing,* detailing the results from a study that involved fifty-eight readings by twenty of our certified mediums, performed between 2009 and 2013. (About 25 percent of the

mediums who attempted our extensive, peer-reviewed eight-step certification procedure did not achieve passing scores.) The sitter participants in the study were randomly selected from a national volunteer
pool.

The fifty-eight readings all took place over the phone using the
more-than-double-blind reading protocol described previously. The
highly statistically significant results demonstrated that sitters scored
more items as accurate in their own readings (target readings) than
items in readings meant for others (decoy readings) using two different methods of analysis. The sitters also gave targets significantly
higher global scores than decoys. In addition, a statistically significant
proportion of sitters correctly chose the target reading over the decoy
in the pair of readings they scored.

Furthermore, this study was a successful replication and extension
of a previous study published in the same journal in 2007. In science,
it hasn't really happened until it happens twice.

But these are just words. What does this all mean?

These statistically significant (that is, real and evidential) accurate data from a combined total of seventy-four mediumship readings
performed under more-than-double-blind conditions that eliminated
fraud, experimenter cueing, rater bias, and cold reading show that
mediums report accurate and specific information about discarnates
without prior knowledge about the discarnates or sitters and with no
sensory feedback. In other words, certain mediums have unexplainable (by current materialist science) abilities to say correct things they
shouldn't otherwise know about dead people.

But, as pointed out previously in this book, while the statistically
significant data demonstrate the reporting of accurate information
about the deceased under controlled conditions, they cannot say *where*
the information is coming from. By addressing the normal, sensory
sources from which the mediums could be getting their information,
we can only say where the information is *not* coming from. It's not
cold reading or other sensory explanations. So it must be a nonlocal,
psi-based source. There are two possibilities: survival psi (from the
discarnate) and what we at the Windbridge Institute call "somatic psi"

(from the medium's own psi, also referred to as "living-agent psi"). Neither one can be proven or disproven as the explanation for where a medium gets her information, and the content of the reading cannot help differentiate between which of these theories is more plausible.

Hitting this wall has been an ongoing frustration for mediumship researchers and one of the reasons why most researchers stopped examining the phenomenon altogether. At the Windbridge Institute, we're also looking at the phenomenology—the study of experiences—since the mediums report being able to easily differentiate whether survival psi or somatic psi is responsible for the different pieces of information they are receiving. When we asked Windbridge Institute mediums to describe the difference between the two sources, a "mediumship reading" being one where they say they use survival psi, one medium stated: "A psychic reading is like reading a book . . . a mediumship reading is like seeing a play." Other mediums noted:

> In a mediumship reading, it feels like someone is talking *to* me. With psychic readings, it's information *about* someone.

> With psychic information, I have to "squint" from the inside out like to focus on something in the distance. When I do mediumship, it's not squinting at all. It's just receiving.

> With mediumship, I get to meet new people all the time. Psychic information is boring.

> It's very different. It's like listening to someone versus looking myself.

> The physical feeling I get is a tingling or a pressure in my head when the medium stuff starts to happen or when they're entering the room. I don't get that at all during a psychic reading.

In a recent quantitative (acquiring numerical data) study, some of the first names we gave to the mediums were of living people and some were deceased. They (and I) didn't know which were which as they performed the readings. In a statistically significant portion of the readings, *the mediums were able to accurately determine if the simple first name belonged to a living person or a deceased person.* This knowledge was obtained through a reading for each name.

After each reading for both the living and the dead name, the mediums completed a questionnaire that allowed us to determine the intensity of each of twenty-six dimensions of their experiences (for example, joy, sadness, the vividness of mental imagery, and alterations in the experience of time). The readings for a dead person and those for a living person provided the same experience for the mediums within these parameters, except for one significant difference: love.

The mediums experienced more love during readings in which the name belonged to a deceased person. Reference to the love that the discarnate and the sitter shared is a common element in a mediumship reading, so this made sense. The really interesting bit, though, is that this difference in experiences happened even when the medium didn't consciously know if a given reading was for a living or a deceased person. *There was something about the information she was reporting that created a loving experience.*

Love seems to be a major component of the real-life mediumistic experience. One Windbridge Institute medium noted that during mediumship readings vs. psychic readings:

> There's more of a loving feeling. When I connect with somebody on the other side, everything's happy and great. I feel like I don't know who I am anymore. I lose myself. My identity is gone . . . I'm just part of the universe; I'm part of love energy . . . Reading psychically is very different. I'm more aware of myself. It's more grounded. It makes me feel alone.

In a study in which we monitored the brain activity of six Windbridge Institute mediums using electroencephalography (EEG), we found differences for four tasks the mediums performed: recollection (think about a living person you know), perception (listen while I read you information about a person), fabrication (make up someone and think about him/her), and communication (communicate with a deceased person you know). We concluded that "the experience of communicating with the deceased may be a distinct mental state that is not consistent with brain activity during ordinary thinking or imagination."

Together, data from modern mediumship experiments and the conclusions drawn from the large body of general psi research support a model of nonlocal (vs. materialist) consciousness that continues to exist after the death of the body.

Chapter 15

How Do They Do It?

A s Julie Beischel points out, studying the phenomenology of mediumship is a way of at least getting some clues that might help differentiate between living-agent psi and survival psi. I too wanted to understand how mediums develop these abilities, so I interviewed Sandra O'Hara about a year after my reading with her. She spoke to me from her home outside Dublin, where she lives with her teenage daughter. Sandra works from home on a schedule that integrates well with her role as a mother. Her clients find her only through word of mouth, yet she has a full-time schedule of readings from all over the world. One time when we spoke, she had just finished reading for someone in Russia, with a translator.

Sandra told me she was never motivated to be a medium, nor did she have to learn anything, because it all just happened to her naturally. "I'm so used to what I do that it's like second nature to me. I don't know how I do it, I just do it. I've never really questioned the process since it's been there since age four," she said. During her early years, she thought everyone else could see spirits and experience clairaudience just like she could. She had three siblings, but none of them had the same abilities, and she learned gradually that this was unique to her. She says her parents didn't discuss it with her much or ask too many questions; she was essentially on her own with this exceptional aspect of her life.

When she entered adolescence, Sandra had had enough of being different, and she was able to shut her abilities down, like closing a door. "I told them, 'I don't really like seeing you.' They stopped showing themselves," she explains. She went to college and studied business and criminology. Beginning when she was married at twenty-three, Sandra worked for a BMW manufacturing company and people started talking to her and asking her questions pertaining to her abilities. She was approached by people she knew, and then eventually by the police, to help solve missing-person cases. She gradually opened that door again, and her mediumship skills developed further. Six years later, she gave up her job to do readings full-time, and has been doing so for twenty-three years (as of 2016).

Many people ask the question that I posed to Sandra: If these are deceased people speaking from another dimension, why do they focus on such mundane things during these readings, rather than communicating profound observations about the nature of life and death? First of all, she explained, the medium has to receive enough verifiable points about the communicator to convince the sitter of the identity of their loved one on the other side. Any messages to be received would be meaningless unless the sitter was sure about whom they were coming from. The purpose of the readings seems to be simply to show that the person has survived, and this is what sitters are usually looking for. "Most of our lives are made up of mundane things," Sandra wrote in an email. "They can't interfere. They are not trying to change our lives. They only want us to know life goes on." She said they come through with the personality they had when alive so that the sitters are able to recognize them.

People often wonder why the discarnate communicator can't just give a string of very specific details right off the bat, rather than being indirect or symbolic with their deliveries. Like Laura had said earlier,

Sandra told me that the connection with Spirit is a bit like playing the game charades. "I think it has to do with the frequency, much like radio frequencies, and it is not always possible for me to fine-tune it. So, I get a series of words, images, or sounds and then translate that into the messages for the sitter. I believe that Spirit knows what they want to say and as the translator I take the responsibility for not always getting it completely right." (As the reader may recall, Laura also said that any miscommunications were her responsibility when I asked her this question.)

I wanted to gain more perspective on the question that most impacts the survival hypothesis, so I asked Sandra the same question posed by Julie Beischel: How does she distinguish information psychically accessed from earthly sources from those received from a discarnate? If living-agent psi fools its users into believing they are speaking to dead people when actually they are not, then a medium would not have a sense of any differentiation between the two modalities during readings. Sandra said that sometimes that's the case—everything merges once she is engaged in a reading, and she has no reason to be concerned about differentiating them because it's the information for the sitter that's important. But she said sometimes there is a clear difference:

> When Spirit energy comes, it's like a breeze, a new vibration,
> that comes into the room and is external to me. My own psychic
> energy feels like heat across my forehead, or in different places in
> my body. The new vibration sometimes arrives before the read-
> ing, and sometimes it even gets impatient waiting for the reading
> to start. Then it stays the whole time.

But how does she know this "new vibration" is a discarnate communicator?

> I can tell it's from Spirit based on the energies that come in—the
> information they give me, the sensations they give me. The de-
> tails of a death come in very specifically and really hit me, and I

don't think I could psychically tune in to that and get the sensations as well. I couldn't get it that way. I definitely can say it's an external source. Absolutely.

I have met Laura Lynne Jackson a few times in person in different contexts, including an extended discussion over lunch in my apartment. I have also witnessed her give spectacular readings within a group setting, where she knew nothing about who was in the audience. Author of the 2015 bestselling book *The Light Between Us*, Laura is entirely sincere, intelligent, radiant, and obviously gifted. She has a brilliant, intense disposition while also being warm with a loving humility about her.

Like Sandra, Laura grew up with natural abilities, which mainly involved an exceptional perception of people's energies and an ESP that she seemed to have been born with. She would know in advance when upsetting events were about to happen, such as the accidental death of a friend or the TWA Flight 800 plane disaster in 1996, which disturbed her profoundly because there was nothing she could do to stop the horror. She eventually learned she could be helpful to people by reading for them, using her psi to provide information without involving any discarnate sources—information about them would just come to her, "like when you get a thought in your head." She was a practicing psychic, not a medium.

But when Laura was twenty-three, suddenly everything changed. During one of her regular psychic readings, she felt a brand-new energy insert itself like "a new distinctly different portal that was open," letting in a "strong forceful presence." She didn't understand it. "I heard a name. Who was this? What was happening? I didn't know. I just let what I was hearing and seeing tumble out." She heard the name Chris, and told her sitter, Paul, that someone by that name was present. She was astonished by how specific and intimate the details were, coming from Chris, mainly about Paul's girlfriend rather than Paul, which confused her even more. Eventually, Paul told her that all the details were accurate, and that Chris was his girlfriend's former boyfriend. Paul's girlfriend had been in the car with Chris when it crashed, and Chris died. Chris was giving Paul his blessing for the relationship with his ex-girlfriend.

This was not something Laura had ever experienced before. It was clearly different from the psychic readings using only LAP that she had been performing regularly, which did not involve access to any "dead people" on the other side. So when Paul confirmed that it was accurate, she was shocked:

> I felt a chill run through my body. What was Paul telling me? That Chris was coming to me from the beyond? That I was hearing from a dead person as clearly as if he was right in my apartment? At that moment, I felt awe. I was coming to grips with my ability as a psychic . . . but I'd never considered that I might also be a medium, someone who is able to communicate with the other side. And yet in that reading I was getting clear specific details from someone who had crossed. I didn't have to root around for it or struggle to pull it out—it just came through like water through an open tap.

This was a turning point for Laura. "I wondered how the reading would affect my path going forward, now that I could connect with people who had crossed. What I didn't yet fully understand was that I wasn't just responsible for conveying information from the other side. I was also responsible for *interpreting* it."

This clearly illustrates that Laura could—and still can—clearly tell the difference between her psychic readings and those in which she communicates with entities from "the beyond." The fact that this use of survival psi came later suggests that these communications may be more unusual or harder to access than simple psychic information. At first, Laura says, it was like learning a foreign language, and she had to determine what certain symbols meant, used consistently in her readings. It seems reasonable to ask, who should know better than those mediums who are able to differentiate between their use of two different types of psi? Does it make sense to argue that Laura is fooling herself, even when the ability surfaced later as it did, and the distinction is as clear to her as night and day?

Laura developed an internal protocol "that allowed me to switch from one gift to another and back again without everything getting confused . . . I came up with a system that made connecting with dead people much more efficient." In fact, during a reading, the two psi aspects do not merge. She described it to me this way in 2015:

> When I read, I get an interior screen—kind of like a wide-screen TV—and it is divided into the left-hand side and the right-hand side. I start my readings on the left—that is where psychic information comes through. The right side is where my mediumship comes through. I get pulled to that side when I see a point of light enter the screen. I have that side divided into three sections: upper right for the sitter's mother's side of the family, lower right for Dad's side, middle for friends, peers, extended family, etc. Once I connect, those on the right-hand side of the screen will show me images, movie clips, make me feel things, hear things, etc.—in order to convey information to me. I don't know of any other medium who has an inner screen divided between left-hand psychic information and right-hand mediumship information.

Psychologist Jeff Tarrant has a PhD in Counseling Psychology and is an adjunct professor at the University of Missouri. In 2103, he began mapping the brains of psychics and certified mediums while they conducted readings. The mediums consistently showed unusual brain-wave activity, sometimes including "significant increases in fast activity in the back of the head—the areas of the brain associated with visual processing," according to Tarrant's website. Of course, such data does not prove communication with the dead but "it does strongly suggest that mediums are entering a very different state of consciousness when they are engaged in their work. They do not simply appear to be faking—something interesting is definitely going on!" Tarrant writes.

Tarrant measured Laura's brain activity twice. He then decided to take his study of Laura's process one step further, by comparing scans of her brain during a psychic reading—when she used her living-agent psi—with those taken during a mediumship reading when she engaged her survival psi. In other words, he wanted to see if what Laura described as her use of two distinct types of psi would actually register as different in her brain. This would be concrete evidence that two different processes were in operation. In fact, Tarrant did discover applicable changes in the area of the brain involved in visual processing. He states:

> One area of the brain is becoming active while she is receiving mediumship information; the other area is becoming activated when she is involved in a psychic reading. Coincidentally—or not—Laura reports that she sees psychic information in her left visual field, and she sees mediumship information on her right visual field. Actually, that is exactly what we see on these brain images. So this appears to be confirmation of what Laura reports from her own experience.

The fact that Laura uses two distinct processes, as shown by changes in her brain, corresponding to how she has always described the operations of her two internal visual screens, strongly supports her statement that indeed the processes are different. This confirmation shows that she is not only aware of her own internal process, but that she is telling the truth. If both types of readings were limited to her use of living-agent psi, it would seem logical that both psychic readings and mediumship readings would register in the *same* place in her brain.

This does *not* prove that the difference between these two brain states is that one involves communications from dead people. But one could argue that Tarrant's study at least supports the survival hypothesis.

Overall, the data show that it is perfectly reasonable—even rational—to interpret the best work of genuine mediums as evidence for survival. But I believe that a true evaluation can occur only once one has experienced a successful reading with a gifted medium; then, one's own perspective and assumptions will enter in as a necessary component, and each person will draw their own conclusion. Otherwise, this is purely an intellectual exercise, looking at this from the outside—like reading about the taste of an apple rather than taking the bite.

Chapter 16

Finding George

Sometimes mediums access information not known to any person anywhere on the planet, which makes the survivalist interpretation even stronger. The problem with this kind of information is the difficulty in verifying it. I discovered one such case, which I found particularly compelling but also surprisingly complex. While in the UK in 2015, I interviewed Mark Lewis, a managing director of Basilica Marketing, which provides marketing solutions for shopping centers in England. He had an extraordinary experience with a medium that he documented through careful notes. Highly skeptical, Mark's intention was to try to find out what happened to someone who died many years ago, whom he never knew. His motivation was strong, so he was willing to give mediumship a shot. Given his clarity, intelligence, and objective approach, I felt fully confident in him as a source for this story.

"I had, for many years, a feeling that there was someone close to me who I did not know," he said. For reasons he could not explain, he knew that this feeling had to do with his grandfather's younger brother, George Draper. Mark never knew George, but his granddad

Walter Draper, who died in 1980, had told him stories about his great-uncle George when he was a boy and said that they looked alike. The memories always stayed with Mark. "I felt a deep affinity with this person," he said, "and as time went on I began to believe that there was more to find out and that it would be important to me."

Mark could find out very little about George. He had been killed during World War I as a very young man. According to official documents, he died in France on July 16, 1916. He was listed as missing and the only record of his name was on the Memorial to the Missing at Thiepval, implying that his body had never been found and he therefore had not been buried. A few years before his reading, Mark had obtained the battalion diary for the Royal Warwickshire Regiment, which George fought with, for July 1916. It referred to fighting outside a village called Pozières on July 15, the day before George was supposed to have gone missing or died. Pozières is about three kilometers from Thiepval.

This was all that Mark or anybody knew about George Draper.

There were a number of British cemeteries in the area, including one at Pozières, but since George was listed as missing, Mark and his family never paid attention to them. The graves either had named individuals or were simply marked as unknown, so they were not relevant to his search for George.

Mark had a reading with British medium Sandy Ingham (the same medium who later whispered "You kept my secret" during that spontaneous reading) over the phone in the spring of 2013, only because his wife highly recommended her. Sandy knew nothing about Mark's grandfather or uncle, and Mark did not reveal why he had scheduled the reading.

Sandy began by talking about Mark's mother, and then suddenly said she had someone there whose name began with "W," then said it was "Wal," and then "Walter." Mark was taken aback, because most people called his grandfather "Wal" for short. Sandy then said she was with someone named George, who was coming forward very strongly. How amazing this must have been for Mark! She said that he was a military man wearing a uniform, and did not have a soldier's cap on, but instead a "funny little hat on the side of his head." Indeed, the one photo Mark had showed George with a small forage cap on the right side of his head.

Sandy also said that George was Mark's granddad's favorite brother, and that he had been a sort of spiritual father to Mark and they were connected in that way. She added that George had died in the war, that he was gassed, and that the number 19 was relevant. She reported "seeing" a field of rows of white crosses. Then Sandy said, "I don't understand what I am telling you, but he [George] is right up close to me and is saying 'G22, G22, G22' over and over again and I can't stop saying it, but he is telling me this is very important and you will know what this means." According to Mark, Sandy was agitated because she had no idea why this was being repeated to her so fast. She also said that G22 was "one of four," but again, she did not know what this meant.

Finally, Sandy said that George died on the same day as Mark's wedding anniversary. Mark did not confirm or deny this. That date was July 19, which resonated with the "19" provided earlier in the reading, and the month was accurate. Actually, there was no combat on July sixteenth when the records said George died, but there was on the fifteenth. It was conceivable that he was wounded on the fifteenth and died sometime later. If this were the case, George could have died on July 19, as Sandy said.

Mark recognized what "G22" meant. From previous research years earlier, unrelated to George, he knew that British cemetery grave records always gave a letter for the row and a number for the plot, indicating where each person was buried. But where would this be? After all, George was listed as missing and was not buried in a war cemetery.

There are hundreds of British, French, and German cemeteries on the Somme battlefields of France, with many thousands of graves for the identified soldiers and unidentified remains of those killed in action or who died of their wounds. After the reading, Mark went to the Commonwealth War Graves Commission website and selected the Pozières British Cemetery, because that was where George's regiment fought the day before he went missing. There were 2,760 men buried there, 1,382 in unnamed graves. Mark went over a map of the large cemetery and saw that there were four main plots, each one containing a grave number G22. This matched what Sandy had said: that G22 was "one of four." After searching further, he discovered that grave G22 in plots one, two, and four were named. So those in the area of G22 in plot three were the only options. Amazingly, they were dated for deaths on July 15, 1916.

Mark also learned that the site of the cemetery was where the main field hospital was located during the war, and those who died at the hospital following battle injuries were buried there along with the casualties.

Even though the July 15 dates matched, and there were four plots as Sandy had suggested, Mark had no way of determining who was buried at the unnamed G22 in plot three. So, in November 2014, he visited Sandy again, this time in person, to see if he could learn more. He told her nothing about any of his discoveries about G22.

They were chatting and Sandy suddenly said, "Oh, Walter's here!" She looked at Mark and said, "You have come about the grave." Mark told her he was seeking more specific details. He took out a copy of the rough plan of the cemetery, which he had printed from the Internet, and asked if she could locate a specific area on it that might be significant. The plan just showed blank rectangular sections for groups of tombstones and no specific gravesite numbers were designated within them. Without looking at it, Sandy asked him to lay the plan facedown on the table, so the front side was not visible. She used a hanging crystal as a sort of antenna, and then touched the back of the empty sheet in a specific spot, and marked it. When they turned it over, the mark corresponded to the location of grave G22 in plot number three.

Sandy was consistent, but how could he be sure this was where George was? Then, at the end of the reading, Sandy said George was telling her something else: that he was close to "Albert." She said that name at first, but then said it was . . . "Albertone" . . . or "Alberone" or something similar. This meant nothing to Mark.

When he got home, Mark went once again to the website cemetery list of the 1,378 unnamed graves on the website. Searching through the extensive database, he located grave G21, to the left of the unnamed G22 in plot three. Buried there was Private G. W. Albone, just as Sandy had said.

Mark had no memory of previously noticing the names on the two named graves on either side of G22 when he looked at the database. "This fact only confirmed that Sandy could obtain information of which I had no previous knowledge," Mark reports. He was now convinced that his great-uncle George was buried at this spot in Pozières. He and his family made an emotional visit to the grave in August 2014.

After returning, Mark had a third phone reading with Sandy, without telling her anything about having gone to France. Sandy mentioned George, and said that his grandfather Walter was there and said, "You went and you found him." He added that Mark went exactly to the right spot and that George had been present when Mark was at the grave.

Mark was convinced that the sources of his information were his two family members, Walter and George. They communicated through Sandy many details that she could not possibly have known, including their names. Most significant was the loudly repeated "G22" from the first phone reading, which Sandy could not understand, and the related statement that it was "one of four." Sandy was struck by the urgency of the G22 message. The rapid repetitions and Sandy's inability to understand the message gave an impression of an animated, external source highly motivated to get the message through.

It had never occurred to anyone that George's body might have occupied an unnamed grave. As for G22 at the Pozières British Cemetery being George's final resting place, the location and the death date fit. Sandy came up with the name on the adjacent grave. There was not one human being who knew that George was buried there, or one written record anywhere on the planet that documented it. Therefore, it seemed logical to assume that George was the only possible source for this information.

Mark had felt a deep spiritual connection with George all his life and was determined to find out what had happened to him. With this deep bond between them, which George confirmed for Sandy, there might have been a strong pull for George to come through and comply with Mark's wishes.

It is clear that telepathy with Mark or any other person can be ruled out as the source for the information about G22. Would it have been possible for Sandy to have acquired the information through other advanced psi abilities—such as clairvoyance—without any help from George or Walter? Without diminishing the significance or emotional impact of this reading, I want to shed light on the difficulty of answering this question definitively.

The initial details that Sandy provided at the first reading could theoretically have been accessed through telepathy or clairvoyance—the information was in Mark's mind, and the photo was at a location. The more-difficult piece to attribute to Sandy's ESP is "G22." But by the time it came through to her, Sandy already knew a certain amount about George. It is conceivable that G22 could have just popped into her psychic field, out of the so-called psychic reservoir, without her knowing what it was, because of her focus on George. If George was buried at this location, perhaps she could have psychically picked that up without knowing it.

But we have no way of proving that George actually is buried at plot G22 in Pozières. Mark was convinced that he was, the final nail in George's coffin being when George told Sandy the name of the person in the next grave. Short of exhuming the grave and doing a DNA test—and there would not likely be any DNA to compare it to, unless there was something left from Walter—there will never be a way to scientifically verify that this G22 belongs to George. But clearly if there was no connection between George and G22, it seems unlikely that Sandy would have perceived that perplexing message repeatedly with such intensity. No matter its source, it was loaded with significance, and it seems unlikely that G22 could have referred to anything else other than this grave.

This is what's important: If George is buried there, Sandy received information that is not available in the mind of anyone on the planet, ruling out telepathy with the living. This means that if the information did come from Sandy's living-agent psi, the only other option would be the use of her clairvoyance to find a grave designation having characteristics that would make sense for George.

If this was the method used, it would have required an extraordinary ability to string together information leading to a satisfactory result. First, she would have to learn telepathically that Mark had come to her for help in finding George. She would have had to use telepathy further to learn from Mark's mind that George died in a specific location (Pozières, France). Then she could clairvoyantly locate the most likely nearby cemetery (the Pozières British Cemetery). She would also telepathically need to acquire when George died (Mark thought it was July 16, 1916), which contradicted the information she provided that the death was on Mark's anniversary (July 19). If human psi is really unlimited, Sandy could then have used her clairvoyance to psychically access the website for the cemetery, locate the grave database, and search the 1,382 unnamed graves—all of this with unconscious clairvoyance, using only her mind. Or perhaps she could clairvoyantly read a hard-copy printout of the database at the cemetery, if it exists. Either way, she would then have to find an unnamed grave associated with deaths from July 15 to 19, 1916. All of this would have to be done almost instantaneously during the reading. Then later, she would have to use a similar faculty to find the name on the adjacent tombstone.

The extreme level of clairvoyance required makes this explanation hard to swallow. But according to the assumption of unlimited psi within the LAP hypothesis, if the information exists in any location on the planet, it in principle could be accessible through a medium's clairvoyance, no matter how convoluted the psychic journey to retrieve it or how many different sources are required. On the other hand, if Sandy received the information from George, one could argue that this transmission was much more straightforward: from a non-local dimension, George, the only "person" who knew his final resting place, could use his psi to transmit "G22" to Sandy. Of course this requires us to accept the assumption that a disembodied consciousness can communicate with us with psi abilities comparable to ours.

This is simply an illustration of our inability to prove that information is being delivered from deceased people *even if we can rule out telepathy* completely. We simply don't know enough about how these refined processes work. This does not by any means rule out the possibility of communication with those who have survived death, which many theorists believe is the simpler and more likely deduction in cases such as this. It simply illustrates our inability to definitively prove it.

For Mark, why should anything else make sense, and why should he be interested in such an abstract alternative analysis anyway? His search for George is now over, and that's what matters.

The survivalist interpretation is certainly a rational one. But beyond that, as I learned in my own readings with Laura and Sandra, there is nothing like the experience of an accurate reading to convince one of its validity. There is so much more that comes through than hard cold facts, which can't be communicated through analysis, as there was for Mark. And certainly Mark's strong desire for resolution and his inner connection to George would impact his relationship to the reading. In any case, as mediumship readings go, this one was extraordinary. And, if one feels with intuitive certainty that a loved one was present, then why wouldn't one accept that as real? The meaning—even the reality—of an experience can be determined only by the experiencer. Mark was able to resolve a lifelong need to find his great-uncle George this way. Others are deeply comforted by an evidential reading in which they become convinced that their recently lost loved one has survived and simply entered another dimension. This is ultimately the value of mental mediumship.

And, we must remember that mediumship is just one aspect of a larger picture pointing toward survival, which includes children with past-life memories and those convinced they have glimpsed the other side in near-death or actual-death experiences. Certainly the possibility that we can communicate with a nonlocal consciousness is now solidly conceivable, and something wonderful to contemplate.

Chapter 17

Trance Mediumship and Drop-in Communicators

By Alan Gauld, PhD, DLitt

The evidence I received in my two readings, and even the G22 given to Mark, pales in comparison to what has been provided by some of the best historical mediums on record. Using a deeper form of mediumship, these mediums would go into a "trance" and allow one consistent deceased communicator to speak directly through their vocal cords. This "control personality" would deliver information from other deceased people, with them in their world. As an analogy, this would mean that rather than Sandy telling Mark what George was saying, her regular control would speak directly to Mark through her body while she remained temporarily unconscious. With George right there with the control, Mark could have a two-way conversation with him in great detail, and observe his characteristic style, language, and sense of humor. The process is not just receptive, like the mental mediumship readings described so far, but it can be interactive. Sadly, I don't know of any trance mediums available today at the exceptional level of those so well studied and documented during decades past, but I suspect that there still are such mediums.

Some of the most intriguing evidence for survival is presented in this chapter by one of the leading scholars and most distinguished researchers in the field. Born in 1932, Alan Gauld is a retired Reader in Psychology, School of Psychology, University of Nottingham in the UK. He spent a postgraduate year at Harvard and then he principally taught biological psychology and neuropsychology at Nottingham. He is the author of Poltergeists (1979) *with Tony Cornell,* Mediumship and Survival: A Century of Investigations (1983), *and* A History of Hypnotism (1992), *among other works. Gauld is a past president of the Society for Psychical Research and has received multiple awards for his research in parapsychology. This chapter was culled from* Mediumship and Survival—*one of the best works ever on this topic that I encourage everyone to read in full—with his permission and review.*

It is not uncommon for persons who have had successful sittings with mental mediums to say afterward something like this: "Here is a transcript of the tape recording with my comments. There were a good many excellent 'hits.' But simply reading the record can give you no idea of just how convincing the communicator really was. So much of the impression he made was due not to what he said, but to the way he said it, to his tone of voice, characteristic humor, to his mannerisms and gestures. They were so completely right!"

These impressions are generated most convincingly by "trance" mediumship, which I consider to be the most "advanced" form of mental mediumship. Here the medium's normal personality, as it were, is completely dispossessed by an intruding intelligence, which achieves a varying degree of control over the medium's speech, writing, and entire neuromuscular apparatus. The medium herself usually retains little or no recollection of what has been said or done in her "absence," while she was in trance. She may feel herself to be overshadowed, influenced, gradually "taken over" by another personality, while her own awareness of her surroundings progressively diminishes. With repetition, the passage to full trance becomes quicker and easier.

The fullest manifestations of the personalities of ostensibly deceased persons have often been obtained through trance mediums, and qualified psychical researchers have shown a corresponding interest in collecting detailed records of this kind of mediumship.

Usually there will be only a few deceased persons who can ostensibly speak through the medium's vocal apparatus directly, while she is unconscious during the trance state. They are generally referred to as "controls." Controls will often relay messages from other deceased persons, called "communicators," with whom they purport to be in touch. (Use of these terms must not be held to imply a belief that the "controls" and "communicators" are anything other than aspects of the medium's own personality; I shall therefore hold myself excused from too frequent a use of such phrases as "ostensible communicator," "alleged control," etc.)

If one had to identify a person whose body one could not see by conversing with him over a somewhat noisy telephone line, one could not identify him unless, for example, he could remember certain things that he ought to be able to remember if he is the person he purports to be; and unless he exhibited certain motives and purposes, skills and personality characteristics known to be his; and so forth. Without these kinds of evidence, one would have no grounds at all for supposing that some human beings may in some sense survive the dissolution of their bodies.

But trance mediumship can add something further through the direct manifestation of the communicator as opposed to the medium simply relaying messages to the sitter like a telephone operator. In the published records, one finds various controls who achieved remarkable verisimilitude in mannerisms, turns of speech, etc. In none of these instances had the mediums any knowledge of the communicators in life as would account for the accuracy of the dramatizations. But it is exceedingly difficult to pin down these characteristic touches in terms that would carry conviction to outsiders. If we are to assume that the medium is acquiring her factual information solely from the living through her powers of ESP, we have now to credit her with the ability to incorporate this assembly of facts into a convincing dramatic representation of the so-called communicator. And this is to credit her with a further kind of unusual gift.

Mrs. Piper

Trance medium Leonora E. Piper (1857–1950) of Boston, Massachusetts, was studied so extensively that the few volumes of case records are still unsurpassed in quantity and detail. She is also one of the very few mediums whose trance speech and writings have been subjected to a serious and extensive psychological analysis.

Mrs. Piper was "discovered" for psychical research by William James of Harvard University, arguably the greatest psychologist of that or perhaps any time. James was sufficiently impressed by his sittings to send some twenty-five other persons to her under pseudonyms. In the spring of 1886 he wrote an account of the results and stated, "I am persuaded of the medium's honesty, and of the genuineness of her trance; . . . I now believe her to be in possession of a power as yet unexplained."

The general procedure at a sitting would be this: Mrs. Piper would pass into a trance. There was never the least doubt that the trance state was, in some sense, "genuine"—William James and G. Stanley Hall, another well-known American psychologist, demonstrated that Mrs. Piper could be cut, blistered, pricked, and undisturbed by a bottle of strong ammonia held under her nose. (The tests were so stringent that Mrs. P. complained bitterly about their painful aftereffects.)

After a few minutes, Mrs. Piper would begin to speak with the voice of her control, who gave the name of "Dr. Phinuit." A soi-disant French doctor with scanty knowledge of the French language, Phinuit spoke in a gruff, male voice and made use of Frenchisms, slang, and swearwords, in a manner quite unlike that of the awake Mrs. Piper. Phinuit would give sitters accounts of the appearances and activities of deceased (and sometimes also of living) friends and relations, and would transmit messages from them, often with appropriate gestures.

On an off day, Phinuit would ramble, flounder hopelessly, and fish for information, and if given any, would blatantly serve it up again as though it had been his own discovery. But when he was on form he could, with hardly any hesitation, relay copious communications from the deceased friends and relatives of sitters, communications that would turn out to be very accurate even in tiny details, and far too accurate for the hypothesis of chance or of guesswork based simply on the appearance of the unnamed sitters, to seem in the remotest degree plausible.

As a result of a report by William James, a leading member of the British Society for Psychical Research (SPR) and an expert in the unmasking of fraud, Richard Hodgson (1855–1905), went to Boston in 1887 and assumed charge of the investigation of Mrs. Piper. He arranged for the careful recording of all sittings, and took the most extensive precautions against trickery. Sitters were introduced anonymously or under false names, and were drawn from as wide a range of persons as possible. For some weeks Mrs. Piper was shadowed by detectives to ascertain whether she made inquiries into the affairs of possible sitters, or employed agents to do so. She was brought to England where she knew no one and could have had no established agents; her sittings were arranged and supervised by leading members of the SPR. Sitters were for the most part introduced anonymously, and comprehensive records were kept. And still Mrs. Piper continued to get results.

The thought of fraud was never far from Mrs. Piper's early investigators. The case against it was powerfully summarized in 1889 by Frank Podmore, a highly skeptical writer, who points out that despite careful overseeing amounting at times to invasion of privacy, Mrs. Piper had never once been detected being dishonest. Yet successful communicators often addressed sitters in exactly the right tone, and might unmistakably refer to trivialities of a wholly private significance. The charge of credulity, said Podmore, rested with those who, without consideration and without inquiry, could lightly attribute all the results to imposture.

In the spring of 1892, Dr. Phinuit was gradually superseded by another control, who, whatever his ultimate nature, was at least not fictitious. This was George Pellew, a young man of literary and philosophical interests who had been killed in New York a few weeks previously. He was known to Hodgson, and five years before had had, under a pseudonym, a single sitting with Mrs. Piper.

Pellew first manifested at a sitting to which Hodgson brought a close friend of his (Pellew's). Then and thereafter the George Pellew control and communicator (GP) showed a most detailed acquaintance with the affairs of the living Pellew. Out of a hundred and fifty sitters who were introduced to him, GP recognized twenty-nine of the thirty who had been known to the living Pellew (the thirtieth, whom he recognized after an initial failure, was a childhood friend who had "grown up" in the interval). He conversed with each of them in an appropriate manner, and showed an intimate knowledge of their concerns, and of his own supposed past relationships with them. Only rarely did GP slip up badly, as he sometimes did when discussing, for instance, the philosophical questions that had so much interested Pellew in life. During the period of GP's ascendancy, Hodgson became convinced (he had not previously been so) that Mrs. Piper's controls and communicators were, at least in many cases, what they claimed to be, namely the surviving spirits of formerly incarnate human beings.

GP remained the principal communicator until early in 1897 (during this period Hodgson continued to keep very full records). In 1905 Hodgson died, and, predictably, he too then became one of Mrs. Piper's controls. The purported communications from him were discussed in an interesting paper by William James. Mrs. Piper's trance mediumship ended in 1911, perhaps in consequence of the harsh treatment that she received at the hands of two American psychologists, G. Stanley Hall and Amy Tanner.

When pushed to its limits, the preferred counterhypothesis to the survivalistic one is that mediums' information can be more simply and satisfactorily explained in terms of ESP by living persons. Since we do not know the limits of ESP we can never say for certain that ESP of the extraordinary extent that would often be necessary—

"super-ESP"—is actually impossible. This is the central dilemma in the interpretation of ostensible evidence for survival.

Sometimes it seems that the hypothesis of telepathy between the medium and persons present at the sitting is the most obvious one. For instance, the world-renowned British physicist Sir Oliver Lodge, a pioneer in the science and technology that led to the development of radio, also tested Mrs. Piper. He gave Dr. Phinuit a chain, entrusted to him by a gentleman abroad, that had belonged to that gentleman's father. Phinuit produced a large number of facts and purported facts concerning the father, which Lodge then transmitted to the son. The son replied, according to Lodge, that Mrs. Piper's reading "recognizes the correctness of those things which I knew, and it asserts the total incorrectness of those things of which I was ignorant. So far as this series of facts goes, therefore, the hypothesis of a direct thought-transferential means of obtaining information is immensely strengthened." The only accurate information Mrs. Piper provided was what was already in the mind of the proxy sitter, the son.

The theory of telepathy between medium and sitters has thus in certain cases a good deal of plausibility, but just how far can we push it? On December 8, 1893, the Reverend and Mrs. S. W. Sutton of Athol Center, Massachusetts, had the first of two readings with Mrs. Piper, introduced under the pseudonym of "Smith." They had recently lost their young daughter Katherine, nicknamed Kakie. With a practiced note-taker acting as recorder, Mrs. Piper went into trance. Her control Phinuit then spoke and sometimes gesticulated on behalf of a child communicator. The following is an excerpt from the transcript of the session, with annotations in brackets added afterward by Mrs. Sutton, the child's mother:

> Phinuit said: . . . A little child is coming to you . . . He reaches out his hands as to a child, and says coaxingly: Come here, dear. Don't be afraid. Come, darling, here is your mother. He describes the child and her "lovely curls." Where is Papa? Want Papa. [He (i.e., Phinuit) takes from the table a silver medal.] I

want this—want to bite it. [She used to bite it.] [Reaches for
a string of buttons.] Quick! I want to put them in my mouth.
[The buttons also. To bite the buttons was forbidden. He exactly
imitated her arch manner.] . . . Who is Dodo? [Her name for
her brother, George.] . . . I want you to call Dodo. Tell Dodo
I am happy. Cry for me no more. [Puts hands to throat.] No
sore throat anymore. [She had pain and distress of the throat
and tongue.] Papa, speak to me. Can you not see me? I am not
dead, I am living. I am happy with Grandma. [My mother
had been dead many years.] Phinuit says: Here are two more.
One, two, three here,—one older and one younger than Kakie.
[Correct.] . . .

Was this little one's tongue very dry? She keeps showing me
her tongue. [Her tongue was paralyzed, and she suffered much
with it to the end.] Her name is Katherine. [Correct.] She calls
herself Kakie. She passed out last. [Correct.] Where is horsey?
[I gave him a little horse.] Big horsey, not this little one. [Prob-
ably refers to a toy cart-horse she used to like.] Papa, want to go
wide [ride] horsey. [She pled this all through her illness.] . . .

[I asked if she remembered anything after she was brought
downstairs.] I was so hot, my head was so hot. [Correct] . . . Do
not cry for me—that makes me sad. Eleanor. I want Eleanor.
[Her little sister. She called her much during her last illness.]
I want my buttons. Row, row,—my song,—sing it now. I sing
with you. [We sing, and a soft child voice sings with us.]

Lightly row, lightly row,
O'er the merry waves we go,
Smoothly glide, smoothly glide,
With the ebbing tide.
[Phinuit hushes us, and Kakie finishes alone.]
Let the wind and waters be
Mingled with our melody,
Sing and float, sing and float,
In our little boat.

. . . Kakie sings: Bye, bye, ba bye, bye, bye, O baby bye. Sing that with me. Papa. [Papa and Kakie sing. These two were the songs she used to sing.] Where is Dinah? I want Dinah. [Dinah was an old black rag-doll, not with us.] I want Bagie [Her name for her sister Margaret.] I want Bagie to bring me my Dinah . . . Tell Dodo when you see him that I love him. Dear Dodo. He used to march with me, he put me way up. [Correct.]

Remarkable though this excerpt is (not more remarkable, however, than the full transcripts of the two sittings, which are, incidentally, documents of social as well as psychical interest), no information was communicated that lay outside the knowledge of the sitters. Does this mean, then, that we can comfortably attribute all Mrs. Piper's "hits" here to telepathy with the sitters?

I know of no instance of undeniable telepathy between living persons, or for that matter of any other variety of ESP, in which the flow of paranormally acquired information has been so quick, so copious, and so free from error. And there is the question of the point of view from which the information is presented. Mrs. Piper would have had to obtain parents'-eye information about Kakie from the sitters, and then with a fair degree of dramatic skill have constructed a Kakie's-eye view of the same facts. Furthermore, incidents at both sittings apparently showed associations that seemed to be in the mind of the child, but that did not awaken the corresponding associations in the minds of the sitters. For instance, when Kakie asked for "horsey," and was given a little toy horse, she said "Big horsey, not this little one." Mrs. Sutton surmised that she referred to another toy horse that she used to like. At the second sitting Kakie requested the horse again, but when given the little horse, said, "No, that is not the one. The big horse—so big. [Phinuit shows how large.] Eleanor's horse. Eleanor used to put it in Kakie's lap. She loved that horsey." It was only these additional particulars that made it clear to Mrs. Sutton which horse was requested—one that was packed away and forgotten in another city.

In a later passage from the first sitting, Kakie asked for "the little book." Her mother supposed that she meant a linen picture book. At the second sitting it became clear that what was intended was a little prayer book that had been read to Kakie just before her death, and then put in her hands. If we are to say that Mrs. Piper could select from the sitters' minds associations conflicting with the ones consciously present and utilize them in order to create the impression that the communicator's thoughts moved along lines distinctively different from the sitter's, we are beginning to attribute to her not just super-ESP but super-artistry as well.

The theory of telepathy from the sitters is, of course, manifestly ruled out when correct information is given that is not at the time known to any sitter. Incidents of this kind are sprinkled throughout the Piper records (and throughout the records of various other mediums too). One example is the case of Sir Oliver Lodge's uncle Jerry, which took place during Mrs. Piper's visit to England in the winter of 1889–90. Sir Oliver Lodge's summary of it is as follows:

> It happens that an uncle of mine in London [Uncle Robert], now
> quite an old man, had a twin brother who died some twenty
> or more years ago. I interested him generally in the subject,
> and wrote to ask if he would lend me some relic of his brother.
> By morning post on a certain day I received a curious old gold
> watch, which his brother had worn . . . I handed it to Mrs. Piper
> when in a state of trance.
>
> I was told almost immediately that it had belonged to one of
> my uncles . . . After some difficulty . . . Dr. Phinuit caught the
> name Jerry . . . and said . . . "This is my watch, and Robert is my
> brother, and I am here. Uncle Jerry, my watch." . . . I pointed out
> to him that to make Uncle Robert aware of his presence it would
> be well to recall trivial details of their boyhood . . .
>
> "Uncle Jerry" recalled episodes such as swimming the creek
> when they were boys together, and running some risk of getting
> drowned; killing a cat in Smith's field; the possession of a small
> rifle, and of a long peculiar skin, like a snake-skin, which he
> thought was now in the possession of Uncle Robert.

All these facts have been more or less completely verified. But the interesting thing is that his twin brother, from whom I got the watch, and with whom I was thus in a sort of communication, could not remember them all.

He recollected something about swimming the creek, though he himself had merely looked on. He had a distinct recollection of having had the snake-skin, and of the box in which it was kept, though he does not know where it is now. But he altogether denied killing the cat, and could not recall Smith's field.

His memory, however, is decidedly failing him, and he was good enough to write to another brother, Frank, living in Cornwall, an old sea captain, and ask if he had any better remembrance of certain facts—of course not giving any inexplicable reason for asking. The result of this inquiry was triumphantly to vindicate the existence of Smith's field . . . , and the killing of a cat by another brother was also recollected; while of the swimming of the creek, near a mill-race, full details were given, Frank and Jerry being the heroes of that foolhardy episode.

It should be noted that Uncle Frank could not remember the snakeskin; so that if Mrs. Piper got all this information by telepathy, she must have ransacked the memory stores of two separate individuals and collated the results.

Mrs. Leonard's Book Tests

The remarkable British medium Mrs. Gladys Osborne Leonard (1882–1968) made a specialty of giving correct information that was not known to any person present at the sitting. A young girl named Feda was her chief control. Feda purported to be the spirit of an Indian girl whom an ancestor of Mrs. Leonard had married in the early nineteenth century. She spoke in a high-pitched voice, with occasional grammatical errors and misunderstandings of word meanings. Feda regarded Mrs. Leonard with something between tolerance and amused contempt, and would sometimes cause her embarrassment; for example, by soliciting small presents, which she thereafter fiercely insisted were her own and not Mrs. Leonard's.

Like Mrs. Piper, Mrs. Leonard was quite prepared to submit herself to critical investigation by members of the SPR, and she too was shadowed by detectives. The first parapsychologist to study her in detail was Sir Oliver Lodge, whose book *Raymond,* describing communications from a son killed in the war, made her famous. She continued to be regularly studied by SPR investigators from then until the early years after World War II.

Certain aspects of Mrs. Leonard's mediumship are not easy to reconcile with anything much less than a form of the super-ESP hypothesis, which allows the medium potential extrasensory access to any identifying detail whatsoever relating to any living or recently dead person in the whole of the Western world. She had remarkable successes (or Feda had remarkable successes) in this regard with "book tests" and "proxy sittings."

A book test worked as follows: A communicator, usually passing the message through Feda, had to specify a page number; the location of the book on a given shelf; the house presumably, or usually, well known to the ostensible communicator. A sentence was found by the sitter on that page that conveyed a message relevant to what had once been said or was appropriate to the past connection of the sitter and the communicator. Since the book chosen need not have been one known to the sitter, *or indeed known in the requisite detail to anyone living,* it is plain, as Lodge says, that "no simple kind of mind-reading can be appealed to or regarded as a rational explanation." Many successful book tests were carried out and studied.

One example involves communicator Edward Wyndham Tennant ("Bim"), a young officer killed on the Somme in 1916. The sitting was held on December 17, 1917.

> Feda: "Bim now wants to send a message to his father. This book
> is particularly for his father; underline that, he says. It is the
> ninth book on the third shelf counting from left to right in the

bookcase on the right of the door in the drawing-room as you enter; take the title, and look at page 37."

We found the ninth book in the shelf indicated was: *Trees* [by J. Harvey Kelman].

And on page 36, quite at the bottom and leading on to page 37, we read:

"Sometimes you will see curious marks in the wood; these are caused by a tunneling beetle, very injurious to the trees . . ."

(Signatures of two testificators to the finding and verifying of this Book-Message.)

GLEN CONNER
DAVID TENNANT

Bim's father was intensely interested in forestry; and his obsession with "the beetle" was a family joke. Thus the message was particularly appropriate, and the bookshelf from which it had been culled was one known to the alleged communicator.

In another case, an anonymous sitter (Mrs. Talbot) received through Feda a message from her late husband advising her to look for a relevant message on page twelve or thirteen of a book in her home bookcase. Feda said the book was not printed, but had writing in it; was dark in color; and contained a table of Indo-European, Aryan, Semitic, and Arabian languages, whose relationships were shown by a diagram of radiating lines. Mrs. Talbot knew of no such book, and ridiculed the message. However, when she eventually looked, she found at the back of a top shelf a shabby black leather notebook of her husband's. Pasted into this book was a folded table of all the languages mentioned; while on page thirteen was an extract from a book entitled *Post Mortem*. In this case the message related to a book unknown to medium and sitter (indeed, so far as could be told, to any living person), but undoubtedly known to the communicator.

These two book tests might be thought to constitute rather striking evidence for survival. Mind reading does not seem a likely explanation, for it was highly improbable that the requisite information was possessed in sufficient detail by any living person. On the other hand, the existence of the books, and of the relevant passages, could have been, and in the second case certainly was, known to the alleged communicator.

Unfortunately the results of many other book tests serve only to confuse the issue: not because they were unsuccessful, but because they were too successful. For the communicators proved equally able to transmit information relating to the contents of books deliberately placed on shelves in houses unknown to them; books, furthermore, having for them no special significance. On the face of it this would imply that the communicators got their knowledge of the contents of these books by clairvoyance (the books, of course, all being closed). Feda certainly talks as though the communicators were independent entities who homed in on the test bookshelves, scanned the books for appropriate passages, and then returned to relay the results through her. But if these communicators could exercise clairvoyance of such remarkable degree, why should not Feda? Why should not Mrs. Leonard herself? In some cases, correct information was apparently given about the contents of books in classical Greek; yet neither Mrs. Leonard, nor the sitter, nor the alleged communicator knew classical Greek, while the person who lent the books (Mrs. Salter), though she knew Greek, had not properly studied several of the volumes. Neither telepathy with the living, nor communication with the dead, nor yet clairvoyance, would seem to supply us with an adequate explanation here.

Still, if we grant for the sake of argument that the books were in some sense open to clairvoyant inspection by an agency other than that of the communicator, there remains the problem of how, from this mass of potentially available material, just those passages were so often selected that were particularly appropriate as messages from the communicator to the particular living recipient. Who selected for Bim's father the passage about the beetle damaging trees? To select a passage as appropriate as this, the medium would have had, e.g., to tap Bim's father's mind, and then, in the light of information tele-pathically gained from it, select that one of the very numerous book passages clairvoyantly accessible to her that would be most likely to impress Bim's family as a message of a kind he might plausibly address to his father.

Proxy Sitters

To remove the sitter even further from the medium, a "proxy sitting" can be used. A sitter goes to the medium on behalf of a third party, about whom both he and the medium know as little as possible. If "evidential" communications are then received, the explanation can hardly be laid at the door of telepathy with persons present. Usually the third party, or absent principal, desires communications from a particular deceased person who has in some way or another to be contacted. To achieve this the proxy sitter may give the medium carefully circumscribed details (e.g., name, identifying phrase) of the desired communicator, or may bring some relic of his to serve as a "token object"; or he may privately appeal to him, or concentrate upon him, before the sitting; or he may request his own "spirit guides" to act as intermediaries. Many proxy cases went on for several sittings.

The best known of all proxy sittings is without doubt the numerous sittings with Mrs. Leonard at which Miss Nea Walker and the Reverend C. Drayton Thomas acted as proxies. These sittings were usually, although not always, the outcome of letters from bereaved, sometimes despairing, parents or spouses.

Drayton Thomas's remarkable "Bobbie Newlove" case extended over eleven sittings. Bobbie was a boy of ten who had died of diphtheria. He proved a fluent communicator through Feda, who made unmistakable references to such details as a dog-shaped saltcellar he had owned, a jack-of-hearts costume he had once worn, visits to a chemical laboratory with his grandfather, gymnastic apparatus that he had set up in his room and exercises carried out therewith, a girl skater of whom he was fond, an injury to his nose, and the topography of his hometown (including place-names). Most curious of all, Bobbie repeatedly insisted, speaking through Feda, that some weeks before his death his constitution had been undermined by contact with "poisonous pipes," and that this had lowered his resistance to the diphtheria. In connection with the pipes he talked of cattle, a sort of barn, and running water. This meant nothing to his family, but upon investigation some water pipes around which he had played with a friend were discovered. The locality answered the description given, and it is possible that Bobbie had drunk bad water there.

In another case, Drayton Thomas was asked by Professor E. R. Dodds, well known as a critic of the evidence for survival, to attempt to contact a certain Frederic William Macaulay on behalf of Macaulay's daughter, Mrs. Lewis. During five sittings in which Thomas served as a proxy, distinctive references were made to Macaulay's work as a hydraulic engineer. The following passages refer to more personal matters. Macaulay's daughter Mrs. Lewis later made annotations to these notes in square brackets.

FEDA: There is a John and Harry, both with him. And Race . . . Rice . . . Riss . . . it might be Reece but sounds like Riss, and Francis. These are all names of people who are connected with him or linked up with him in the past, connected with happy times. I get the feeling of an active and busy home in which he was rather happy.

[This is a very curious passage . . . Probably the happiest time of my father's life was in the four or five years before the war, when we, his five children, were all at school, and the home was packed with our friends during the holidays. John, Harry, and Francis could be three of these . . . But the most interesting passage is "It might be Reece but it sounds like Riss" . . . My elder brother was at school at Shrewsbury and there conceived a kind of hero-worship for one of the "Tweaks" (sixth-form boys) whose name was Rees. He wrote home about him several times and always drew attention to the fact that the name was spelled "Rees" and not "Reece." In the holidays my sister and I used to tease him by singing "Not Reece but Riss" until my father stopped us . . .]

FEDA: I get a funny word now . . . could he be interested

in . . . baths of some kind? Ah, he says I have got the right word, baths. He spells it, BATHS. His daughter will understand, he says. It is not something quite ordinary, but feels something special.

[This is, to me, the most interesting thing that has yet emerged. Baths were always a matter of joke in our family—my father being very emphatic that water must not be wasted by our having too big baths or by leaving taps dripping. It is difficult to explain how intimate a detail this seems . . . The mention of baths here also seems to me an indication of my father's quaint humor, a characteristic which has hitherto been missing . . .]

FEDA: . . . Godfrey; will you ask the daughter if she remembers someone called Godfrey. That name is a great link with old times.

[My father's most trusted clerk, one who specially helped in the hydraulic research, was called William Godfrey. He was with my father for years and I remember him from almost my earliest childhood . . .]

FEDA: What is that? . . . Peggy . . . Peggy . . . Puggy . . . he is giving me a little name like Puggy or Peggy. Sounds like a special name, a little special nickname, and I think it is something his daughter would know . . .

[My father sometimes called me "pug-nose" or "Puggy."]

Altogether, 124 items of information were given, of which 51 were classified as right, 12 as good, 32 as fair, 2 as poor, 22 as doubtful, and 5 as wrong. Dodds, the instigator of this experiment, remarks: "It appears to me that the hypotheses of fraud, rational influence from disclosed facts, telepathy from the actual sitter, and coincidence cannot either singly or in combination account for the results obtained."

Many of the details given in these two proxy cases could be verified only by consulting the memories of friends and relatives of the deceased persons; there were, so far as we know, no pictures, no records, written or printed, and no other physical state of affairs that, clairvoyantly perceived, might have yielded the information. Often there was no single living person who possessed all the information. In the Bobbie Newlove case some of the relevant information (about the pipes and their location) was not known to any member of the communicator's family. We are forced to attribute its production either to telepathy between Mrs. Leonard and Bobbie's one friend who played with him around the pipes, or to clairvoyant scanning of the neighborhood plus skillful guessing about Bobbie's likely habits. We would on the ESP (or super-ESP) hypothesis have to postulate that Mrs. Leonard located (telepathically or clairvoyantly) two separate sources of information, tapped them, and collated and synthesized the results.

An obvious underlying problem that successful proxy sittings present for the ESP hypothesis is of course that of *how* the medium manages to locate (telepathically or clairvoyantly) sources of information appropriate to the case in hand. These sources are remote from the sitting and the sitter, to whom the very existence of some of them is likely to be unknown. We might propose that the medium learns from the sitter's mind the identity of his principal (the person for whom he is acting as proxy), and that this somehow enables her to home in on the mind of the principal; from the mind of the principal further clues to other sources of information may be obtained; and so on. One has only to ask oneself what would be involved here to see that the proposed process is grotesquely implausible.

It must be added, of course, that the survivalist theory too must cope with the problem of how Feda managed to locate Bobbie Newlove, F. W. Macaulay, etc., on the "other side" in order to extract evidential messages from them. Did she do it by ESP? Certainly she often spoke as though her awareness of communicators was of a fluctuating and uncertain kind. However, if there is "another world" to which our spirits pass at death, it is perhaps reasonable to suppose that it contains some form of established communication network or heavenly post office directory.

In some proxy cases the principals have felt the messages received contained not just correct information, but hints of the personal characteristics (humor, interests, turns of phrase, and so forth) of the ostensible communicators. If they are correct in this, we have additionally to attribute to the medium the power to glean the relevant facts and then, instead of presenting them in statement form ("He had a dry sense of humor"), to enact them in dramatic form by reproducing the communicator's characteristic dry humor (or whatever it may be). Certainly the more numerous the unusual gifts we have to attribute to mediums in order to support the super-ESP hypothesis, the more cumbersome that hypothesis becomes.

Drop-in Communicators

Even in successful proxy sittings, there is still—it is often, however implausibly, argued—some kind of link between the medium and some absent person or persons possessing the relevant information. However, in another class of cases, even those tenuous and exceedingly ill-defined links are absent. The class concerned is that labeled by Dr. Ian Stevenson as "drop-in" communicators—communicators who arrive unexpectedly and uninvited, and are ostensibly unknown to medium and sitters. We have on record a number of cases in which drop-in communicators have made statements about themselves and their careers that have subsequently proved possible to verify, showing they once were real people who had died in the past, unbeknownst to the medium or any of the sitters.

Such cases are of obvious interest and their potential theoretical implications are, in general, hostile to the super-ESP hypothesis, and favorable to some form of survival theory. Why, in any verified drop-in case, should the medium's supposed ESP have lit upon facts about that particular deceased person, who has no connection to her or the sitters? The facts about the great majority of drop-in communicators are not in any way especially eye-catching; nor have medium and sitters any special motive for desiring information about that particular deceased person. Most come from the medium's own country and speak her own language. But these constraints aside, we seem reduced, on the super-ESP hypothesis, to supposing that selection of communicator depends upon the random operation of wholly unknown factors.

In most drop-in cases there is some single possible source, such as a printed record, or the organized memory system of a living person, from which the medium could through her supposed extrasensory powers have obtained the whole of her information. But what if (and some cases may at least approximate to this type) the requisite information could have been assembled only through the tapping of a number of discrete sources; e.g., the memories of several different persons or a variety of printed records? How is the medium, having selected the deceased person she will present to her sitters, to discriminate from among all the innumerable items of information telepathically and clairvoyantly available to her, those and only those that are relevant to that person? So far as I am aware we do not have, from outside the mediumistic situation, a single properly authenticated example of a clairvoyant managing to read a concealed passage of prose in anything like the necessary detail.

It is thus possible to construct an idealized drop-in case that pushes the super-ESP hypothesis to the verge of unintelligibility; indeed beyond that verge. Such a case would have the following features:

(a) The drop-in communicator in question would have a strong and comprehensible reason for wishing to communicate; a reason clearly stronger than any that the medium might have for wishing to contact him.

(b) The information that he communicates would be such that the medium could not have obtained it all by extrasensory contact with a single living person or document.

(c) We can be tolerably certain that the medium could not have obtained the information by ordinary means.

The survivalist theory has obvious advantages when it comes to explaining why the medium selects one unknown deceased person rather than another: the deceased person selects himself. As Stevenson remarks, "Some 'drop-in' communicators have explained their presence very well and their motivation to communicate is an important part of the whole case which has to be explained as well as the provenance of any information communicated." It is difficult indeed to decide how seriously communicators' own explanations of their presences ought to be taken; but sometimes at least the professed explanations are "in character."

Cases of verified drop-in communicators are fairly scarce in the "reputable" literature of psychical research; how far this reflects an overall scarcity it is hard to say. There are often pressures on those mediums investigated to exclude communicators other than those with whom the sitter wishes to speak. Also, the verification of drop-in cases requires a good deal of time, and, very often, a working knowledge of the country's public records system and access to a large library. Drop-in communicators of the utmost veridicality could march into and out of the average home circle without its occurring to anyone that it would be feasible to check up on them. And where such checks have been undertaken, they have often fallen far short of the required standard of thoroughness.

There is in the literature at least one carefully investigated case in which a drop-in communicator made a series of correct statements, the totality of which could not have been obtained either clairvoyantly from a single document, obituary, etc., or telepathically, from the mind of a single living person. I refer to the case of Runolfur Runolfsson ("Runki") of Iceland, for which the medium was Hafsteinn Bjornsson and the investigators were Erlendur Haraldsson and Ian Stevenson.

Between 1937 and 1938, in Reykjavik, the capital of Iceland, a highly eccentric communicator began to manifest through the entranced medium. He showed a yearning for snuff, coffee, and alcohol, refused to give his name, and kept reiterating that he was looking for his leg. Asked where his leg was, he replied, "in the sea."

In January 1939 Ludvik Gudmundsson, the owner of a fish factory in the village of Sandgerdi, about thirty-six miles from Reykjavik, joined the circle. The unknown communicator showed great interest in this new sitter, and eventually stated that his missing leg was in the latter's house at Sandgerdi. After a good deal of further pressure from the sitters, he made the following statement:

My name is Runolfur Runolfsson, and I was fifty-two years old
when I died. I lived with my wife at Kolga or Klappakot, near
Sandgerdi. I was on a journey from Keflavik [about six miles
from Sandgerdi] in the latter part of the day and I was drunk.
I stopped at the house of Sveinbjorn Thordarson in Sandgerdi
and accepted some refreshments there. When I went to go, the
weather was so bad that they did not wish me to leave unless
accompanied by someone else. I became angry and said I would
not go at all if I could not go alone. My house was only about
fifteen minutes' walk away. So I left by myself, but I was wet and
tired. I walked over the kambinn [pebbles] and reached the rock
known as Flankastadaklettur which has almost disappeared now.
There I sat down, took my bottle, and drank some more. Then I
fell asleep. The tide came in and carried me away. This happened
in October 1879. I was not found until January 1880. I was
carried in by the tide, but then dogs and ravens came and tore
me to pieces. The remnants [of my body] were found and buried
in Utskalar graveyard [about four miles from Sandgerdi]. But
then the thighbone was missing. It was carried out again to sea,
but was later washed up again at Sandgerdi. There it was passed
around and now it is in Ludvik's house.

The communicator also revealed that he had been a very tall man.
Runki's extraordinary tale was subsequently verified in considerable
detail, although it did not appear that he had in fact stopped at the
house of Sveinbjorn Thordarson. Ludvik knew nothing about any
thighbone in his house, but after inquiries among older local inhabi-
tants, he found that sometime in the 1920s such a bone, believed to
have been washed up by the sea, had been placed in an interior wall. It
was recovered, and turned out to be the femur of a very tall man. No
one knew whose bone it was, and there was no record that indicated
whether or not the thighbone was missing from Runki's remains. One
wonders, indeed, why, even if the deceased Runki were the source of
the communications, and even if the thighbone were actually his, he
should have had any special knowledge of the matter.

The remaining statements were nearly all verifiable from entries distributed between two manuscript sources, the church books of Utskalar (in the National Archives at Reykjavik), and the Reverend Sigurdur Sivertsen's *Annals of Sudurnes,* which rested unpublished and little known in the National Library at Reykjavik. That Runki had been tall was confirmed by his grandson, who, however, had not known him, and was not aware of the bone and of other relevant facts. He could therefore not have been, either through telepathy or through normal channels, a source for all the information communicated. It is possible that an editor who in 1953 prepared *Annals of Sudurnes* for publication was aware even in 1939 of the major details of the story, but he did not know about the bone. Nor did he meet Hafsteinn before 1940.

Haraldsson and Stevenson sum up the possibilities as follows:

> . . . it does not seem feasible to attribute all of this information to any single person or any single written source. And this would be true, we believe, whether the medium acquired the information normally or by extrasensory perception. We think, therefore, that some process of integration of details derived from different persons or other sources must be supposed in the interpretation of the case. It may be simplest to explain this integration as due to Runki's survival after his physical death with the retention of many memories and their subsequent communication through the mediumship of Hafsteinn. On the other hand, sensitives have been known to achieve remarkable feats of deriving and integrating information without the participation of any purported discarnate personality.

If communication between the living and the dead is possible, and can be carried on through the agency of mediums, we should expect to meet with drop-in communicators, for there must be many recently deceased persons who earnestly desire to send messages of comfort, reassurance, and advice to their bereaved relations. Had there been no records at all of verified drop-in communicators, the survivalist position would necessarily have been seriously weakened. As it is, the onus is still on the survivalist either to explain away, or else to present reasons for denying, the supposed fact that such cases are relatively rare.

Conclusion

To conclude, it seems to me that there is in each of the main areas I have considered a sprinkling of cases that rather forcefully suggest some form of survival. But what we know stands in proportion to what we do *not* know as a bucketful does to the ocean.

And even if one accepts that in the present state of our knowledge some sort of survival theory gives the readiest account of the observed phenomena, many issues remain undecided. In the vast majority even of favorable cases, the "surviving" personality that claims continuity with a formerly living, or previously incarnated, personality, is only able to demonstrate such apparent continuity on a very limited number of fronts, and may, indeed, markedly fail to demonstrate it on others. This does not, of course, mean that behind the observed manifestations there does not lie the fullest possible continuity; but equally it means that the hypothesis of complete continuity is unproven, and all sorts of possibilities remain open. Is there partial or complete survival? Sentient survival, or (far worse than mere extinction) survival with just a lingering, dim consciousness? Is there long-term survival or survival during a brief period of progressive disintegration? Is there enjoyable survival, or survival such as one would wish to avoid? Survival as an individual, or survival with one's individuality for the most part dissolved in something larger? Is survival the rule, or is it just a freak? To these and many other questions I can at the moment see no very clear answers.

I can only conclude that it is possible from a properly informed consideration of the evidence to build up a rational case for belief in some form of survival, and also a rational case against it. And a rational case, of either tendency, built on evidence, however difficult to interpret, is to be preferred to any amount of blind belief or blind disbelief.

Chapter 18

Seeking the White Crow

In the last chapter, Alan Gauld presented some of the most convincing cases from trance mediumship ever studied. The hypothesis that mental and trance mediumship can involve communications with deceased personalities is certainly plausible, even if impossible to prove. There are of course other compelling examples of mediums who allowed themselves to be subjected to strict controls and demonstrated similar capacities to Mrs. Piper and Mrs. Leonard.

Drop-in communicators—"spirit" entities who are completely unknown to the medium or sitters and simply show up uninvited—are especially evidential. Alan Gauld is a highly objective, meticulous investigator with decades of experience who tends to err on the side of caution in interpreting events occurring during sittings with mediums. (I am privileged to have had lengthy email discussions with Alan about many issues, including his own attendance at various sittings.) He stated in his chapter that drop-in cases that have been "solved"— meaning the personality providing information when dropping in has been shown to actually have lived on this earth—are "hostile to the super-ESP hypothesis, and favorable to some form of survival theory." There are not many cases like this that are on the record—although there are likely others that remain unknown—but it only takes one white crow to prove that not all crows are black.

In addition to being unconnected to the medium and the sitters, these uninvited communicators show up with a logical reason for wanting to communicate that serves only themselves, and not the people in the room. If the medium were using his or her "super-ESP," as Alan calls it—living-agent psi defined as unlimited—the facts of the communicator's life would often have to be culled from various types of sometimes obscure sources in multiple locations and pulled together to create the personality. The highly refined level of telepathy and clairvoyance needed to do this would be almost unimaginable. And for what reason? Even Stephen Braude, an expert on LAP, agrees with Alan Gauld. "Drop-in cases make particularly good sense in terms of the ostensible communicator's expressed motives for communicating," he says. "As a result, survivalist interpretations of those cases seem more parsimonious than their super-psi alternatives. Although the best cases are by no means coercive, the evidence for drop-ins, overall, seems to strengthen the case for survival."

The case of Runki's leg that Alan presented, investigated by University of Iceland psychologist Erlendur Haraldsson and psychiatrist Ian Stevenson, is a case in point. Haraldsson will describe another stunning case of a drop-in communicator—one I think is even stronger than Runki's leg—in his upcoming chapter about physical medium Indridi Indridason.

I also find it significant that some mental mediums are clear about the difference between the use of their LAP (receiving information from sources on earth) and survival psi (their receiving information from discarnates). Brain scans show that there is at least a difference between the two modalities by documenting that they operate from different parts of the brain. In the case of medium Laura Lynne Jackson, the location of the scans in her brain for each function corresponded to the side of her "inner screen" used to distinguish a psychic reading from one where the information is accessed "from the other side." Although the scan cannot tell us what the difference is between these two functions, they point toward the most highly developed mental mediumship—Laura being an exceptionally accurate medium—involving something else besides psychically acquired information, just as the mediums describe.

Evidence from verified past-life and intermission memories, and from varieties of near-death, actual-death, and end-of-life experiences, suggest that consciousness can function independently of the brain and may carry over from one life to the next. When all of this is considered together, with its different components interconnected and mutually supportive, our case for survival grows. The data all seems to point toward the same reality. Even Braude concludes after three hundred pages of discussion in *Immortal Remains*, "I think we can say, with little assurance but with some justification, that the evidence provides a reasonable basis for believing in personal postmortem survival." After the rigor of his analysis of the LAP hypothesis, this was a very welcome conclusion!

I am pausing here for a moment to reflect on the powerful evidence presented so far. But let us now take another step forward. I will pose the next question, which naturally follows the previous section: If disembodied entities can communicate through mediums to us here in the physical world, can these entities show themselves to us *directly,* by communicating without an intermediary? If they are really so close, capable, and aware that they can locate a medium linked to a sitter they once knew, why shouldn't they be able to manifest enough for us to see them or hear them ourselves, or be able to impact our environment in such a way that we can perceive their presence? We will now consider different types of communications that can come to us directly. For those on the receiving end of such transmissions, the impact often supersedes even the best reading with a medium. In the next chapter, I will share with the reader my own unexpected experiences, which occurred while I was researching this book.

Chapter 19

After-Death
Communications

I suspect that many of you have had experiences during which you felt that some kind of communication was occurring from a deceased friend or family member—or if not, you know someone else who has. Some people may be uncomfortable talking about these often strange events (as I am, although I'm biting that bullet by describing them here). "After-death communications" (ADCs) are spontaneous, personal signals perceived as coming from a departed loved one, which seem unmistakably clear and highly meaningful to the one receiving them. They are usually unasked for, and can arrive as a shock into the otherwise ordinary world of someone who may not even consider such things possible. At other times, they can come as a direct response to a request to receive a sign or physical manifestation from the deceased consciousness.

Because they come and go quickly, and are rarely documented,

ADCs are not evidential in a strict sense. Yet, these experiences can be the most potentially life-changing link to belief in survival for their recipients, because the messages can be so profoundly personal and specific. Many ADC experiencers are in a state of grief, full of longing for the departed person. It is reasonable to ask if the perceived communications are unconsciously self-generated in order to satisfy a psychological need—what could help more than a sign that their loved one has not really died? Perhaps ADCs are all unconscious manifestations through living-agent psi, having nothing to do with the perceived messenger. But some involve multiple recipients or highly unusual physical phenomena. And for the more powerful ones, the recipient has no doubt about where they are coming from. The reader can be the judge.

After-death communications manifest in many forms. There are "dream visits" that are unusually vivid and seem "real," which one never forgets; moving forms or apparitions; electrical effects on appliances, lights, radios, or computers (such as going on and off); movement of objects or the unexplainable appearance of a meaningful object; lights without any source; audible external voices or other sounds; smells related to the departed person; feeling a touch; or simply strongly sensing a presence.

Loyd Auerbach, parapsychologist and author of the next chapter on apparitions, lost a mentor, friend, and kindred spirit when Martin Caidin died on March 24, 1997. An aviation authority and pilot, Caidin wrote over fifty books including the novel *Cyborg*, the basis for the *Six Million Dollar Man* franchise. He also developed the ability to move objects with his mind (psychokinesis) and was very interested in the paranormal. Later in his life, he taught workshops and spoke about this interest, and Loyd began working with him then.

Nine days after Marty's death, Loyd was driving along a California freeway listening to the radio. Suddenly he sensed a presence in the car with him. Then his new car, which had always been smoke free, filled up with the strong smell of cigar smoke. There was no way to explain this, but Loyd knew what it was. He recognized the distinct smell of the type of cigar that Marty had often smoked in his presence, which lingered in the car for about five minutes. Loyd felt that his friend had come to say goodbye.

Later that morning, Loyd called a pilot friend of both his and Marty's who lives on the East Coast to tell him about the cigar smell in his car. But before he could say anything, the pilot told Loyd that he could hardly believe that Loyd was calling. He said that, around 10 a.m. EST, he felt a presence in the cockpit of his airplane followed by the smell of cigar smoke. Like Loyd, the pilot recognized this as Marty. The time of the two events coincided. And to make it even more remarkable, another pilot friend of Marty's had the same experience in his cockpit, a few minutes later.

None of these rational and competent professionals had any doubts that this was Marty visiting them. The fact that it happened three times, for three different people at almost the same time, is what makes the incident remarkable. Could all three have unconsciously created this experience themselves because they expected Marty to contact them? If so, it seems highly unlikely that the self-created sign would be identical for all three and that it would be experienced at the same time.

Jane Katra holds a PhD in public health, was a professor at the University of Oregon, and coauthored two books on nonlocal consciousness and healing with physicist Russell Targ, who was a pioneer in the development of the laser. In 2002, psychiatrist Elisabeth Targ, her close friend and Russell's daughter, died. Elisabeth had spent a decade at Stanford University, becoming a certified Russian translator and then earning her medical degree. In January 2002, she was awarded a National Institutes of Health grant of $1.5 million to carry out two distant-healing prayer studies, one on patients with glioblastoma multiforme, a rare and aggressive brain tumor. Two months later, Elisabeth received the devastating diagnosis of a fast-growing tumor of the same type she was about to study. She died at the age of forty, in Palo Alto, California.

Coming from a "science-minded family" of intellectuals, Jane did not accept that communications could come from someone who had died. That changed for her and others after Elisabeth seemingly sent so many messages and signs to such a range of people that the source of the communications became incontestable. Jane explains:

> I have been the recipient of or witness to over thirty surprising and spontaneous communications from Elisabeth. The most evidential ones were those received by more than one person at the same time; a communication in a foreign language unknown to the recipient; lights flashing on and off or books about healing moving themselves off shelves when people talked about her; messages to two people regarding serious health problems unknown to either of them; and a prediction wherein several people received different, incomplete communications, and when we put them together, they completed an idea.

One of the more striking examples occurred only a few days after the memorial service for Elisabeth. Elisabeth's husband received a letter from Kate, a close friend of Elisabeth's, who lived in Washington State. Kate said that she had had a dream in which Elisabeth asked her to give him a message. She said Elisabeth began chanting nonsense syllables to her over and over, first in the dream, but then so persistently that Kate was awakened from a sound sleep. She continued to hear the syllables, so she got up and wrote them down, as if she was taking dictation. Kate had no idea what they meant or how they were spelled, but they were repeated so many times that she was able to transcribe them phonetically. To her they were simply odd sounds. She wrote:

YAA TEE BAA VEE SHOO.
YAA TEE BAA LOO BLUE.
YAAZ DEE YES. YAAZ DEE YES.

Since she was told the message was for Elisabeth's husband, Kate mailed it to him. He brought out the letter when he was eating lunch together with Jane and Russell Targ, and suggested that Jane read it aloud for all to hear. After Jane had read the sequence of nonsense syllables out loud a few times, Russell exclaimed, "Wait a minute! Those words aren't nonsense! They're Russian!" It meant:

I see you (YAA TEE BAA VEE SHOO)
I love you (YAA TEE BAA LOO BLUE)
I'm here! I'm here! (YAAZ DEE YES, YAAZ DEE YES)

The actual Russian is:

Я тебя вижу
я люблю тебя
Я здесь

Kate verified that she had never spoken any Russian, been to Russia, or heard people speaking Russian. A specific after-death message in a foreign language had been delivered through a third person who did not understand a word of it.

"I wanted to make my mark in the world by being intelligent," Jane says. "Science and good research were my framework. We didn't do religion. I did not believe in survival of consciousness after death, or in ADCs. I certainly did not believe that they happened to people like me. But eventually it became clear to me and many others that these communications were indeed coming from Elisabeth Targ. I no longer had any doubt."

The full range of ADCs are more common than one would think. In the mid-1970s, Erlendur Haraldsson, professor emeritus of psychology at the University of Iceland, conducted surveys asking 902 Icelanders whether they had ever been aware of the presence of a deceased person. Thirty-one percent answered yes. Another 1980 survey conducted in Western Europe found that 25 percent reported that they had been in contact with someone who had died, and in the United States the figure was also 31 percent. In the years following his survey, Haraldsson conducted in-depth interviews with over 450 people who had had ADCs.

Beliefs by the general public certainly do not make it so. And it's reasonable to assume that some of Haraldsson's reports are questionable, imagined, or based on wishful thinking, despite his protocols for careful research and meticulous interviews. But most people do not take the time to respond to detailed questions if they are confabulating. And some ADCs involve multiple witnesses. Others come from someone who the recipient did not know had died. Sometimes a message might come from a deceased person to a recipient who does not understand it, because it is meant for a third person, as happened to Jane Katra. "When all the accounts we have collected are considered, it seems impossible to reject all of them as deceptions and mistaken perceptions," Haraldsson concludes. "Something real is there, at least in some of the accounts."

Haraldsson discovered that about half the events occur within the first year after the death, and three-quarters before the end of the fourth year, which does not seem surprising to me, since the connections between the loved ones left behind and the deceased person would be most intense closer to the time of death. What's most interesting is that for 86 percent of the cases occurring within twenty-four hours of death, the percipient did not know that the perceived person had died or was dying. In the cases occurring within an hour of death, 89 percent of the people reported encounters with someone they had not known had died.

In the Iceland surveys, 28 percent of the deaths of both males and females who ostensibly provided ADCs was due to sudden, unexpected, and violent causes, mostly accidents. This is much greater proportionally of violent deaths for that country than occurred in the general population (only 7.8 percent from 1941 to 1970). Most of these communicators are men, which makes sense, because men are more likely to die violently than women.

This corresponds somewhat to the data from cases of children with past-life memories. Dr. Jim Tucker reports that 70 percent of the lives remembered by children involve a violent death, which includes accidents, murders, and suicides. And three-quarters of these violent death cases involve males. In examining the death statistics for five years in the United States, Tucker discovered that 72 percent of the unnatural deaths in the general population involved males. This matched almost exactly the proportion of past-life memories involving males, suggesting that the children are not fantasizing. In addition, after many years of research, Haraldsson found that apparition cases also contained a much higher percentage of appearances from those who had suffered a violent death, when compared with the general population. Haraldsson points out this finding in other areas:

> Persons suffering a violent death feature predominantly in cases of apparitions of the dead and in cases of the reincarnation type, as well as in mediumship, including both direct communicators and drop-ins. The cases tend to have an invasive character, in that the deceased persons are frequently unknown to those who experience them and thus seem to assume an active role in their appearance. All of these findings tend, in my view, to support the survival hypothesis.

I take ADCs seriously partly because I received some dramatic ones myself over a two-year period (from 2013 to 2015) while researching evidence included in this book. Although they are very personal and remain puzzling, they made a deep impression on me, and after much thought I decided it would be dishonest for me to withhold them from my narrative. They are part of my investigation—the timing was fortuitous—and I kept an open and receptive mind throughout the process, sometimes even asking for an ADC to occur through directed thought. Some of the experiences had an interesting link to aspects of my mediumship readings. These paranormal events may be hard to believe (they were for me), but in reporting on them here, I trust myself as the most reliable source I know! You can be absolutely certain that everything I describe is exactly as it occurred, down to the smallest details. As with my mediumship readings, I made notes immediately after each event and analyzed them afterward. I understand why ADCs have so much impact, and how profoundly mysterious, and provocative, they are. They evoked a complex set of emotions in me—expanded awareness, elation, incomprehension, questioning, doubt, and hope—and always a sense of connection to something nonlocal.

As previously described, my younger brother died unexpectedly in January 2013. He was a troubled person and spent most of his adult life living in Scotland. We were always bonded though, and throughout his life he was closer to me than he was to our other two siblings. Sadly, I don't think I realized how much I cared about him until after he died. The shock of his sudden departure, and our unfinished relationship, was a different kind of emotional pain than anything I had ever known, and I never could have predicted the deep effect it had on me.

My first ADC came out of the blue before any mediumship readings or before I had entertained even the slightest thought of any such communications. I was lying on my bed alone, in deep mourning with the overwhelming pain of my brother being gone forever. Suddenly his voice burst onto the scene. It startled me, because as I experienced it, it was not generated from my brain; it was from the outside. I heard his familiar voice clearly say, "Leslie . . . I'm fine. It's okay." The way he said my name was unique to the way he spoke; it was so clearly his tone. His emphasis was: "Hey—stop! Everything is totally okay and I'm fine!" I was stunned because it was like a sudden and jolting external intrusion, completely different from a thought or memory.

This seemed like an experience of telepathy: I felt like I was hearing with my mind and not my ears. It wasn't *in* my mind, but was perceived *by* my mind, as if my consciousness had its own nonphysical ears. It had sound: it was loud, but not quite like someone talking, because it wasn't localized to one spot. I was completely taken aback.

There were other experiences such as a dream visit and electrical disturbances (lights going on and off by themselves) that seemed strange, but I had no idea if they meant anything. But then I had my reading with mental medium Laura Lynne Jackson (described in a previous chapter). She told me that my brother had been "throwing his energy," and "he's working hard to communicate through electrical things. He has already done something—a light went on and off?" This was uncanny—the night I had returned from Garry's memorial service in Scotland, I was falling asleep and suddenly the light next to my bed came on by itself and stayed on. I remember feeling like it was him, but who knows? It was a nice thought, but I didn't make much of it.

Laura continued: "With the refrigerator too! And he's laughing!" I didn't know what this meant during the reading; it made no sense to me at all . . . something amusing involving an attempt to communicate using a refrigerator? But when I listened to the recording afterward, suddenly it hit me. A couple of months earlier, my refrigerator had built up solid ice along the inside back wall. For a few days, I melted it off with matches and kept resetting the temperature, raising it up to warm the inside, but for some reason that didn't solve the problem. So finally I called the repair company, which sent two technicians over. They took one look and showed me that a simple button, located on the outside and above the door, controlling the internal fan, had been turned off. I couldn't understand how this had happened, because I knew for sure I had not touched this button and there had been no one else in my apartment that could have done so. I felt silly! The repairmen apologized for having to charge me a hundred dollars for simply pressing the button. It was ridiculous—and Laura said my brother was laughing! Could he have been playing a prank on me? Or did he try to do something else with the refrigerator, and it went awry?

A skeptical viewpoint would assume that of course there was some mechanical explanation for this. Maybe Laura had picked up on the incident psychically. I can see the validity of that perspective, but when you're in the middle of it and open to something else, that alternative seems real also. Who is to say?

Some months later, I was staying at my family's summer house on the coast in Massachusetts. One afternoon I was in the woods and sat on a rock near the ocean, and in a deep, lengthy, heartfelt meditation I connected to my brother and asked him for a sign. I wanted more "proof" that he was there—something physical that would make it obvious to me.

The next morning, I woke up and groggily went into the kitchen, turned on the light, and made coffee. After adding milk to my cup, I was just about to put it in the microwave when the ceiling light blinked twice—off, on; off, on—and then went off. The microwave went off also, along with the light above the stove on an adjacent wall. The other lights in the kitchen remained on. I checked the lights in rooms nearby, and they were all working. Well, all I wanted was a hot cup of coffee, so I picked up the microwave and plugged it into a working socket on another counter. Then suddenly it hit me: Is this Garry? Then the lights came back on. They had been off about three or four minutes. This could have been the sign I had requested! The fact that the lights blinked before going off and the microwave went out literally at the moment I was putting my cup into it could be seen as two good ways to get my attention and force me to notice what was happening. If all the lights had just suddenly gone off at once, it would not have meant anything to me. What would cause some kitchen outlets to blink twice and go off, and not the others? I will never know. In the moment, this was my sign. At times I still believe that is what it was. At other times, I have no idea.

However, much stranger things were to come. During my birthday reading with Laura, she had said that my brother was handing me a red balloon. We then agreed (all "three" of us) that a red balloon would be a concrete sign to be delivered by my brother from then on as a way for him to show his presence to me—a red balloon along with the continuing electrical effects. Laura told me I would see real red balloons within the next few days. I found that hard to believe, and I took this prediction with a large grain of salt. She also said I could ask for these signs when I needed them, and he would show himself to me by delivering them. I honestly thought at the time that this would be too miraculous—it was just a medium engaging in wishful thinking, and it could never happen.

Well, I saw two red balloons within the next few days—one outside a bookstore in Concord, Massachusetts, and another in a Manhattan subway station. However, Valentine's Day was that same weekend, so I assumed there were a lot of red balloons floating around, and this could easily have been a coincidence.

Two weeks later I was alone at home one evening, thinking about my brother and feeling connected to him. I lit a candle for him, and asked him to move the flame, or to do something physical for me . . . to send me a sign of his presence. (This was the first such request since Laura had suggested I ask.) I kept focusing on this throughout the evening, but nothing happened. Without thinking too much about it, I went to bed. When I woke up the next morning, I could not believe what I saw. In the tree outside my third-story New York City window, stuck in the branches, were three red balloons and one black one, together in a bunch. I had never seen a balloon in that tree before, nor have I since. What are the chances of red balloons getting caught in the branches of the tree opposite my window at the same time that I asked for a communication—something physical—having established that this was our specific sign? My brother and I had agreed on this one. It's hard to communicate the impact this had. I was awestruck and elated. This time I could not believe it could be a coincidence. Impossible! Could I have created this myself? That also seemed impossible. Yet how could a deceased entity find balloons in our world and deliver them to a location? It seemed inconceivable to me, but I had no other way of explaining it.

Some requests I made for signs after that were not answered. But on May 15, 2014, I went into a meditative state and once again passionately and deeply asked my brother Garry to do something definite, something obvious, to show his presence. I need more proof! I never get enough physical manifestations to convince me! I need to dispel my doubt! The request was not made casually and I spent much time delivering it.

The next day, I was cooking and using Spectrum organic sesame oil. In one bottle there was only a little left, and I had a second bottle about a third full. So I emptied the remaining sesame oil from that jar into the second one, and put the now-empty bottle down on the counter with the cap loosely on top. (The standard sixteen-ounce jar had a narrow neck with a plastic opening allowing the cap to be screwed on.) About a minute later, suddenly the top went shooting straight up into the air about five or six inches, and fell on the counter. There was a force there, seeming to be coming from inside the empty bottle, strong enough to send the cap flying into the air. But there was nothing inside the empty bottle. I admit that I was elated. My brother was delivering in spades!

Shortly afterward film producer Larry Landsman came by with a contract for a documentary he was going to make on the topic of my book. I will never forget showing him the very ordinary empty bottle and asking if he could explain how this could possibly happen. It was like a pop of the champagne bottle celebrating the launch of the film project. I don't know what Larry thought, but he certainly couldn't explain it.

And it didn't end there. The next day, I was pondering all this. A top had somehow shot up in the air from an empty bottle on my kitchen counter, with a force of something behind it. What caused this? I meditated again and, feeling a deep connection to my brother, I implored him to answer me: Who was this? I thought it was him. Was it you? I asked. Can you keep on doing things like this? I told him how much I love the physical stuff—it makes me so so happy, because it makes me feel connected to him like nothing else.

I went back to work for a while in my office, and then went into the kitchen to make tofu and vegetables. I opened the bottle of sesame oil that was about half full, poured some in the pan, and put the bottle down with the cap resting on top, but not screwed on. A few minutes later, I was more than shocked. The same thing happened! The top went flying off straight up, and made a popping sound, like there was pressure inside pushing it off. How could it have that sound? There was no cork, no gaseous bubbles trapped inside . . . just air and oil. The bottle was a few inches from the edge of the counter and this time the cap landed on the floor. What could I think? It was as if Garry was responding and saying, "Yes, it was me!" I was laughing, and filled with wonder and disbelief. It was miraculous. In that moment, I was sure it was him.

I had experienced psychokinesis, macro-PK—the movement of an object by nonphysical means—twice in my kitchen. It was one of the more bizarre experiences I've ever had. Perhaps it was caused by me—my strong desire and intention to have a communication from my brother, perhaps a deep psychological need manifesting itself through PK, like a positive poltergeist effect (more on poltergeists in a later chapter). It certainly didn't feel like this, but unconscious events are just that—outside our awareness. Could simply the intensity of my longing to hear from my brother, and my request for a physical manifestation, have created the result of the repeated flying bottle caps? That is certainly one possible explanation. On the other hand, maybe my sincere and deeply felt request for communication opened up some kind of energy field, similar to what happens with a medium, making it possible for my departed brother to reach into this reality.

In either case, it's hard to describe how startling this was. I asked him for a sign the first day, and the first cap popped off. Then I asked again, "Was that really you? Show me!" and a second cap popped off. Another component was the popping sound, which could not have come from the movement of the loose bottle cap. Both requests were deeply rooted within me, from a meditative state that was unusually heartfelt and that lasted for at least half an hour. But if it somehow was my brother, why would he choose such a strange way of demonstrating his presence to me? Was this simulation of a popping cork meant to be a reference to the fact that he enjoyed a good drink in his day? Perhaps it symbolized a joyful celebration of his saying, "I am here!" No matter what, some unknown force was in operation here and no rational framework can encompass it.

In thinking about this, I reflected on what Pim van Lommel wrote earlier:

I refer to this consciousness beyond time and space, which has no material or biological basis, as "nonlocal consciousness." Its wave functions store all retrievable memories, and all other aspects of information. It features an interconnectedness that offers the chance of communication with the thoughts and feelings of others, and with those of deceased friends and relatives. Its roots lie in another invisible, immaterial realm that is always in us and around us.

Finally, the most disarming event of all occurred over a year later, in August of 2015. I had not experienced any ADCs for about a year and was no longer focused on them at all. Once again I was staying at our family's summer house, where we had spent every summer while growing up. My brother had always loved this special place as his lifetime home.

We had a full house that summer night—my father and stepmother, my other brother and his wife, and my grown son were all staying there as well—and my sister had been with us for dinner. It was unusual for the whole family to be together like this. The full moon in a clear dark sky made a path of light on the ocean water as magical as it was when we were children. When I went to bed, the night was still, with no nearby neighbors or lights, or any human sounds. I was sleeping in Garry's former room, where his bed was a few feet from the wall. There was a window at the foot of the bed, and a second, open window was across the room. When I went to sleep at around midnight (I had had nothing to drink or smoke), the moonlight was coming in the open windows, making it relatively easy to see inside the room.

I had just dropped off to sleep when, suddenly, I was woken by something in the room. In a split second, I was totally and completely awake. This was not normal; usually there is a transition between sleep and waking up, but this was instantaneous. I saw a dark figure standing nearby, beside the window toward the end of the bed. I saw it move very slightly from the window toward me in the moment I woke up. I blurted out, with alarm and without any forethought, "Hey, somebody's here!!" My heart was beating fast and I was scared, like when your breath is taken away and you're frozen in shock. This figure was right next to my bed! I thought for a second that maybe it was my other brother snooping around the room for some reason, but I could hear him snoring through the wall. The thought that this could be an intruder never crossed my mind; it was so safe there that we have never locked the doors at night.

I could see the shape of a head, and the body was like a dark cloak—no arms or legs, just a cloaked form. I stared, and the head was slightly lighter in tone than the darker, rounded body underneath. I couldn't see any features of the face but I felt it to be a male. The lower part was blocked by the bed, in a dark space. The figure seemed full-size, and I saw clearly in the moonlight that it blocked out the picture on the wall behind it. It was so close, I could have sat up and touched it.

But I lay there without moving, fixated on it. Somehow I knew it wasn't going to hurt me. Then it registered that this was not a normal person. My fear increased. As I felt the fear, the form began to slowly dissolve. I felt intuitively that it was reacting to my fear—as if to say, "Okay, you don't like this, I'll go . . ." and I watched it dissolve like a fog slowly melting in the sun. That was unbelievable—watching what appeared to be a solid figure disintegrate before my eyes into shimmering little particles, and then nothingness, leaving empty space where it had stood moments earlier. That was when I knew: this really, actually, and without question was something otherworldly, ghostly, inexplicable, an apparition that I had witnessed right there next to me. As it evaporated before my eyes, I could only think, Oh my God, it's for real. I honestly did not want that to be the case in that moment.

Shaken with disbelief, I lay immobile for a long time with my heart pounding, staring at the space in the moonlight where it had been. I thought right away that this must have been my brother. It was about forty-five minutes before I managed to move and get myself up to turn on a light. I kept it on all night and barely slept. Anxious and exhausted, I couldn't stop thinking about this throughout the next day, but I didn't tell anyone in the family about it—what would they think? It would only make them uncomfortable. Instead, desperate to talk to someone, I emailed a friend in the UK who was experienced with such things, and that helped.

I thought about all the times I had asked Garry to show himself to me. But this just seemed over the top; something for which I was entirely unprepared. If this was him, maybe he felt drawn to make contact at that moment because all the family were present in the place he loved most, and I was sleeping in his room. It seemed that the full moon created perfect conditions, because although it was dark in the room, it was light enough that I could see in the moonlight streaming through the window next to the bed. But I was so disarmed that I did not experience it as something positive.

Of course I have no way of knowing who or what this apparition was, and I could never prove to anyone that this occurred. I was wide awake and I was not hallucinating, of this I am absolutely certain. The form seemed completely foreign and external to me, and really frightened me. This presence woke me up, suddenly and instantaneously. By what mechanism? And how could a form dense enough to block out the space behind it disintegrate in the moonlight as I watched? If I had welcomed it and tried to communicate, what would have happened, and how long would it have stayed? Could I have captured it on my cellphone camera if I'd thought of it? In retrospect, I wish I had it to do over again, and I regret that I was too unnerved to think along these lines.

At that time I had been grappling with the question of whether my previous ADCs could have been self-generated by my unconscious mind—by "motivated psi," as defined by Stephen Braude and others. I found this hard to come to terms with; the inner conflict it generated was on my mind during that summer. I felt as if Garry were saying, "Okay, I've tried hard and you're still not convinced. Let me *really* show you something and you will never doubt again!" It was so totally unbelievable that in the moment it seemed clearly to be a manifestation of another reality, more than anything that came before. This time, I could not possibly conceive of it being a creation of my own psi, even though my detached rational mind knew that this is what some experts would suggest. This was an adult-size form, which moved and then dissolved from shiny particles into empty space. And if indeed it was my brother, then some aspect of him survived death.

. . .

After this, I wanted to speak to other credible recipients of ADCs with experiences more evidential than mine. I discovered one exceptional person who had received communications objectively more convincing, often involving multiple participants. Jeffrey Kane is an academic vice president and has a PhD in the philosophy of science; he has written and edited scholarly books on the philosophy of knowledge and educational policy.

Jeff's oldest child, Gabriel, died in a car crash in June 2003, four days before his twenty-second birthday. In 2005 Jeff wrote *Life as a Novice,* a powerful book of meditative poems describing the journey of his deep grief, inspired by his son's continuing presence in his life. A profound, gifted poet and a true contemplative, Jeff describes repeatedly waking up in the morning to "a hole torn in the side of the world where once you stood." Jeff's connection to his son seems to be as strong as any human bond could possibly be.

"Perhaps the shock and incomprehensible nature of the loss of a child leave the parents somehow more receptive to messages from the spiritual realm," he told me. "We are often so confused that the comfortable realities of daily life no longer hold their solidity. The real becomes unreal; the sounds and sights of a familiar room seem as if they come from a foreign land. There is not so much pain as utter confusion about how a child you watched come into the world is no longer in it."

On Gabriel's birthday just days after his death, Jeff and his wife, Janet, heard a crash inside the house somewhere but didn't think much of it. When Jeff went into his walk-in closet before going to bed, all shelves on the right side had collapsed onto the floor, so that everything slid off them to the center of the closet. There had not been any changes to the closet shelves, or the items on them, for years and there was no explanation for why all the shelves on one side would suddenly cave in. And there, on top of the pile of clothes, shoes, and photo albums lying in a heap on the floor, square in the middle with its front cover facing Jeff, was the album of Gabriel's birth. None of the photo albums had been touched for seven years prior, yet on Gabriel's birthday, his birth album lay there staring Jeff in the face. This was the first tangible event that occurred, and Jeff interpreted it as "either cruel fate or meaningful." It was at least enough to leave a question in his mind saying perhaps this was more than coincidence.

Soon after, Janet had a reading with a medium, who told her Gabriel would leave dimes for them to show he was around. Jeff told his wife this was "absolute nonsense": the medium had planted the notion in their minds to look for dimes so that it would become a circular and self-fulfilling prophecy. A few days later, Janet and their daughter Emily went to the beach, and while in the water swimming, Emily felt a dime float into the palm of her hand. How often does such a thing happen? Still, Jeff attributed that to an "amazing coincidence."

Yet a few days later he questioned that interpretation. He was sleeping, woke up, and in the dim light saw something that looked like a dime or a penny about seven or eight feet away on the floor. He mused cynically to himself, snidely dismissing the idea with sarcasm: "Oh, I wonder if that's a dime from Gabriel!" He turned away and then suddenly heard Gabriel's voice. "I absolutely heard him, clearly, in English; it was loud and precise and unmistakably his voice," Jeff told me. The voice said, "Aha! Check the date. It's a 1981!" That was the year of Gabriel's birth. Jeff picked up the coin—a penny—but couldn't read the date on it, so he woke his wife. It was 1981. "He was telling me something I couldn't possibly have known," says Jeff. I remembered what it was like to hear my brother's voice, as clear as day. But Gabriel's message was longer, very specific, and less generic than my brother's message was.

That summer, Jeff and Janet went on a trip to Bar Harbor, Maine, and were driving in Acadia National Park. "I wish Gabriel could give us some kind of sign to let us know he's around," Jeff said. At that moment, the car clock jumped one hour. They both saw it. Was this a sign from Gabriel? They drove around to see if somehow they had entered a different time zone, or had been affected by a nearby tower, trying to find a rational explanation—without success. Three days later, they were driving again and Jeff mentioned to Janet that, yes, the hour shift might have been a fluke caused by a malfunctioning cell tower or something. He added that if the clock changed by two hours, that explanation would not make sense and there had to be something else going on. Within two or three minutes, the clock changed by two hours.

Needless to say, the immediacy of the response to Jeff's comment about the clock is astonishing, as well as its repetition. I was reminded of the two times the bottle caps shot into the air in my kitchen, but in my case a day passed between my asking and the receiving, and I hadn't asked for a specific sign like Jeff did the second time. (Although I did say, "Show me that this was you!"—what better way to do that than to repeat the sign again?)

Effects on electrical appliances seem to be among the more common ADCs. On another occasion, Jeff told me he was sick and home in bed, when he strongly felt Gabriel's presence and even thought he felt the mattress depress next to him. Jeff said, "Gabe, if you're really here I need a validating sign." The electricity in the house went off—once again the effect was immediate—and came back on a few minutes later. There was nothing unusual about the weather, no rain or wind, and nothing wrong with the electricity to explain the incident. Similarly, my brother seemed to have blinked the kitchen light twice and then turned it off along with the microwave—at least that is one interpretation of what might have happened—but once again, there was a delay in time after I asked him for a sign.

For discriminating, thoughtful people, there is always an element of doubt. "When I'm out of the experience, I'm back in that intellectual mode which ultimately can't grasp what literally does not make sense," Jeff explained. "I'm not in a high intuitive state most of the time; I'm facing the world dealing with the practicalities of daily life. The times I have certainty is when I'm in the middle of the experience. The way we normally think with our intellects is reflective; it looks at things. Reality apprehended intuitively is engaged, connected. You don't look at things as much as dwell in them." I understood his words very well.

And Jeff's journey continued. Two extraordinary ADCs involved people outside the family. Early on, Jeff had been getting what he perceived as thoughts coming into his mind from Gabriel, and he was writing them down in the form of letters. "They made so much sense, and were wise, comforting, and beautiful," Jeff told me. "But I also felt I might be losing my mind. How could I know I'm not just trying to comfort myself, to help myself cope? I had no answer to that question." So he said to Gabriel, "Gabe, if this is you and not me, tell me something I couldn't possibly know, something that would make no sense to me, that is completely illogical, but that I can validate." In response, he received a phrase from Gabriel: "I am red." Jeff laughed. "This didn't mean anything to me, and clearly it was absurd." He looked it up anywhere he could and tried to find some meaning for it, without success. A few weeks later he reasoned that no resolution was forthcoming. Resigned, he told his wife, "These thoughts have been *me* speaking. There is no validation. It must just be me comforting myself. This shows I'm making this stuff up."

About an hour after making that statement, a package arrived at the door. It contained a painting of an angelic figure. Jeff said it reminded him of Gabriel immediately, and he began to cry. Janet exclaimed, "It's red!" and only then did he notice the color. The package came with a note from the mother of someone Janet knew through her teaching, who wrote that she had passed the painting in a store window and for some reason she bought it. Something compelled her to send it. She stated clearly that she didn't know why she did so. She said they could throw it out, put it in the bathroom, do whatever they wanted with it, and she hoped it didn't offend them. Jeff then discovered that with the painting was a card from the artist. It said that the magenta color of the robes was the nearest color in our spectrum to the light emitted by *those who have died in their youth;* it is the color of communication, of love, from the so-called dead to the living. "I am red" had now been validated, made even stronger by the strange involvement of another person.

"I couldn't have made this up," Jeff says. "My son had a hand in making sure that woman sent that painting, confirming something that was a complete absurdity for me to begin with."

On another occasion, Jeff's wife heard from a medium that Gabriel's message for her was to "take care," and this didn't sit right with her. Having had breast cancer in the past, Janet was beside herself with worry, not knowing what he meant by this. Should she go to the doctor? Was she sick again? Jeff was angry. He said to Gabriel, "I want to talk to you. I don't want any more cryptic bullshit. I have to know how Mom is. I have to know. I will talk to you in my sleep." And he lay down on the couch. It was 10:30 p.m. and he tried to sleep, but couldn't settle down. Frustrated, angry, restless, he heard the phone ring. It was now about 10:45 p.m. On the line was a clairvoyant friend whom he had not spoken to in about six months. "Jeff," she told him, "I was on the phone with my mother just now, and I heard Gabriel yelling at me. He said, 'Hang up! My father needs to speak with me! Hang up and call him now!' He was so persistent, I had to get off and call you. What is going on?" She was able to converse with Gabriel and communicate to Jeff that Janet was fine and there was nothing to worry about.

"Nothing in psychology can explain this. Where did it come from?" Jeff commented. "People can discount this stuff if they are tied to that easy sense of the world I lost when Gabe died. They will not know what to do with it if their view of reality is bound by what makes sense; that is, what can be sensed." Jeff told me that one thing that drives him crazy is when people say with a patronizing tone, "Well . . . if it helps you get through it . . ." His response is: "I'd rather live my life in absolute desperation and misery as long as I'm living in truth, than to live with a sense of hope and meaning in a world where I'm simply deceived." He has been absolutely careful to probe every ADC, and he is the kind of astute intellectual who goes out of his way to avoid deceiving himself.

Jeff also experienced something similar to an apparition, but perhaps more beautiful. Three or four months after Gabriel died, he was in his son's room in deep mourning. He was sitting on Gabe's bed with all the lights off and it was totally dark. At the foot of the bed and to his right, he saw a golden, oval ball of light about twelve inches wide by eighteen inches high, suspended in the air six or seven feet away. It had soft edges and a distinct shape. He tried to determine what it could be. Moonlight reflecting off a car window, or maybe a streetlight? No . . . if that were the case, the light would be on the wall or ceiling, not suspended in one place in midair. He thought, well, maybe there is some particulate matter there; but light would still go through the matter. No, this was a self-contained, suspended ball of light; there was no unusual particulate matter. Jeff watched it for over a minute, and intuitively he felt he might be seeing Gabriel so he concentrated on the light intently. Then it slowly faded away. He told Janet later, "I think I just saw Gabriel . . ."

Several months later, Jeff went to see the well-known mental medium George Anderson. Anderson told him in the middle of the session, "You've seen him. You saw him as a light in a darkened room. You didn't know if it was him, but he's telling me to tell you that it was." Jeff was astounded. He gained the confidence to meditate and ask Gabriel why he showed himself like that rather than as an apparition, which would be something recognizable. Gabe answered that he came like that in order to teach an important lesson. "Gabriel explained that the light I saw was the very same light that exists in all human souls," Jeff said. "Everyone has, everyone is, that same golden light."

Even so, on the question of the survival of consciousness after death, Jeffrey Kane recognizes that the most anyone can actually say is "I don't know." There is no certitude about it, and there never will be. "We will never have proof because the knowledge that life after life is possible emanates from an intuitive level of experience. If you think that even proof within a high degree of probability is ever going to satisfy you, it won't. But there are sufficient questions here so that you can't just dismiss this. I'm not saying life after life is the only answer, although I do believe it is correct, but I'm saying that no materialist framework can accommodate it."

Ultimately, experiences like this teach us something; they are transcendent. If one embraces them, their power and intimate quality of connection are very hard to convey in words. Those with similar experiences understand. Jeff's final thought to the question of survival was "I can't see a reason not to believe."

That statement helped me find some kind of resting place with my own inexplicable experiences. No one can prove any of these events and we will never know for sure what ADCs actually are. The experiences described here either came from the energy of a surviving consciousness with whom the recipient was deeply bonded, or they were created by internal unconscious forces that we don't understand. So I too can't see a reason not to trust the intuitive certainty that comes during the experience, when one steps unintentionally outside the materialist framework. In those moments, I can't see a reason not to believe.

Chapter 20

Interactive Apparitions

By Loyd Auerbach, MS

The apparition I witnessed was silent and disappeared quickly, possibly in "reaction" to my fear. But apparitions were also alluded to in a positive light by neuropsychiatrist Peter Fenwick in his chapter about end-of-life experiences; they can be experienced by the dying person as welcoming presences assisting with their journey to the next world. How do we explain these strange, otherworldly forms?

Apparitions are more complex and even refined than either of these examples would suggest. Many people consider them to be the stuff of scary movies or ghost hunting shows, but in fact they have been seriously studied and documented for over a century. Most persuasive are "collective apparitions"—those that are seen by multiple witnesses at the same time or by several witnesses at different times. Apparitions can directly affect the environment and are not solely visual; they also create sounds or smells, and sometimes pets or other animals demonstrate awareness of them. Like a drop-in communicator or a familiar personality speaking through a medium, apparitions can exhibit purpose and provide identifying information to recipients that can later be verified— but this time directly to the recipient, without an intermediary. How can that happen?

Loyd Auerbach, a leading authority on this topic, has a master's degree in parapsychology and has been a professor at Atlantic University, JFK University, and HCH Institute in Northern California. He has been investigating cases of apparitions, hauntings, and poltergeists for over thirty-five years and is the author of ESP, Hauntings and Poltergeists: A Parapsychologist's Handbook *(2016) and* A Paranormal Casebook: Ghost Hunting in the New Millennium *(2005), among other works.*

The concept of a "ghost" conjures up a variety of thoughts and images in our minds, which may or may not be true to fact. Popular culture has impacted beliefs about what ghosts might be and how they affect the living and the physical world. For most people, a ghost is a spirit of someone who has died. For many, it is scary.

Along with the phenomenon of mediumship, ghostly encounters were a major focus of the early days of serious research into the paranormal. Investigators documented experiences from credible people, under good conditions, including cases with more than one witness able to access verifiable information. Several important volumes and papers were published by the Society for Psychical Research (SPR) and the American Society for Psychical Research (ASPR), including the classics *Phantasms of the Living* by Edmund Gurney, Frederic W. H. Myers, and Frank Podmore; and *Human Personality and Its Survival of Bodily Death* by Myers. (Contemporary research on the phenomenon can be found in the *Journal of the Society for Psychical Research* in the UK and the *Journal of Scientific Exploration* in the US.)

Some of the early researchers preferred the term "phantasm," but (fortunately) they moved on to "apparition," which we use today since it does not have the cultural baggage of "ghosts." While the very definition indicates something visual, apparitions are sometimes perceived in other ways, such as hearing their voices or footsteps, smelling their perfume or cologne, feeling their presence or even their touch. In some cases apparitions appear to be able to move objects. They interact with us and with the immediate environment.

There are categories for such sightings within parapsychology. Apparitions of the dead appear to be an aspect of the human personality (mind, soul, spirit, consciousness) surviving the death of the body and somehow existing in our physical world. They are either recognizable as a once-living person or provide information that allows that identification to be made later. For the apparition to represent evidence for survival past death, it must be capable of communicating or interacting with those around it in a conscious way.

Sir William Barrett (experimental physicist and parapsychologist, 1844–1925) reported on an experience investigated by Henry Sidgwick (economist and philosopher, and first president of the SPR) in 1892. Sometimes "the phantasm is not only seen but also apparently heard to speak; sometimes it may announce its presence by audible signals," Barrett wrote. This particular case involved "rapping" made by an apparition seen by Rev. Matthew Frost of Bowers Gifford, Essex, who made the following statement:

The first Thursday in April 1881, while sitting at tea with my back to the window and talking with my wife in the usual way, I plainly heard a rap at the window, and looking round at the window I said to my wife, "Why, there's my grandmother," and went to the door, but could not see anyone; still feeling sure it was my grandmother, and knowing, though she was eighty-three years of age, that she was very active and fond of a joke, I went round the house, but could not see anyone. My wife did not hear it. On the following Saturday, I had news my grandmother died in Yorkshire about half-an-hour before the time I heard the rapping. The last time I saw her alive I promised, if well, I would attend her funeral; that was some two years before. I was in good health and had no trouble, age twenty-six years. I did not know that my grandmother was ill.

Sidgwick learned that when Frost last saw his grandmother two years earlier, she had promised to appear to him at her death. The conditions were decidedly nonspooky: he saw her in full daylight and even, for a moment, thought it was his grandmother physically present. "Had there been a real person Mrs. Frost would both have seen and heard her; nor could a living person have got away in that time," Barrett states. The house stood in a garden a good way back from the road, and Mr. Frost immediately went out to see if his grandmother was really there. Actual news of her time of death came to Frost by letter two days later.

As described earlier by Peter Fenwick, deathbed apparitions are those encountered by people who are in the process of dying, sometimes involving an apparition of someone the dying person did not know had died. Dying people do not always describe the apparitions as being interactive, but if they say they are coming to greet them or help them move on, even that perceived intention indicates some level of consciousness.

Much more common than encounters with any of the categories of apparitions are experiences that, on the surface, may seem to be apparitions, but actually are something quite different. People perceive figures, sounds, and voices related to people or activity, smells, and even sensations that they conclude are caused by a "ghost." However, these ghosts seem to be acting in repetitive patterns and are essentially locked to a location such as a house, bar, restaurant, hotel, plot of land, or on rarer occasion to an object. And here there is no interaction evident, even after communication is attempted. These phenomena are called hauntings, or, alternatively, place memory.

A haunting is a kind of echo, or recording of sorts, of actual people and events. A location (or object) holds/records information about its history. Our own psychic abilities—or perhaps our brains, interacting with some element of the physical environment—allow us to pick up certain playbacks of this history, including sightings of people. However, these are more like holograms, not conscious beings. They are like a loop of a videotape playing itself over and over. And these "recordings" seem to have been made by the environment while the subjects were alive, not deceased.

The key element distinguishing apparitions from hauntings is consciousness. Video or audio recordings are not conscious and cannot interact or adapt to new people or new situations. In the same way, hauntings cannot interact, but apparitions, ostensibly representing a person's consciousness, can. Hauntings are not evidence for survival past death.

If an apparition's presence leads to things breaking, or causes electronic malfunctions, such activity typically seems purposeful or directed. Any such movement caused by intention only—conscious or unconscious, living or dead—is by definition "mind-matter interaction," known as psychokinesis (PK). Apparitional PK appears to be more deliberate than the more common, chaotic PK stemming from living people (caused by "poltergeists," discussed in the next chapter).

Our personal perception of the "mind" of apparitions, and the process of possible communication or receiving of information from them, involves use of telepathy, in the same way a medium might receive information from a deceased loved one for a sitter. And how does a postmortem apparition, effectively a consciousness without physical senses, perceive the world and people around itself? This too involves psi, and is the same mechanism by which a medium understands her communications—the consciousness speaking through her uses its psi to send the messages to her, which she is able to access through her own similar faculties.

The best apparition cases have always included multiple witnesses, involving a number of individual people experiencing the apparition separately over a period of time, or two or more people doing so at the same time. These cases can include verifiable information gleaned from the apparition that was not previously known to the witnesses. Many have had a personal element to them, involving people seeing or otherwise experiencing the apparition of a relative, loved one, or friend.

During my earlier studies and career in parapsychology, I was personally undecided as to whether survival of consciousness was the best explanation for even some of the most convincing apparition cases, although I certainly leaned toward it. I also considered the abilities of young children to recall details of another life, studied extensively by Ian Stevenson as described earlier in this volume, to be well beyond the norm for psi. I was unclear as to whether mental mediums were using ESP with the deceased or with living sources. I had little trouble considering the merits of both explanations.

But as I spent more time examining historical cases as well as conducting my own investigations, I gradually shifted my opinion more toward survival as the most likely underpinning of many of the experiences reported. However, some instances were explainable also by living-agent psi, and one must always consider each case from both perspectives before reaching a conclusion. The following cases will give you specific details that may illustrate why I lean toward the survivalist position.

In 1985, Donna McCormick, a knowledgeable and very careful researcher whom I worked with for a few years, provided me with an example of an interesting, ongoing apparition case. In the following interview, Donna mentions three psychics, "Alex, Ingrid, and Ann." One is Alex Tanous, a well-known, gifted psychic with many academic degrees, who taught theology at Manhattan College and St. John's University in New York City.

> It began shortly after her [the woman of the couple] grandfather died. She was extremely close to him. They lived on the second floor of a two-family house. They would hear footsteps coming up the stairs, the lock being turned, the door opening, the door closing, the footsteps coming in, then ending up at the children's bedroom, the nursery, or going straight to their room. They'd go out and look. They wouldn't see anybody, they wouldn't hear the footsteps anymore. This was a repeated pattern.
>
> They'd see apparitions of this individual. Some of them were clear sightings, very concrete seeming, to the point where people who were visiting would ask, "Who's that in the house?" Other times, just vague shadows would be seen.
>
> They determined on their own that it was her grandfather.

We brought Alex in, and Ingrid, and Ann, and they all gave descriptions of the grandfather. She had a picture of him, so we put that among several others for the psychics to choose from, and each one picked the grandfather's. They all gave good descriptions of what he was like in life, interactions that occurred, where the phenomena occurred, really an excellent case of everything being very clear-cut.

Also, the family moved recently, and the phenomena are still continuing at their new location, which suggests that it's person-related rather than house-related. The psychics had given the explanation that the grandfather was watching over them. He's not "earthbound," as some people like to characterize these things. He knows he's dead and is just keeping an eye on the family.

The family really doesn't mind at all. And it's not like they're clinging to this for any strange purpose. It's just not frightening to them. In some ways it's a little reassuring. They have had experiences that suggest that the children are being looked upon; blankets being pulled up over the children. The baby a few months old lying in the crib wouldn't have a blanket on him, but then they'd find a blanket on him.

The grandfather had not lived with the family, and the activity was seemingly independent of the activity of the grandfather when he was alive. But one case in particular, early in my career, pushed me much more firmly into the survival camp.

During the early-to-mid-1980s, when I was on the Core Faculty of John F. Kennedy University's Graduate Parapsychology Program (which ended in the late 1980s), I received a call from a woman named Pat in Livermore, a city east of Oakland, California. It was a bit atypical of the usual fear-filled "help us" calls; Pat was simply refreshingly curious.

Pat was an attorney and lived with her husband, Mark, and twelve-year-old son Chris. Her mother lived nearby. Only a short time before the call, she learned that her son had been having conversations with a "ghost" he identified as that of the woman who had been the previous owner of their home. She also learned that these almost daily conversations had been going on for well over a year.

They had purchased a more-than-seventy-year-old home a couple of years after the 1980 death (by natural causes) of the owner, who had lived in the house since her birth in 1917. Along with the house, the family bought some of the original furniture and a porcelain doll collection. The original owner's only living relative, himself quite elderly, had arranged for the sale through his private attorney. Neither Pat nor her husband had any communication with that relative.

Since moving into the house, Pat, as well as her husband, her mother (on visits), and more frequently her son Chris, had seen an apparition appearing and disappearing in the house. The initial sightings had come shortly after they moved in, when Chris was eleven. They spotted the apparition of an elderly woman walking through the living room, typically toward the stairs. In a number of instances, the figure waved at the percipient and would disappear a few seconds later. This kind of behavior appeared to demonstrate an awareness of the presence of the witnesses and an attempt by the apparition to interact, but it also could have been a minor variation of a psychic imprint of the woman's activity when she was alive. Based on what else Pat told me, the former was much more likely than the latter.

Pat had grown up in a family environment that acknowledged and even discussed psychic experience, and she was not afraid of the apparition. Still, she didn't tell the other family members about seeing it until after her son had spoken up. Nor had her mother or husband told any other family member about their own experiences. It seemed that each was worried about scaring the others in the household. For research purposes, this withholding of information is important, since we can be reasonably certain that no one influenced anyone else's recollections or descriptions. Also, the fact that the sightings occurred at many different times and were seen by independent witnesses who were alone at the time adds credibility to the existence of the apparition as something external and consistent over time.

Things came to a head when Chris began talking about the origins of some of the antique furniture, and specifically dolls, in the collection that had belonged to the former owner. When Pat asked if he had found some kind of diary or letters describing the items and their stories—something they'd been looking for throughout the house since they moved in—Chris simply replied, "Lois told me."

"Who's Lois?" asked Pat.

"You know, Lois—the ghost you, Dad, and Grandma have been seeing since we moved in."

"How do you know we'd been seeing a ghost?"

"Lois told me."

Lois was the name of the late owner who had been born in the house and spent her life there until she died at age sixty-three. Naturally, Pat and Mark would have learned the name of that former owner during the process of buying the house, and Chris might have learned it as well. At this point, all the family members admitted to one another that they too had seen the apparition on several occasions. But it was Chris whom Lois apparently felt most comfortable around. Chris reported to his family that she had appeared to him every day since the first time he saw her, when he waved back at the figure he saw. He said that the woman did not disappear once he waved at her, but rather approached him and began communicating.

Pat wasn't concerned about getting rid of the spirit of Lois, but she was a little concerned about the implications of having this ghost in the house with a developing preteen. In fact, by the time she called me, Pat had already taken her son to see a local psychological counselor to make sure he was "okay" and that it was not damaging to have him continue conversing with this apparition while he grew up.

I was quite excited to interview the family and observe the environment, especially since Pat stated that Chris was able to get verifiable information from Lois. This is a rarity when it comes to apparition cases. Pat did pass along a concern of Lois's about my visit, however, which she learned about from Chris. Apparently Lois not only spoke with Chris, but she also watched television quite a bit with him (and even, he said, helped him with his homework). They had seen a commercial for the movie *Ghostbusters* (and Chris had seen the movie) and were worried we'd bring along "blasters" to get rid of her. I assured Pat that our only equipment would be a still camera and a cassette recorder. We made an appointment for several days later.

In the meantime, Pat arranged for me to have lunch with the therapist who had seen Chris. He admitted that he was an agnostic when it came to ghosts, but told me that he was convinced that Chris was well adjusted, incredibly mature for his age, and not prone to making things up, consciously or otherwise. In fact, he stated that if his other clients were as well adjusted as Chris, they wouldn't need therapy at all. While based only on a single session, he commented that it seemed the boy's relationships with his parents and grandmother were all very good. This is something I observed on my visit, though with Mark away on business, I could not observe Chris's interaction with his father. I did speak with Mark on the phone prior to the visit, and his experiences matched those of the others, although he seemed a bit less accepting of the idea of living with a ghost in the house.

On the day of our scheduled trip to Livermore, the parapsychology students who usually accompanied me were unavailable. My wife at the time, Joanna Rix, was very interested in coming along on this "friendly ghost" case. The third member of our "team" was a student, Kip Leyser.

As we drove, we talked about a number of things, such as the problems I was having with the car I was driving and what kind of car I might buy in the near future. Joanna was seriously contemplating quitting her secretarial job at a law firm that week and spoke of a real dislike of her place of employment. Kip spoke about the ten or so years he'd been out of school between college and graduate school when he had been a professional dancer. None of this is directly relevant, of course; I mention it only because it became so later, when it more or less came back to "haunt" us at the house.

We arrived at the Victorian-style house and were greeted by Pat, her mother, and Chris. I got the impression that Chris was giving us the visual once-over to make sure we had no ghost traps or portable particle accelerators. We started the audiotape running as we entered, recording as we walked around the house discussing their sightings of the apparition.

Pat and her mother said they had seen the figure for fleeting moments, and she always appeared as an elderly woman. Chris, on the other hand, told me himself that he had been seeing her almost every day for more than a year and a half, since that first time he waved back at her. He told us she didn't always appear as an old woman. She often shifted her appearance, looking like a teenager, a six-year-old, a woman in her thirties, and sometimes middle-aged. When I asked him about her clothes, Chris said they changed all the time. Pat and her mother also admitted to seeing Lois wearing different clothing, even though she was always the same elderly woman when they saw her. This was important to me, as was the appearance of Lois at different ages. Changing clothing and even changing ages in the perceived visual, especially when coupled with interaction and communication, is an indicator of self-awareness and consciousness.

We finished the tour, which included hearing some history of Lois, her family, and the house, which Chris learned from Lois. For a twelve-year-old, Chris was an articulate purveyor of anecdote. I had little trouble believing someone else was feeding him the information.

At first assessment, Chris could have been using his own unconscious but highly developed psi abilities to access the information from within the house loaded with history. Psychometry is a form of psychic practice in which one perceives information about an object's owner and history by touching/holding it—and what is a house but a big object? However, Chris (really Lois, through Chris) was including some stories about Lois's family and activities that took place outside the home. Pat had considered whether Chris had found and memorized diaries that would have provided such stories, but she could not imagine how that was possible.

Was Lois—an apparition of a woman who died a few years earlier—actually communicating intelligently with Chris? And, was she there when we were in the house? According to Chris, the communications were on a daily basis, and she was by his side the whole time we toured the house. He remarked that she was suspicious and was keeping an eye on us as well (the *Ghostbusters* thing again).

We ended up in the living room and sat down in a semicircle facing Chris, to ask Lois some questions. Chris was seated next to an empty easy chair he identified as Lois's favorite spot to sit. According to the boy, she was sitting right there. None of us could see her though.

At that moment, I felt like I was in some kind of weird sitcom. The three of us pitched questions at an empty chair as a young boy looked and listened to "someone" sitting there, repeating or translating "her" answers. In essence, he was functioning as a medium, even though most mental mediumistic interactions with ostensible deceased spirits do not involve extensive, clear, two-way conversations like this one (and Chris was not in any kind of trance state).

Joanna and Kip asked questions more related to Lois when she was alive, including any information on the cousin who was executor of the estate, and whose attorney had blocked Pat from any personal contact. This was information for which we could seek verification later. Personally, I was more interested in learning about her current incarnation as an apparition.

All the answers were specific and to the point. More and more information came out about Lois, giving us the picture that she was a local social butterfly, often hosting parties at her home throughout her life. Most of her relatives had died, but she thought there might be one or two still alive besides the cousin who was responsible for selling the house. We didn't pursue that any further, but I got the feeling that any other relatives who might have been alive were ones she didn't care for.

I brought my questioning back to the issue of how Lois appeared in a form that people could see—how was that possible? Through Chris, Lois said she believed she did not have a "form." She believed she was some kind of "ball of energy" that was able to communicate by "projecting her thoughts" to others. These thoughts included visual and verbal information that she would "project into the minds of others" so they would "see" and "hear" her as if she were really there.

The process by which information bypasses the physical senses and is merged with our perceptual process has been called "perceptual insertion." To me, this explanation made much sense. It meant that Lois was aware that she was literally telling Chris's mind what to perceive. They were not really, visually, seeing or hearing Lois. The information she "broadcast" added to their own perceptions. In communicating with Chris, her "broadcast" was more intentional, directional, while with the others she was just putting out a "signal," which they turned out to be capable of perceiving. This explains why only some people might experience apparitions—their perceptual processes are susceptible to such insertion by telepathic projection. It also explains why one doesn't expect to see genuine photos or videos of ghosts. They have no form to reflect light.

"Why was Lois appearing in different forms and clothing?" I asked.

"Because that's how she felt that day," he replied. In other words, it was Lois's own sense of self, her perceptions about the way she viewed herself that day (at a particular age in particular clothing), that shaped her "projection" of herself. So why do ghosts have clothes? Because that's how most people visualize themselves . . . with clothing on. Lois declined to appear to us (she still didn't quite trust us, she said), and admitted she wasn't even sure she really could, telling us that the family seeing her might have to do with their current attachment to the house and how psychic they were.

Most of what Lois said about her form as an apparition was more than a bit familiar, as I had read similar accounts over the years, but at the time I think one would have been hard-pressed to find the relevant, rather scholarly books or papers in public or middle-school libraries. This description was not something I expected from a twelve-year-old boy who, according to his mother, had never read anything on ghosts.

I asked Lois why she was still hanging around her old house, why she had not passed on. The answer was that she had done much socializing, had many parties in her life, and hadn't been an avid churchgoer. A believer in heaven and hell, she thought too much partying and not enough church might see her to hell, so she figured, why take a chance? From her deathbed in the hospital, she focused on being back at home. She felt herself slipping away and the next thing she knew, she was in the house. In case you're wondering, she did not see "the light" and knew nothing of what was ultimately the afterlife. When the family moved in, she had further reason to stay—she liked the new family and felt very happy with them, especially Chris.

I finally asked if Lois had any questions for us. Apparently she decided to use this as a way to show off. Chris looked to the empty chair and then asked us each a question.

"Loyd, she wants to know if you've decided on a color for that new car you want.

"Joanna, have you really thought about the kind of job you want after you quit the one you have?

"Kip, how long were you a professional dancer?"

I think our jaws probably hit the floor at the same time. We each, in hollow voices, answered the questions. Then after telling Pat and the others that the questions related to our in-transit conversation, I asked how Lois knew to ask these questions. Chris looked over to the chair, then back at us a bit sheepishly. "You're probably not going to like this, but Lois wanted to make sure you weren't bringing blasters to get rid of her, so she hitched a ride with you here and eavesdropped." We all got a big (though nervous) laugh out of that—though Kip looked a little uncomfortable, having been sitting in the backseat where presumably Lois "hitched" her ride.

On the drive back, we skimmed through the tapes to listen for any indication that we'd somehow told them about our previous conversation. We concluded that either Chris (or Lois) read our minds while we were there or that Lois somehow really was present in the car with us. No matter what, telepathy by either Chris or Lois would have been enough to explain this and seems a reasonable interpretation.

Shortly thereafter, I learned something very significant from Pat. After our meeting, based on information provided by Lois, they were able to track down the elderly cousin who had arranged the sale of the house. I spoke with him, and he verified the information about Lois's youth and life as true, as well as facts about the family and Lois's house that Chris said Lois provided.

We had a tape of the information Chris provided from Lois, recorded when we were present before any attempts were made to verify the information. Like the child reincarnation cases in which a prior written record is very important for the evidential value of the case, we had the equivalent before anyone knew if Lois's points were accurate or not. Her cousin had no vested interest in the accuracy or inaccuracy of the facts we brought to him (although he was very interested to hear that Lois had survived her death, since he was getting on in years himself). In a number of instances, as I began some of the family-related anecdotes, he finished the stories for me, in a manner that corresponded to the information Chris had given me. Pat conducted even more thorough checks to see if Chris had somehow found diaries or other papers Lois might have left behind. None was ever found.

Chris continued to see Lois on a daily basis for a while, but then lost interest as he grew up and discovered (and was discovered by) real girls. However, I was informed that Lois continued to help him with schoolwork, and even offered advice about his girlfriends. When last I spoke with Pat in the early 2000s, Lois was still in the house, still seen on occasion by members of the family, and still apparently happy to be earthbound in her lifetime home. Surprisingly, nobody in the family seemed to mind.

This case was a kind of turning point in my own belief about survival as it relates to apparitions. First, the verified information was enough under the circumstances to convince me that normal sources of information could be ruled out. Lois was either there interacting, or else Chris was some kind of super-psychic who was able to pick up the information from the house itself through clairvoyance or retrocognition. But since there were other witnesses to Lois actually manifesting visually, a heavier emphasis can legitimately be placed on the former possibility rather than the latter. Add to that Chris's utter lack of any other psychic perceptions or experiences, and I think we're left with a likely apparition as opposed to a one-note super-psychic.

The family members were well adjusted, got along well with one another, and were seemingly without psychological issues about the unusual recurring visits by this apparition. Most people who contact me about seeing or hearing a ghost have the impulse to turn and run.

This family was not prone to overreacting or exaggeration; they were levelheaded, honest people motivated by curiosity more than anything else.

Lastly, the information Lois provided about how she was able to appear and communicate was far beyond what most people would be able to read about easily at the time, let alone the kind of information that a twelve-year-old would spout about ghosts. It's rare to be able to ask about the "how" and "why" of apparitions. Lois showed herself to be a person first, and an apparition second. She was a shining example that human personality seems to persist after death.

As part of another investigation, I actually experienced an apparition myself—directly, and closer than one might imagine possible. The Moss Beach Distillery restaurant, south of San Francisco, had reports of a woman in a blue dress (who became known as "The Blue Lady") going back to the early 1930s. People over time reported seeing her individually and on occasion in small groups. Since the late 1970s, the activity at the location became more physical (things moved on their own) but people were still occasionally seeing her, especially psychics and mediums. My work on this case began in 1991, and by 1999, I'd brought in different environmental sensors, worked with many other investigators, and interviewed dozens of witnesses (staff, patrons, locals, and psychic practitioners).

One night that year, I was alone taking magnetic readings behind the bar well after two in the morning, with lights fully on. Suddenly, my magnetometer spiked quite high. At first, I thought I was picking up the ice machine or some other powered piece of equipment from the bar area. But there was no apparent source for the spiked reading based on where I was standing.

Then, a moment later, I felt a tingling sensation on the back part of my body, followed by a sort of rippling effect. The tingling sensation passed completely through my body, stopped, then returned from the other direction. There was a pause, and it repeated. I began timing the experience. For me, having intense personal paranormal experiences is pretty rare, and my curiosity always overrules any potential anxiety. Plus, having been involved in looking into the behavior of this particular apparition for so long, I knew there was absolutely nothing to fear.

As the experience continued, I knew that somehow The Blue Lady was getting my attention by moving through my body. I even got a "mind's-eye" perception of a woman in her twenties walking back and forth through me, giggling. After several passes and about two minutes of this, three mediums who had been working with me entered the room and stopped, all staring at me. One began laughing, and another said, "Hey, she's walking right through you"—followed by more laughter from all three. One of them then said, "I think we scared her off" and, indeed, the tingling sensation ceased. They observed this without me saying a thing.

I asked them each, separately and independently, to note whom they'd seen, what she was wearing, her hairstyle, and what she was doing. Their descriptions not only agreed with one another's, but also with the mental image I'd received (and even the giggling).

What did it feel like? In general, the "energy" of the experience rocked my body a bit, somewhat like what one feels standing in ocean surf as the waves come in and out. The tingling sensation was a very light, positive feeling possibly because The Blue Lady's intentions were positive, or perhaps because of my own curiosity-based attitude. In fact, it actually felt good.

Really spectacular apparition cases such as this are rare, but I would like to briefly describe one more. The World War II aircraft carrier USS *Hornet,* a registered State and National Historic Landmark and now a museum, is moored at the former Naval Air Station Alameda on San Francisco Bay. Since 1999, I've been investigating multiple sightings there. Well over a hundred witnesses have reported seeing dozens of different sailors and officers, and in most cases the apparitions were aware of them and also reacted to their presence.

Some verifiable information has been communicated, mostly through mediums and other psychics, and it has been consistent. In the early investigations, before the press became involved, many details were withheld from the psychic practitioners. Granted, they could have telepathically pulled them from my mind (or that of others present). But on a few occasions, an apparition told the psychic about a previous witness encounter that I knew nothing about. Also, the manifestation of a distinct personality, as with the best mental mediumship readings, was sometimes clear and present. There has been consistent communication with at least two particular entities. One clear message has been that the majority of the apparitions present on the USS *Hornet* were not representative of those who died aboard, but rather of those who served aboard the ship during their lives.

Most apparition cases are onetime and personal in nature—involving the perception of a just-deceased loved one, relative, or friend—rather than continuing over time. The USS *Hornet* case exemplifies the kinds of evidence sought in the best apparition cases that lend themselves to scientific study: numerous multiple witness sightings, including several witnesses seeing the same apparition(s) at the same time; apparent interactivity and definite responses to requests, including some purposeful psychokineses; consistent communications to different people over time; and some veridical information communicated. Most people have no idea that such "otherworldly" events really do take place. But in fact, they do.

The philosophical divide in parapsychology is not whether such phenomena exist, but whether they are caused by human psi alone or some other human manifestation, rather than by a disembodied consciousness. The best cases would require a complex form of "super-psi" that goes well beyond what is generally reported or what we have seen in controlled laboratory conditions. Many have proposed that such experiences could be either psychological hallucinations or hallucinations resulting from the recipient's use of telepathy or clairvoyance in learning unconsciously of the death of someone represented by the apparition.

These kinds of interpretations are much harder to accept when the apparition has no connection to any of the witnesses. Also, interactivity does not seem possible with a nonconscious environment, and certainly the interactivity of several witnesses with the same apparition suggests something distinct and external in their environment, as does the existence of the same apparition over time. Based on my many years of investigations and experiences, I think the evidence is weighted heavily toward the survival hypothesis in explaining apparitions.

But the question certainly remains open. If there is no upper limit to psi's range or strength, which itself is as non-falsifiable as the survival hypothesis, this can always be used to explain any paranormal experience, no matter how unusual or complex. After all, an interactive dead person may be just as difficult to conceptualize as unlimited psi by those who have not experienced something like this themselves.

Multiple witnesses to the same apparition at the same time would require some kind of unconscious telepathic cooperation. Each person would experience the same mental animation of the character and somehow experience the same new piece of the story consistent with the previous incidences unknown to them.

In general, the framework from which one approaches cases of interactive apparitions may determine what conclusions or explanations are possible and acceptable. If one is not of the opinion that consciousness is more than the brain and separate from it, one is more likely to approach these cases from the human-psi angle. If one deduces, as Pim van Lommel and Peter Fenwick described earlier, that consciousness can function independently of the brain, survival seems to be a simpler explanation, and certainly a preferable one (since we all die, don't we?). In terms of my own experience, when encountering what seems to be an aspect of someone who has survived the death of the body, I don't personally feel comfortable discounting the possibility of their sentience.

Of course, upon death, all of us will find out if we're right or wrong—that is, if we're still conscious afterward.

PART FOUR

The Impossible Made Real

There is no more fascinating field than this—the borderland of the Unknown; the dim, obscure region that lies between mind and matter, between physical and spiritual forces and energies, between the noumenal and the phenomenal worlds.

—HEREWARD CARRINGTON

Chapter 21

Human-Generated Phenomena

After-death communications and apparitions provide a taste of what is to come in this section. Imagine if groups of open-minded people could sit together and create an environment in which the types of phenomena described in previous chapters—or even more spectacular phenomena—would occur repeatedly and reliably. Then, many people could experience them in a controlled setting. We could also be certain the seeming miracles actually occurred, because multiple witnesses would be present, and scientists could observe and document them. Wouldn't this be an ideal scenario, offering the possibility of proof? Welcome to the strange but scientifically revolutionary world of physical mediumship, and all the other physical phenomena in various contexts that you will encounter in the next few chapters.

In previous chapters, we have seen examples of object movements occurring without anyone touching the objects—these are manifestations of macro (large-scale and visible to the observer) psychokinesis

(PK), or "mind over matter." The movements occurred spontaneously—a houseful of clocks stopped at the time of death, as described by Peter Fenwick; the car clock jumped first one hour and then a second hour for Jeffrey Kane and his wife; my bottle tops flew up with a popping sound in my kitchen. These displays might have been caused by the consciousness of a recently deceased person, as it seemed to those of us who witnessed them, or by the focused minds of the human agents in unusual states of consciousness. And in terms of the question of survival, this distinction is obviously critical. But before moving on to physical mediumship, it is also important to understand that certain macro-PK *can* be generated by human agents alone, the prime example being those arising in poltergeist cases.

Poltergeists are "outbreaks of spontaneous paranormal physical phenomena centering upon the organism of some particular individual," according to expert investigators Alan Gauld and A. D. Cornell. Some scientists today refer to the phenomenon as "recurrent spontaneous psychokinesis" (RSPK), which usually appears to be caused by unconscious psychological disturbances and emotional imbalances within someone in the household, often a troubled adolescent. This person releases stress through a "telekinetic temper tantrum," as Loyd Auerbach describes it, affecting the physical environment. The most common effects are percussive sounds such as raps, thumps, and banging, and household objects tilting, being knocked over, or hurled across a room. Gauld and Cornell reference five hundred cases from the literature in their 1979 classic book *Poltergeists*.

What's important to contemplate is the nature of the force involved. The poltergeist phenomenon often appears to be controlled by an "intelligence which not infrequently seems to organize and direct the various happenings," Gauld and Cornell say. In some cases communication, such as responsiveness to questions by rapping in code, occurs; the phenomenon seems to exhibit a purpose; and sometimes it focuses on one particular object. In an attempt to understand the nature of this intelligence, the two investigators explored the possibility that in a minority of cases, the intelligence may stem from a discarnate entity, as originally proposed by Ian Stevenson in a 1972 paper titled "Are Poltergeists Living or Are They Dead?" Stevenson highlights circumstances in which an object is flying through the air and suddenly changes speed; turns at a sharp angle and continues in a new direction; or goes from hurtling through the air to suddenly floating or gently coming to rest. "I think such cases suggest some discarnate agency actually carrying the objects transported or somehow otherwise controlling their flight," Stevenson writes. "I have not myself been able to imagine how such effects could be produced solely by the unconscious mind of the living agent." But when objects appear to be recklessly knocked over, which is usually the case, their movements are more likely to be caused by the chaotic energy of the adolescent agent.

Along these lines, Gauld and Cornell's "discarnate agency hypothesis" proposed that the physical effects and the purposes manifested would be different if discarnate entities were the source rather than human beings. Although rare, a case can be considered as a candidate for discarnate status if the paranormal incidents are not strictly tied to the comings and goings of one particular person or they switch from association with one person to another. If multiple witnesses see the same "phantasmal figure" or "misty shapes" in connection with the phenomena, this would also suggest a possible association with a discarnate entity. And most bizarre of all are the phenomena that "so far as is known exceed the capacities of any living agent," such as objects materializing in midair, direct voices speaking fluently from the air, or objects becoming animated. Along with Stevenson, the two investigators propose these could be caused by discarnates.

These sorts of phenomena also occur within physical mediumship in a more positive framework, as we will soon see. And as I'm sure is obvious, we do not understand how the process works, regardless of the source of its generation. What's important to understand is that, without question, objects can move "on their own" propelled by a mysterious force. This is not just the stuff of movies, hoaxing, or fantasy. To the contrary, small groups have conducted experiments in which table levitations and other physical phenomena have been generated through their own focus and intention, and not through eliciting the assistance of any mediums or discarnate agents. These human-generated events can be repeated and documented.

A well-known 1966 paper by K. J. Batcheldor describes a series of eighty sessions in which sitters experienced brisk movements and levitations from a forty-pound table. A six-pound table levitated six feet, beyond the reach of the small group, and other paranormal events were noted. "One cannot push a table into the air, either consciously or unconsciously, when the hands are on top of it," Batcheldor writes. "When it happened it came as quite a shock." In 1968, Alan Gauld and three others experienced table levitations so high that the ends of the legs, touched by the sitters, were at or above head level. A few years later, C. Brookes-Smith and D. W. Hunt described their group's ability to induce "powerful displays of psychokinesis with ostensible levitation and telekinetic phenomena" in a journal paper. The authors describe this ability as "a psychological 'skill' which can be acquired through aptitude and experience by virtually all human beings." Indeed, psychokinesis expert Stephen Braude first became interested in parapsychology, and particularly in psychokinesis, when he experienced table movements in his living room one day with two friends from graduate school. "The table rose *under* our fingers, all fingers were visible atop the table, and I could see clearly that the table made no contact with our legs or knees," he says.

In the 1970s, a group of eight Canadian researchers decided to create a fictitious "spirit" communicator, a thought-form they called an "imaginary ghost," through intense concentration and focus over a period of time. They fabricated the persona of a seventeenth-century British knight they named "Philip Aylesford," who had an affair with a Gypsy girl. Every detail of his imaginary life was visualized and discussed by the group over a period of months, as if he were a real person.

Led by George Owen, who had previously taught genetics and mathematics at Trinity College, Cambridge, the group sat together beginning in 1972 and engaged their "Philip" personality through table movements, followed by unexplained raps coming from inside the table. Philip communicated by giving one knock for yes or two for no. He was able to answer questions correctly only if they pertained to the fictitious history created by the sitters that was known to them. Otherwise, he could not reply. Yet he developed into what *seemed* like a full personality, with likes and dislikes, reactions and opinions. All of the physical effects were caused by a force created by the imaginations and focus of the human participants, which evolved and eventually inexplicably demonstrated intelligence, preferences, and independence. William G. Roll, Oxford-educated parapsychologist and psychologist from the University of West Georgia, made the somewhat amusing comment that "to judge by Philip the poltergeist can be domesticated."

It may be hard to accept such reports until you experience this yourself. I was fortunate to have that opportunity. In 2015, Stephen Braude invited me to be part of a small team, under his supervision, which would document table levitations and possibly more phenomena facilitated by Kai Muegge, a German physical medium. I had met Kai previously and had experienced the phenomena of his sittings in a more relaxed setting, so he welcomed my participation. Steve had conducted a successful study on Kai's phenomena in 2013 and published the results in a leading journal. This time, he wanted to see if he could improve on some of those results by introducing stricter controls. Robert Narholz, a documentary filmmaker, would participate and our goal was to film a full table levitation in red light with the latest advanced low-light cameras.

We went to Hanau, Germany, where Kai lives, in October 2015. During our first sitting, five of us sat around a plastic garden table, 33.5 inches in diameter and 28 inches high. At Kai's suggestion, Steve and I each tried to lift it and make it rise straight up while the tabletop remained horizontal. We had our hands and knees pressed upward against it from under the table, but it was impossible to do so. "Any movements we could produce resulted in table movements that felt obviously different from the way ostensibly genuine levitations feel—namely, slow, buoyant, and weightless and not as if pushed," Steve wrote in his journal paper about the sessions. "Levitated tables seem to float."

During the sessions, the lights were off and the music turned on, with a low red light nearby to be activated as needed. Like many other mediums, Kai believes that darkness facilitates the phenomena and that it is much harder to achieve results in the light (more on this to be discussed later). We were careful to make sure Kai was "controlled" during the sittings, meaning that someone on either side of him held his hands and touched his legs with theirs at all times to confirm that he was in no way physically influencing the movement of the table or any other phenomena. I was controlling Kai for most of the time on his left side. We inspected the round plastic table thoroughly to make sure there was no hidden contraption lodged within it that could cause independent movement.

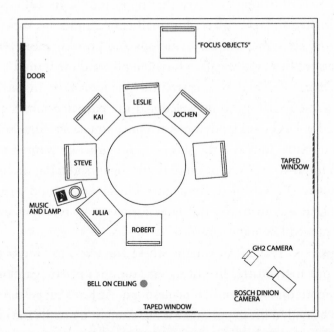

Our setup in Hanau. Kai's wife, Julia, and investigator Jochen (pseudonym) joined us. *Copyright © Robert Narholz*

Once we got started, sitting with our hands or fingertips resting lightly on top of the table, we experienced a lot of table tilting, and erratic circular movements. Sometimes the table would tilt sharply to one side on two legs and then loudly bang the two raised legs back onto the floor. Our hands were barely touching it. But it was the longer, more relaxed levitations—with the tabletop horizontal and not tilted—that really stood out. One of them lasted about fifteen seconds. The table rose at least two and a half feet straight up, and while suspended in the air, it swayed and dipped, gliding as if rocking on waves in what seemed like a swimming motion. It was as if it had suddenly become light and fluid, floating effortlessly, almost "alive."

In addition, we heard some strong raps on the wall a few times, which sounded like something knocking quickly in rapid succession. A bell hanging from the ceiling rang strongly once. All the sounds were recorded. These physical phenomena occurred completely on their own while we were anchored to the table with Kai controlled— much to our delight.

Before beginning the next sittings with the cameras, Steve, Robert, and I cleared the sitting room of anything unnecessary and thoroughly inspected every inch of the space and its contents. Steve locked the doors leading to the outside and kept possession of the keys. This ruled out any possibility of an accomplice entering the room or for any apparatus for raising tables to be present.

We continued to experience more levitations, some between two and three feet off the ground, including one with that remarkable back-and-forth "swimming" motion. Once, Robert pressed down on the table in front of him to see whether it would go down. He was sitting across from Kai, and if Kai was somehow lifting it from his side, the table would have yielded to Robert's pressure. "It was spongy, like pushing down on a spring," Robert told me. "It did not feel at all as if someone was forcing the table up from one side only, but rather, as if it was lifted by a force applied uniformly to the whole table, from beneath." Unfortunately, Robert did not capture our best levitations on camera, with the table going straight up, due to problems introducing the light quickly enough at the right moments. But all of us were able to see the levitated table when the red light was switched on.

On one side of the room, we had rested a large, flat circular drum leaning against the legs of a chair out of anybody's reach (with the "focus objects" shown in the diagram). While I was controlling Kai, we heard a loud bang come from the drum in the pitch dark. Afterward, we observed that its position against the chair had not changed. I got up and hit the drum moderately with my hand, and we all agreed that the resulting sound was significantly softer than it was during the sitting. Even so, the rather light pressure I put on the center of the drum easily knocked it from its position. How could this more forceful, much louder bang have left it intact in its position? What was it that hit the drum, and how did it generate this sound?

These phenomena might have been examples of a "domesticated poltergeist" created solely by Kai with the help of the group's focused desires and intentions. This is how it seemed to me, and this certainly was Steve's perception. However, Kai said there were "spirit controls" making it happen, and he asked them to perform throughout the sessions and talked to them regularly, even sometimes scolding them for not delivering. He threatened to end the session and warned them not to be afraid of the camera. Was he actually talking to himself while somehow making these unexplainable things happen?

In January 2016, I asked Steve Braude—who has studied Kai Muegge extensively and is arguably the leading expert in the world on macro-PK—for his thoughts:

I think it would be hasty to conclude that there was only one agent. Some of the participants felt tense enough for the emotions to have yielded a poltergeist effect. Kai may well have been the repository of most of the tension and the likely (paranormal) cause of the drum thwack and some other phenomena. But the table movements are particularly ambiguous. In the final séance we were not getting much table activity until I made the suggestion that we talk about the weather and tell jokes. Now, does that show that Kai's PK "force" was inhibited by the group until we got our minds off the job, or does it show that getting our minds off the job left several of us free, collectively, to influence the table? No one has a clue. I do believe there's little reason to suppose that discarnates caused any of the phenomena, most of which seemed too closely tied to the psychodynamics of the occasion.

As for what exactly it is that could make any of those effects occur, I can't say anything helpful except to note that if it's PK, we don't know what that is. We didn't feel cold breezes like those reported with some other mediums prior to object movements. So we can't make any moderately conservative appeals to more familiar sorts of energy transfer. We can only appeal to the mystery of PK. And even then, we don't know if the different effects all had a similar cause. We don't know if there's any lawlike connection between whatever can ring a bell, hit a drum, raise a table, or make lights appear. We don't know a thing about whether the various phenomena classed as PK share any underlying nomological unity.

As Steve implies, not much science has been applied to the study of PK. However, one fascinating study on the acoustics of paranormal rapping sounds, like the ones we heard in Hanau, establishes the truly unexplainable nature of these "otherworldly" noises. In a 2010 paper, scientist Barrie G. Colvin reported results from his examination of ten recordings of genuine poltergeist raps made from 1960 to 2000. He compared them with the waveforms of raps produced normally on the same materials. By measuring the amplitude of the sound waves on a computer program, which also indicates the strength of the sound, he obtained diagrams of the waveforms. The pitch of the sounds was also determined.

For normal rapping sounds, such as a knuckle tapping on a wall, the amplitude is at its strongest point at the moment the knuckle hits the wall—at the instant the sound begins—and then decays quickly. In the ten poltergeist raps Colvin studied, the loudest part of the sound was not at the very beginning. Instead, the sound started relatively quietly and gradually built to a maximum before it decayed, and the decay took longer.

The famous Enfield case of 1977 in North London was extensively documented by experienced investigators. They recorded mysterious raps along with some similar, normal raps on the bedroom door with the same equipment (a reel-to-reel device at $^{15}/_{16}$ inch per second), providing ideal data for comparison. The diagrams show the striking difference between the sounds. Colvin showed that this difference between normal and poltergeist raps was consistent for all ten cases, with the same anomalous characteristics in all the unexplained raps.

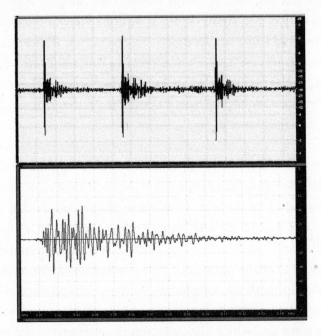

The normal raps at the location of the Endfield case (*top*) are strikingly different from the anomalous rap (*bottom*), which builds and decays gradually.
Copyright © Barrie Colvin

Colvin concluded that the rap-like sounds caused by poltergeists seemed to not be actual raps at all. Instead, they "appear to involve the relatively slow buildup of a stress within a material, culminating in an audible sound when the level of stress reaches a specific magnitude. The reasons and physics of this mechanism are unknown . . ." He states that no one has been able to produce sounds with similar waveforms to those of the unexplained raps, even when attempting to do so. His theory is that the anomalous raps originate from the vibration of molecules *inside* something like a table, and not from something striking the surface, which creates a very different sound. The waveforms more closely resemble seismograms from earthquakes, the only waveform of this type that is produced by normal means. The loud bang on Kai's drum might have been generated this way—from inside the drum—which could explain why it didn't fall over. Even though the vibration was strong, it might have affected the drum in a way we don't understand.

It's hard to communicate how magically thrilling it is to feel a levitated table swim, to hear a bell ring and a drum banged with no human agent involved. The mystery of it evoked my deepest curiosity. Such events are important for our investigation here not because they relate to the survival of consciousness beyond death, but because they establish for the reader that these physical phenomena really do occur. They have been reliably documented time and time again, by qualified, skeptical observers in situations where hoaxing or faulty observation can be ruled out. Objects are moved and sounds made by some force we don't understand—a force that sometimes seems to act with intelligence. A first step to understanding physical mediumship—which in contrast may offer evidence for survival past death—is to recognize the reality of macro-PK. The reader's mind should now be able to expand to accommodate the more elegant, refined, and even beautiful events of genuine physical mediumship.

Chapter 22

From Object Movements to Materialized Hands

The object movements described in the previous chapter, as unusual as they are, represent the most rudimentary, even commonplace PK manifestations on the scale of what's possible. Facilitated by the unconscious drives of human agents alone, they are in fact trivial. But they take on a different meaning in the context of physical mediumship. During a group sitting with a physical medium, usually called a "séance" (from the Old French *seoir*, "to sit"), the medium goes into a trance similar to that of the well-studied trance medium Mrs. Piper, as described by Alan Gauld, only perhaps deeper. A "spirit control" then occupies the medium's body and communicates through body language or by speaking through his or her vocal cords. The medium has essentially "stepped aside" to allow the use of the body by these forces.

The more exceptional manifestations within physical mediumship include the levitation of objects that sometimes fly around the room; the creation of moving lights; the playing of instruments without any-

Copyright © Dan Callister/Alamy

Copyright © Lisa Kean

Copyright © Lisa Kean

Courtesy of Sandra O'Hara

Mediums Laura Lynne Jackson (TOP LEFT) and Sandra O'Hara (BOTTOM RIGHT) provided readings for me, which included recognizable personality traits and numerous accurate facts about my brother Garry Kean (ABOVE at age 12) and close friend Budd Hopkins (BELOW), who both died within recent years. Did Laura and Sandra acquire this information from earthly sources through their own extraordinary telepathy and clairvoyance? Or were these two discarnate beings present delivering their memories and messages as the mediums describe?

George Draper (RIGHT), a World War I soldier missing in action. His great nephew Mark Lewis attempted to find his remains with the help of a medium, who provided many specific details she said came from George. Mark located George's unmarked grave in France after the medium said George gave her "G22" (the grave location) and the name "Albone" on the adjacent grave (BELOW LEFT). Mark brought a plan of the potential graveyard, and the medium pointed to the location of the grave (red dot) with the map upside down and invisible to her (BOTTOM RIGHT). The location corresponded to "G22" provided earlier.

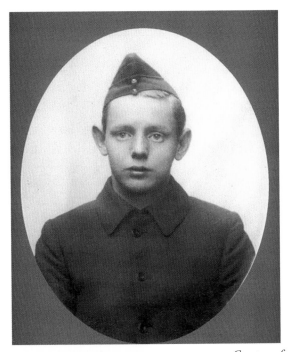

*Courtesy of
Mark Lewis*

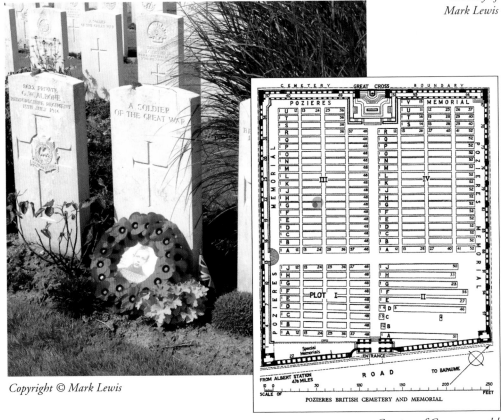

Copyright © Mark Lewis

*Courtesy of Commonwealth
War Graves Commission*

LEFT: American trance medium Leonora Piper was studied extensively by William James and others. She is arguably the greatest and most well-documented trance medium of all time. *Courtesy of Mary Evans Picture Library*

BELOW: With investigator Stephen Braude (LEFT) and German physical medium Kai Muegge (CENTER) at Kai's home in Hanau, Germany, in 2015. *Courtesy of Stephen Braude*

The séance room where we documented the anomalous table movements and other phenomena facilitated by Kai. The drum, which made a loud bang "on its own," is to my left, leaning on its chair. Kai sat where I am, with his hands and legs controlled by me on one side and Stephen on the other. *Courtesy of Leslie Kean*

Thomas Mann and others were deeply impressed by the séances of the young physical medium Willi Schneider, shown here in trance with luminous pins on his clothing to keep him visible in the low light. He is controlled by zoologists Karl Gruber (CENTER) and Karl Zimmer (RIGHT), who were present for the séance Mann describes. *Courtesy of Peter Mulacz*

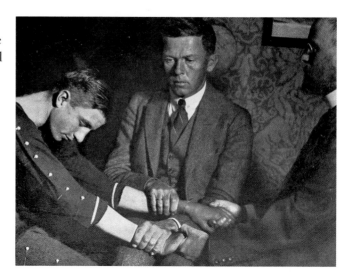

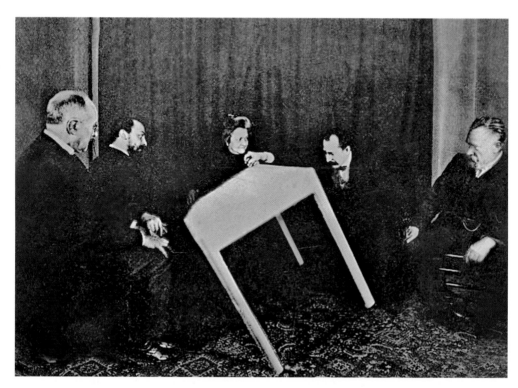

Eusapia Palladino facilitates the independent movement of a table for investigators who are holding her hands and watching her feet. The table has risen off the ground and tilted. *Courtesy of Stephen Braude*

Eusapia Palladino, the most thoroughly investigated physical medium ever. Born in Italy, she was scrutinized under rigorous controls by scientists all over Europe and in America, most famously in Naples in 1908. *Courtesy of Peter Mulacz*

Iceland's physical medium Indridi Indridason manifested numerous independent voices in multiple languages unknown to him, some singing operatic duets. He died at age twenty-eight. *Courtesy of Erlendur Haraldsson/White Crow Books*

Professor Erlendur Haraldsson of the University of Iceland researched the work of Indridi Indridason. He has published on after-death communications, drop-in communicators, and many other areas in scientific journals and books for over forty years. *Copyright © Jón Örn Gudbjartsson*

ABOVE: 63 Store Kongensgade, Copenhagen, on the far left, where the fire broke out, observed by Indridi's drop-in communicator Emil Jensen. The house on the right is 67, where Jensen lived on the second floor. *Courtesy of Erlendur Haraldsson/White Crow Books*

RIGHT: Welsh physical medium Alec Harris, one of the greatest materialization mediums on record. His full-form materializations in low light were witnessed by hundreds of observers. *Courtesy of the Harris family and Saturday Night Press*

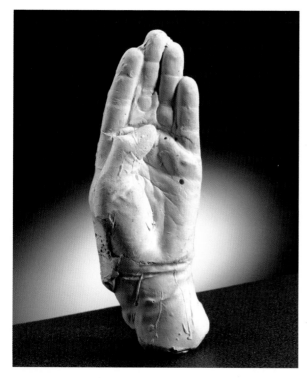

A series of plaster casts were made from materialized hands that were dipped into molten paraffin wax during the séances of Polish physical medium Franek Kluski under tightly controlled conditions. *Copyright © Yves Bosson/Agence Martienne/Institut Métapsychique International (IMI), Paris*

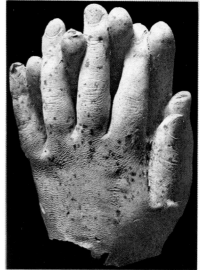

A cast with crossed fingers showing much detail. Human disengagement from the paper-thin glove would have been impossible without damage. Everyone in the room had linked hands, and Gustave Geley and others could see the materialized hands dipping into the hot wax, which splashed on the sitters. *Courtesy of the Institut Métapsychique International (IMI), Paris/Agence Martienne*

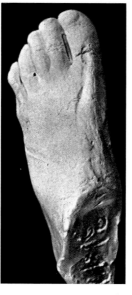

LEFT: The glove from this mold was flattened. The soft, warm glove was dropped on the back of Geley's hand, which was holding Kluski's hand, so he did not move it until the séance was over. *Courtesy of IMI, Paris/Agence Martienne*

RIGHT: A child's foot was also provided; no children were present in the séance room. *Courtesy of IMI, Paris/Agence Martienne*

The page in the book test conducted by physical medium Stewart Alexander's guide, Freda, for an American whose home Stewart knew nothing about. Freda referenced a specific location on the shelf, p. 84 on the left side, an animal near the top, and farther down the names "George" and "Smith." All were found as specified. *Courtesy of Kevin Kussow*

After the Cheyenne delegation departed, Anthony ordered Left Hand and Little **Raven** to disband the Arapaho camp near Fort Lyon. "Go and hunt **buffalo** to feed yourselves," he told them. Alarmed by Anthony's brusqueness, the Arapahos packed up and began moving away. When they were well out of view of the fort, the two bands of Arapahos separated. Left Hand went with his people to Sand Creek to join the Cheyennes. Little Raven led his band across the Arkansas River and headed south; he did not trust the Red-Eyed Soldier Chief.

Anthony now informed his superiors that "there is a band of Indians within forty miles of the post. . . . I shall try to keep the Indians quiet until such time as I receive reinforcements." [17]

On November 26, when the post trader, Gray Blanket John Smith requested permission to go out to Sand Creek to trade for hides, Major Anthony was unusually cooperative. He provided Smith with an Army ambulance to haul his goods, and also a driver, Private David Louderback of the Colorado Cavalry. If nothing else would lull the Indians into a sense of security and keep them camped where they were, the presence of a post trader and a peaceful representative of the Army should do so.

Twenty-four hours later the reinforcements which Anthony said he needed to attack the Indians were approaching Fort Lyon. They were six hundred men of Colonel Chivington's Colorado regiments, including most of the Third, which had been formed by Governor John Evans for the sole purpose of fighting Indians. When the vanguard reached the fort, they surrounded it and forbade anyone to leave under penalty of death. About the same time a detachment of twenty cavalrymen reached William Bent's ranch a few miles to the east, surrounded Bent's house, and forbade anyone to enter or leave. Bent's two half-breed sons, George and Charlie, and his half-breed son-in-law Edmond Guerrier were camped with the Cheyennes on Sand Creek.

When Chivington rode up to the officers' quarters at Fort Lyon, Major Anthony greeted him warmly. Chivington began talking of "collecting scalps" and "wading in

Stewart Alexander in his garden in Northern England. *Copyright © Leslie Kean*

Stewart's séance room. He is strapped into the armchair; the table is lit from underneath during the materialization of the hand. The trumpets, which fly around the room, are on the table next to drumsticks, which are banged loudly on the table by whatever force is present. *Copyright © Leslie Kean*

one touching them; the passing of living matter through inert matter; voices that speak out of thin air; and the physical materialization of hands or full human forms. This may be hard for many readers to accept as real. It was for me too, until I not only studied the scientific literature documenting studies of genuine mediums but also sat with two of them myself. No, these cases do not only involve hoaxes and parlor games, despite the better-known disreputable séances that seem to get all the attention.

We all know that fraudulent mediums have fooled gullible and vulnerable people for a long time, and continue to do so. But some genuine physical mediums have been willing to subject themselves to rigorous observation and strict controls by scientists who are able to rule out any fraud or trickery. Numerous volumes of reports and detailed books about these historical studies are available beginning in the late 1800s, with Braude's 1997 study *The Limits of Influence* taking the contemporary lead. David Fontana, the British investigator and author of *Is There an Afterlife?*, also provides recent case details, some based on his own observations.

Physical mediumship is unique in that "it provides us with objective visual evidence of the interaction between different dimensions," according to Fontana. Genuine physical mediums facilitate such unbelievable physical phenomena that it's understandable uninitiated people would reject such reports. What happens in these séance rooms defies our intellectual grasp of the natural order of things. But in fact, these phenomena are part of Nature, because they do occur.

In terms of survival, the question is whether "spirit communicators" are manipulating the physical world, as the mediums understand to be the case. During the heyday of physical mediumship, between 1850 and 1930, most if not all mediums believed that their physical phenomena and verbal evidence from loved ones came by way of spirit beings from the "afterlife" world. Today there appear to be fewer physical mediums. Many may simply work quietly with a consistent small group, keeping it private. Given the materialistic and fast-paced, technological orientation of Western culture, and the negative attitude of the establishment toward mediumship, this is understandable. But many outstanding scientific studies of physical mediumship under the strictest controls were published in the 1920s and '30s, and they are absolutely astonishing.

Séance-room phenomena are so radical that they can be overwhelming, even disturbing, the first time one has to face them. German writer and critic Thomas Mann, winner of the Nobel Prize in Literature, described his first séance in a whimsical, elegant, and very honest 1929 essay. Mann, one of the most influential German writers of the twentieth century, described himself as a skeptic, with the following caveat: "I aver that there can be no true skepticism which is not skeptical of itself; and a skeptic, in my humble view, is not merely one who believes the prescribed things and averts his eyes from everything that might imperil his virtue. Rather your true skeptic will, in ordinary language, find all sorts of things possible, and he will not, for the sake of convention, deny the evidence of his sound senses." This attitude, coupled with his brilliance, made him the perfect person to test the validity of physical mediumship.

Mann was invited to a séance at the palatial home of Baron Albert von Schrenck-Notzing, a physician, psychiatrist, and notable psychic researcher who had been studying a young Austrian medium, shy and still a teenager, by the name of Willi Schneider (1903–1971).

Mann was impressed by the quality of those in attendance—two zoology professors and other intelligentsia, medical professionals and scientists. He inspected the séance room and the objects in it to make sure there was nothing suspicious, and the baron invited him to witness Willi strip and dress in a one-piece cotton garment covered by a dressing gown with luminous ribbons covering it, which would make him visible in low light. Willi also wrapped a luminous ribbon around his head, and the team peered into his wide-open mouth. Once in the séance room, Willi was always controlled by at least two people who held his arms and legs. Mann had this job during much of the séance, even though Willi was visible to everyone in his luminescent clothing.

A table was placed inside the circle five feet away from the medium. On it was a lamp with a red shade, a bell, a plate with flour on it, a little slate and piece of chalk. An upside-down wastepaper basket stood next to the table with a music box on it, both with luminous ribbons attached; a typewriter was on the floor near the baron; and luminous felt rings were strewn about the floor, some with luminous strings attached. The room was illuminated by a covered dark red ceiling light and the little table lamp. Mann states that Willi gave off light, as did the rings and the objects, so "the field of operations was visible; and after a little while the top of the table seemed really quite well lighted."

Willi went into a deep trance, as if he was asleep. His head drooped sideways on his chest until his familiar "spirit communicator" Minna made her presence known through his body movements, and responded to questions by squeezes of Mann's hand while he controlled Willi. Initially nothing happened, so they took a break; and even after that, almost an hour passed with nothing at all. Then, with Willi in a deep trance, Minna returned. The baron and another sitter encouraged and cajoled her into performing, and she requested the handkerchief. Familiar with what this meant, the baron dropped a handkerchief on the floor near the table, where it lay, "a white gleam in the twilight," while the participants leaned toward it and chattered at Minna's request. Mann describes what happened next as he watched the handkerchief:

> Before all our eyes, with a swift, assured, vital, almost beautiful movement it rose out of the shadow into the rays of light, which colored it reddish; I say rose, but rose is not the word. It was not that it was wafted up, empty and fluttering. Rather it was taken and lifted, there was an active agency in it, like a hand, you could see the outline of the knuckles, from which it hung down in folds; it was manipulated from the inside, by some living thing, compressed, shaken, made to change its shape, in the two or three seconds during which it was held up in the lamplight. Then, moving with the same quiet assurance, it returned to the floor.
>
> It was not possible—but it happened. May lightning strike me if I lie. Before my uncorrupted eyes, which would have been

just as ready to see nothing, in case nothing had been there, it happened. Indeed, it presently happened again. Scarcely had the handkerchief reached the floor when it came back up again into the light, this time faster than before; plainly and unmistakably we saw something clutching it from within, the members of something that held it—it looked to be narrower than a human hand, more like a claw. Down, and up again, for the third time up. The handkerchief was violently shaken by the something inside it, and tossed toward the table, with a poor aim, for it hung by one corner and then fell to the floor.

Mann was shaken. "Never before had I seen the impossible happening despite its own impossibility." He held Willi's wrists while someone else had custody of his knees. "Not a thought, not a notion, not the shadow of a possibility that the boy sleeping here could have done what was happening there. And who else? Nobody. And still it was done. It gave me a queasy feeling."

Next, the bell with its gleaming ribbons and shiny metal was placed on the overturned wastepaper basket by the baron. Then it too was lifted up—"impossible, of course, but it is taken by a hand, for what else can take a bell by the handle?"—and it was rung violently, carried through the air, rung again, and flung under one of the sitters' chairs. "Slight seasickness. Profound wonderment, with a tinge, not of horror, but of disgust," Mann writes.

The wastebasket was knocked over, then lifted high into the air illuminated by its ribbons and the red light, and then tumbled to the floor. Again, reacting to the intellectual affront of these events, Mann felt "a mild form of seasickness." He left Willi's side and sat in the circle near the table, while somebody else took the job of holding Willi's wrists. Minna then made an effort to turn the handle of the music box. "Tell it to stop," the baron told Mann. Mann commanded her several times to stop and start the music box, and she obeyed each time. "You sit there, bending forward, you command the impossible, and you are obeyed, by a spook, a panic-stricken little monster from behind the world . . ."

Then Minna shoved and tossed the illuminated rings on the floor and carried one with a string to the table and put it down. She made knocking sounds on the table. "Tut, tut, you hole-and-corner fish out of water, why, and with what monstrous knuckles, are you knocking like that on our good table, before our face and eyes?" Mann thought to himself. At that moment, Minna flung a felt ring into his face.

The baron suggested that Minna "do something useful" and go to the typewriter on the floor, which had paper in it ready for use. Mann writes:

> The thing seems able to listen to reason, it desists from its efforts at the box. We wait. And, on my honor, the writing-machine begins to click, there on the floor. This is insane. Even after all we have already seen, it is in the highest degree startling, bewildering, ridiculous; the fantasticality of the thing is even fascinating. Who is it writing on the machine? Nobody. Nobody is lying there on the carpet in the dark and playing on the machine, but it is being played on. Willi's arms and legs are held fast. Even if he could get an arm free, he could not reach the machine with it; and as for his feet, even if they could reach that far they could not touch single types on the machine, they would tread on several at once. No, it is not Willi. But there is nobody else. What else can we do but shake our heads and laugh? The writing is being done with the right touch, a hand is certainly touching the keys—but is it really only one hand? No, if you ask me, there are surely two hands; the sounds are too quick for one, they sound as though proceeding from the fingers of a practiced typist; we come to the end of a line, the bell rings, we hear the carriage being drawn back, the new line begins—the sound breaks off and a pause ensues.

Then, in front of a dark black curtain, a little apparition appeared. It was "vague, and whitely shimmering," lighted by a sort of flash of white lightning that came from within it. Then it was gone. The baron asked Minna to put her hand in the plate of flour and leave an impression, but she didn't. The séance ended. A "nonsensical jumble of large and small letters" was found on the previously blank typewriter page. Mann writes:

> I am in that intriguing and confounded state of mind in which reason commands us to recognize what reason on the other hand would reject as impossible. The nature of the phenomena I have described makes it inevitable that the idea of deception should afterward haunt the minds even of those who saw with their own eyes; only to be laid, over and over, by the evidence of the senses, by the reflection that deception was definitely impossible.

Despite feeling seasick, Mann writes that he couldn't resist going to one more séance, so that he could see the handkerchief rise up into the red light before his eyes. "For the sight has got into my blood somehow, I cannot forget it. I should like once more to crane my neck, and with the nerves of my digestive apparatus all on edge with the fantasticality of it, once more, just once, see the impossible come to pass." I can strongly relate to his reaction—it is unforgettable and deeply compelling to witness these unnerving, "impossible" events, and all these years later, I too felt the strong calling to relive them after attending my first séance. Thankfully my digestive tract was not affected; I did not feel queasy or seasick—quite the opposite—as I will explain in a coming chapter.

I have to wonder if Mann would have needed to be rushed to the hospital if he had witnessed something even more impossible: the creation of a visible, moving hand. As hard as it is to believe, some mediums can facilitate the materialization of hands with joints and fingernails that are warm and fleshy, that touch people, bang on solid objects, and carry things around the room. In some rare cases, they dissolve while people are actually holding them.

In 1908, the well-known Italian medium Eusapia Palladino (1854–1918) was subjected to controlled studies in Naples by three of the world's most skeptical and seasoned investigators, who knew every trick in the book used by fraudulent mediums. Eusapia was exceptional—no other physical medium has ever been studied so carefully, for so long, with such extreme precautions, and by so many scientists. Eusapia had acknowledged that if she was not tightly controlled, she might try and cheat while in trance when her actions were completely out of her control and she was not aware of her own behavior. She had done so in the past, although her unsophisticated, obvious tricks were easy to detect, and only possible when the controls were lax. (She welcomed the most stringent limitations possible to prevent this, which were in place here.)

The Society for Psychical Research (SPR), the leading scientific research organization of its day, sent these emissaries for the purpose of exposing Eusapia as a fraud. American investigator Hereward Carrington had recently published the lengthy book *Physical Phenomena of Spiritualism,* detailing the trickery and devices used by fraudulent mediums, after observing and exposing them for many years. With a reputation as one of the keenest investigators in the US, he was also an amateur magician and could reproduce many séance-room phenomena produced by disingenuous mediums. British researcher W. W. Baggally had spent over thirty-five years attending the séances of physical mediums, was also a magician, and had rarely if ever met with anything that appeared genuine. The Honorable Everard Feilding was likewise highly educated in dealing with fraudulent mediums. While he had an open mind and a good sense of humor, his skepticism was extreme.

Carrington, Baggally, and Feilding, nicknamed the "Fraud Squad," conducted eleven séances with Eusapia in a room entirely under their control. They constructed the cabinet—a corner area enclosed with a curtain around it that many mediums say helps concentrate energy allowing for materializations. Eusapia and the team sat at a small table outside of the cabinet. The door was locked; any possibility of an accomplice was eliminated. Eusapia, usually in trance, was physically controlled at all times. There was always enough light in the room to see everything that happened. The men noted, out loud, anything and everything that developed, describing also the controls on Eusapia, all of which was recorded by a stenographer present in the room.

The official "Report on a Series of Sittings with Eusapia Palladino" documented, explained, and analyzed the proceedings in 295 pages. Not only are the actual phenomena stunning, but these great skeptics also document the progression of their transformation as they are forced to face the unavoidable reality of the genuine phenomena.

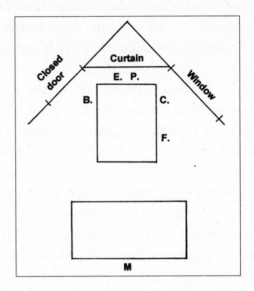

The diagram of the séance room included in the report. "M" is the stenographer.

"We were still fresh at the game, still alertly suspicious of every movement of Eusapia; somewhat annoyed, to speak frankly, at our failure to detect any fraud at the first séance, and determined to get even with her," Feilding wrote after the second séance on November 23, 1908. In the same comment, he also stated that "my mind was not prepared to accept the phenomena which occurred, and yet I was unable to suggest any loophole for fraud in the production of any of them." In that particular session, the team documented a range of object movements, sounds, and the plucking of a guitar string. The light "was strong enough not only to enable us to see every object all over the room, but even to read, at our places at the table, small print," the notes say.

Materialized hands first appeared in Séance V. "The light was always sufficient to see the exact whereabouts of her face, as well as of her hands, even from the further side of the table," Feilding wrote. The notes state:

> At 11.10 an entirely fresh phenomenon occurred, viz., the appearance over the medium's head, from between the two curtains, of a hand, dead white in color. It came somewhat slowly out, palm downward, then clenched its fingers and withdrew again between the curtains, the medium's own hands being held separately and distinctly by B. and F.

In addition, when Carrington pushed against the curtains a little later, "something solid and tangible within the curtain, like a hand," pushed back strongly against his hand—"a material and responsive agent." Of course Eusapia was outside the curtain and under control.

Eusapia believed she was under the influence of her spirit control John King, ostensibly her father in a previous incarnation. He was "supposed to regulate her séances and produce most of the phenomena," says Carrington. Sometimes John would tap answers to questions by table tilting or rapping on the table. He would touch a specific person immediately when asked while both Eusapia's hands were under control. On one occasion Eusapia was tired and wanted to end the session but John said "No, no" through the table. A little later he signaled yes. "Here, then, we have evidence of an external intelligence, differing from that of Eusapia, and expressing wishes in direct opposition to her own," Carrington writes.

In Séance VI, on December 4, the hand manifestations progressed to actually grasping people outside the cabinet, but through the cabinet curtain, so that separate fingers, a thumb, and fingernails could be felt. How freakish! This may sound creepy, as it did to me when I first read it. Imagine feeling these hands for the first time! The report states:

> 1. I am touched by something coming straight on to the points of my fingers.

12:11 a.m. F. I am touched again; I am taken hold of by fingers, and I can feel the nails quite plainly.

[My forefinger was pressed hard by three separate fingers above it and by a thumb below, through the curtain. I felt the nails quite distinctly as they pressed into my finger. F., Dec. 6/0 8.]

C. Her head pressing against my head. I am absolutely holding her left hand on the table, both her legs are around my right leg under the chair.

B. I am absolutely certain that her right hand is on my left hand on her right knee.

2. I am touched again. Grasped. this time as though by the lower part of the thumb and fingers. [The grasp was round the palm of my hand. F., Mar. 1 1/0 9.]

And a little later:

12:17 a.m. F. I have asked John if there was enough force for him to show himself. Immediately afterward—

C. I saw a white thing over her head clearly.

[So did I ; it was just as though something showed itself obligingly in reply to my request. F., Dec. 5 /0 8.]

[The medium squeezed my hand, and immediately afterward I saw the white thing. C., Dec. 5/0 8.]

B. I saw the white thing over her head and immediately after that a hand came out from behind the curtain and forcibly pulled me toward the cabinet, quite tightly on my sleeve.

[The pull was so violent that it almost pulled me off my chair. B., Dec. 5 / 0 8.]

Carrington comments that the touches of human hands were "the most extraordinary and the most incredible of any of the phenomena produced through Eusapia's mediumship." He continues:

That human hands—having all the peculiarities of hands, even to the presence of fingernails, should become visible and tan-

gible during a séance—these hands not being Eusapia's nor any
of the sitters'—this is so utterly at variance with common sense
that one finds it next to impossible to believe it. And yet these
hands are real, and by no possible means could they have been
Eusapia's.

Next, in Séance VII, along with many other phenomena, a *visible*
hand grasped someone. The report states:

It was the first séance, indeed the only one, at which a hand
came out from within the curtain and was both felt and clearly
seen. This occurred at 12.9 a.m., when B. was grasped on the
shoulder by a hand visible to himself and C. (see B.'s note). Further, at 11.20 p.m. a hand came out over the medium's head,
visible to F., C., and M. from the stenographer's table, ringing a
large tea-bell which had been placed on the table inside the curtain. It attached it with extraordinary rapidity to the medium's
hair, leaving it there, and disappeared, to return about a quarter
of a minute afterward, detach it, ring it over the medium's head
and throw it onto the séance table. Both the medium's hands
were separately and adequately controlled at the time.

Baggally adds:

I had felt the touch and grasp of a hand at the previous séances.
For the first time, at this one, I clearly saw a hand. It appeared
from behind the right-hand curtain at about 2½ feet from the
floor, advanced toward my right shoulder and gave it a strong
grip, after which it disappeared behind the curtain. The hand
appeared to be a man's hand of a natural color, larger than
Eusapia's, which I subsequently examined.

Baggally concludes that a "supernormal force" was able to "produce the effects of tangible matter and assume the form of a hand."

What is the nature of this "supernormal force"? The report's fourteen-page conclusion ends with Feilding, who says he will refrain from speculating upon its nature, even though he acknowledges that "it is just in this speculation that the whole interest of the subject lies." He points to the same two possibilities that are still debated today, now known as the LAP hypothesis ("an extension of human faculty") and the survival hypothesis ("something apparently intelligent and external to her") as being the two possible explanations. The phenomena, he adds, are "the playthings of the agency which they reveal."

Eusapia Palladino was not the only physical medium who facilitated the materialization of visible, "living" hands that were observed by leading scientists of the day. Daniel Dunglas Home (1833–1886), considered along with Eusapia to be one of the most impressive mediums ever, demonstrated for twenty-five years and was never accused of cheating. Born in Scotland but raised in America, Home (pronounced "Hume") was under carefully controlled observation for many years by Sir William Crookes, a prominent chemist and physicist noted for his discovery of the element thallium and for his cathode-ray studies. According to Stephen Braude, who researched Home extensively, among fifteen different "mind-boggling" types of phenomena that Home repeatedly generated were:

> Hands, supple, solid, mobile, and warm, of different sizes,
> shapes, and colors. Although the hands were animated and
> solid to the touch, they would often end at or near the wrist and
> eventually dissolve or melt. Sometimes the hands were said to be
> disfigured exactly as the hands of a deceased ostensible communicator (unknown to Home) had been.

Crookes himself made some observations in published notes:

> On another occasion a small hand and arm, like a baby's,
> appeared playing about a lady who was sitting next to me. It
> then passed to me and patted my arm and pulled my coat several
> times.

A hand has repeatedly been seen by myself and others playing the keys of an accordion, both of the medium's hands being visible at the same time, and sometimes being held by those near him.

To the touch the hand sometimes appears icy cold and dead, at other times warm and lifelike, grasping my own with the firm pressure of an old friend.

No one can explain with any certainty what was behind the creation of these hands, which often responded with intelligence to the words of the experimenters, but other mediums manifested them as well. The work of these sophisticated investigators was impeccable, reported in lengthy papers available to readers today. And, I will later describe witnessing the materialization of a hand myself, with contemporary medium Stewart Alexander.

A range of other extraordinary phenomena, perhaps suggestive of survival, such as drop-in communicators who can later be verified as having lived on earth, also occur within physical mediumship. Another is independent voice. In these cases, ostensible disembodied communicators speak either in midair or through a simple cone known as a "trumpet," which helps amplify the voice, at an objective distance from the medium that can be easily determined by the sitters. Some mediums, such as the well-known Leslie Flint, had their mouths taped, were wired to a throat microphone, held water in their mouths, or were rendered speechless by investigators in other ways while the voices carried on across the room. I find these otherworldly yet conversational voices to be one of the more wondrous aspects of physical mediumship, as described in the next chapter.

Chapter 23

Possible Evidence
of Survival

By Erlendur Haraldsson, PhD

Erlendur Haraldsson is a professor emeritus of psychology at the University of Iceland, where he taught from 1973 to 1999. Before that, he studied philosophy at the Universities of Copenhagen, Edinburgh, and Freiburg, and received his PhD in psychology from the University of Freiburg in 1972. Haraldsson has been researching psychic phenomena, apparitions, child reincarnation cases, and mediumship since the 1970s. In a previous section, I described his studies of after-death communications. He has published widely on these and related topics in psychology, parapsychology, and psychiatric journals, as well as writing numerous books, the most recent being Indridi Indridason: The Icelandic Physical Medium *(2015). Although not as well known as many others, Indridi Indridason is undoubtedly one of the greatest physical mediums of all time.*

I will present two incidences within the physical mediumship of Indridi Indridason of Iceland, whom I have personally investigated in great detail. One exceptional case of a verified drop-in communicator, and another of independent voices singing in a language unknown to the medium, provide evidence that points toward the possibility of human survival of physical death. In fact, these two events within Indridi's mediumship are among the best evidence I have ever encountered for that possibility.

Indridi Indridason grew up on a farm in northwestern Iceland, and moved to Reykjavik, the capital of Iceland, at age twenty-two to become a printer's apprentice. His extraordinary gifts were discovered by chance in 1905 when he was invited to sit with a group of intellectuals and other prominent members of Icelandic society interested in his mediumship. Einar Kvaran, a well-known writer and editor, established a research group, the Experimental Society, to study Indridi. Indridi's period of activity lasted until the summer of 1909, when he and his fiancée both caught typhoid fever, from which she died and he never recovered. He died in a sanatorium in 1912, when he was only twenty-eight years old.

The mediumship of Indridi Indridason was investigated and tested extensively by members of the Experimental Society. With Einar Kvaran as president, its leading members included Haraldur Nielsson, professor of theology at the University of Iceland; and Björn Jonsson, newspaper editor and later the prime minister after home rule was established in Iceland. Indridi's remarkable psychokinetic and mediumistic phenomena are described in numerous contemporary reports. His séances were documented in notes written immediately after a séance or the following day, called minute books, which were usually signed by a second person who checked the document for accuracy. Papers on his mediumship were presented at professional conferences in Copenhagen and Warsaw in 1921 and 1923.

His phenomena, some of which occurred in full light, included movements and levitations of various objects, sometimes of the medium himself; knocks on walls and clicking sounds in the air; light phenomena and materializations of hands and forms; "invisible" playing of musical instruments; independent voices sometimes singing; dematerializations and apports. (Apports are physical objects paranormally transported into the room from other locations.) Although he is not that well known, the strength and variety of the observed phenomena resemble those associated with Daniel Dunglas Home, considered to be one of the most remarkable physical mediums ever studied.

From 1908 to 1909, Indridi's mediumship was also scrutinized by Gudmundur Hannesson, an outstanding scientist who received many honors in Iceland and abroad, and became professor of medicine at the University of Iceland two years later. A member of the Reykjavik city council, he was known for his skepticism, as well as his integrity and impartiality. "You may state as my firm conviction, that the phenomena are unquestionable realities," Gudmundur concluded after applying the most rigorous and meticulous controls.

Indridi was a trance medium, and various communicators spoke through him. On November 24, 1905, a new communicator appeared who was not recognized by any of the sitters. He could therefore be categorized as a drop-in communicator, similar to that of the case of "Runki's leg," which I investigated and was described previously by Alan Gauld. The hypothesis of telepathy among living persons and/or clairvoyance does not adequately explain the strongest drop-in cases, thus establishing them as being of particular significance for the question of the survival of the human personality past death.

The unexpected visitor spoke Danish and introduced himself as "Mr. Jensen," a common Danish surname, and gave his profession as a "manufacturer." According to Kvaran, "The time was about nine o'clock when he came. Then he disappeared and came back an hour later." Indridi took a break during that hour, and when Jensen returned, he said that during the break, he had been to Copenhagen and a fire had been raging in a factory on one of the streets there. It was brought under control within an hour.

Witnesses to the statements wrote them down, and the next day a written account was deposited with the Bishop of Iceland. It is important that a written record was on file before any verification was attempted.

Copenhagen is over thirteen hundred miles from Reykjavik. In those days, there was no telephone or telegraph connection between Iceland and Europe. The people of Iceland had to wait for newspapers to arrive later by boat. Almost a month later, the newspapers were delivered. They confirmed that a fire had indeed broken out on November 24 in a factory located at Store Kongensgade 63, a major street in Copenhagen, and that the fire was brought under control in an hour. Given the time change, Jensen discovered the fire at about 11:15 Danish time; the handwritten fire brigade report on the fire says they were called at 11:52, and the fire was already raging. Kvaran's statement about the timing when Jensen spoke of the fire must be an estimate, and our records indicate that the fire is likely to have started sometime after nine (eleven Danish time).

In summary, Jensen made four specific statements that were confirmed later:

1. There was a fire on a street in Copenhagen.
2. The fire was in a factory.
3. The fire started just before midnight on November 24, 1905.
4. The fire was brought under control within an hour.

There is no conceivable normal explanation to account for the fact that Jensen—or, for that matter, Indridi—described in real time a fire that was taking place some thirteen hundred miles away.

But there was more to come years later. In 1991, two books of minutes of the Experimental Society that had been lost for over half a century turned up in the estate of the widow of a former president of the Icelandic SPR, Rev. Jon Auduns. They cover a period of about seven months between 1905 and 1908 and describe over sixty séances. It was not until 2008 that I took a careful look at them. I then made an unexpected discovery, perhaps the most memorable finding of my life.

Who was that mysterious Jensen? Was he just a figment in the mind of Indridi, or had he ever been a real living person? After Jensen's first appearance on November 24 he appeared frequently; however, not a word had been found about his corporeal identity in the minute books that we had.

The newly turned up books revealed more details about Jensen. In a sitting on December 11, 1905, apparently in response to being asked, he made the following highly specific statements about his life:

> It (my Christian name) is Emil. My name: Emil Jensen, yes! I have no children. Yes, (I was a bachelor). No, (I was not so young when I died). I have siblings, but not here in heaven.

Apparently no attempt was ever made to verify any of this. In 2009, I went to the Royal Library in Copenhagen, and found a series of annual volumes listing businesspeople there in the nineteenth century. I looked up Jensen in the volume for 1890. There were hundreds listed, but there was only one manufacturer named Emil Jensen. And his address? Store Kongensgade 67, which is two doors away from number 63 where the fire broke out. This seemed to be more than a mere coincidence.

Later that year, I searched census documents in Copenhagen. In 1885, Thomas Emil Jensen, single, thirty-seven years old, born in Copenhagen, is listed as manufacturer and coffee merchant. The census record of 1860 showed that his parents lived at that time at Store Kongensgade 40 with seven children—four daughters and three sons. In fact, the records show that for his whole life, beginning at the age of eight, Emil Jensen lived on Store Kongensgade or on streets crossing Store Kongensgade.

Emil Jensen died in 1898, living only some three hundred yards away from the house where the fire broke out. His certificate of burial from the City Archives states that he was single and fifty years old when he died. His four sisters all died after him, the first one in 1908, and his older and younger brothers both died in the 1920s, also after him. I then found a document of the probate court, written when Emil Jensen's estate was divided, which states that he had no children and confirms that his siblings were all alive when he died.

Jensen's statements given in the minute book on December 11, 1905, were all verified:

1. My Christian name is Emil. (Various documents)
2. I was a bachelor. (Certificate of burial)
3. I have no children. (Probate court)
4. I was not so young when I died. (Certificate of burial)
5. I have siblings. (Census records, probate court)
6. My siblings are not in heaven (are living). (Probate court)
7. I was a manufacturer. (Various documents)

The "hit-rate" with respect to the identity of Emil Jensen is 100 percent, as is the description of the fire in Copenhagen, which was detailed earlier.

Could there be a normal explanation of this case? A great advantage of historical cases such as this is the impossibility of fraud and/or leakage based on modern communication equipment. Since there were no telephones yet, the only potential explanation that one can speculate about is that Indridi had an accomplice who started the fire at a predetermined time so that they could impress those around them. This possibility is so absurd that it can safely be excluded. Perhaps Indridi might have read an obituary of Emil Jensen in a Danish newspaper. I checked this possibility. No obituary of Emil Jensen was found in *Politiken* or *Berlingske Tidende*, the papers of that time.

Is this a case of clairvoyance by the medium? Perhaps an out-of-the-body experience with a perception of a fire in distant Copenhagen? Or a case of telepathy? Indridi had never been to Copenhagen. As far as is known, that fire should not have interested Indridi more than fires anywhere else in the world. And how could he clairvoyantly acquire specific information a few weeks later about the life of Emil Jensen—which I confirmed as accurate—that later was found to connect him to the location of the fire? That seems like a near impossibility. And Indridi stated that he knew no person in Copenhagen who might have felt the need to think of him at the time of the fire.

Let us assume for a moment that Jensen existed as a discarnate entity communicating through Indridi. Then, this would have been a case of spirit communication. Let us ask what might be the reasons Jensen might have had to observe the fire. He might have felt compelled, during a pause from mediumistic work with Indridi, to return to Copenhagen to observe an event that must have been important to him because it took place on the street where he had lived all his adult life. Therefore he could have had a strong motivation to follow the development of this fire. By contrast, Indridi does not seem to have had any particular motivation to do so.

Also important is the fact that Jensen spoke Danish at the sittings, "with a typical Copenhagen accent" as Kvaran described it. Indridi received minimal education in the rural area where he was brought up. He could not speak in Danish, and certainly not with a Copenhagen accent.

The case of Emil Jensen displays the importance of motivational factors in assessing the evidential value of drop-in cases. In this instance, the event was highly relevant to the drop-in communicator and had no significance whatsoever for the medium. The event occurred in a place Indridi had never been to, and the communication was provided in the language spoken at that distant location. Furthermore, the identity of the communicator Emil Jensen was established over a century later. He was an actual living person, who died prior to his visits in Indridi's séance room and was never known to Indridi.

The case opens up the important question: Who was the percipient, the living Indridi or the deceased Jensen? The weight of the motivational factor tips the scale heavily toward the deceased Emil Jensen. It offers an intriguing argument for Emil Jensen being an independent entity distinct from the person of Indridi Indridason.

To move on, direct-voice phenomena were a prominent feature of Indridi's mediumship; that is, voices that would be heard away from the medium in other parts of the room, and not coming from his mouth. They were heard speaking or singing in sittings in which adequate controls were in place, and the sitters were known well enough to the investigators to assure that no accomplice could have played a part.

It is highly unusual in physical mediumship that direct voice is the most common phenomenon. Yet for Indridi, these spirit voices were documented in 77 percent of the ordinary sittings recorded in the minute books. Each voice had its own characteristic and style of speech. The voices might be high- or low-pitched, whispers in the ear of a particular sitter, or in song; they could be softly spoken or as though shouting. And they could be either male or female. They were in most cases recognized by the sitters as voices of deceased people whom they had known, and were mostly unknown to the medium. They might address particular sitters and would respond to questions. A few spoke in French, Norwegian, or Dutch, and Emil Jensen in Danish. None of these languages were known to Indridi.

What is most extraordinary is that two very different voices even sang the same melody together at the same time. Haraldur writes that the independent voices very often sang beautifully, and "we could sometimes hear two voices singing simultaneously: the soprano voice of a lady and the bass voice of a man." Einar Kvaran confirmed this observation.

The vigorous skeptic Gudmundur Hannesson reports that on June 11, "while music was being played so that the medium would fall deeper in trance, there sang (outside) first a bright feminine voice . . . and then a strong male voice." Once, for a short while, Gudmundur heard them "sing at the same time . . . Both voices were heard very close to me."

One of the frequent voices belonged to a female French singer. She spoke sometimes in French, and tried also to speak in English and German. Few Icelanders spoke French in those days but some people attended who could test her French. In September 1907, the minutes relate that the French-speaking G. T. Zoega addressed the singer in French and "apprehends that she understands him. He hears clearly French words and phrases in her speech, though he could not hear whole sentences." At a later time, Thor Gudmundsson and Kvaran conversed with her in both French and English and checked carefully that she understood both languages. That description from one of the minute books indicates responsive xenoglossy.

On one occasion, some sitters ingeniously tested the accuracy of Indridi's statements about the movements of deceased persons he claimed to see, providing further evidence of xenoglossy. Two sitters on each side of Indridi were holding both his hands, his right arm, and had their legs wrapped around his legs. Indridi said that he saw the French singer standing between the cabinet and a chimney that stood close by. One of the sitters spoke French, so he addressed the French singer in French and asked her to do something; Indridi and the rest of the sitters could not understand what he was saying. Indridi said: "Now she bows down." And that is exactly what she had been asked to do—in French. Since Indridi didn't understand any French, her responsive movements that he could see verified that she—or something perceptible to him that he saw to be her—was there and able to understand a language unknown to him.

Brynjolfur Thorlaksson, the organist at Reykjavik Cathedral, describes an incident that in his view threw light on the identity of the French singer as someone who had actually lived:

> At a meeting of the inner circle we heard a male voice speak French at a distance from the medium that we had never heard before. It seemed that his words were not directed at us but to someone on the other side. At the same time we heard some other voices around the medium, but rather unclearly. We did though discern among them the voice of the French singer and heard her suddenly scream in distress. It seemed as if there had been an uproar or disagreement of some kind. We did not distinguish individual words except at one time a male voice said, "Madame Malibran."
>
> We asked the control what had happened. The answer was that the man, who had used the name to address the woman, was Malibran, and he had been the husband of the French singer

who had also been there. They had not seen each other since their passings. He had learned about her whereabouts and came to the meeting in order to get her to go with him, but she had refused. That was the cause of the uproar. More we were not told.

None of those present had the faintest idea about "Madame Malibran" and her husband. The next day some of us looked for the name in some encyclopedias. Unexpectedly, we found that in America (USA) there had been a wealthy French plantation owner by the name of Malibran. He had married the singer Maria Felicia who was of Spanish descent. She was born in Paris 1808 and died in Manchester 1836. He went bankrupt three months after they married; she divorced him and returned to Europe.

With further research, they found that the celebrated mezzo-soprano named Maria Felicia Malibran sang leading roles in opera houses in Paris, Naples, London, and New York. She was considered one of the greatest opera singers of the nineteenth century. Born in Paris, her father was one of Rossini's favorite tenors, and she trained as a singer from an early age. While in New York, she hastily married François Eugène Malibran, a man old enough to be her father, whom she left a year later. She died when she was only twenty-eight, from injuries suffered when she fell from her horse. François Malibran died the same year she did.

Perhaps her sudden death at such a young age could explain her desire to return and continue singing. Her outstanding career was cut short when she still had many unfulfilled years ahead of her.

Another wonderful incident, which took place in full light outside the séance room, is reported by the organist Thorlaksson:

Once in the middle of the day, as often occurred, Indridi was at my home. While he was there I played on the harmonium a melody by Chopin. Indridi sat to the left of the harmonium. I expected that Mrs. Malibran knew the melody that I was playing, for I heard her humming it around Indridi. Then I saw him falling into trance . . .

I heard many voices, both of men and women singing behind me, but especially to my right with Indridi being on my left. I did not distinguish individual words, but the voices I heard clearly, both higher and lower voices, and they all sang the melody that I was playing.

This singing differed from ordinary singing as it sounded more like a sweet echo. It seemed to come from afar, but was at the same time close to me. No single voice was discernible except the voice of Malibran. I always heard her distinctly.

Indridi is perhaps the most extraordinarily gifted medium able to demonstrate direct singing of many voices simultaneously. The French female voice sang beautiful duets with a male voice, seemingly coming from the air, without the use of vocal cords. This occurred in a language unknown to Indridi. Not only did she speak the language, but she was also responsive in conversations with sitters in that language. This responsive xenoglossy strongly suggests independence from the medium. In addition, the French singer displayed a skill that neither the medium nor anyone else present possessed: her extraordinary professional singing. In fact, no one in the whole country had this skill, for there were no opera singers living in Iceland at the time of these sittings.

I believe that the exceptional variety of phenomena can be interpreted as pointing toward human survival of bodily death. The manifestation of these phenomena may indicate the existence of another realm of reality of which we rarely have a glimpse. Seen that way, Indridi was a middleman (the direct translation of the term "medium" in Icelandic is "middleman"), or an interface of rare quality between these two realms.

Chapter 24

The Enigma of Full-Form Materializations

The discarnate Emil Jensen did not only appear as a drop-in control personality speaking through Indridi, as Haraldsson described. He also materialized into physical form, apart from the medium, and touched some of the sitters or allowed them to touch him. Jensen made his first entrance between the curtains at Kvaran's house during a séance there, stated his name, and shouted, in his familiar Copenhagen accent, "Can you see me?" Kvaran and Nielsson each reported independently about one such appearance in 1906. Nielsson writes:

> The new visitor [Jensen] was dressed in very fine white drapery, of which many folds hung down to the floor; and the light was radiating from him. We saw him at different places in the room. Once he stood on a sofa, and behind him was a red light, which was similar to a little sun, with whitish light streaming out from

it. This sight I shall never forget. Frequently he managed to appear seven or eight times the same evening in different places in the room. Many times we saw the medium and this materialized being simultaneously.

In 1907, the Bishop of Iceland, the Magistrate of Reykjavik (later one of the five Supreme Court judges in Iceland), and the British consul attended a séance with Indridi. Along with forty sitters, they witnessed Jensen materialize eleven times in bright, luminous light. The bishop declared that he was completely convinced that these observations, and others of Jensen's, were genuine. Since Haraldsson documented that Emil Jensen was someone who actually lived in Copenhagen and died in 1898, does this establish that Jensen had survived death? It would seem so . . . but for some scholars and investigators, this is not a simple question. Some further examples are in order.

But first, I assume that many readers may be overwhelmed by the boggle factor at this point. How can the mind deal with the notion of a materializing and dematerializing, walking, talking, and touching physical human form? Perhaps you are throwing up your hands and wondering whether to stop reading. But the problem is, such materializations have actually occurred—this has been documented. And if you stop and think about it, that is quite wonderful, is it not? But it is also one of the strangest and most confounding aspects of nature, or biology, or spirituality, or whatever it is, that perhaps anyone has encountered.

Were you able to accept the appearance of a hand more easily? To put it in perspective, PK expert Stephen Braude believes that full-form manifestations are no less plausible than partial materializations or other forms of PK. Given all the evidence we have of the materialization of hands, "the evidence for full-form materializations does not seem to present any additional conceptual obstacle," he writes.

French physiologist Charles Richet (1850–1935) was awarded the Nobel Prize in Physiology or Medicine in 1913. He spent decades as the editor of leading journals and published papers on physiology, physiological chemistry, experimental pathology, and normal and pathological psychology. In short, he was highly respected and knew how to conduct rigorous experiments. We are fortunate that he also devoted his attention to the study of rare physical mediums who produced materializations, and wrote hundreds of pages about the results and his attempt to understand them.

Richet made the same point as Braude. After witnessing many partial and full materializations, he commented that it is just as difficult to understand the materialization of a living, mobile hand, or even a finger, as it is to understand "the materialization of an entire personality, which comes and goes, speaks, and moves the veil that covers him." In 1934, he wrote:

> I shall not waste time in stating the absurdities, almost the impossibilities, from a psycho-physiological point of view, of this phenomenon. A living being, or living matter, formed under our eyes, which has its proper warmth, apparently a circulation of blood, and a physiological respiration, which has also a kind of psychic personality having a will distinct from the will of the medium, in a word, a new human being! This is surely the climax of marvels. Nevertheless, it is a fact.

Polish medium Franek Kluski (1873–1943) was also a Warsaw banker, author, playwright, and poet—intelligent and well-educated. In the interest of science, he willingly subjected himself to study by Richet and physician Gustave Geley (1860–1924), another outstanding investigator from the French Institut Métapsychique International who is well known for his studies of physical mediumship. Alan Gauld wrote that Kluski must have been "the most remarkable medium of his time, probably of any time."

Kluski's mediumship was witnessed by over three hundred people, which included the Polish intelligentsia, experts from the Polish Society for Psychical Research, and, in addition to Geley and Richet, Everard Feilding from Eusapia Palladino's "Fraud Squad." Most important, Geley and Richet and others working with them brought Kluski to a windowless laboratory at the institute in Paris, where in

1920 they conducted eleven successful séances. The strictest controls were in place—the simple room was inaccessible, except during experimentation, with no possibility of confederacy; a red light was on; and the medium's hands were held by an investigator on either side at all times. While the investigators linked hands, the medium remained completely still and was in a trance throughout the sittings. Under these conditions, fraud was physically impossible. In this context, as well as during many other séances with Kluski, materialized forms with "human" faces were observed.

These forms were similar to the hands in that they were solid and "alive." In situations without red light, the forms became visible when they picked up radiant luminous plaques that were available in Kluski's séance room; other times they were self-illuminating. In sittings involving additional visitors, the entities were often recognized as friends or relatives of those present—eighty-four people confirmed such recognition. They would touch people and sometimes respond to the unexpressed thoughts of sitters.

F. W. Pawlowski, professor of aeronautical engineering at the University of Michigan, attended several séances with Kluski in 1924. In a published paper he said:

> It is impossible for anyone to reject or deny these phenomena, and it is impossible to explain them by clever trickery. I realize perfectly that it is difficult for anyone to accept them. To accept the possibility of creating in a few minutes live and intelligent human beings, whose bones one can feel through their flesh, and whose heartbeat one can hear and feel, is beyond our comprehension.

Pawlowski wrote a chilling description (they were *not* "apparitions" according to today's terminology; they were solid):

> The light from the plaque was so good that I could see the pores and down on the skin of their faces and hands. On the nose of an older man-apparition I could see clearly the complicated pat-

tern made by the crooked, tiny red blood vessels; I could examine closely the texture of the material of their clothes. I examined
a number of them at such close distance that I could hear their
breathing and feel their breath upon my face.

Through ingenious experiments that may provide the most convincing evidence ever for the reality of materialized forms, Geley and
Richet created a permanent record of their existence. For the Paris
sittings and later in a series of sittings in Warsaw in 1921, the researchers placed a circular tank containing a layer of hot liquid paraffin
wax floating above electrically heated water in the center of the séance
circle. They then asked the beings to dip their materialized hands into
the hot wax, making thin gloves around them. The sitters could hear
the sound of something splashing in the wax, and wax would splatter
on the floor and onto people nearby. Sometimes a wax-covered hand
would touch them after dipping into the hot pot. The forms would
then dissolve their hands from the dried wax, dropping the empty
gloves in the sitters' laps or onto the table. They were fragile—thinner
than a sheet of paper. Geley writes:

> We had the great pleasure of *seeing* the hands dipping into the
> paraffin. They were luminous, bearing points of light at the
> finger-tips. They passed slowly before our eyes, dipped into the
> wax, moved in it for a few seconds, came out, still luminous, and
> deposited the glove against the hand of one of us.

It was not possible for Kluski or anyone else in the room to have
produced these seamless gloves. A human hand could not slide out of
the narrow wrists because the necessary movement would damage the
very thin layer of wax. In the Warsaw experiments, gloves were produced with interlocking fingers, with two hands clasping one another,
and with the five fingers spread wide apart. Needless to say, removal
of a human hand from such formations would be impossible. Dematerialization was the only method that would leave the molds intact.
The investigators also made sure that no wax gloves could have been

smuggled into the room ahead of time. Unknown to anyone else, in one instance Geley and Richet added a bluish coloring agent to the paraffin just prior to the séance; for another experiment they secretly added cholesterin. These additions assured the identity of the specific wax as being from the séance room only.

After the gloves dried, the investigators poured plaster into them, and once this hardened, they submerged them in boiling water and stripped away the thin wax layer. The Paris experiments yielded nine molds—seven of hands, one of a foot and one of a mouth and chin. The hands and foot were the size of a five- to seven-year-old child and had no resemblance to those of the medium. Although miniature, the perfect anatomical details of the hands were those of adults, and not smooth and round like a child. The molds were extensively photographed for publication by Geley in 1927, and they remain to this day at the Institut Métapsychique International in Paris.

"We were able to obtain objective and formal proofs, absolutely incontrovertible, of the reality of the materializations," Geley states, and "to secure absolute certainty of the supernormal origin of the moulds." I find these molds to be so compelling—physical copies of materialized entities whose nature is a profound mystery—that I spent much time staring at the photographs and reading Geley's descriptions of their formations. If one studies the literature on this, it is impossible to refute the authenticity of the molds. How wondrous is this? Even Geley let his scientific guard down at one point: "In these rough forms the enigma of universal life—the relations of the Idea to Matter—is revealed in the splendour of its beauty," he wrote in 1927.

But does this documentation of full-form materializations tell us anything about survival past death? Zofia Weaver, a contemporary expert who has researched Kluski in his native language, likens his manifestations to those of sophisticated poltergeist cases, simply involving more advanced, refined, and spectacular phenomena. Like the physical phenomena resulting from conjuring up the fictional Philip, the manifestations might have been created by the thoughts, moods, focus, and intention of the sitters—"a group mind at work . . . united by enthusiasm, mutual rapport, lack of inhibition, and a common goal," as Weaver describes it. But in addition, they "interact with the world in a very physical way that requires physical energies." It is impossible to explain or interpret them with any certainty.

In relation to the question of survival, it would be helpful to know something about how these solid beings are created in the séance room.

Most of the time, physical mediums, unconscious in deep trance, exude a strange substance that Richet called "ectoplasm." Ectoplasm is used by the creative force to build physical forms, which seem to be imbued with "life" that can then interact with the physical world. Hands independent of an attached body, like those described earlier, were also seen to emerge from ectoplasm. Many competent researchers in addition to Richet, Schrenck-Notzing, and Geley have observed the formation of moving forms from this substance, in the light and under conditions eliminating the possibility of fraud. Sometimes they went so far as to search the medium's every orifice and give her natural dyes, which would color anything coming from out of her stomach, since ectoplasm usually emerged from the medium's mouth. In his extensive study of French medium Eva Carrière (known as Eva C.), Richet describes . . .

> . . . a whitish steam, perhaps luminous, taking the shape of gauze or muslin, in which there develops a hand or an arm that gradually gains consistency. The ectoplasm makes *personal* movements. It creeps, rises from the ground, and puts forth tentacles like an amoeba. It is not always connected with the body of the medium but usually emanates from her, and is connected with her.

Viewing it in a low white light, Schrenck-Notzing writes:

Without the help of the hands or knees, a flowing white substance emerged from the medium's mouth, which was inclined toward the left. It was about 20 inches long and 8 inches broad.

It lay on the breast of the dress, spread out, and formed a white head-like disk, with a face profile turned to the right, and of life size.

Ectoplasm has been shown to be so sensitive that if light is introduced unexpectedly, or someone touches an ectoplasmic form when not invited to do so, it will recoil violently and return swiftly to the body of the medium, causing serious harm or even death. (This is why the "rules" of the séance room—which are apparently determined by the guides in charge—must always be respected by those in attendance.)

British medium Alec Harris (1897–1974), one of the finest materialization mediums of the twentieth century, offered sitters the experience of witnessing formations from ectoplasm in red light. British investigator David Fontana, who spent more than thirty years researching psychic and mediumistic phenomena, writes that Harris belongs "in the very front rank of physical mediums."

Like Minnie Harrison (1895–1958), another well-known physical medium of the same time period, Alec Harris was not subjected to the rigorous scientific scrutiny of some of the earlier mediums. However, careful notes were written by astute participants; and accounts by credible people over many decades describe enough controls to be convincing that genuine phenomena did indeed occur. Both Harrison and Harris sat quietly within their own small groups composed of committed family members and trusted friends—known as a "home circle"—for many years, without accepting money or seeking publicity, allowing guests to visit. Harris spent about forty years "demonstrating the reality of survival," as Fontana describes it.

In 1952, Oxford-educated Theodore Johannes Haarhoff, with two doctorates in classical languages and professor at the University of the Witwatersrand in Johannesburg, attended a séance with Alec Harris. He examined the room first, and noted that Harris had brought nothing with him. "The materializing powers of Mr. Harris are astounding, unique, and entirely above suspicion," he wrote in a published article. "I make these statements after many years of investigation and many disappointments and experience of fraudulent mediums." Haarhoff described the materialization of a Greek philosopher he had worked with who came close to him and spoke in ancient Greek, using the correct pronunciation, which is different from that of modern Greek, as explained in his article. "The ectoplasm which issues in abundance from his [Harris's] body and which the etheric entities use to make themselves visible, streams like a mist and assumes all sorts of shapes yet can be compacted into something absolutely solid while the power lasts—and what amazing power it is!" he declared.

Maurice Barbanell, the editor of the journal *Psychic News,* wrote that he saw thirty forms materialize in good red light with twenty-seven sitters present for almost three hours. "I was so close to the cabinet that several of the forms had to walk over my feet," he wrote. "On several occasions I handled the flowing ectoplasmic draperies, which were soft and silky to the touch. I shook hands with two forms. Their hands were firm and normal." A number of the forms were recognized by sitters. He was most impressed by the materialization of a girl, who "disposed of any suggestion that the results could be explained away by trickery by revealing part of her feminine form, nude from the waist up! Then one materialization parted the curtains so we could see the figure and the medium at the same time."

And a very skeptical Albert Fletcher-Desborough, professional stage illusionist who did not believe anything he had heard about these séances, did such a thorough examination of the room and cabinet, looking for structural mechanisms like floor escapes and wall slides, that he was certain no one could come in or out. As he wrote in the *Liverpool Evening Express* and for *Psychic News* in 1974, "There was no chance for deception." He wrote that first he recognized his father, who emerged from the cabinet and called Fletcher-Desborough by the nickname "Bertie," which was known only to his family. Then his brother, who had been shot in the ankle, hobbled out, gave his name, and took his hand. "Why all these manifestations on my behalf? Because I was an unbeliever," he concluded.

With Alec Harris, many people also witnessed the dematerialization of the solid entities, dissolving and sinking into the floor. Some sitters interacted with their loved ones, easily recognizable, and they had no doubt about the reality of survival after such an experience.

In 1961, two journalists who concealed their identities attended a séance with Alec Harris as guests. They stationed hidden camera crews outside the window, with the intention of catching Alec committing fraud. According to Alec's wife, Louie, Alec's "guide" materialized during the séance and spoke to the sitters, then walked among them while taking their hands in his. The guide showed them the entranced Alec to establish his separate identity, but this was not enough to convince the journalists. When the materialized form walked over to one of them, the man threw his arms around the solid figure, grabbed him and held on tightly. Louie reported the journalist shouted, "I've got you!" He "was obviously convinced he had captured the draped medium in the act of duplicity, masquerading as a spirit form," she wrote. She said that the figure quickly dematerialized, and Alec cried out in pain as the ectoplasm returned to his body "with the impact of a sledgehammer." Alec became very ill and was under medical care for months as a result. It took two years before he became himself again, but he was never able to fully relax as a medium in the same way as before.

Could these full-form materializations be the most striking form of evidence for survival past death, especially when they are recognized as someone who once lived? Perhaps they are in a class by themselves. I asked investigator Stephen Braude for his thoughts. "Just as it may be practically impossible to distinguish survival psi in a mental mediumship setting from living-agent psi, why wouldn't the situation be the same in the case of materializations?" he wrote in an email. He points out that we don't know if all psychokinetic phenomena are one continuum—everything from a levitating table to a materialized object, to a waving hand emerging from ectoplasm to Eusapia's proto-hand carrying objects from the cabinet to a full-form materialization, could be instances of some kind of single psychokinetic process.

"If a discarnate can manifest in materialized form, that's PK. Living agents also have PK abilities including the ability to materialize things, and in those cases there's no need to posit entities for which we have no other direct evidence," Braude states. Human-generated, group PK was behind the Philip experiments; Kluski's forms seemed to morph in response to the shifting wishes of the sitters. Braude also notes the fact that a large bird materialized in Kluski's séance room. "Are we to suppose that a discarnate bird was using Kluski as a medium in order to manifest in the 'flesh'? Why must full-figure (stable) human forms be treated any differently?"

Understanding Braude's logic, I have struggled with such questions. For reasons that may not be based on logic, I will acknowledge that I find it harder to accept the idea that human-agent psi has been solely responsible for cases involving materialized forms walking, talking, and touching their family member while providing personal information unknown to anyone else. This hypothesis proposes that somehow the combination of the medium and that specific family member—who may have been a one-time guest and unknown to anyone in the group—bolstered by the intense focus and anticipation of the other sitters, would have been the creator of the responsive, intelligent "living" being in question. However, Braude's logic is impeccable. "Typically, within mental mediumship, good trance manifestations resembling people unknown to the medium are recognized by sitters, who are all part of the full psychic nexus and thus possible causal agents," he says. "A materialization strikes me as different only insofar as it adds a PK component to the mix. The Philip case was an apparent instance of PK by committee, and this scenario could presumably be the same." Since the living-agent psi hypothesis makes the assumption that human psi is unlimited, a proponent can argue that theoretically it can do just about anything.

It's fair to point out that Steve Braude has never experienced any partial or full materializations himself. Experience and its context certainly have a way of profoundly impacting one's perceptions, as we saw with Thomas Mann, although obviously Steve does not deny the reality of phenomena that he has not personally witnessed. And neither did Mann, who studied the work of Geley and others concerning ectoplasmic materializations. Mann rebuffed the "spiritualistic" hypothesis despite its greater simplicity, and wrote that more likely the phenomena were created by the medium partly externalizing himself. He believed that "the medium's magically objectified dreams" were mingled with the subconscious ideas of the sitters and energetically projected to another location, which resonates with Weaver's comments about Kluski's process.

Longtime British investigator David Fontana questioned this interpretation. He stated that the best cases of physical mediumship make it difficult to argue that the physical phenomena produced "can be accounted for solely by the action of living agents." In fact, Fontana, who *has* witnessed partial and full materializations with a number of mediums, argued that genuine physical mediumship "provides an additional and very powerful argument against the super-ESP theory." He says that since laboratory demonstrations and experiments studying PK have never come close to demonstrating macroeffects, this suggests that some unknown agency is involved. These extraordinary human powers—such as the ability to materialize other living beings or produce independent voices speaking in languages unknown to the medium—have not been demonstrated in any other contexts. "The experiences that I've had have convinced me that it is very difficult to explain any of these things by an alternative explanation to that of survival," he said in a 2004 interview.

In addition, Fontana was not willing to dismiss the fact that the good mediums (which he noted are very hard to find) are absolutely clear that the energy involved comes from discarnate spirits. As far as he was concerned, they know far more about what's happening "than investigators like myself, who are just sitting there observing what is going on." He explained further:

> I could go in with all sorts of grandiose theories of my own and try and tell mediums that the experiences that they have are not what they think they are. But there are grave dangers in that, just as there are in the rest of psychology, if you try to dictate to people and say that you know their experiences better than they know them themselves. So, from the point of view of the medi-

ums, the answer to the question is clear: survival is a fact, and people are communicating.

We must consider whether all the very best and most well-tested physical mediums have been consistently deceiving themselves and us for over a century. Philosopher Michael Sudduth says this is certainly possible. "I don't think it's antecedently improbable that all the relevant subjects have misinterpreted their experience, nor anything improbable in supposing that they've been unconsciously motivated to do so," he told me in 2016.

These arguments can go on forever. Could there ever be something like the Philip experiment established with the intention of achieving materializations, which could generate walking and talking materialized forms purely through intention and thought? Given how few mediums are able to perform like this after many years of development, this would be extremely difficult to achieve, if it were even possible. The mediums are in a deep trance state, rendered unconscious by what they say are the discarnate entities speaking through them. Ectoplasm is usually a requirement, and we know very little about how this substance is created or manipulated. And if the more advanced phenomena could be human created, being part of one continuum, why wouldn't poltergeist phenomena normally include disembodied hands or physical forms? These are complicated and unresolvable questions, but they all have a bearing on the question of survival.

Steve Braude asked me why I would suppose that it should be easier for the deceased to create a materialization than for a living human being. It'a a good question. I have my own thoughts about this, even though they could never win an academic philosophical argument. While allowing for certain assumptions about the nature of the afterlife, one could postulate that a deceased spirit is materializing *itself* through some kind of memory it carries from life on earth by which it can reconstitute its previous form using ectoplasm, as if putting on an old overcoat. For a medium to do this on his own, he would have to have the power to create a form entirely *separate* from himself, which could walk and talk independently—a functioning "other." In addition, he would have to use telepathic information to make the form match a once-living person completely unknown to him, and then imbue the form with the obscure verbal information and physical appearance that would prove its identity to a family member. Through the ectoplasm, he would have to give this form *life*. Which seems more feasible: for a spirit entity such as Emil Jensen to re-create his own physical form, or for an unconscious human being to have the power to create another independent "living" human being?

We can't logically settle these questions. Any discussion must eventually boil down to the context and the experience of individual observers. But let's pause and reflect for a moment. What's extraordinary is that these phenomena occur at all. The existence of full-form materializations cannot be disputed; scientific studies have shown that they are real. What can we make of this? It so boggles the mind that it is almost unthinkable.

After witnessing these phenomena myself, as I will describe shortly, I felt intuitively that it made sense to separate the more "advanced phenomena"—moving materialized hands and full forms demonstrating intelligence and a quality of being "alive"—from those that seem more mechanical, such as poltergeist-style object movements or table tilting. Despite the brilliant logic of Braude and Sudduth, which has kept me up at night, I often find myself unable to lump these two types of manifestations together. Maybe this has to do with my direct experiences of séance-room phenomena, but I was relieved when I discovered that Nobel Prize–winning scientist Charles Richet also noted this distinction:

> That a mechanical energy of an unknown kind should emanate
> from the human body and move a table, and shake a piece of
> board with knocking, is not entirely incomprehensible. But that
> this force should produce word-making sound, lights, and living
> human forms—this indeed goes beyond all our concepts of the
> possible. A warm and living hand, a mouth that speaks, eyes that

see, and thought that thrills, like the hand, the mouth, the eyes, and the thought of a human being—these are phenomena that put us to utter confusion.

He echoed my thoughts exactly! Hereward Carrington—the extreme skeptic who studied Eusapia Palladino—also deduced that phenomena showing intelligence were in a different category from object movements. For phenomena such as materializations, "since this is not the medium, what can it be but some external intelligence—some entity with a mind and thoughts of its own?" he wrote. "And what can that be but a spirit?"

Carrington acknowledged living-agent psi as "some force, under the control of the medium's own brain and mind, is in operation and not that of any spirit." And, similar to Michael Sudduth's arguments about the need to recognize certain auxiliary assumptions when interpreting the evidence in favor of survival, Carrington lists the assumptions he's making in conjunction with his concept that spirits exist. They are: our consciousness persists past physical death; it retains memory and personal identity; first it inhabits some kind of astral body "of the same shape as our physical body"; it is in our surroundings and possesses supernormal, psychic powers; it's normally invisible but can become visible and communicate with those present; it can only act on the physical world through an intermediary.

And that intermediary is "the nervous, vital force of the medium, externalized by her beyond her body and utilized by the manifesting spirit for the purposes of its manifestation." By clothing itself with this vital energy (ectoplasm), like a sheath or cloak, the nonphysical intelligence "can come in contact with the material world, move material objects, be seen, felt, and even photographed," Carrington says. The link supplied by the medium enables the "spirit" to become material. "By postulating this intermediary, this vital connection between the material and the spiritual worlds, can we explain all the facts at these séances, and in no other way," Carrington states. He does acknowledge, however, that sometimes the phenomena can manifest spontaneously;

we have seen just that with regard to after-death communications and apparitions, for example. After spending ten years investigating physical mediumship and spiritualism, Carrington concluded:

> When hands, faces, and forms appear, when conversations are carried on with these forms, in a language unknown to the medium, about matters private and unknown to her, it seems preposterous to attempt to explain these facts in any other way than to admit that a spiritual entity is present and active there. The spiritistic hypothesis is the only one that in any way explains the facts, and I shall accordingly adopt it, until some better explanation be forthcoming.

Carrington went from extreme skeptic to accepting survival, and this was only because of his own personal observations of physical mediumship under controlled conditions, which he could not explain to his satisfaction in any other way. Now, so many years later, perhaps more convincing arguments have since been formulated in favor of alternative explanations. But they remain as theoretical postulations only, and it seems we have no more scientific understanding of events in the séance room now than we did in the days of these earlier investigators.

Stephen Braude recognizes that a scientific argument isn't going to resolve the question of survival. "So you pick and choose assumptions that are acceptable to you, which will be highly colored by personal experience and by what has impacted you." This is what Carrington did, after conducting extensive investigations. The fact is, these phenomena represent the manifestation of the impossible, like magic made real. And I too had the good fortune of experiencing them for myself. This changed everything for me—moving the problem from one of theoretical perplexities into a paradigm-changing, real-life series of events.

Chapter 25

My Astonishing Second "Personal Experiment"

We now move into the present. Physical mediumship is not a lost art that belongs only to an earlier time. The traditions have been carried on, even though many mediums now work outside of the public eye.

I first encountered British physical medium Stewart Alexander in the fall of 2014 through his 2010 memoir, *An Extraordinary Journey,* which includes accounts by many sitters of the phenomena that have repeatedly manifested in his séance room for decades. In reading his life story, I was deeply impressed by Stewart's integrity and modesty, and had no doubt that he was "the real deal." He had an honest, un-cluttered clarity and sincerity that impressed me, a purity of character, and an integrated, natural quality of spirituality that had no dogma or self-consciousness attached. His core belief is that the purpose of his mediumship is to allow "spirit people" to enter our world and demon-strate that we survive death. For close to fifty years, Stewart has given his life to this task. In addition, he is a scholar regarding the history of physical mediumship, with a home library full of historic papers and books, and he has interviewed countless people who sat with Alec Harris, Minnie Harrison, Helen Duncan, Hunter Selkirk, and other great mediums.

It all started in 1968 when he was twenty-two. Stewart happened upon the classic 1931 book *On the Edge of the Etheric* by Arthur Findlay, describing Findlay's personal investigation of the independent voice medium John C. Sloan (1869–1951). Stewart was so inspired by it that he spent several years reading everything he could about physical mediumship. Eventually he formed his own home circle with friends, family, and neighbors; they sat together weekly in the dark for many months with no results. Stewart was not looking to become a medium himself; he simply wanted to help create the right conditions for phenomena to possibly occur.

However, one evening, without warning, he was entranced by an entity or presence called "White Feather," who was to become his principal "spirit guide" and who, over a period of many months, developed the ability to speak through Stewart when he went into a trance state. It took over ten years, but eventually White Feather was able to speak independently through what is called a "trumpet"—a simple eighteen-inch cone made of lightweight materials with one narrow opening and one larger, like a small megaphone—while it was levitated in the air. Stewart describes this turning point as "akin to the breaking of a dam"—it took tremendous patience and commitment to get there.

Other phenomena developed gradually over time, including the unexplainable appearance and transport of objects, known as "apports," into the room. A second guide arrived, also speaking through Stewart, who called himself Christopher and said he had died as a young boy, so he presented himself as a very lively child. Cheerful, mischievous, and amusing, Christopher conducted some successful book tests—stating specific information to be found on a specific book page in a distant unfamiliar location, like those of Mrs. Leonard as described previously by Alan Gauld—and he also brought through evidential information from loved ones.

In 1988, Stewart's current home circle was formed. By this time his trance state was so deep that when implements were screwed into his flesh, he showed no reaction. He gave his first public séance in 1992, when even then, he says modestly, "my physical mediumship was still in an embryonic state." It was during these larger séances that sitters were invited to test Stewart in the light to show that he was really in a deep trance. On one occasion, an experienced sitter performed his operations "with the skill of a master butcher," according to a report by an observer. To the horror of nearby attendees, he "nipped, sliced and screwed the implement into the medium's flesh but to no avail. On returning from trance there was not a mark on Stewart's arm and he was not aware of what happened until told later in the bar." I spoke to reliable witnesses who confirmed this account.

Walter Stinson, a Canadian who had lived in Boston and died in his twenties during a train accident in 1911, arrived as another member of Stewart's "spirit team" in 1992, and was in charge of developing the physical phenomena. Walter said he was the brother of the famous Boston medium Margery Crandon (1888–1941), who was the subject of rigorous testing by investigators for many years. Walter worked with his sister in her séance room after his death, and he intended to continue this work through Stewart. Next, Freda Johnson, a strong and nurturing proper lady who provides evidence from loved ones, completed the team in 1996. The young and witty Christopher now has the job of relaxing people and making them laugh. Some years later, another "spirit person," Dr. Barnett, who has been a physical healer for many sitters, was able to regularly speak independently of the medium and materialize fully during séances.

The notion of different personalities speaking through Stewart must sound very strange, and perhaps hard to imagine. They were, remarkably, all present in the séances I attended, and I will try to convey what this was like. From now on I will dispense with the qualifying quotes around such phrases as "spirit people," because it is cumbersome. We are entering this world, as we did earlier with mental mediumship, on its own terms, and it is a necessity that I respectfully use the language inherent in it.

Stewart has always lived his life as only a part-time medium. Throughout the many years of his development, he ran a business with his wife seven days a week and raised two children, and he now spends a great deal of time with his two young grandchildren. He always kept his home and business life entirely separate from his mediumship life—remarkably, his two sons never knew of his deep involvement as a medium until he gave them copies of his 2010 book. "I could not allow the two worlds to mix," he told me. "When I walk into the séance room I do so as Stewart the medium, always willing to give everything I possibly can to the spirit team. When I walk out, I do so as Stewart the family man." I have seen firsthand that this is indeed the case, after visiting and spending time with Stewart and his family at his home.

Stewart has been sitting with the same small group—his current home circle—for almost thirty years. In this way, he is an "old school" medium, more like Alec Harris or Minnie Harrison than many of the new and younger mediums, who are either embroiled in controversy or charging high fees for sittings while traveling from place to place. Many of this new breed have not developed their mediumship for very long, yet have been eager to join the "professional" circuit and develop a following nonetheless. In contrast, Stewart simply sat with the same group week after week, year after year, decade after decade, with his priority being his continued development within his home circle, while sharing his mediumship with sincere and interested people who sought him out and requested to sit with him. This is partly why he is unique, and why I was drawn to him.

In November 2014, Stewart and I began a long email correspondence that lasted for months. He has always been a very private person, and despite the fact that he published his memoir, he prefers to avoid publicity. Unsure about what relationship he would have to this book, he invited me to attend a retreat/conference he gives twice a year and to present a talk on UFOs there. After this event, in April 2015, he suggested I come back to his hometown in Northern England and sit for two sessions with the home circle. Needless to say, I was overjoyed by the invitation.

I was aware that Stewart's séances have always been conducted mainly in the dark. He set it up this way when he first began, because history has shown that it is easier for physical phenomena to occur in darkness. Although some of the better-known mediums were able to work in the light, as we have already seen, many others did not. Stewart always wears luminous tabs on his knees, visible at all times; each curtain of his cabinet has the same visible markers, as do the trumpets with a ring of illumination around the larger opening. A red light is switched on when the spirit communicators permit, and much has been witnessed this way during his séances—so they are not always in the dark.

Perhaps your red flag has gone up—it is understandably hard to accept that the darkness required by most mediums is for legitimate reasons. Researcher David Fontana, after sitting with many mediums including Stewart Alexander, explained that "many natural phenomena, such as the germination of seeds, gestation in the womb, and the development of images on photographic plates, take place in the absence of light or in the presence only of a dim red light." And even those mediums who worked in the light years ago worked best in darkness. According to Hereward Carrington, Eusapia Palladino's sensitivity to light heightened as the depth of her trance increased and he notes the fact that her phenomena originated inside the closed cabinet, where it was dark. "Rarely do phenomena take place in good light, outside the curtains; and when they do they are almost invariably telekinetic in character and of simple nature," Carrington wrote. Light rays "are extremely energetic, and liable to disintegrate and disrupt any excessively fine and subtle body."

Gustave Geley concurred that the detrimental effect of light on ectoplasmic forms is "only natural and logical." He made an important point:

If light hinders the biologic process in the first stages of organic growth, considering that this process is very slow, it is easy to conceive that it should actually paralyze the same processes during materialization, when the rapidity of vital action is greatly accelerated. The human embryo, for instance, requires weeks to be built up in the womb, shielded from light; in a séance, a quasi-human being or a human organ is completely formed in a few seconds. The rapidity of the process must be taken into account in order to understand the injurious action of light in materialization séances.

According to Fontana, we need to accept darkness if we want to experience physical phenomena, simply because it is the condition under which they best occur. "The extraordinary thing is not that it happens in darkness, but that it happens at all," he wrote in his foreword to Stewart's memoir. Nonetheless, Stewart, probably more than anyone else, would like nothing more than to be able to introduce more light into the séance room (and so would the spirit guides working with him). They are working toward this goal.

Despite his distaste for travel, Stewart has held séances in Scotland and Wales, as well as in Sweden, Switzerland, Germany, and Spain. He has sat for skeptics, researchers, and parapsychological organizations. For these public sittings, he was often bodily searched, and his chair and every aspect of the various rooms were thoroughly inspected. "Apart from the very few and unconvincing accusations made against him by ill-informed individuals," David Fontana wrote in 2010, "Stewart's long career has been free from attempts to cast doubt on the genuine nature of the phenomena associated with his mediumship."

I attended two séances that week in April 2015, and returned for two more the following August. Ray Lister, the circle leader, and his wife, June, had designated a room in their home as the séance room, and this is where I was fortunate to join the circle twenty-seven years after they began sitting in that space. I have come to know Stewart and his circle members well, and Stewart agreed to be part of this book once we had met and talked at length.

For my first séance, there were only four other sitters, all of whom had been with the circle for years. The small size was ideal. Stewart encouraged me to not let go of my analytical journalistic side in the séance room, affirming to me that "logic and reason should never be sacrificed under any circumstances." Before we began, I searched the nine-by-ten-foot séance room and everything in it. It had one window, which was boarded up and covered over to prevent any light from coming in. In one corner was a high shelf for the remote-controlled audio recorder, and in another was the cabinet—a curtain rod with two curtains opened all the way. In the center was a low table with some cable ties, wooden rings, drumsticks, and a bell, and the two trumpets were nearby. The table had a red light underneath it that could be turned on to shine through the red cloth covering on the glass top, and there was a standing red LED light along with another light on the ceiling. The chairs were almost touching, as the room

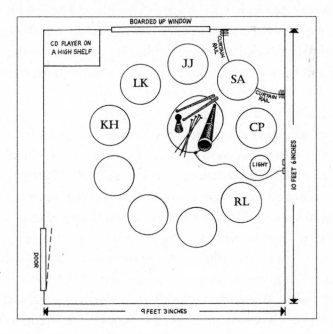

A typical setup in Stewart Alexander's séance room. *Copyright © Katie Halliwell*

could hold only about twelve sitters; anyone getting up would be noticed. I determined that nothing was hidden in the room, and no accomplices could enter or leave. The room remained empty between the time I inspected it and the sitting began.

When the six of us entered the room at 8 p.m., Stewart was secured to the wooden arms of his chair with thick cable ties, which are looped through an opening attached to the arm and can be removed only with a noisy wire cutter. (Ray showed me the cable ties package from the local store; for the August séances I brought my own.) I made sure that the ties were locked in place tightly enough that neither hand could possibly slide out of them. His hands were flat against the arms of the chair when they were secured and the plastic dug into the skin above his wrist, which he didn't mind. Luminous markers were attached to his knees. The door was locked and the lights were turned off.

Music—the same every week—was played to help trigger Stewart's trance state. This transition happens very fast; within a minute or two. Later, I asked him what this feels like. He said he can feel "them" coming; he feels the muscles in his face stiffen up and senses energy on top of his head and a pulling in his solar plexus. He surrenders all control, and then instantly, he's gone. He trusts the spirit people completely, and puts his life in their hands.

The communicators Walter and Freda have tried to explain how this happens, saying they disconnect Stewart's mind from his brain and thereby acquire access to his vocal apparatus. Freda explained that the mind, which is all that we are, is eternal and indestructible. Like Pim van Lommel and Peter Fenwick described earlier, she said that the physical brain is merely an instrument for the mind to give it physical expression, rather than the source of the mind, so that therefore consciousness can be separated from it. In this case, one consciousness departs and another one somehow makes use of the body. In one séance I attended, Walter told me that they ideally want about 80 percent control of the medium in order to avoid being overly influenced by his mind. (Some influence is unavoidable. If they took 100 percent control, he would be dead.)

Once Stewart was in trance, the music was turned off and White Feather arrived—the dignified Native American doorkeeper who always opens the sittings with a short welcome, speaking through Stewart. Then the playful but brilliant Christopher took over with his lovable high voice, causing Stewart's body to wiggle and jump with his energy, and he had all of us in hysterics. Walter came next, with a charming, deep voice, a seriousness but also a particular liking for the ladies. I noticed how distinctly different each of the voices and personalities were. To the circle members, they were old friends. Between their appearances, Stewart slumped in his chair with his head down as if deeply asleep; when they took over, he came alive again.

Walter asked me to come sit next to Stewart, and I sat to his right. Following instructions, I placed my left hand on top of Stewart's right hand, which was at the end of the arm of the chair with the cable tie tight around his arm just above his wrist. At Walter's direction, I took my other hand and felt that locked cable tie holding Stewart tightly to the chair. "Do you feel the strap, ma'am?" Walter asked, and I confirmed it. I slowly moved my right hand away, but my left hand remained on top of Stewart's right hand, gripping it tightly. "If I can now take Stewart's arm through the strap I think that would be somewhat impressive!" Walter stated. Then, suddenly, his arm flew upward, with my hand gripping his and riding up along with it, with a quick snapping sound.

Walter immediately said to feel the strap on the arm of the chair with my other hand, while my left hand remained in the air still holding on to Stewart. The cable tie remained there, still locked in place, unbroken, just as I had felt it a second before with Stewart's arm inside it. I had just witnessed "living matter through matter" as Walter described it—Stewart's arm moved right through the locked cable tie, which remained closed on the arm of the chair. This experiment has been performed many times, and I spoke to two sitters who once observed it in red light.

Walter then passed the intact cable tie, still closed in its loop, through the solid arm of the chair, and said "it is yours, take it!" So this was "matter through matter," but not living matter. "Is there a spare strap on the table?" Walter asked. This to me was the most star-tling part of all: we could then hear the rasping, clicking sound of a new cable tie being pulled through the ratchet that locked it in onto Stewart's arm and the arm of the chair, replacing the one that I had in my hand. This maneuver takes two hands! No one in the room had moved. There was no other sound in the silence. Somehow a new, opened cable tie had been transported from the table and secured onto Stewart's arm again. I then felt that new strap tightly locked around his arm, pinching into his flesh.

I identified with Thomas Mann's reaction to hearing the clicking of typewriter keys by "nobody" with two hands—his seeing the impos-sible happening, despite its own impossibility. And, it reminded me of Sir William Crookes's description of an incidence of matter through matter involving D. D. Home. The spirit communicator stated: "It is impossible for matter to pass through matter, but we will show you what we can do." There was a bouquet of flowers on the center of the table. "In full view of all present, a piece of china-grass fifteen inches long, which formed the center ornament of the bouquet, slowly rose from the other flowers, and then descended to the table in front of the vase between it and Mr. Home. It did not stop on reaching the table, but went straight through it, and we all watched it till it had entirely passed through," Crookes wrote. Home's hands were visible to all, and the grass stem showed no signs of pressure or abrasion.

Walter said his purpose here was to demonstrate for me "the great reality of our own survival, we who have passed through the change called death." He said this experiment demonstrates "how close our worlds truly are" because its success depends on the sitters coming to-gether in love and harmony, providing sufficient energy for it to occur. It may seem like a miracle to us, but it isn't for them.

Next, the trumpets were placed on the floor in front of Stewart. After the sitters sang for a few moments to add energy to the room, one trumpet started tapping rapidly up and down on the floor. It then rose upward, completely on its own; we could clearly see its illumi-nated band around the larger end. It went up to the ceiling. It moved both slowly and fast, now banging loudly on the ceiling, now gracefully drifting and swooping among the sitters. It touched my forehead very gently with a few taps. Navigating perfectly in the pitch dark, it never bumped into anyone or touched them too forcefully or with any awkwardness. Stewart came out of trance off and on, commenting groggily from his chair ("Is everything going okay?"), his arms strapped and knee tabs always visible in the dark.

There was something utterly beautiful and mesmerizing about the silent display of this material object that had come alive like some kind of magical bird from another world, responsive and intelligent. It was one of the most marvelous spectacles I have ever witnessed. The trumpet also could stop in its tracks in midair. When it rested at my eye level, suspended in front of me, a human voice spoke through it, trying to form words. It was absolutely bizarre to hear a disembodied voice emanating from a cone in midair. Stewart could be heard breathing heavily, gurgling and coughing due to the ectoplasm. The second trumpet then went up as well, and it too danced around from floor to ceiling, sometimes nodding up and down, or shaking as if laughing, in response to questions or comments from the delighted sitters. It stroked my hair and tapped my face gently. I was so filled with joy and wonder that I wanted the trumpet dance to go on forever. Finally, a male voice, mostly unintelligible, came again from inside the hovering trumpet, like a lost soul struggling to come up for air.

(At a later séance, I was astonished when the levitated trumpet stroked my nose and my cheek, maneuvering around my glasses so well that it never touched them—a feat that could not be accomplished by any human in the blackness.)

The trumpets returned to the floor, and suddenly the bell on the table rang vigorously.

Then the voice of Dr. Barnett introduced himself from near to Stewart, speaking independently. He had constructed an "artificial mechanism"—a voice box made from ectoplasm—through which he could speak, and he said he was planning to materialize and walk among us.

The drumsticks banged hard and quick against the table—on their own, like the bell. The sitters wondered whether the little boy Christopher was having fun.

I felt as if I had stepped into an entirely different world, an alternate reality with its own natural laws. It all may seem entirely outrageous. But I am only describing what I actually saw with my eyes, felt against my skin, and heard with my ears, along with the other sitters, and I assure you I am not exaggerating. I was able to maintain my clarity of mind, even while enjoying myself immensely, and I carefully studied the digital recordings of the sessions afterward to be sure my memories were accurate. I made a point of noting my observations out loud so they would be captured as a record of what happened to me.

How do the trumpets fly around like this? Like the mediums of the past, Stewart's ectoplasm makes it possible. In May 2000, Freda said all the physical phenomena depend on this "vital energy substance," which is both spiritual and physical. It can be manipulated by the spirit energy to change from a smoky substance to something solid; from something unsubstantial to something very substantial. "From the ectoplasm the scientific people are able to create either pseudopods or ectoplasmic arms. It is these that are connecting themselves to the trumpets, dear," she said. The other end is attached to the medium; it is part of him. I was amazed that, just as Geley had noted so many years earlier, Freda pointed out that the séance room creations are very fast as compared to development of life in the womb. "What takes nine months to reach fruition is created in seconds within the séance room," she said, reiterating that this is why ectoplasm is so extremely sensitive to light.

Somehow the ectoplasm can be used by the spirit people to move objects around the room. While Eusapia Palladino was in trance, her spirit control John King explained in a similar way how the slates in the séance room were transported. He referred to the emanation as fluid, saying it "forms bundles of straight rays, which are like stretched threads and support the slates. When these threads or rays are sufficiently strong, the object may perhaps be raised above the heads . . ."

And the replica of the human voice box? "We are able to vibrate your atmosphere and convert our thoughts into audible sounds," Dr. Barnett explained, adding that it is exceedingly difficult and the structure is unstable. He says it happens the same way our thoughts from our brain are converted into sound—for them, the mind is the equivalent of the brain in the physical world. The voices speaking through the trumpet are also using the ectoplasmic voice box, formed close to the medium. Their voices are carried through a hollow ectoplasmic tube into the smaller end of the trumpet, where they are amplified and heard through the larger end. That is all hard to imagine, but we know ectoplasm exists, and other accomplished mediums have explained the independent voices in the same way.

And beyond the many reliable reports (and strange photographs) from the past, I know ectoplasm exists because I was fortunate enough to see it. Walter, still speaking through Stewart, told me he wanted to demonstrate the materialization of his own hand. This was what I had been waiting for! I pulled my chair up to the other side of the small table, which was cleared of all objects. The red light under the glass tabletop was turned on, illuminating the surface and the area above it.

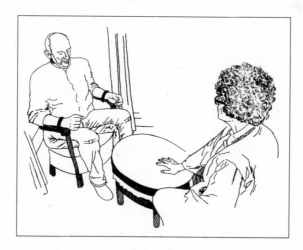

For the hand experiment, Stewart remained strapped in his chair and in trance while I followed instructions. *Copyright © Katie Halliwell*

Walter spoke to me throughout. The ectoplasm formed a grayish-black, foggy cloud that moved slowly toward me over the table, coming from Stewart's side opposite me. Gradually, I saw it grow, form

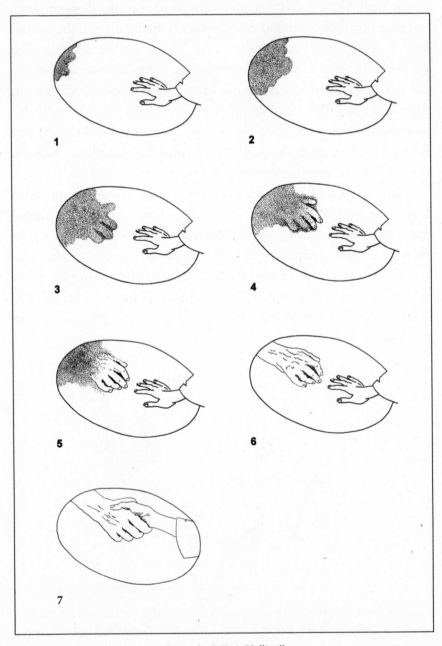

into a rounded shape; then it looked more like a hand, then I saw emerging fingers and a thumb, and suddenly it morphed into a three-dimensional, solid human hand that formed a fist and banged three times loudly on the table to demonstrate its solidity. It then withdrew off the edge of the table. From the gaseous ectoplasmic energy, a solid living hand had emerged.

Walter then asked me a question: "Would you like to feel the hand of a man dead to your world for over a hundred years?" You can imagine my answer.

He asked me to place my right hand on the table, palm down. The same thing happened: the ectoplasm crept over the edge of the table and I watched it form again into a living hand, which moved close to my hand and touched it. I held that materialized hand in mine. It felt completely normal and human, with joints, bones, and fingernails, but much warmer than my hand and larger, with sort of stubby fingers and very soft skin. Once again, it withdrew.

Stewart, his arms still locked to his chair, was too far from the center of the table to reach it. In any case, this hand was larger and fleshier than Stewart's; I could tell the difference, especially after having held on to Stewart's more delicate, thinner hand for the "matter through matter" display. Regardless, I saw this hand form in front of me from a cloud, from nothing, into a full hand; it could not possibly have belonged to anyone in the room. During my following three séances, I observed the materialization of Walter's hand twice from close by while others sat at the table, once with a sleeve hanging on the arm, and was myself the recipient of its touch one more time. This experiment had an element of shock and surrealism to it the first time, but I found it to be joyfully astonishing beyond my ability to describe.

At a sitting in 2005, Walter explained how he does this:

When the energy [ectoplasm] has been converted into a form visible to you, when it becomes pliable, when I know that it is of a molecular state which will allow me to work further upon it, I then dip my etheric hand into the energy, into the ectoplasm which I find clings to my etheric hand. This organized mass,

from which I create my etheric hand, has constituency and it has
weight. It is the weight that creates the problem. It is difficult for
us to manipulate physical weight, physical mass, because I come
from a world as you know which exists on a finer vibrational
level than your own. So I have to slow down my vibrations.

Once again, I have to acknowledge that the reader may be so
baffled by the strangeness of this as to feel quite disturbed by it, or
even unwilling to believe it. Perhaps you just want to close this book.
Please remember that I am simply reporting honestly and accurately
what happened and what was said; the other sitters experienced the
same phenomena. Also, let me remind you that, as noted in previous chapters, materialized hands have been scientifically documented
under the strictest controls. In fact, some such reports sound almost
exactly like what I experienced with Stewart. Sir William Crookes saw
a luminous cloud "condense into shape and become a perfectly formed
hand. At this stage, the hand is visible to all present." It moved like
any normal hand, and then faded off back into the cloud.

Charles Richet watched a mass of "grayish, gelatinous" ectoplasm
emanate from Eva C.:

Little by little it seems to split into digits at its end. It is like the
embryo of a hand, ill-formed but clear enough to enable me
to say that it is a left hand seen from the back. Fresh progress:
the little finger separates almost completely: then the following
changes, very quick but very clear: a hand with closed fingers,
seen from the back, with a little finger extended, an ill-formed
thumb, and higher up a swelling that resembles the carpal bones.
I think I see the creases in the skin.

And Walter's materialization reminded me of Geley's experience
also—he observed ectoplasm and wrote that "this kind of bud ex-
pands into a perfectly modeled hand. I touch it, and it gives me the
feeling of a normal hand; I feel the bones and the fingernails. Then it
retreats, diminishes in size, and disappears . . ."

Many people, including David Fontana, have also touched Walter's fully animated, materialized hand in Stewart's séances. I was moved to realize that this is not something lost to the past that one can only read about; the legacy of these remarkable phenomena from the great historical mediums had fortunately continued into the present. This astounding contemporary manifestation links Stewart to these mediums throughout history and allows people now to see the hand—and touch it—for themselves.

During my fourth séance, on August 20, 2015, with nine other sitters, I was fortunate to experience something else unbelievable but real: the full materialization of Dr. Barnett. Unlike the hand, this required darkness. Initially, Stewart was levitated in his chair; he woke up as we saw his knee tabs rise about a foot, saying how much he disliked being levitated (on some occasions he has risen five feet, and even to the ceiling, while strapped in his chair, often waking up). By watching the knee tabs, we could see him being moved inside the cabinet by whatever the force was that could accomplish such a heavy task. Walter then told us to link hands and sing, to build up the energy. My heart was beating with anticipation as I waited for the miraculous to unfold.

Shortly, the sitters nearest the cabinet felt hands touching them; some said they were small hands, and we noted four. I was told that these were Dr. Barnett's helpers; one was a child. When Dr. Barnett started walking and touching people, I could hear his footsteps. I also heard his voice as he moved around—the same voice I had heard before when he spoke through that voice box. He said how difficult this was for him, and when it seemed as if Stewart might wake up, he commanded, "Sleep!" Stewart's knee pads were visible except when they were blocked by the forms moving in front of him; this was another way we knew that something "solid" was actually there. When Dr. Barnett stood before me, he tapped me gently and repeatedly on the head with both hands. In response to a question, he said, "I have a helper with me," and his voice was clearly right in front of me. Stewart started coughing, and then I heard the cabinet curtains shake as if someone had grabbed them and was rattling them strongly.

It seemed quite inconceivable, but a walking and talking "human" form, not present in the room before that moment, materialized, came out of the cabinet, and then dematerialized into the deep, mysterious darkness inside it. How could this be? Stewart told me afterward that the spirit people exist in an etheric body at a higher vibration. It's like taking a bamboo pole and swinging it so fast that the eye can't see it anymore. The pole is still there, but it's moving too fast, vibrating too rapidly, for us to perceive it. If you slow it down, then it is in a physical state that we can observe. The spirit people have to slow themselves down in the same way when they materialize. They then use the ectoplasm to manifest themselves. They have said how very difficult and unpleasant, even painful, it is to do this, describing it as similar to walking through thick mud, or like wearing a heavy, wet overcoat.

The love and harmony in that séance room were like nothing I have known before; and this seemed to help create the magnificent meeting of two worlds. By the end, I felt as if the room were filled with a palpable energy, almost like a substance filling the space. That may not sound journalistic, but I can only reflect on the words of Jeffrey Kane provided earlier: "Reality apprehended intuitively is engaged, connected. You don't look at things as much as dwell in them." The experience of dwelling in that room was almost indescribable, yet I kept my objective mind intact at the same time.

But as far as Stewart is concerned, the physical phenomena are only part of the picture. Although they present a powerful argument for survival, he says that the case becomes much stronger when backed up by other types of evidence, especially evidence in the form of verifiable messages from sitters' loved ones. I witnessed this a number of times, but no such messages were delivered to me.

For example, I was given the tape of an October 2015 sitting, which took place at a seminar before many witnesses. I studied it carefully. The room was illuminated, and Freda spoke through Stewart while he was in a light trance. Freda said that she had a gentleman with her in her world, anxious to speak to a friend; the gentleman had died just over four years ago, and his name was Derek. A woman named

Violet Eccles from Australia came forward, and said this applied to her. Freda invited her to come sit next to the medium, and continued.

There was some kind of celebration also around four years ago, Freda said, and it had to do with Derek's "good son." He had a son? she asked. Violet said yes. Freda kept listening. "Good son . . . good-ee-son . . . good is son . . . No, it's *not* his son," she said. "Goodison, Goodison Park!" Violet exclaimed. "I spread his ashes there." (This is a soccer stadium in Liverpool; Derek loved soccer.) "He feels as if he's at home there," Freda said. (Derek lived in Liverpool before moving to Australia; it was home to him.) Next Freda said Derek was sending love to his wife, Joan. (His wife's name is Joan.) And she brought up his friend Joe, saying he had been ill. (Joe was his best friend and was ill.) She said Violet's sister Dolly was also on the other side. (Correct.) "What's this about playing the piano?" Freda asked. Violet said her brother, also deceased, was a trained pianist. "Who is Allie, Allison?" asked Freda. "My daughter-in-law," Violet replied. "They are all here!" Freda told her with delight, as if observing a gathering at a party.

Throughout, the deceased communicators gave messages of love, Violet made comments to them, and she was sometimes quite emotional. "Now there is something to do with Phil," Freda said. "Your people are all shouting at me!" (Violet thought this was her nephew. Later she realized it was her friend Phil who had died.) Finally, Freda said that Violet's people were telling her to say one word: "duck." Violet chuckled, and Freda exclaimed in her amused, schoolteacher's voice, "They are laughing like drains . . . too many shouting at me, dear! I must mention the word 'duck'!" Violet explained that when she was very young, she tried to rescue a duck from drowning because it had its head under the water. This had become a family joke.

I contacted Violet to confirm that Stewart knew absolutely none of this (which he told me he was certain he did not), and to check the accuracy of what had happened. Violet told me Derek's wife informed her after the reading that her husband had indeed died four years and two months prior, as Freda had said. This reading contained eight specific names (including the reference to "duck"), an accurate time of death, and a specific celebration (the ashes at Goodison Park). Four times Freda communicated the correct relationship of a named person to Violet. There were no errors. But these simple facts cannot convey the power and emotion that this held for Violet, who had no doubt her loved ones had survived death.

In 2014, Reville Mohr, a skeptic who did not believe in mediumship or the afterlife, flew from Australia with his sister Leone Holdsworth to attend a sitting with Stewart. Deeply depressed about the loss of his wife nine months prior, Reville "was very negative and I was worried that he might be so rude that the séance would be closed," Leone told me. Still, she thought it might help him. To everyone's surprise, Freda, speaking through Stewart, invited Reville to come sit by Stewart. She asked him, "Are you thinking of getting married ?" "No" was the reply. Then Freda said that she might not be hearing it correctly, but that she had a lady there saying, "Marry Lynn." Then she corrected herself by saying, "Oh, no—it's Marilyn. Reville, would you be surprised if I told you that I had your wife here with me?" Again he replied no. "Would it also surprise you if I told you that she had your daughter Kimberley and your son Thomas that you never got to meet with her also?" With that, Reville broke down and cried. He and his wife, Marilyn, had lost their infant daughter Kimberley to crib death, and it was Reville who discovered her lifeless body. Marilyn had miscarried their baby boy Thomas at five months. No one else in the séance room knew anything about this other than his sister.

Reville had been so emotional that Stewart texted his host, a circle member, the next morning to ask how he was doing. "Her reply has stuck in my mind ever since," Stewart told me, tearfully moved by the memory. "She said he had gone for a walk and on his return he was like a man who had just won the lottery." He was forever changed, with a huge weight lifted from his shoulders. "I would give up all the flying trumpets, materializations, everything, if it meant that the trance mediumship could be far, far more evidential than it is. To me, this kind of evidence is everything," Stewart told me in 2016.

Another important component is the healing performed by Dr.

Barnett either when he materializes, or through Stewart when he occupies his body, sometimes for serious illnesses such as cancer.

In 2011, Robin Hodson and his wife visited the circle. Robin was told to sit in front of the cabinet by Dr. Barnett, who was speaking through Stewart. Stewart's hands were placed against Robin's open palms, and "immediately it was like receiving electric shocks," Robin says, which lasted for a few minutes. Dr. Barnett announced that Robin's "organisms had been changed," which resulted in much laughter among the sitters, and that Robin would not know the results for three months. Unknown to Stewart and the circle members, Robin was suffering from cardiomyopathy, an incurable disease of the heart muscle making it difficult for the heart to pump blood, and was under constant medical supervision. After this experience in the séance room, his legs felt weak and he could only stumble back to his chair.

During his next visit to the cardiologist at Brighton Hospital, the usual echocardiogram was taken. According to Robin, the doctor asked what he had done since his previous visit. He had been alarmed then because Robin's heart efficiency test was at an all-time low of just over 20 percent, and the heart was enlarged. Now he told Robin that his heart efficiency had substantially increased to 55 percent (within the normal range) and his heart had also reduced to a near normal size. The doctor said it was rare that patients suffering from cardiomyopathy ever had such a miraculous recovery. And this visit was exactly three months after the visit to Stewart's circle, as Dr. Barnett had said (it had been booked prior to the séance). Robin says he has no more symptoms and his condition no longer needs any medical supervision. And this is only one example of such a healing.

I must also note that sometimes evidence from loved ones does not make sense or can be inaccurate, and sometimes healings are not successful. There are also times when Stewart sits with his circle and nothing happens at all. Séance results are not predictable, and Stewart worries greatly about this when people travel long distances to sit with him. What happens each time is beyond his control.

I asked Stewart about the living-agent psi hypothesis, which postulates that all the phenomena are solely a product of his own psi and that of the sitters, using psychokinesis to create the physical effects. "Is Dr. Barnett created by me?" he replied. "Someone who cannot only speak to people independently of me, but can walk among them, put his hands on them and heal them? Is this me? Nonsense!"

One more remarkable event occurred only a few months before I completed this book. Kevin Kussow of Otto, North Carolina, the owner of a successful business, had been sitting in a small circle led by his father for over thirty years. Kevin had emailed Stewart early in 2016 to ask his advice. The circle had not convened for a while due to Kevin's father being ill. A few months later, Freda said during a séance that she wanted to do a book test for Kevin, two days after Kevin's father died on March 2, 2016. (The reader may recall Mrs. Leonard's remarkable book tests described previously by Alan Gauld.)

Freda began by providing some accurate details identifying Kevin's father who had just arrived into spirit. She then said that his bed faced a bookcase that also had many ornaments on it, and to its left was a door. She mentioned a pair of shoes she said Kevin's father was speaking of. Kevin was told to go to the second shelf, take the second or third book from the left, and open it to page eighty-four, which would be the page on the left side. Near the top would be a sentence mentioning animals or an animal. Farther down would be the names "George" and "Smith." This was recorded at the séance and the tape was sent to Kevin.

The description of the location of the bookcase relative to the bed and the door, and its being full of ornaments, was accurate. With his mother and two sons present, Kevin went to the second shelf and counted the second and third books from the left. The second book was a thin paper pamphlet, but the third was *Bury My Heart at Wounded Knee*, about the slaughter of Native Americans. Kevin turned to page eighty-four, which was on the left side. Two sentences down was a reference to the name "Little Raven" and on the next line to hunting buffalo—the animals that Freda had referred to. Farther down the text referred to a post trader named Smith and a "half-breed son" named George—also exactly as Freda had said. His father's favorite shoes—Crocs—were sitting right there near the bookshelf.

Freda had pinpointed three accurate details on the page, as well as the specific page of the book containing them, in a specific location on a specific shelf, in a house across the Atlantic Ocean. Stewart had never met Kevin and knew nothing about his home. Did Freda travel there, or somehow project her consciousness there, to view the book? Or could Stewart have such extraordinary clairvoyance that he could have "seen" the five words on that specific book page, along with the book's location on the shelf, while unconscious? He considers that possibility preposterous. "The book tests are important to the survival argument," he told me. "This is the kind of experiment that the critics conveniently ignore." I spoke with Kevin who never knew the book test would ever be made public, and I have no reason to doubt his integrity. And this is not the first time that Freda has performed like this.

Does Stewart's mediumship show that we survive death? Not if the varying independent voices, sometimes recognized by sitters, are all manifested only by Stewart and the sitters; not if the five consistent spirit people are simply unconscious multiple personalities, and the walking and talking materialized forms are creations by human beings alone; not if the powers of ectoplasm, yet to be explained, do not require external forces; not if Stewart has the capacity to heal ailing people he doesn't know are sick through touch, provide accurate details from deceased loved ones, and read books miles away, all through his own psi while completely unconscious. Is this conceivable? Is it just as difficult to conceive of discarnates reaching into our world with their psi as it is to imagine Stewart and his sitters being unconsciously responsible for all of it with their psi? You be the judge. Maybe it's a combination of both. But I can share through personal experience that the message that we survive death permeates the interchanges, the laughter and tears, and the physical demonstrations within the séance room. It is the lifeblood of all that goes on there. It's quite impossible to cross the threshold into this "other world" without entering into that reality. I can't prove anything, but I only wish everyone could have the experience.

Just last night, I was in downtown New York City when I received a text message from one of Stewart's circle members: "Dr. Barnett walked among us last night and did some healing . . ." This popped in as I stood waiting for the subway on a crowded platform. Suddenly the implications of the casual text hit me in a new way. How simply extraordinary! In a small room in England, a man materialized, walked out through a curtain, talked and touched people, and then vanished to from where he had come. This man says he once lived on this earth. To Stewart's circle members, this is such a normal occurrence that it can be texted to me in two lines. And we all just go about our regular lives. Should the rest of the world know that this is happening?

Chapter 26

A Life in Two Worlds

By Stewart Alexander

Stewart will now speak directly to the readers in his own chapter. He has never written for any mainstream publications before, and this is a rare opportunity to hear from this unusual physical medium about his own experiences and unique perspective.

I have always welcomed the many reasonable questions about my physical mediumship that naturally arise. To begin with, I am often asked how I can be sure that the Spirit People who allegedly communicate through me are not simply aspects of my own unconscious mind, each as a unique, developed personality. The fact is that I cannot be sure. That is a truthful answer. However, my many years working as a medium (private and public) in which countless people have interacted with these Spirit "controls" suggests forcefully to me that they are exactly who they claim to be: denizens from the next world. Whilst I am not in any way religious, I will quote the Bible in saying, "By their fruits ye shall know them." I shall explain.

My longtime guide White Feather was the first to make himself known to me. I had been sitting for months with a small group, and nothing at all had happened. On one such occasion I was with only my brother and sister-in-law, and we sat with our hands on the table in front of us with a dim red light, as always. After our hour together had almost passed, my thoughts were beginning to turn to the cup of tea and the biscuits that always awaited us afterward. That was the highlight of those sittings at that point!

Then suddenly I heard a voice—it was as clear as a bell, in my left ear. It said, "Switch the light out; continue to sit." The strange thing is, I didn't find that extraordinary in any way and I wasn't startled by it in the moment. This voice continued to repeat, over and over again, like a loop on a tape, "Switch the light out; continue to sit. Switch the light out; continue to sit." And this went on and on and on. When my brother suggested we bring the sitting to an end and put the kettle on, I said, "No, switch the light out." He reached up and switched off the red light. And now I pause as I write this, because I have a problem: How does one describe the indescribable? I will do my best and try.

At the moment the light went out, something approached me from behind. Whatever it was, as it came toward me, everything in my entire body, every nerve, every muscle, began to twitch and jump, and suddenly he was there—inside my body—and I was outside. And then I heard "myself" talking from a distance: "I come, speak, brother, sister." Just those few words, but those few words were the beginning. No sooner were they said than whatever it was, or he was, came out of my body and I found myself back in. A few moments later my brother brought the sitting to an end and switched on the light. We then sat in relative silence drinking tea and eating biscuits. Hardly anything was said, and I went home. The experience, to say the least, unnerved me.

The next morning I arrived at my office—at the time I was a de-sign engineer at a large international engineering company—and the phone was ringing. I picked it up and it was my brother, and he said excitedly, "Are you coming round for a sitting tonight?" And I replied, "Not bloody likely!!" Honestly, that was the first and the last time that I was ever frightened in a séance room. Never since. But I was still very nervous about what had taken place.

Still, we continued to sit. If White Feather was going to control me, it would always be in the first few minutes—otherwise nothing would happen. Whenever he did come, the first thing that would happen was that my left hand would become almost deformed. It would curl in on itself. It was as if I had severe, crippling arthritis, except it was not painful.

It was a long journey. Following several years of sitting in a home circle, as I began to develop further, I must confess to suffering constant nagging doubts. Was White Feather a product of my own making, which I had, in some mysterious way, inadvertently conjured up after all the years of hoping for a breakthrough? Or was he really dwelling in the next world, with my body as a vessel for communication between our world and his? That precise dilemma, I fervently believe, is one that confronts most genuine developing trance mediums. To be of good conscience, no one wants to be guilty of fooling themselves and, even worse, fooling others. So repeatedly I asked myself if all of this was merely a figment of my own imagination or perhaps a so-called secondary personality that I had unconsciously created to meet expectation. In short, I was literally filled with self-doubt.

Still, I continued to sit in that circle. It would be several more years before I could finally accept that the voices that spoke through me were who they claimed to be. My persistent doubts would finally be relieved when I attended a séance with the English medium Leslie Flint in the early 1970s. At that time, he was celebrated internationally as one of the finest "direct-voice" mediums in the world, in whose presence the voices of the dead were heard speaking independently of him in another part of the room as if coming out of the air, while he sat quietly in his chair. (This ability was similar to that of Indridi Indridason, as described in an earlier chapter.) On some occasions Flint even joined in with the conversations. As I was privileged to discover firsthand, to sit there and listen to the voices of men, women, and children talking to their loved ones on this side of life was absolutely fantastic.

On the third or fourth time I sat with Leslie Flint, I encountered what I consider to be one of the milestones in my development. A variety of voices spoke to various sitters from different parts of the room, and Flint spoke only from his chair. We had been sitting for over an hour when suddenly I heard the voice of my grandmother coming from the center of the room. She had been like a mother to me, my brother, and my two sisters, taking a central role in raising us following the collapse of our parents' marriage when I was ten. On the day she passed over, just two or three weeks before that séance—a fact entirely unknown to Flint—I had sat alone with her at her hospital bedside. She had been unconscious but I had held her hand, and something had passed between us not known to anyone else. Suddenly, there in that small séance room a few weeks later, she mentioned this to me—something known only to me, on the earth, and to her, on the other side. The voice I was listening to belonged to her. The way she said it, and certain words she used, were characteristic of her alone, and there was no question in my mind that this was she. Thus, she proved to me that she had survived death. As her words faded away, I was left with a feeling of intense gratitude, not only to her for making the supreme effort to return to me, but also to everyone at both sides of death who had made that wonderful communication possible.

But it did not end there! As I sat reflecting on that emotional conversation, suddenly, out of the darkness, another voice began to speak, and it was one that I knew only too well from recordings I had listened to of my own séances. It belonged to White Feather, who had consistently endeavored to develop me despite my conflict about his authenticity. As he spoke independently of Flint, from another part of the room, it suddenly occurred to me that here was my golden opportunity to establish once and for all if he indeed was who he claimed to be. Was he really an autonomous individual, or an aspect of myself? Suddenly the solution popped into my head, and I said, "Can I ask a question?" He said, "Yes," and I inquired if, during his earthly life, he had had any kind of physical deformity. Instantly, he replied: "Do you mean my left hand?"

My feelings as he uttered those words are impossible to convey. The unalterable fact is that in that room—in the presence of Leslie Flint, who was a virtual stranger and knew nothing of my mediumistic development—the communicator had uttered just six potent words: "Do you mean my left hand?" The effect on me was profound.

Following such a wonderful experience I would never doubt again that he was who he claimed to be.

From that moment on I dedicated myself to the "great work." And on it went, over many many years, very slowly. In time, the "team" of Spirit People (White Feather, Christopher, Freda Johnson, Walter Stinson, and Dr. Barnett), who are now like close friends, became part of our weekly sittings. The consistency of the distinctive personalities and the extraordinary abilities our Spirit friends have demonstrated for so long defy all the rules of our physical world as we currently understand them, and have led me to firmly believe that they are who they say they are. Hundreds of séances have been recorded and the love that the Spirit People radiate and express is palpable. Sitters are often moved beyond words. I honestly cannot imagine that this represents my own psychological manifestation of complex multiple personalities who somehow can work seeming miracles, heal illnesses, and read the minds of people while I am "asleep" in a deep trance.

Also, the physical manifestations rest upon the use of an energy substance (referred to as ectoplasm), which the Spirit People use to manipulate objects and to partially or fully materialize. While this generally occurs within dark conditions, there have been occasions when a red light has been switched on long enough for people in the room to observe the ectoplasm in action, while attached to my body. When Walter (our Spirit worker responsible for physical phenomena) materializes his hand, it comes from a cloud of ectoplasm that is always visible in the red light. If this were purely psychological, and the effects were due to unconscious psi, it seems highly unlikely that such a mysterious substance would be generated and could be seen by those in the room.

Unfortunately very few people will ever experience the wonders of the séance room, since so few genuine mediums and reputable circles are accessible to people today—many may work only in private. In this regard, I want to address a question that I have been asked on many occasions and that I have thought about very carefully. Leslie Kean posed this question to me in 2015. She asked if she could videotape the materialization of Walter's hand using a newly developed small camera that could shoot in the low red light we always have on for this experiment.

Knowing the nature of her book, I seriously considered throwing caution to the wind and agreeing to this. But upon reflection, I realized, as I have before, that this would throw my life, and that of the circle, into turmoil that would be destructive to the purpose of our circle and problematic for my family. And such an investigation would ultimately lead nowhere. Please allow me to explain.

I have spent almost fifty years involved in an exhaustive study of the history of physical mediumship. Historic fact shows that many of the known physical mediums cooperated at some point with researchers. Yet this exposure ultimately led to suspicions or allegations of suspected fraud even for the genuine mediums. Sometimes the findings were labeled "inconclusive" and the researchers demanded more and more tests, or they looked for loopholes that they suspected had allowed the medium to produce bogus phenomena. And again, more tests were demanded.

Even favorable reports by investigators with impeccable credentials were questioned or doubted, and sometimes even ridiculed. For the authentic mediums, the phenomena were never proved to be genuine beyond any doubt as the investigators wanted, nor could they be shown to be fraudulent—so nothing was conclusively proved and accepted by the larger scientific community. This pattern has repeated itself from Eusapia Palladino to Eva C.; from Margery Crandon to Helen Duncan. They cooperated, and they all met the same fate.

Margery, one of the most extraordinary physical mediums of the 1920s and '30s, was the subject of vicious controversy after subjecting herself to years of rigorous testing. Selective critics totally ignored remarkable phenomena, manifested under tightly controlled conditions, that simply could not be explained away. These have been conveniently forgotten since Margery's death and today she is widely considered to have been a very clever fraud who used her feminine charms to dupe many a male researcher. The contemporary research world continues to ignore this cruel and disgraceful injustice, which ultimately led to the death of this courageous woman through alcoholic poisoning.

I often wonder how Margery and others might have developed if they had chosen to sit exclusively within their private, harmonious home circles. We can only speculate what phenomena might have occurred if they had not been subjected to the cold clinical atmosphere of the tests and the pressure to perform. Sometimes photographs were part of the research they allowed. Of course it is well known that many fraudulent mediums have attempted to deceive gullible people, and photos of ectoplasm and other phenomena were indeed faked. But even the legitimate images taken under controlled conditions can look very strange to anyone who has not sat with a physical medium. This does not excuse the accusations these photographs have generated against the genuine mediums willing to take the risk of allowing photography in the séance room.

At best, a film of Walter's hand would show that paranormal action was a reality, but it could be explained away as an abnormal physiological function possessed by and unconsciously directed by myself. It would not be seen as anything close to proving survival beyond death—although there would be much debate about that. Following scientific scrutiny and authentication, the world press and broadcast media would quickly descend. My cherished family life would be severely disrupted, along with my séance room circle, due to the uproar. Our small circle would be unsustainable under the pressure of world scrutiny. And no doubt there would be demands for further studies and more filming, and it would never stop.

At worst, the footage might be questioned as fraudulent. Then I would take my place among all those mediums before me who chose a similar path. The stigma that has long been attached to their names would forever be attached to mine. In that event, my children and my grandchildren would always wonder if their father/grandfather had been capable of engaging in fraud, because they would wonder whether the film was genuine or bogus. The thought of that is frankly unbearable.

My mediumship functions as a direct result of an innate, acute sensitivity that I have lived with from the beginning, and has intensified over time. This might wither and die under such pressure. My further development as a physical medium would be threatened. I see absolutely no point in engaging in such an ambitious project while knowing that success or failure would be a literal calamity, to me, my family, and circle, and would not prove anything anyway. I hope that is understandable to all those who would love a séance room video, for reasons I certainly understand.

You may wonder, what about me? Wouldn't I like to have this video so that I can witness the hand being materialized since I am in trance when it occurs? For many years I was invariably unconscious when the physical phenomena occurred. Eventually, however, I began to briefly regain consciousness at such times and I have to say that I was delighted to observe what, until then, I had only been told about—such as the levitated trumpets gliding around the room. Sometimes I am levitated in my chair above the heads of the sitters—something I admit I do not like—and I wake up then. There is also another purpose in my emerging from the trance condition at such times. In hearing my voice the sitters have further confirmation that I am where I am supposed to be—in my chair and not several meters away fraudulently manipulating the séance trumpets or engaging in other covert activity.

And I have seen more than simply these glimpses within my own séance room. Some years ago, I was able to witness a full range of physical manifestations while attending a séance with another physical medium. These observations literally changed my life—without them, it is possible that I would have forever remained unknown. On this occasion, I was one of sixty sitters. I witnessed some of the exact same manifestations that had been produced within my circle for years. After the séance, I saw the joy on the faces of everyone who had attended and the buzz among them and I saw how, in that short time, lives had been deeply affected. A belief in the possibility of survival beyond death and communication between the two worlds had been converted into certainty in the minds of so many of those people. In that moment I knew that I could no longer remain a private medium sitting solely within my small home circle, as I had done for many years. I felt that it was a duty to sit before the public. And so began my years of public demonstrations.

But regarding the materialization of the hand, I can only say that this was the most wonderful phenomenon I ever personally witnessed. It was at one of my public demonstration séances some years ago. I had heard repeatedly from sitters about Walter materializing his physical hand from a cloud of ectoplasm, but never expected to see it myself. One memorable night I regained consciousness and there it was. I must say that I bubbled over with excitement when I saw it, and I was still talking about it months later. There is a very big difference between hearing about a phenomenon and actually observing it—a very big difference—even for the medium.

Sometimes the Spirit People are playful, and there is often much laughter during the séances. I will never forget one occasion decades ago when I was sitting as the medium with a circle at the home of friend, mentor, and colleague Alan Crossley. As we chatted together prior to the sitting, we observed a window shade flapping in a breeze coming in from the open window, and the shade kept noisily hitting the back of a vase of flowers on the window ledge. Inevitably, the vase toppled over onto the floor. We all saw it, and water shot out all over the carpet. Alan immediately got a cloth and crouched down on the ground to wipe it up. But then he sat right up and laughed and said, "Come feel this, the carpet is totally dry!" It was thoroughly and completely dry, despite the pool of water that was there moments before. And that is the truth! The absolute truth.

Six hours later in Alan's séance room, I woke up during the sitting. Christopher, our young boy in the Spirit world who is still with us today, had said, "Do you want a present?" When everyone exclaimed yes, we heard a "whoosh" and all this water fell down and we were all soaked. This was an occasion when we were delighted to be soaked! They must have taken the water from the toppled vase and suspended it somewhere. Isn't that fantastic? With experiences like that, how can you ever doubt?

On another occasion, when I was with a group hosted by a wonderful medium called Kath Matthews (who was to become my first mentor), we had a blank sitting—nothing happened at all. When we turned on the light, there on the floor in front of each member of the circle was a little plastic animal—dogs, cats, cows, horses, etc.! But to our dismay, nothing had been left for Kath. We were a bit upset, because it seemed she had been ignored by the Spirit world. However, the next morning, Kath called me in a very excited voice. She lives alone and her house had been locked after the sitters left. She told me that when she woke up in the morning, there was a little plastic pink pig sitting on top of the book that she had placed on her nightstand prior to falling asleep. So you see, this is the power of the Spirit world.

However, as wonderful as these events are, I have long maintained that genuine physical phenomena do not alone prove communication with the departed. Unquestionably, physical manifestations are (or can be) a wondrous spectacle, but it is the evidential information transmitted at a physical séance that, in my view, is the absolute acid test of such mediumship. If this is outside the knowledge of the medium, unconscious during the sittings, then surely this would forcefully suggest that an outside intelligence is indeed involved.

Physical phenomena are often much harder for people to accept. I am confident that should the dead be able to fully materialize as living, breathing, solid forms in a well-lighted room in my presence, doubts would still remain in the minds of many researchers and irrational skeptics, who, because of their belief systems, simply would not accept that this could be possible.

I have been asked many times what the experience of my mediumship means to me personally. Truthfully, for a long time I found it difficult to answer this. For many years following a séance, guest sitters would thank me for the experience and tell me that their loved ones had communicated with them. I never knew what to say, especially since I had been in trance the whole time, so my ridiculous response would invariably be "Well, I'm so pleased for you." However, this was to dramatically change following one particular séance a few years ago, when the realization of what occurs within our séance room and how it affected people really hit me full on.

On that night, a lady had traveled over two hundred miles to attend. We knew nothing about her other than the fact that she was evidently very sincere. Arriving at our circle leader's home that night (in which the séances have been held now for over thirty years), I was introduced to her. She was shy, and other than exchanging pleasantries, little else was said. Eventually we went up into the séance room and the sitting commenced. Two hours later and just prior to it ending the lady found herself in communication with her beloved partner, who, tragically, she had lost twelve months earlier. Needless to say, none of us knew anything about this—a loss that, we were to discover later, had almost destroyed her. We subsequently learned that she had been extremely close to her partner, who died unexpectedly, and she was such a wreck that she couldn't eat or sleep and had considered suicide.

When the séance drew to a close, all the sitters went down to the lounge on the floor below. Shortly afterward, when I had recovered from the trance condition, I made my way down the stairs and as I walked into the lounge the lady stood waiting for me. Throwing her arms around me, she said the following: "Thank you for saving my life." This literally meant the world to me, and I remember this moment vividly and with much emotion. Never again would I utter an insipid phrase such as "Well, I'm so pleased for you." I realized, this is why we have sat all these years. This is what it's all about.

In addition, I wish to play my part in encouraging and inspiring others to form their own circles and sit for the development of mediumship. For those who want to achieve contact themselves, I will give one crucial bit of advice. I have sat with the same group week after week, for over thirty years. The most difficult thing in today's frenetic, technological world is to get a group of committed people to sit in harmony like this. The group must meet regularly at the designated time, be free of conflict, and be consistent and committed. It must be seen that this is a commitment to the Spirit world. The development of a circle can be excruciatingly slow and very frustrating on occasions, requiring much patience. But all you can do is be there, and have trust and confidence in the Spirit world, because it is a collaboration between the two worlds. It's as simple as that.

Two-world communication is tenuous—it is fragile, and frankly we have little conception of the conditions that may affect and influence it. All we can do—all we can ever do—is to work in full cooperation with the Spirit People, listen to them and let them guide us, and give always of our best.

My personal journey, which commenced in 1968, has not yet reached its end. What I have learned primarily is that the Spirit world wants desperately to prove the reality concerning the nature of life; that they are who they claim to be; and that death will be the most wonderful journey we will ever make.

And what does this mean in terms of my life here and now? I live with the belief that it is essential to cause no one harm; to help others; to be true to oneself. I believe that we all have a spark of "God" within us—God being the all-pure state toward which we are all returning. We are a part of that pure state and as such we are all a part of one another.

I have long been in a privileged position that has allowed me (and others) to momentarily peer beyond the curtain. Repeatedly the Spirit People have done their best to inform us—to give to us an understanding of their glorious world, that world that awaits us all. But, always, they have failed. One imagines that for them to succeed would be akin to an effort we might make to explain to a man without sight what color is, or to explain to someone deaf since birth what the sound of rain is like. We know from what we have been told that the world of eternity far surpasses in every conceivable way that of our present one. As our Spirit guide Freda has said, "Your world is a world of illusion; our world is a world of ultimate reality."

And she has assured us that we do not lose our individuality, personality, character, and our memories when we make that transition to the world of ultimate reality. So I continue to hold one single-minded vision: that my mediumship may offer comfort and reassurance that death is not the end, but is simply a passage into that other world into which, one day, we all shall pass.

Conclusion

We have come to the end of a multilayered, interconnected journey—from past-life memories to actual-death experiences, from mental mediumship to after-death communications to physical mediumship. Perhaps you have come to agree that the material presented provides evidence highly supportive of the survival hypothesis.

The living-agent psi versus survival debate is an unsolvable one since the LAP alternative can never be ruled out beyond a shadow of a doubt. But, as Alan Gauld concluded in his chapter, "A rational case, of either tendency, built on evidence, however difficult to interpret, is to be preferred to any amount of blind belief or blind disbelief." My intention therefore has been to offer a certain level of insight and resolution for those seeking objective answers to the question of survival past death. Although as an investigative journalist I yearn for rational, factual answers that are universally true, unfortunately they cannot always be definitive when dealing with issues like this, even if the evidence is highly suggestive.

It is also valuable to realize that there may be other ways of approaching this problem, rather than limiting its resolution to LAP vs. survival psi; there is so much we don't know. For example, perhaps the distinction between the two forms of psi is not really as drastic as it seems. Longtime survival researcher Daniel Drasin sees it this way:

> For millennia, philosophies and wisdom traditions have insisted that consciousness is an irreducible, primary property of nature. So to explain away mediumship and other forms of apparent afterlife communication as being caused by psi among the living is to overlook the strong possibility that all psychic functioning occurs within the same general realm or field, which we crudely term the "other side" or the "spirit world." Since copious evidence seems to confirm that consciousness can function independently of the brain, perhaps our "true selves" actually reside on the "other side" whether we are in a physical body or not. If so, then the distinction between deceased people communicating through their psi to a medium and the medium using her own psychic functioning to acquire information may be a false one, since in this view both sources operate within the same domain.

In any case, those of us who lean toward survival as the best explanation of the data are in good company. Despite Stephen Braude's thorough assessment of psi and its relationship to survival, he writes that he can say "with little assurance but with some justification, that the evidence provides a reasonable basis for believing in personal postmortem survival"—at least for a limited time. David Fontana, as we know, concluded that the living-agent psi argument is not adequate to explain the evidence. He attended sittings with a number of experienced physical mediums over many years and witnessed the full range of phenomena—unlike Braude, who has not experienced any phenomena he is convinced are genuine beyond the types of PK I described in our sessions with Kai Muegge.

Clearly, for many of us who do end up accepting survival, this determination may ultimately come not only from evidence we can study, but also, as Fontana says, "from personal experience and from some inner, intuitive certainty about our real nature." Michael Sudduth comments along the same lines: "My position and arguments do not rule out there being an experiential justification for belief in survival. Subjects who have near-death experiences, who have ostensible memories of past lives, or mediums who experience 'communicators' in particular ways may very well be in possession of experiential grounds that confer justification of their belief in survival."

There is certainly much compelling evidence, even if it does require acceptance of the auxiliary assumptions spelled out earlier. Emil Jensen, as described by Erlendur Haraldsson, was a drop-in communicator who provided enough details to be identified years later as someone who actually lived. He materialized before the eyes of many reliable witnesses in the séance room of Indridi Indridason. Does the appearance of someone like this, who is known to have walked the earth, constitute proof that we survive death? I suspect the witnesses who conversed with Jensen were convinced of that. But how can we be sure that the materialized form was actually the same "person" as the Danish drop-in communicator, or that this form was not somehow generated by the medium and sitters themselves?

There are also those who report experiencing the continuity of consciousness before birth and after death. If a young child remembers many emotionally charged details about someone he says he was in a previous life, which are verified when that person is identified, does this mean that the child lived before? It's not proof in a strict sense, even though this is certainly hard to explain in any other way. And, many people are convinced, including medical doctors and other expert investigators, that "dead" people leave their bodies, enter into an afterlife realm, and return to tell us about it. Maybe disembodied entities can communicate with us, move objects, or even materialize their hands, after they make the final one-way trip into what we call death.

For me, such convincing studies and case accounts have not had the same impact as have my personal experiences, even though these experiences are likely to be less convincing to anyone else. The after-death communications that I perceived to be from my brother, especially his voice breaking into my space from outside my thoughts, red balloons appearing in the tree outside my window, bottle caps flying off, and a dark form presenting itself to me in the moonlight, are more alive in me than anything I have read. These feel so clearly external to me, that I am compelled to allow them that reality. And why not? As Jeffrey Kane described it, "The times I have certainty is when I'm in the middle of the experience." The doubts only arise later.

My two mental mediumship readings, described in detail here, gave me the gift of a perception that the two people who came through had continuity. I felt a sense that my brother had not fully disappeared and was present in a different way. The readings filled the painful void of his premature death, upending that finality. Whether this is an objective truth or not, I will never know. But I can certainly vouch for the power of a highly evidential reading (which is a rarity) in helping to heal the pain of losing a loved one.

And, as I stated previously, the séances with Stewart Alexander have changed my life. Since I witnessed the materialization of a human hand, touched it, and felt its life and warmth, a door was opened in me. I encountered something utterly incomprehensible yet physically real. I have come to know Stewart's spirit guides quite well, through laughing with them, asking them questions, and being indescribably moved by their purity of intention and distinct personalities. I can't deny that this seemed like entry into an extraordinary space where two worlds come together, challenging my previously held concept of reality. However, I also can't explain these things and they will always generate questions in me that will likely never be answered.

No matter where the force that produces these extraordinary phenomena comes from, any intellectually honest person who studies the literature and engages directly with authentic, skilled mediums cannot deny that psi is real. Maybe the disconnect between these unexplained phenomena and the laws governing physical reality (as it is now understood) reinforces the hypothesis that, indeed, consciousness stands apart from the physical body. I'm not a scientist, but I would think that if consciousness is nonlocal and if there are nonphysical realms, these would naturally exist outside the confines of the material world and would therefore not be subject to the laws of physics. My only request of those who deny that any of this is possible is to simply look at the evidence with an open mind.

Stephen Braude began studying the literature on psychokinesis and telepathy in the 1970s, and until then he had dismissed such reports as "confused or delusional," like his "equally ignorant" mentors (and like so many contemporary skeptics). He expected that his investigation would reveal information to further support his belief in the worthlessness of the material. "But the evidence bowled me over," he reports. "The more I learned about it, the weaker the traditional skeptical counter hypotheses seemed, and the more clearly I realized to what extent skepticism may be fueled by ignorance." He acknowledges that he was uniquely situated to recognize the intellectual cowardice and dishonesty that he came to see in the severe skeptics because he had previously observed these traits in himself. "They are demons with whom I am intimately acquainted," he says. Braude writes:

> I am hardly comfortable about announcing to my academic colleagues that I believe, for example, that accordions can float in midair playing melodies, or that hands may materialize, move objects, and then dissolve or disappear. . . . But I have reached my present position only after satisfying myself that no reasonable options remain. Actually, I find that my discomfort tends to diminish as I discern more clearly how little the most derisive and condescending skeptics really know about the evidence and how their apparent confidence in their opinions is little more than posturing and dishonest bluffing.

Looking back to the early twentieth century when courageous researchers faced the same derision from their colleagues, investigator Hereward Carrington stands out in the same way Braude does today. Initially highly skeptical, Carrington has valuable advice for all of us:

> I did not go to Eusapia's seances any too ready to be convinced; and the fact that I was so convinced (this being the first case of genuine physical mediumship I had ever seen during ten years' continuous investigation) proves, it seems to me, that the severest skeptics are likely to become converted if they would but deign

to stop criticising the reports and sittings of others, and go and have sittings themselves. Only in that manner can one's mental attitude be changed, and the genuine nature of the facts be forced upon one—as they were forced upon me.

We each have a choice about how to engage with these unique human capabilities and mysterious forces, which lie hidden behind the facade of our material world. They have the power to redefine who we are, and to change our perception of life and death. Someday conventional science will come around and recognize them, but until then, we are one step ahead. We can draw our own conclusions, based on consideration of the evidence, our own experience, and our sense of inner knowing and connection, all of which inform our relationship to the question of survival. I hope this book has opened doors that will allow you to engage meaningfully in that process and to take some solace in the fact that there is abundant mystery all around us, and that death may very well not be the end.

Notes

INTRODUCTION

3   **producer for a documentary film on this topic** *The Afterlife Investigations,* 2010, NTSC, 86 minutes. Written, produced, and directed by Tim Coleman, with Daniel Drasin as associate producer. www.timcolemanmedia .com.

3   **he was able to live a normal life in the present** I recommend viewing the documentary "The Boy Who Lived Before," produced for BBC Channel 5's *Extraordinary People* series in 2006, available on YouTube.

3   **The stated purpose of the Scole experiments** I recommend: Grant and Jane Solomon, *The Scole Experiment* (Campion Books, 1999). These two journalists wrote a readable, illustrated book about the Scole work.

3   **documented the events as genuine in a lengthy, scholarly report** Montague Keen, Arthur Ellison, and David Fontana, "The Scole Report," *Proceedings of the Society for Psychical Research,* Vol 58, Part 220 (Society for Psychical Research, November 1999). For those more seriously interested in physical mediumship, I highly recommend this 450-page report. It is available on Amazon, reprinted as Keen, Ellison, Fontana, *The Scole Report* (Saturday Night Press Publications, 2011).

4   *UFOs: Generals, Pilots, and Government Officials Go on the Record* (Harmony Books/Crown Publishing Group/Random House, 2010; Three Rivers Press/Random House, paperback edition, 2011). With a foreword

by John Podesta, the book was a *New York Times* bestseller and has been published in eleven additional languages. See UFOsOnTheRecord.com.

4   **more hard data is needed** For those interested, I am on the board of UFO-DATA, a nonprofit organization that will capture new data on UFOs at a level never done before and make it available to the scientific community. See UFODATA.net.

8   **more than all the energy of the stars and galaxies combined** Michio Kaku, *Physics of the Impossible* (Doubleday, 2008), 270.

8   **"experimental evidence for it is staring us in the face"** Ibid.

8   **"the most profound mystery in all of science"** Richard Panek, "Dark Energy: The Biggest Mystery in the Universe," *Smithsonian* magazine, April 2010.

8   **"there is nothing that is harder to explain"** David J. Chalmers, "Facing Up to the Problem of Consciousness," *Journal of Consciousness Studies* 2 (3) (1995): 200–19, http://consc.net/papers/facing.html.

8   **"the most sophisticated thinkers tongue-tied and confused"** Daniel C. Dennett, *Consciousness Explained* (Back Bay Books, 1992), 22.

9   **One exception to that is Dean Radin** Radin is adjunct faculty at the Department of Psychology at Sonoma State University and the author or co-author of over 250 technical and popular articles. Among his books are *The Conscious Universe* (HarperOne, 1997), *Entangled Minds* (Simon & Schuster, 2006), and *Supernormal* (Random House, 2013).

9   **"evidence collected over a century by scores of researchers"** Dean Radin, *The Conscious Universe* (HarperOne, 1997), Chapter 1 excerpt: deanradin.com/NewWeb/TCUindex.html.

9   **"and yet retain credibility as an unbiased observer"** David Fontana, *Is There an Afterlife?: A Comprehensive Overview of the Evidence* (O Books, 2005), 470.

9   **survivalists are confused, or even disingenuous** For more information on this argument, see Michael Sudduth, "What's Wrong with Survival Literature?" on his blog *Cup of Nirvana* (September 2015). For an extensive analysis by Sudduth, see his book *A Philosophical Critique of Empirical Arguments for Postmortem Survival* (Palgrave Macmillan, 2016).

10   **allowing them to find someone through whom they can communicate** Michael Sudduth, "Is Postmortem Survival the Best Explanation of the Data of Mediumship?" from Adam Rock, *The Survival Hypothesis: Essays on Mediumship* (McFarland & Company, Inc., 2013), 47–48.

10   **"the mental states or causal powers of immaterial persons"** Ibid., 49.

10 a "strengthened" or "robust" survival hypothesis Ibid., 48.

12 **Stephen Braude, professor emeritus of the University of Maryland** Braude is also editor in chief of the *Journal of Scientific Exploration* and author of *The Limits of Influence: Psychokinesis and the Philosophy of Science* (Routledge, 1986; revised edition, University Press of America, 1997); *Immortal Remains: The Evidence for Life After Death* (Rowman & Littlefield, 2003); and *The Gold Leaf Lady and Other Parapsychological Investigations* (University of Chicago Press, 2007), among others.

12 **"No scientific theory renders any form of psi improbable"** Braude, *Immortal Remains*, 16.

13 **"can survive the death of our bodies, at least for a time," he states** Ibid., xi.

13 **"not the hypothesis of survival itself"** Sudduth, personal communication, January 17, 2016.

13 **"it stretches the hypothesis way beyond the breaking point"** Fontana, *Is There an Afterlife?*, 471.

13 **"Unusual Suspects," defined as "abnormal or rare processes"** Braude, *Immortal Remains*, 11.

14 **"if you prove one single crow to be white"** William James's 1896 "Address of the President Before the Society for Psychical Research" (reprinted in *Subtle Energies & Energy Medicine* 7, 1 (1996): 23–33.

CHAPTER 1: "AIRPLANE CRASH ON FIRE!"

18 **his emotional and spiritual transformation throughout** All excerpts and comments in this chapter from Bruce Leininger were provided in personal emails and telephone interviews in 2014 and 2015.

22 **no Corsair at the flight museum that James visited** Jim Tucker, *Return to Life: Extraordinary Cases of Children Who Remember Past Lives* (St. Martin's Press, 2013), 69.

25 **"trying to work through a traumatic event"** Ibid., 73.

25 **parachuting down after being hit** Ibid., 84.

26 **"always wanted to turn left when they took off"** Bruce and Andrea Leininger, *Soul Survivor: The Reincarnation of a World War II Fighter Pilot* (Grand Central Publishing, 2009), 109.

29 **matched those of the G.I. Joe dolls that had their names** Gwen Connor told them that her cousin Leon Conner had blond hair. Wallace Peeler, Billie's younger brother, described him as looking very much like James's G.I. Joe, with dark hair. They could not locate any of Walter Devlin's

family, but veterans who knew him said he had a lot of red hair, and they recollected that he was nicknamed "Red" or "Big Red." Leininger, *Soul Survivor,* 170, 180–86.

32   **the ABC show *Primetime* covered the case** Originally aired on April 15, 2004, anchored by Chris Cuomo. It is on YouTube along with other clips on the case.

32   **she said in the 2004 *Primetime* show** Ibid.

CHAPTER 2: THE CASE OF JAMES 3

36   **Psychiatrist Ian Stevenson, the pioneer of this work** For a list of Stevenson's books and papers, see the website for the Division of Perceptual Studies (DOPS), University of Virginia.

37   **just as Huston was for the Leiningers** All information above from Jim Tucker, personal communication, January 2016.

37   **published two books on children with past-life memories, and numerous papers in scientific journals** Jim Tucker, *Return to Life: Extraordinary Cases of Children Who Remember Past Lives* (St. Martin's Press, 2013) and Jim Tucker, *Life Before Life: A Scientific Investigation of Children's Memories of Previous Lives* (St. Martin's Griffin, 2008). See www.jimbtucker.com. Academic papers listed at the DOPS website.

38   **after jumping out of a burning building in Chicago** For more on this interesting case, watch news coverage on YouTube.

38   **that were not dated and recorded** Andrea kept a notebook where she made notes on them, and Bruce often made notes, but unfortunately these were lost after the couple completed their 2009 book *Soul Survivor,* written when James was eleven, which incorporated them.

38   **"occupation or skills of the previous person"** Tucker, personal communication, September 12, 2016.

39   **the "cockpit" he created in the closet** Tucker, *Return to Life,* 84.

39   **the scores of aircraft drawings he made,** Ibid., 73.

39   **as a missing antenna on a model airplane** Ibid., 81.

39   **Japanese Zero plane being miscalled a "Tony"** Ibid., 81–82.

39   **"actively discourage their children's talk about a previous life"** Jim Tucker, unpublished letter to the editor of *Harper's,* February 2015.

40   **"There is no evidence to indicate the latter"** Jim Tucker, "The Case of James Leininger: An American Case of the Reincarnation Type," *EXPLORE* 12, no. 3 (May–June 2016): 206.

40   "information gathering and telepathic influence over the subject" Braude, *Immortal Remains*, 217–18.

41   makes "the survivalist position seem stronger still" Ibid., 216–17.

42   "or James Huston appear to have been made either" Tucker, "The Case of James Leininger," 206.

42   "how difficult apparent past-life memories can be for children to have" Tucker, Ibid.

42   "this explanation warrants serious consideration" Ibid.

CHAPTER 3: INVESTIGATING CASES OF CHILDREN WITH PAST-LIFE MEMORIES

43   "The Uncomfortable Facts About Extrasensory Perception" Ian Stevenson, "The Uncomfortable Facts About Extrasensory Perception," *Harper's* 219 (1959): 19–25.

43   "Scientists with Half-closed Minds" *Harper's Magazine*, 1958, 217, 64–71.

44   a two-part paper summarizing a group of forty-four such cases in 1960 Ian Stevenson, "The Evidence for Survival from Claimed Memories of Former Incarnations. Part I. Review of the Data," *Journal of the American Society for Psychical Research* 54 (1960): 51–71.3. Ian Stevenson, "The Evidence for Survival from Claimed Memories of Former Incarnations. Part II. Analysis of the Data and Suggestions for Further Investigations," *Journal of the American Society for Psychical Research* 54 (1960): 95–117.

45   and all of us have now published numerous papers Antonia Mills, Erlendur Haraldsson, and H. H. Jürgen Keil, "Replication Studies of Cases Suggestive of Reincarnation by Three Independent Investigators," *Journal of the American Society for Psychical Research* 88 (1994): 207–19; Satwant Pasricha, *Claims of Reincarnation: An Empirical Study of Cases in India* (New Delhi: Harman, 1990); Jim B. Tucker, "A Scale to Measure the Strength of Children's Claims of Previous Lives: Methodology and Initial Findings," *Journal of Scientific Exploration* 14 (2000): 571–81.

45   An example is a little girl in India named Kumkum Verma Ian Stevenson, *Cases of the Reincarnation Type, Volume I: Ten Cases in India* (Charlottesville: University Press of Virginia, 1975), 206–40.

46   reported as adults that they still remembered some details of a past life Erlendur Haraldsson, "Persistence of Past-Life Memories: Study of Adults Who Claimed in Their Childhood to Remember a Past Life," *Journal of Scientific Exploration* 22 (2008): 385–93; Erlendur Haraldsson and Majd Abu-Izzedin, "Persistence of 'Past-Life' Memories in Adults Who, in Their

Childhood, Claimed Memories of a Past Life," *Journal of Nervous and Mental Disease* 200 (2012): 985–89.

48   Sukla became distraught upon hearing the news and demanded to be taken to her Ian Stevenson, *Twenty Cases Suggestive of Reincarnation* (sec. rev. ed.) (Charlottesville: University Press of Virginia, 1974), 52–67. (First published in 1966 in *Proceedings of the American Society for Psychical Research*, vol. 26.)

48   Others show phobias related to how the previous person died Ian Stevenson, "Phobias in Children Who Claim to Remember Previous Lives," *Journal of Scientific Exploration* 4 (1990): 243–54.

48   she fell into a flooded paddy field next to the road and drowned Ian Stevenson, *Cases of the Reincarnation Type, Volume II: Ten Cases in Sri Lanka* (Charlottesville: University Press of Virginia, 1977), 15–42.

48   often appear in the children's play activities as well Ian Stevenson, "Unusual Play in Young Children Who Claim to Remember Previous Lives," *Journal of Scientific Exploration* 14 (2000): 557–70.

48   his mother felt he was never able to fully catch up Stevenson, *Twenty Cases,*109–27.

49   act out a scene of trying to escape from a sinking boat Ian Stevenson, *Reincarnation and Biology: A Contribution to the Etiology of Birthmarks and Birth Defects* (Westport, CT: Praeger, 1997), 1403–10.

49   behavior that must have been unsettling to his parents Ibid.,1406.

49   that contributes to the development of human personality Ian Stevenson, "The Phenomenon of Claimed Memories of Previous Lives: Possible Interpretations and Importance," *Medical Hypotheses* 54 (4) (2000): 652–59; Ian Stevenson and Jürgen Keil, "Children of Myanmar Who Behave like Japanese Soldiers: A Possible Third Element in Personality," *Journal of Scientific Exploration* 19 (2005): 171–83.

49   Chanai Choomalaiwong, a boy in Thailand Ibid., 300–23.

50   exit wound on the body of a gunshot victim Ibid., 933–34.

50   only stubs for fingers on his right Ibid., 1186–99.

50   only a linear stump for his right ear Ibid., 1382–1403.

50   twenty-two-hundred-page collection of over two hundred such cases Stevenson, *Reincarnation and Biology.*

51   can sometimes produce very specific effects on the body Ibid., Chapter 2.

51   numerous statements about a past life in another town Stevenson, *Twenty Cases,* 131–49; H. S. S. Nissanka, *The Girl Who Was Reborn: A Case-Study Suggestive of Reincarnation* (Colombo, Sri Lanka: Godage Brothers, 2001).

52   **over fifty of the details Ryan had given were accurate** Tucker, *Return to Life*, 88–119.

52   **a group of twenty-seven children, including sixteen boys** Tucker, *Life Before Life*, 141–43.

52   **a paper on seventy-nine American cases in 1983** Ian Stevenson, "American Children Who Claim to Remember Previous Lives," *Journal of Nervous and Mental Disease* 171 (1983): 742–48.

53   **the children tended to be very intelligent and very verbal** Jim B. Tucker and F. Don Nidiffer (2014), "Psychological Evaluation of American Children Who Report Memories of Previous Lives," *Journal of Scientific Exploration* 28 (2014): 583–94.

53   **including those of James and Ryan, in my latest book,** *Return to Life* Tucker, *Return to Life*.

CHAPTER 4: "THE OLD ME"

56   **carrying a big book about Hollywood** Don Shiach, *The Movie Book: An Illustrated History of the Cinema* (Smithmark Pub, 1996).

56   **1932 movie called** *Night After Night* **starring George Raft** The Paramount Pictures movie was directed by Archie Mayo and starred George Raft, Constance Cummings, and Mae West.

CHAPTER 5: FIFTY-FIVE VERIFIED MEMORIES

69   **"was that I was so old!"** Marisa Martyn Rosenblatt, personal communication, August 30, 2016.

72   **"Cyndi and I have had over a long period of time"** Jim Tucker, personal communication, July 13, 2015.

73   **"we were looking to see if Marty Martyn's did"** Tucker, *Return to Life*, 109.

73   **It was clear that the two photos showed the same man** All information about Kate Coe's search comes from Russ Stratton's documentary piece *A Life in the Movies,* shown on The Biography Channel.

73   **there was nothing else online about Martyn** Jim Tucker, personal communication, March 20, 2015.

74   **"we could get back to some kind of normalcy"** This letter was provided to me as part of Cyndi's journal.

74   **aired in April 2011 on The Biography Channel** *A Life in the Movies* for *The Unexplained,* produced by Air Extreme, LLC, for the A&E Network,

2011. Unfortunately, the piece is not available for public viewing. I hope to be able to make that possible in the future.

76   **"I know about things Marty knows about"** From Cyndi's journal, August 7, 2010.

77   **he was elated and clearly was totally at home there** From Stratton's film *A Life in the Movies* for The Biography Channel.

78   **Marty Kolinsky's birth date clearly typed as May 19, 1903** Presumably this information was provided by the passenger and conformed with his passport. All documents referenced here are from the National Archives and available on Ancestry.com.

79   **"the idea can be judged on its merits," Jim said** From an interview for NPR, "Searching for the Science Behind Reincarnation," aired on *Weekend Edition,* Sunday, January 5, 2014.

CHAPTER 6: THE SHOE ON THE LEDGE

90   **on television, using the actual tennis shoe** This documentary clip shows the actual shoe and early interviews with me. It can be viewed on YouTube.

91   **addressing their objections and laying them to rest** My reply to the most scathing doubters can be found in "The Other Shoe Drops," *Journal of Near-Death Studies* 25, no. 4 (Summer 2007): 245–50.

91   **researching their reports, and writing about them** This led to the founding of the Seattle International Association for Near-Death Studies in 1982. More than ten thousand people—NDErs, people in need of support for other spiritual experiences, dying people, grievers, and the curious public—have since come through that door. And I wrote the book *After the Light* (William Morrow & Co., 1995), which includes Maria's story, that of the first blind person to be interviewed about an NDE, and many other veridical near-death experiences.

CHAPTER 7: JOURNEYS OUT OF BODY

92   **"say, a thirty-minute OBE to immortality"** Mark B. Woodhouse, "Out-of-Body Experiences and the Mind-Body Problem," *New Ideas in Psychology* 12, Issue 1, March 1994.

93   **"associated with a body that *has* lost that potential"** Janice Miner Holden, "Veridical Perception in Near-Death Experiences," *The Handbook of Near-Death Experiences* (Praeger Publishers, 2009), 187.

93   "imagery-rich manifestations of ESP," Stephen Braude points out Braude, *Immortal Remains*, 253.

93   "extrasomatic interpretation"—perception from outside the body—involved Michael Sudduth, "In Defense of Sam Harris on Near-Death Experiences," *Cup of Nirvana*, December 21, 2015.

94   "consciousness to function independent of the physical body" Holden, *Near-Death Experiences*, 186.

94   "it continues to function beyond irreversible death," she writes Ibid., 188.

95   "dead people to participate in their studies" Ibid., 188.

95   Vicki doesn't see anything—no light perception All quotes and much of the information in the four-paragraph section on Vicki Noratuk came from an interview conducted with her by filmmakers Daniel Drasin and Tim Coleman, on November 15, 2004, in Seattle. They provided me with an exclusive transcript.

95   she found herself up near the ceiling For more about Vicki Noratuk's case, I recommend the 2002 BBC documentary *The Day I Died*, available on YouTube. The section on Vicki is in Part 6; all of it is worth watching.

96   psychologist Sharon Cooper, in their book *Mindsight* Kenneth Ring, Sharon Cooper, and Charles Tart, *Mindsight: Near-Death and Out-of-Body Experiences in the Blind* (Institute of Transpersonal Psychology, 1999).

96   the largest clinical, multi-hospital study ever conducted Sam Parnia et al., "AWARE—AWAreness During REsuscitation—A Prospective Study," *Resuscitation* 85 (2014): 1799–1805.

97   "until the heart has been restarted" "Is There Life After Death? Study Suggests Consciousness Continues After Heartbeat Stops," *Huffington Post UK*, October 2014.

97   "how long the experience lasted for" Adam Withnall, "Life After Death? Largest-Ever Study Provides Evidence That 'Out of Body' and 'Near-Death' Experiences May Be Real," *Independent*, October 7, 2014.

97   an automated voice repeating, "Shock the patient" Parnia et al., "AWARE," 1804.

97   "in transcendent dimensions beyond the physical world" Holden, *Near-Death Experiences*, 185.

98   "experience of a transcendent or mystical domain" Bruce Greyson, "Western Scientific Approaches to Near-Death Experiences," *Humanities* 4 (2015): 788.

98   **"distractions and limitations of the physical brain"** Bruce Greyson, "Seeing Dead People Not Known to Have Died: 'Peak in Darien' Experiences," *Anthropology and Humanism* (2010) 35, Issue 2, 160.

98   **as the man he had seen during his NDE** Greyson, "Western Scientific Approaches," 783.

98   **brother who died before she was born** Ibid.

98   **"hallucinations based on expectation," Greyson writes** Ibid.

99   **"perceived although not lived in the reality"** Marie Thonnard, Vanessa Charland-Verville, Serge Brédart, Hedwige Dehon Didier Ledoux, and Steven Laureys, "Characteristics of Near-Death Experiences Memories as Compared to Real and Imagined Events Memories," *PLoS ONE* 8 (3) (March 2013): 1.

99   **"memories of both real and imagined events"** Arianna Palmieri, Vincenzo Calvo, Johann R. Kleinbub, Federica Meconi, Matteo Marangoni, Paolo Barilaro, Alice Broggio, Marco Sambin, and Paola Sessa, " 'Reality' of Near-Death-Experience Memories: Evidence from a Psychodynamic and Electrophysiological Integrated Study," *Human Neuroscience* 8:429 (2014):1.

99   **"events experienced in a peculiar state of consciousness"** Ibid.

CHAPTER 8: "ACTUAL-DEATH" EXPERIENCES

100   **what happened with Pam in a 2007 interview** This interview was conducted by filmmakers Drasin and Coleman and has never been published before. I chose to use this one rather than seek an interview now, since it was made closer to the time of Pam's surgery.

101   **former BBC radio broadcaster Tim Coleman and researcher Daniel Drasin** See the first note (on page 363 of this book) for information on Coleman's film. Drasin is the producer and director of *Calling Earth* with Coleman as associate producer, a 95-minute feature documentary about international research into instrumental trans-communication (ITC)—voices and images apparently from the "other side" that manifest through modern electronic devices such as audio recorders, telephones, video systems, and digital cameras. A short trailer is available at tinyurl.com/callearth-trailer. The full film can be viewed free of charge at tinyurl.com/callearth.

109   **Some skeptics have argued that Pam woke up during the process** Gerry Woerlee, "An Anesthesiologist Examines the Pam Reynolds Story. Part Two: The Experience," *SKEPTIC* 18 (2) (Summer 2005); published by CSICOP and the *Skeptical Inquirer*—with an agenda. Woerlee is a committed skeptic. For further information, see Alex Tsakiris, "Near-Death

Experience Skeptics Running Out of Excuses," April 16, 2010—an interview with Woerlee.

109   **11 to 33 clicks per second at 90 to 100 decibels** Holden, *Near-Death Experiences,* 198. Holden provides an excellent analysis of the Pam Reynolds case, addressing skeptical arguments, on pp. 191–99.

109   **"to hear through normal auditory pathways"** Kate Broome, producer and director, BBC documentary *The Day I Died,* 2002. Available on YouTube.

110   **"about this shadowy boundary between the two states?"** Fontana, *Is There an Afterlife?,* 404.

110   **"absolutely implacable and final,"** Parnia wrote in 2013 Sam Parnia, "Erasing Death," *Huffington Post,* April 28, 2013.

111   **"the woman had, in fact, died," Parnia reports** Ibid.

111   **after having been dead for 101 minutes** Robin Marantz Henig, "Crossing Over," *National Geographic,* April 2016, pp. 41 and 48.

111   **"even many hours after it has taken place"** Parnia, "Erasing Death."

111   **"who have objectively and medically died"** Ibid.

111   **calling it an "actual-death experience"** Terry Gross for *Fresh Air,* "NPR Interview with Dr. Sam Parnia," February 20, 2013 (on YouTube).

112   **"in which death is fully reversible," he says** Parnia, "Erasing Death."

112   **"to experience when we go through death"** "NPR Interview with Dr. Sam Parnia."

112   **"that apparatus is completely nonfunctional"** Ibid.

112   **"but somehow their memories get wiped"** Ibid. (All information in this paragraph is sourced to that NPR interview.)

CHAPTER 9: THE NDE AND NONLOCAL CONSCIOUSNESS

114   **bestseller *Endless Consciousness: A Scientific Approach to the Near-Death Experience*** This book has been published in English as *Consciousness Beyond Life: The Science of the Near-Death Experience* (HarperOne, 2010).

116   **by psychiatrist George Ritchie, *Return from Tomorrow*** George G. Ritchie with Elizabeth Sherrill. *Return from Tomorrow: A Psychiatrist Describes His Own Revealing Experience on the Other Side of Death* (Chosen Books, 1978).

116   **Moody's famous bestseller *Life after Life* in 1971** Raymond Moody, *Life After Life* (Mockingbird, 1971).

119   **study, published in December 2001 in** *The Lancet* Pim van Lommel, Ruud van Wees, Vincent Meyers, and Ingrid Elfferich, "Near-Death Experience in Survivors of Cardiac Arrest: A Prospective Study in the Netherlands," *Lancet* 358 (2001): 2039–45.

120   **told the Belgian press** Betz's comments appeared in the Belgian newsmagazine *De Tijd* on December 29, 2001.

120   **three additional prospective studies with an identical design** They are: S. Parnia, D. G. Waller, R. Yeates, and P. Fenwick, "A Qualitative and Quantitative Study of the Incidence, Features and Etiology of Near Death Experiences in Cardiac Arrest Survivors," *Resuscitation* 48 no. 2 (2001):149–56; Penny Sartori, Paul Badham, and Peter Fenwick, "A Prospectively Studied Near-Death Experience with Corroborated Out-of-Body Perception and Unexplained Healing," *Journal of Near-Death Studies* 25, no. 2 (2006): 69–84; and Bruce Greyson, "Incidence and Correlates of Near-Death Experiences in a Cardiac Care Unit," *General Hospital Psychiatry* 25 (2003): 269–76.

120   **"that consciousness is localized exclusively in the brain"** Greyson, "Cardiac Care Unit."

121   **8 percent contained minor errors, and 2 percent were false** Holden, *Near-Death Experiences.*

122   **"Four weeks later he left hospital as a healthy man"** van Lommel, *Consciousness Beyond Life.*

124   **In 2005, the journal** *Science* **published 125 questions** This was a 125th-anniversary special issue on July 1, 2005: vol. 309, issue 5735.

125   **consciousness is not physically rooted** This paragraph was adapted from the following: *World Futures: The Journal of New Paradigm Research* 62, Issue 1–2 (2006).

126   **all past, present, and future is enclosed** Ibid.

CHAPTER 10: INTERMISSION MEMORIES: LIFE BETWEEN LIVES

128   **intermission memories tend to arise in the stronger reincarnation cases** Poonam Sharma and Jim B. Tucker, "Cases of the Reincarnation Type with Memories from the Intermission Between Lives," *Journal of Near-Death Studies* 23(2) (Winter 2004): 116

128   **"a stronger memory for items preceding their current lives"** Ibid., 116.

128   **referring to three main phases** Ibid., 107.

129   **Ratana Wongsombat, a girl born in Bangkok in 1964** Tucker, *Life Before Life*, 102, and Ian Stevenson, *Cases of the Reincarnation Type, Volume IV: Twelve Cases in Thailand and Burma* (Charlottesville: University of Virginia Press, 1983), 12–48.

129   **or not realizing they were dead** Sharma and Tucker, "Intermission Between Lives," 107.

129   **a case study on Patrick Christenson** Satwant K. Pasricha, Jürgen Keil, Jim B. Tucker, and Ian Stevenson, "Some Bodily Malformations Attributed to Previous Lives," *Journal of Scientific Exploration* 19, no. 3 (2005): 359–83. Tucker covers this case in the first chapter of *Return to Life*.

129   **as shown by medical records** Pasricha et al.,"Bodily Malformations," 367.

130   **"ever heard about Billy or his nickname before"** Tucker, *Return to Life*, 12.

131   **before death to the same body (NDEs)** Sharma and Tucker, "Intermission Between Lives," 112.

131   **brilliant light that is so common to them** Ibid.

131   **"that encompasses NDEs," Tucker and Sharma conclude** Ibid., 116.

131   **"reports from healthy, young children"** Ibid., 117.

CHAPTER 11: END-OF-LIFE EXPERIENCES

135   **personnel or relatives present shared the dying patient's vision** William Barrett, *Deathbed Visions* (Methuen & Co, 1987; originally published in 1926).

135   **We drew up a questionnaire asking about these phenomena** Sue Brayne, Hilary Lovelace, and Peter Fenwick, "An Understanding of the Occurrence of Deathbed Phenomena and Its Effect on Palliative Care Clinicians," *American Journal of Hospice and Palliative Medicine* 23, no. 1 (January/February 2006): 17–24.

135   **we also carried out the study in three Dutch hospices** Peter Fenwick, Hilary Lovelace, and Sue Brayne, "Comfort for the Dying: Five Year Retrospective and One Year Prospective Studies of End of Life Experiences," *Archives of Gerontology and Geriatrics* 2009; DOI:10.1016/j.archger .2009.10.004.

136   **they occur in over 60 percent of those people who die while conscious** A. Mazzarino-Willett, "Deathbed Phenomena: Its Role in Peaceful Death and Terminal Restlessness," *American Journal of Hospice and Palliative Care* 27 (2010): 127 (originally published online October 8, 2009).

136   **often reported by, nurses and relatives who care for the dying** Dewi Rees, "The Hallucinations of Widowhood," *British Medical Journal* 4 (1971): 37–41.

137   **witness the positive effect on their relative** Peter Fenwick, Hilary Lovelace, and Sue Brayne, "End of Life Experiences and Implications for Palliative Care," *International Journal of Environmental Studies* 64, Issue 3 (2007): 315–23; C. W. Kerr, J. P. Donnelly, S. T. Wright, S. M. Kuszczak, A. Banas, P. C. Grant, and D. L. Luczkiewicz, "End-of-Life Dreams and Visions: A Longitudinal Study of Hospice Patients' Experiences," *Journal of Palliative Medicine* 17 (3) (2014):296–303. DOI: 10.1089/jpm.2013.0371. Epub January 11, 2014.

138   **out-of-brain mechanism rather than a within-brain generation** Sue Brayne, Hilary Lovelace, and Peter Fenwick, "End-of-Life Experiences and the Dying Process in a Gloucestershire Nursing Home as Reported by Nurses and Care Assistants," *American Journal of Hospice and Palliative Care* 25 (3) (June–July 2008): 195–206.

138   **higher prevalence—about 80 percent—than we found in our own study** Cheryl L. Nosek, Christopher W. Kerr, Julie Woodworth, Scott T. Wright, Pei C. Grant, Sarah M. Kuszczak, Anne Banas, Debra L. Luczkiewicz, and Rachel M. Depner, "End-of-Life Dreams and Visions: A Qualitative Perspective from Hospice Patients," *American Journal of Hospice and Palliative Care* 32 (3) (2014): 269–74.

138   **they talked to the caregivers over 60 percent reported visions** P. Grant, S. Wright, R. Depner, and D. Luczkiewicz, "The Significance of End-of-Life Dreams and Visions," *Nursing Times* 110(28) (July 9–15, 2014): 22–24.

138   **possibly 60 percent and more, experienced this** M. Renz, Schuett M. Mao, A. Omlin, D. Bueche, T. Cerny, and F. Strasser, "Spiritual Experiences of Transcendence in Patients with Advanced Cancer," *American Journal of Hospice and Palliative Care* 32(2) (March 2015): 178–88; Epub November 20, 2013.

139   **certainly color the specific aspects of some of them** Bernard Lo, Delaney Ruston, Laura W. Kates, Robert M. Arnold, Cynthia B. Cohen, Kathy Faber-Langendoen, Steven Z. Pantilat, Christina M. Puchalski, Timothy R. Quill, Michael W. Rabow, Simeon Schreiber, Daniel P. Sulmasy, and James A. Tulsky, "Discussing Religious and Spiritual Issues at the End-of-Life," *JAMA* 287, no. 6 (2002): 749–54.

143   **Thus expectation cannot be used as an explanation** Michael Nahm, "Terminal Lucidity in People with Mental Illness and Other Mental Disability: An Overview and Implications for Possible Explanatory Models," *Journal of Near-Death Studies* 28(2) (2009): 87–106.

145 **The best we can say is that they are transcendental experiences** Franklin Santana Santos and Peter Fenwick, "Death, End of Life Experiences, and Their Theoretical and Clinical Implications for the Mind-Brain Relationship," in Alexander Moreira-Almeida and Franklin Santana Santos, eds., *Exploring Frontiers of the Mind Brain Relationship: Mindfulness in Behavioral Health* (Springer Science and Business Media 2012), DOI 10.1007/978-I-4614-0647-1-9.

146 **"brains existing in a material world"** John C. Eccles, *Evolution of the Brain: Creation of the Self* (Routledge, 1991), 241.

146 **the fifth dimension that these conscious experiences are stored** B. Carr, "A Proposed New Paradigm of Matter, Mind and Spirit," *Network Review: Journal of the Scientific and Medical Network*, nos. 102 and 103 (2012).

146 **Lisa Randall, theoretical physicist from Harvard University, and Raman Sundrum** Randall and Sundrum, "Four Dimensional Brain in a Five Dimensional Bulk," *Physical Review Letters* 83 (1999): 4690.

147 **David Lawton, who has made studies of the NDE** David Lawton, https://www.scimednet.org/event-speaker/david-lawton.

147 **The theory implies that death of consciousness simply does not exist** Robert Lanza, *Biocentrism: How Life and Consciousness Are the Keys to Understanding the True Nature of the Universe* (BenBella Books, 2010).

147 **L. Stafford Betty has described this as "the merging of two worlds"** L. Stafford Betty, "Are They Hallucinations or Are They Real? The Spirituality of Deathbed and Near-Death Visions," *Omega* 53 (1–2) (2006): 37–49.

148 **sister of Steve Jobs reported that just before he died** Mona Simpson, "A Sister's Eulogy for Steve Jobs," *New York Times*, October 30, 2011 (op-ed).

CHAPTER 12: MY FIRST "PERSONAL EXPERIMENT"

151 **"by future advances in cognitive neuroscience"** Michael Sudduth, "Awakening Survivalists from Dogmatic Slumber," *Cup of Nirvana* (blog), September 28, 2015.

152 **"that is always in us and around us"** van Lommel, Chapter 9 of this book, 123–24.

154 **Forever Family Foundation (FFF)** For more information see www.foreverfamilyfoundation.org.

154 **the Windbridge Institute in Tucson, Arizona** For more information see Windbridge.org.

157 **"like a nickname; there's another name too"** All quotes from Laura's and Sandra's readings throughout this chapter are from the audiotapes of the sessions.

CHAPTER 13: AN ALMOST PERFECT READING

168 **"and it was not for anyone else to hear"** This impromptu reading was recorded; these are exact quotes.

168 **"by the appearance of evidence suggesting survival?"** Stephen E. Braude, "The Possibility of Mediumship: Philosophical Considerations," from Rock, *The Survival Hypothesis*, 30.

169 **"And that percentage is generous"** Robert Ginsberg, personal communication, August 6, 2015.

CHAPTER 14: RESEARCH INTO MENTAL MEDIUMSHIP

171 **they are in good mental health, socially adjusted, and productive** Alexander Moreira-Almeida and his team examined spiritist mediums in Brazil; Elizabeth Roxburgh and Chris Roe have performed studies with spiritualist mediums in the UK.

180 **"during ordinary thinking or imagination"** Arnaud Delorme, Julie Beischel, Leena Michel, Mark Boccuzzi, Dean Radin, and Paul J. Mills, "Electrocortical Activity Associated with Subjective Communication with the Deceased," *Frontiers in Psychology* (2013), 834: 8.

CHAPTER 15: HOW DO THEY DO IT?

181 **She spoke to me from her home outside Dublin** All quotes from Sandra to follow are from this interview and follow-up emails in 2015.

184 **the 2015 bestselling book *The Light Between Us*** Laura Lynne Jackson, *The Light Between Us: Stories from Heaven. Lessons for the Living* (Spiegel & Grau, 2016).

184 **"like when you get a thought in your head"** Ibid., 65.

184 **"I was hearing and seeing tumble out"** Ibid.

185 **"like water through an open tap"** Ibid., 66.

185 **"also responsible for *interpreting* it"** Ibid., 67.

185 **to determine what certain symbols meant** Ibid., 85.

186   **"connecting with dead people much more efficient"** Ibid., 85–86.

186   **"and right-hand mediumship information"** Laura Jackson, personal email communication, July 17, 2015.

186   **Jeff Tarrant has a PhD in Counseling Psychology** For more on Jeff Tarrant see drjefftarrant.com. Quotes from the website are at this address.

187   **"something interesting is definitely going on!" Tarrant writes** Jeff Tarrant, "The Mind of the Medium: The Art and Science of Psychic Mediumship" (article at his blog), November 8, 2014.

187   **"confirmation of what Laura reports from her own experience"** Jeff Tarrant, from a video of Tarrant describing his study of Laura's brain on Laura's website. Go to lauralynnejackson.com/dr-tarrant/.

CHAPTER 16: FINDING GEORGE

189   **"close to me who I did not know," he said** All information and quotes for this chapter came from personal communications (mainly emails) with Mark Lewis between August and December 2015, and from a written report he provided about his readings with Sandy Ingham. All the information from the readings was confirmed by Sandy.

CHAPTER 17: TRANCE MEDIUMSHIP AND DROP-IN COMMUNICATORS

199   **corresponding interest in collecting detailed records of this kind of mediumship** Among prominent trance mediums who have been subjected to extensive and careful study are: Mrs. L. E. Piper, Mrs. "Smead" (Mrs. W. L. Cleaveland), Mrs. "Chenoweth" (Mrs. M. M. Soule), Mrs. R. Thompson, Mrs. E. J. Garrett, and Mrs. G. O. Leonard.

200   **writings have been subjected to a serious and extensive psychological analysis** The most comprehensive general account of her mediumship is that contained in Holt, H. *On the Cosmic Relations* (2 vols. London: Williams and Norgate, 1915); see also Sage, M. *Mrs. Piper and the Society for Psychical Research* (London: Brimley Johnson, 1903) and Piper, A. L. *The Life and Work of Mrs Piper* (London: Kegan Paul, 1929).

200   **"in possession of a power as yet unexplained"** Myers, F. W. H., Lodge, O., Leaf, W., and James, W. "A Record of Observations of Certain Phenomena of Trance," *Proceedings of the Society for Psychical Research*, 1889–90, 6, 653.

201   **assumed charge of the investigation of Mrs. Piper** Hodgson, R. "A Record of Observations of Certain Phenomena of Trance," *Proceedings of the Society for Psychical Research*, 1892, 8, 1–167.

201   **and comprehensive records were kept** Myers, Lodge, Leaf, and James, *A Record of Observations.*

201   **powerfully summarized in 1889 by Frank Podmore** Podmore, F. "Discussion of the Trance Phenomena of Mrs Piper," *Proceedings of the Society for Psychical Research,* 1898–9, 14, 50–70.

202   **surviving spirits of formerly incarnate human beings** Hodgson, R. "A Further Record of Observations of Certain Phenomena of Trance," *Proceedings of the Society for Psychical Research,* 1897–8, 13, 284–582.

202   **in an interesting paper by William James** James, W. "Report on Mrs Piper's Hodgson Control," *Proceedings of the Society for Psychical Research,* 1910, 23, 2–121.

202   **G. Stanley Hall and Amy Tanner** Tanner, A. E. *Studies in Spiritism* (New York: Appleton, 1910).

203   **The son replied, according to Lodge** Myers, Lodge, Leaf, and James, *A Record of Observations,* 461.

203   **the Reverend and Mrs. S. W. Sutton of Athol Center, Massachusetts** Hodgson, *A Further Record of Observations,* 485–86.

205   **when given the little horse, said** Ibid., 387.

206   **records of various other mediums too** Gauld, A. "Discarnate Survival," in Wolman, B. B., ed., *Handbook of Parapsychology* (New York: Van Nostrand Reinhold, 1977), 587.

206   **Sir Oliver Lodge's summary of it** Myers, Lodge, Leaf, and James, *A Record of Observations,* 458-59.

208   **"or regarded as a rational explanation"** Glenconner, P. *The Earthen Vessel* (London: John Lane, 1921), xvi.

208   **Many successful book tests were carried out and studied** Sidgwick, E. M. "An Examination of Book-tests Obtained in Sittings with Mrs Leonard," *Proceedings of the Society for Psychical Research,* 1921, 31, 241–400; and Thomas, C. D. *Some New Evidence for Human Survival,* London: Collins, 1922. In the above paper by Sidgwick, she analyzed the results of 532 such tests. She classified 92 (17 percent) as successful, 100 (19 percent) as approximately successful, 96 as dubious, 40 as nearly complete failures, and 204 as complete failures. In a control experiment (Salter, H. de G. "On the Element of Chance in Book Tests," *Proceedings of the Society for Psychical Research,* 1923, 33, 606–20; cf. Besterman, T. "Further Inquiries into the Element of Chance in Booktests," *Proceedings of the Society for Psychical Research,* 1931–2, 40, 59–98, 1800 "sham" book tests were subjected to a similar analysis. There were 34 successes (under 2 percent) and 51 partial successes (under 3 percent).

208   **The sitting was held on December 17, 1917** Ibid., 60.

209   In another case, an anonymous sitter (Mrs. Talbot) Sidgewick, *An Examination of Book-tests,* 253–60.

211   Walker and the Reverend C. Drayton Thomas acted as proxies Thomas, C. D. "A Consideration of a Series of Proxy Sittings," *Proceedings of the Society of Psychical Research,* 1932–3, 41,139–85; Thomas, C. D. "A Proxy Case Extending over Eleven Sittings with Mrs Osborne Leonard," *Proceedings of the Society for Psychical Research,* 1935, 43, 439–519; Thomas, C. D. "A Proxy Experiment of Significant Success," *Proceedings of the Society for Psychical Research,* 1938–9, 45, 257–306; Walker, N. *The Bridge,* London: Cassell, 1927; Walker, N. *Through a Stranger's Hands,* London: Hutchinson, 1935; cf. Thomas, J. F. *Beyond Normal Cognition,* Boston: Boston Society for Psychic Research, 1937.

211   Drayton Thomas's remarkable "Bobbie Newlove" case Thomas, C. D. "A Proxy Case Extending over Eleven Sittings with Mrs Osborne Leonard," *Proceedings of the Society for Psychical Research,* 1935, 43, 439–519.

212   following passages refer to more personal matters Thomas, C. D. "A Proxy Experiment of Significant Success," *Proceedings of the Society for Psychical Research,* 1938–9, 45, 265–69.

215   that labeled by Dr. Ian Stevenson as "drop-in" communicators Stevenson, I. "A Communicator Unknown to Medium and Sitters," *Journal of the American Society for Psychical Research,* 1970, 64, 53–65.

216   As Stevenson remarks, "Some 'drop-in' communicators Ibid., 63.

217   fairly scarce in the "reputable" literature of psychical research For examples see Gibbes, E. B. "Have We Indisputable Evidence of Survival?" *Journal of the American Society for Psychical Research,* 1937, 31, 65–79; Hill, J. A. *Experiences with Mediums,* London: Rider, 1934, 97–102; Myers, F. W. H. *Human Personality and Its Survival of Bodily Death,* London: Longmans, Green and Co., 1903, Vol. 2, 471–77; Stevenson, Ibid.; Stevenson, I., "A Communicator of the 'Drop-in' Type in France: the Case of Robert Marie," *Journal of the American Society for Psychical Research,* 1973, 67, 47–76; Tyrrell, G. N. M., "A Communicator Introduced in Automatic Script," *Journal of the Society for Psychical Research,* 1939, 31, 91–95; Zorab, G., "A Case for Survival," *Journal of the Society for Psychical Research,* 1940, 31, 142–52.

217   and the investigators were Erlendur Haraldsson and Ian Stevenson Haraldsson, E., and Stevenson, I. "A Communicator of the 'Drop in' Type in Iceland: the Case of Runolfur Runolfsson," *Journal of the American Society for Psychical Research,* 1975, 69, 33–59.

217   he made the following statement Ibid., 39.

219   sum up the possibilities as follows Ibid., 57.

CHAPTER 18: SEEKING THE WHITE CROW

222 "seems to strengthen the case for survival" Braude, *Immortal Remains,* 51.

223 "for believing in personal postmortem survival" Ibid., 306.

CHAPTER 19: AFTER-DEATH COMMUNICATIONS

225 when Martin Caidin died on March 24, 1997 This story comes from: Loyd Auerbach, *A Paranormal Casebook: Ghost Hunting in the New Millennium* (Atriad Press LLC, 2005), 19–24.

226 Jane Katra holds a PhD in public health Jane is the coauthor with Russell Targ of *Miracles of Mind: Exploring Nonlocal Mind and Spiritual Healing* (New World Library, 1999) and *The Heart of the Mind: Using Our Mind to Transform Our Consciousness* (White Crow Books, 2011).

227 Elisabeth seemingly sent so many messages and signs There were many other ADCs from Elisabeth Targ to Jane, and to others. To learn more, go to janekatra.org.

227 "when we put them together, they completed an idea" Jane Katra, personal communication, January 12, 2016.

228 "I no longer had any doubt" Katra, Ibid.

228 Thirty-one percent answered yes Erlendur Haraldsson, *The Departed Among the Living: An Investigative Study of Afterlife Encounters* (White Crow Books, 2012), 1.

228 in Western Europe found that 25 percent reported Erlendur Haraldsson and Joop Houtkooper, "Psychic Experiences in the Multinational Human Values Study: Who Reports Them?" *Journal of the American Society for Psychical Research* 85 (April 1991): 145.

228 in the United States the figure was also 31 percent Haraldsson, *Departed Among the Living,* 1.

228 over 450 people who had had ADCs Ibid., 2.

229 "at least in some of the accounts" Ibid., 233.

229 three-quarters before the end of the fourth year Ibid., 53.

229 encounters with someone they had not known had died Erlendur Haraldsson, "Alleged Encounters with the Dead: The Importance of Violent Death in 337 New Cases," *Journal of Parapsychology* 73 (2009): 107.

229 sudden, unexpected, and violent causes, mostly accidents Haraldsson, *Departed Among the Living,* 62.

229 in the general population (only 7.8 percent from 1941 to 1970) Ibid., 63.

229 **more likely to die violently than women** Ibid., 61.

229 **which includes accidents, murders, and suicides** Tucker, *Return to Life*, 136.

230 **72 percent of the unnatural deaths in the general population** Ibid., 137.

230 **a violent death, when compared with the general population** Haraldsson, "Alleged Encounters," 113.

230 **"to support the survival hypothesis"** Ibid., 114.

237 **"immaterial realm that is always in us and around us"** van Lommel, Chapter 9 of this book, 123–24.

240 **on the philosophy of knowledge and educational policy** Kane authored *Beyond Empiricism: Michael Polanyi Reconsidered* (Peter Lang Publishing, 1984) and edited and contributed to *Education, Information, and Transformation: Essays on Learning and Thinking* (Prentice Hall, 1998).

240 **In 2005 Jeff wrote *Life as a Novice*** Jeffrey Kane, *Life as a Novice* (Confrontation Press, 2006).

240 **"you watched come into the world is no longer in it"** I conducted a phone interview with Jeff Kane on October 30, 2015, from which most of this information and his quotes were drawn. Additional material was acquired through follow-up emails in early November 2015.

243 **he received a phrase from Gabriel: "I am red."** Watch a short video of Jeff describing the "I am red" story by searching "Jeff Kane stories from the other side" on YouTube.

CHAPTER 20: INTERACTIVE APPARITIONS

248 **among other works** Auerbach, *ESP, Hauntings and Poltergeists: A Parapsychologist's Handbook* (Warner Books, 1987); *A Paranormal Casebook: Ghost Hunting in the New Millennium* (Atriad Press, 2005). Other books include *Hauntings and Poltergeists: A Ghost Hunter's Guide* (Ronin Publishing, 2004); *Ghost Hunting: How to Investigate the Paranormal* (Ronin Publishing, 2003); *Mind Over Matter* (Kensington, 1996).

248 **and *Human Personality and Its Survival of Bodily Death* by Myers** One can find the above books and other key books in the field, as well as reports on these experiences and investigated cases and commentary from the early decades of the SPR and ASPR, fairly easily (and for free). Those books, as well as volumes of the journals and proceedings, are out of copyright and available by searching the Internet Archive (archive.org) or Google Books.

249 **"I did not know that my grandmother was ill"** From William Barrett's *On the Threshold of the Unseen* (Kegan Paul, 1917), 147–48. Retrieved from http://www.survivalafterdeath.info/articles/barrett/apparitions.htm and www.archive.org.

CHAPTER 21: HUMAN-GENERATED PHENOMENA

270 **"upon the organism of some particular individual"** Alan Gauld and A. D. Cornell, *Poltergeists* (Routledge & Kegan Paul, 1979), 17.

270 **"telekinetic temper tantrum," as Loyd Auerbach describes** Auerbach, *Paranormal Casebook*, 6.

270 **"seems to organize and direct the various happenings"** Gauld and Cornell, *Poltergeists*, 339.

270 **1972 paper titled "Are Poltergeists Living or Are They Dead?"** Ian Stevenson, "Are Poltergeists Living or Are They Dead?" *Journal of the American Society for Psychical Research* 60 (1972): 233–52.

271 **"produced solely by the unconscious mind of the living agent"** Ibid., 247.

271 **Gauld and Cornell's "discarnate agency hypothesis"** Gauld and Cornell, *Poltergeists*, 353 (for all information to follow in this paragraph).

272 **A well-known 1966 paper by K. J. Batcheldor** K. J. Batcheldor, "Report on a Case of Table Levitation and Associated Phenomena," *Journal of the American Society for Psychical Research* 43, no. 729 (September 1966): 339–56.

272 **"When it happened it came as quite a shock"** Ibid., 340.

272 **ends of the legs, touched by the sitters, were at or above head level** Alan Gauld, "Experiences in Physical Circles," *The Psi Researcher*, 14, Autumn 1994, 5.

272 **"levitation and telekinetic phenomena" in a journal paper** C. Brookes-Smith and D. W. Hunt, "Some Experiments in Psychokinesis," *Journal of the American Society for Psychical Research* 45, no. 744 (June 1970): 266.

272 **"made no contact with our legs or knees," he says** Braude, *Immortal Remains*, x.

272 **the group sat together beginning in 1972 and engaged their "Philip" personality** The sessions went on for many years, and table levitations were videotaped; search "the Philip experiment" on YouTube for numerous video reports. Other paranormal phenomena occurred as well, and the findings were published in the book *Conjuring Up Philip* by Iris Owen and Margaret Sparrow (Harper & Row, 1976).

273 **"by Philip the poltergeist can be domesticated"** J. R. Colombo, *Conjuring Up the Owens* (Colombo & Co. 1999), 39.

273 **and published the results in a leading journal** Stephen E. Braude, "Investigations of the Felix Experimental Group: 2010–2013," *Journal of Scientific Exploration* 28, no. 2 (2014): 285–343.

273 **Robert Narholz, a documentary filmmaker** Narholz is an Austrian American filmmaker, currently completing two feature documentaries—*Finding PK* (working title) and *The One Who Comes After*. He is investigating physical and mental mediumship, as well as psychic phenomena in different cultures, to gain an understanding about the nature of consciousness and its place in physical as well as spiritual reality. www.robertnarholz.com.

273 **"Levitated tables seem to float"** Stephen E. Braude, "Follow-up Investigation of the Felix Circle," *Journal of Scientific Exploration* 30, no. 1 (2016): 34–35.

275 **"applied uniformly to the whole table, from beneath"** Robert Narholz, personal communication, January 21, 2016.

275 **a large, flat circular drum leaning against the legs of a chair** The diameter of the drum was eighteen inches.

276 **This is how it seemed to me, and this certainly was Steve's perception** I encourage anyone who wants more details on these sessions with Kai to read Braude, "Follow-up Investigation of the Felix Circle."

277 **"as PK share any underlying nomological unity"** Steve Braude, email communication written exclusively for this book. January 21, 2016.

277 **In a 2010 paper, scientist Barrie G. Colvin reported results** Barrie G. Colvin, "The Acoustic Properties of Unexplained Rapping Sounds," *Journal of the Society for Psychical Research* 73.2, no. 899 (2010): 65–93.

277 **The famous Enfield case of 1977 in North London** For more information on one of the most well-witnessed and -documented poltergeist cases of all time, see: Guy Lyon Playfair, *This House Is Haunted: The Amazing Inside Story of the Enfield Poltergeist* (White Crow Books, 2011). Playfair was one of two investigators who was on the case for its duration. Interesting footage can be found on YouTube.

278 **"reasons and physics of this mechanism are unknown"** Colvin, "Acoustic Properties," 21.

CHAPTER 22: FROM OBJECT MOVEMENTS TO MATERIALIZED HANDS

281   **"the interaction between different dimensions," according to Fontana** Stewart Alexander, *An Extraordinary Journey: The Memoirs of a Physical Medium* (Saturday Night Press Publications, 2010), 14.

282   **the strictest controls were published in the 1920s and '30s** There are too many to list here, but some of them will be referenced as this section progresses. Many more are available online.

282   **elegant, and very honest 1929 essay** Thomas Mann, "An Experience in the Occult" from *Three Essays,* translated from the German by H. T. Lowe-Porter (Alfred A. Knopf, 1929), 219–61.

282   **"deny the evidence of his sound senses"** Ibid., 227.

282   **Baron Albert von Schrenck-Notzing, a physician** He wrote the well known classic *Phenomena of Materialisation: a Contribution to the Investigation of Mediumistic Teleplastics* (London: K. Paul, Trench, Trubner; New York: E. P. Dutton, 1923). This book features his study of the medium Eva Carrière (known as Eva C.) and is available on Internet Archive.

282   **by the name of Willi Schneider** Willi's younger brother Rudi Schneider (1908–1957) became a well-known physical medium who was the subject of extensive scientific study. For more information see Anita Gregory, *The Strange Case of Rudi Schneider* (Scarecrow Press, 1985).

283   **"top of the table seemed really quite well lighted"** Mann, "Experience in the Occult," 236.

284   **"hung by one corner and then fell to the floor"** Ibid., 246.

284   **"It gave me a queasy feeling"** Ibid., 247.

284   **"not of horror, but of disgust"** Ibid., 248.

284   **"little monster from behind the world"** Ibid., 250.

285   **"the sound breaks off and a pause ensues"** Ibid., 252.

286   **"deception was definitely impossible"** Ibid., 254.

286   **"see the impossible come to pass"** Ibid., 261.

287   **over thirty-five years attending the séances of physical mediums** Hereward Carrington, *Eusapia Palladino and Her Phenomena* (B. W. Dodge & Company, 1909), 153.

287   **had rarely if ever met with anything that appeared genuine** Braude, *Limits of Influence,* 112.

287   **and a good sense of humor, his skepticism was extreme** Ibid.

287 Carrington, Baggally, and Feilding, nicknamed the "Fraud Squad" Ibid., 111.

288 **"Report on a Series of Sittings with Eusapia Palladino" documented, explained** Everard Feilding, W. W. Baggally, and Hereward Carrington, "Report on a Series of Sittings with Eusapia Palladino," *Proceedings of the Society for Psychical Research* 23 (November 1909): 306–569.

288 **"for fraud in the production of any of them"** Ibid., 374.

288 **a range of object movements, sounds, and the plucking of a guitar string** Ibid., 358.

288 **"at our places at the table, small print"** Ibid., 359.

289 **"even from the further side of the table"** Ibid., 437.

289 **"being held separately and distinctly by B. and F."** Ibid., 420.

289 **"a material and responsive agent"** Ibid., 438.

289 **"and produce most of the phenomena"** Carrington, *Eusapia Palladino*, 24.

289 **"and expressing wishes in direct opposition to her own"** Ibid., 273.

290 **"it almost pulled me off my chair. B., Dec. 5 / 0 8"** Feilding et al, "Report on a Series of Sittings," 451.

291 **"by no possible means could they have been Eusapia's"** Ibid, 456.

291 **"separately and adequately controlled at the time"** Ibid., 464.

291 **"larger than Eusapia's, which I subsequently examined"** Ibid., 482–83.

291 **"the effects of tangible matter and assume the form of a hand"** Baggally has a footnote here that reads "The conditions under which I felt grasps and touches on other occasions at these seances than those referred to above offered me also strong evidence that the touches and grasps were independent of the physical organism of Eusapia." Ibid., 565.

292 **the survival hypothesis ("something apparently intelligent and external to her")** As he describes it, the force "must either reside in the medium herself and be of the nature of an extension of human faculty beyond what is generally recognized; or must be a force having its origin in something apparently intelligent and external to her, operating either directly from itself, or indirectly through or in conjunction with some special attribute of her organism." Ibid, 568.

292 **"the playthings of the agency which they reveal"** Ibid., 569.

292 **Daniel Dunglas Home (1833–1886)** For an overview of Home's mediumship I would recommend Braude's chapter in *Limits of Influence*. For more detail, see Home's book *Incidents on My Life* (first published in 1864) and

any of the papers written by William Crookes in the *Quarterly Journal of Science* (1870–1874) and in the *Proceedings of the Society for Psychical Research* (1889 and 1897).

292   **phenomena that Home repeatedly generated were** Braude, *Immortal Remains,* 65–66.

292   **"ostensible communicator (unknown to Home) had been"** Ibid., 66.

292   **"and pulled my coat several times"** William Crookes, "Researches in the Phenomena of Spiritualism," *The Quarterly Journal of Science,* 1874, 92.

293   **"and sometimes being held by those near him"** Ibid.

293   **"with the firm pressure of an old friend"** Ibid., 93.

293   **while the voices carried on across the room** William Bennett, Professor of Electrical Engineering at Columbia University, ruled out accomplices when an impromptu séance occurred with Leslie Flint in Bennett's apartment and the voices conversed with his guests. See Flint's Columbia University lecture, 1970 at www.leslieflint.com. Rev. C. Drayton Thomas of the Society For Psychical Research tested Flint by gagging him and binding him in his chair. The voices of his communicators were still heard. Flint also had plastic molding pressed over his lips, which was then bandaged, while tied to a chair; the voices spoke with their usual clarity, some even shouted. See "Medium Gagged: But Guide Spoke In Direct-Voice," *Psychic News,* February 14, 1948, 1–2. Journalist Alexander Walker with the *London Evening Standard* stated: "In one test, Flint held a measured quantity of coloured water in his mouth, throughout a voluble seance. In another, a throat microphone registered no vibrations from his larynx, while the voices continued in full spate." May 10, 1994, leslieflint.com.

CHAPTER 23: POSSIBLE EVIDENCE OF SURVIVAL

294   **Indridi Indridason** Icelanders use a patronymic system of names and few have family names. They refer to each other by their given name, like Indridi. The second name, Indridason, refers to the fact that his father's name was Indridi. (His sister's name would be Indridadottir, "the daughter of Indridi.")

294   **Indridi Indridason of Iceland** Erlendur Haraldsson, *Indridi Indridason: The Icelandic Physical Medium* (White Crow Books, 2015).

296   **He could therefore be categorized as a drop-in communicator** Erlendur Haraldsson and Ian Stevenson, "A Communicator of the 'Drop-in' Type in Iceland: The Case of Runolfur Runolfsson," *Journal of the American Society for Psychical Research* 69 (January 1975): 33–59.

296 **the Bishop of Iceland** He was the Right Reverend Hallgrimur Sveinsson.

297 **Almost a month later, the newspapers were delivered** Denmark's second-largest newspaper, *Berlingske Tidende,* gave this report:

"Last night at around twelve o'clock the Fire Brigade was called to Store Kongensgade 63, where fire had broken out in a house in the backyard in the warehouse of the Copenhagen Lamp Factory. The fire had spread considerably when the fire brigades arrived from the Main Fire Station and Adelsgade Station. Still, the firemen managed to get the fire under control in about an hour. The damage was substantial."

Politiken, the leading Danish newspaper, states that when the janitor called the Fire Brigade at about twelve o'clock, "the first floor was already ablaze with powerful flames reaching out of the windows and breaking the glass in the windows on the second floor where there is a factory for making cardboard boxes."

The fire was brought under control in half an hour according to *Politiken,* and in one hour according to *Berlingske Tidende.* Here, then, we find a reasonably close correspondence.

298 **I searched census documents in Copenhagen** I also learned that at that time he was living with four single sisters at Store Kongensgade 67, again close to number 63 where the fire broke out. In 1880 Emil Jensen had been living with three unmarried sisters and his brother.

301 **They were heard speaking or singing in sittings in which adequate controls were in place** These independent voices were reported in the two minute books and by Gudmundur Hannesson, Haraldur Nielsson, Einar Kvaran; and by Sigurdur Haralz Nielsson, the eldest son of Haraldur Nielsson, who observed this phenomenon in broad daylight and without Indridi being in trance.

301 **"the soprano voice of a lady and the bass voice of a man"** H. Nielsson, "Some of My Experiences with a Physical Medium in Reykjavik," in Carl Vett, ed., *Le compte rendu officiel du Premier Congrès International des Recherches Psychiques à Copenhague* Copenhagen, pp. 450–65.

301 **Einar Kvaran confirmed this observation** Einar Kvaran, "Metapsykiske faenomener paa Island," *Sandhedssögeren* 6 (1910): 42–51.

301 **"sing at the same time . . . Both voices were heard very close to me"** Gudmundur Hannesson, "Tveir fundir hja Tilraunafelaginu," *Morgunn* 5 (1924): 217–26.

302 **minute books indicates responsive xenoglossy** Ian Stevenson, *Unlearned Language: New Studies in Xenoglossy* (Charlottesville: University Press of Virginia, 1984).

302 **providing further evidence of xenoglossy** That this may have been a genuine case of xenoglossy also gets some support from the fact that a few other

of Indridi's communicators spoke foreign languages that Indridi did not know.

302 **French singer as someone who had actually lived** Thorbergur Thordarson, *Indridi Midill* (Reykjavik: Vikingsutgafan, 1942), 79–81.

303 **outside the séance room, is reported by the organist Thorlaksson** Ibid., 88.

CHAPTER 24: THE ENIGMA OF FULL-FORM MATERIALIZATIONS

306 **"Many times we saw the medium and this materialized being simultaneously"** Haraldsson, *Indridi Indridason*, 72.

306 **they witnessed Jensen materialize eleven times** Ibid., 74.

306 **"to present any additional conceptual obstacle," he writes** Braude, *Limits of Influence*, 135.

307 **"speaks, and moves the veil that covers him"** Charles Richet, *Thirty Years of Psychical Research: Being a Treatise on Metapsychics* (The Macmillan Company, 1923), 491.

307 **"This is surely the climax of marvels. Nevertheless, it is a fact"** Ibid., 467.

307 **Polish medium Franek Kluski (1873–1943)** The definitive work on Kluski is: Zofia Weaver, *Other Realities? The Enigma of Franek Kluski's Mediumship* (White Crow Books, 2015).

307 **"remarkable medium of his time, probably of any time"** Ibid., x.

308 **eleven successful séances** Gustave Geley, *Clairvoyance and Materialization: A Record of Experiments* (T. Fisher Unwin Limited, Bouverie House Fleet Street, E.C. 1927), 207.

308 **eighty-four people confirmed such recognition** Weaver, *Other Realities?*, Ibid., 58.

308 **"heartbeat one can hear and feel, is beyond our comprehension"** F. W. Pawlowski, "The Mediumship of Franek Kluski," *Journal of the American Society for Psychical Research*, 19, no. 9 (September 1925): 503.

309 **"I could hear their breathing and feel their breath upon my face"** Ibid., 486.

309 **"and deposited the glove against the hand of one of us"** Geley, *Clairvoyance and Materialization*, 234.

310 **Geley and Richet added a bluish coloring agent** Ibid., 223.

310 **they secretly added cholesterin** Ibid., 224.

310   **not smooth and round like a child** Ibid., 232. When Kluski's energy was low, his materializations were often undersized. See Mary Rose Barrington, "The Kluski Hands," *Journal of the Society for Psychical Research* 59 no. 834 (1994): 348–49.

310   **extensively photographed for publication** See Geley, *Clairvoyance and Materialization,* for more than two dozen photographs of the molds.

310   **"certainty of the supernormal origin of the moulds"** Ibid., 220.

310   **"revealed in the splendour of its beauty"** Ibid., 240.

310   **"lack of inhibition and a common goal"** Weaver, *Other Realities?,* 132.

311   **"physical way that requires physical energies"** Ibid., 136.

311   **"emanates from her, and is connected with her"** Richet, *Thirty Years of Psychical Research,* 523.

312   **"profile turned to the right, and of life size"** Baron von Schrenck Notzing, *Phenomena of Materialisation* (Kegan Paul, Trench & Co. Ltd., London; New York, E. P. Dutton & Co., 1923), 289.

312   **causing serious harm or even death** The best-known mediums harmed in this way were Helen Duncan and Alec Harris.

312   **"in the very front rank of physical mediums"** Louie Harris, *Alec Harris: The Full Story of His Remarkable Mediumship* (Saturday Night Press Publications, 2009), 9.

312   **"demonstrating the reality of survival"** Ibid., 13.

313   **"and what amazing power it is!"** Theophilus Haarhoff, *Psychic News,* December 13, 1952; and Ibid., 177–78.

313   **"we could see the figure and the medium at the same time"** Harris, *Alec Harris,* 138–39.

313   **"Because I was an unbeliever"** Albert Fletcher-Desborough, "No Chance for Deception—Conjurer," *Psychic News,* March 2, 1974, 1.

314   **In 1961, two journalists who concealed their identities** This incident is reported by Louie Harris and all quotes are from Harris, *Alec Harris,* 237–41.

315   **"human forms be treated any differently?"** Braude private communication, February 8, 2016.

315   **"this scenario could presumably be the same"** Ibid.

316   **"the medium's magically objectified dreams"** Mann, "An Experience in the Occult," 259.

316   **"accounted for solely by the action of living agents"** Fontana, *Is There an Afterlife?,* 353.

316   **"powerful argument against the Super-ESP theory"** Ibid., 247.

316   **that some unknown agency is involved** Ibid.

316   **"an alternative explanation to that of survival"** Video interview with Tim Coleman and Daniel Drasin, April 2004. I recommend the 13-minute video on YouTube titled "Afterlife Investigations Bonus Interview."

317   **"survival is a fact, and people are communicating"** Ibid.

317   **"they've been unconsciously motivated to do so"** Sudduth, private communication, February 9, 2016.

319   **"these are phenomena that put us to utter confusion"** Richet, *Thirty Years of Psychical Research,* 617.

319   **"And what can that be but a spirit?"** Carrington, *Eusapia Palladino,* 292.

319   **"is in operation and not that of any spirit"** Ibid.

319   **lists the assumptions he's making** Ibid., 293.

319   **"move material objects, be seen, felt, and even photographed"** Ibid., 300.

319   **"all the facts at these séances, and in no other way"** Ibid.

319   **that sometimes the phenomena can manifest spontaneously** Ibid., 301.

320   **"until some better explanation be forthcoming"** Ibid., 299.

320   **"and by what has impacted you"** Braude, personal conversation, November 14, 2015.

CHAPTER 25: MY ASTONISHING SECOND "PERSONAL EXPERIMENT"

321   **through his 2010 memoir,** *An Extraordinary Journey* In addition to this memoir, I also recommend a video of an informal lecture Stewart presented in the UK about his development as a medium. Not only is the information fascinating, but one can also get a very good feel for Stewart as a person by listening to him speak. Go to YouTube and search his name.

322   **Alec Harris, Minnie Harrison, Helen Duncan, Hunter Selkirk** Besides the book on Alec Harris mentioned previously, books on these other mediums are also available.

323   **"until told later in the bar"** Hylton Thompson, "Mischievous Spirit Boy Destroys Noah's Trumpet," *Noah's Ark Society Newsletter,* No. 20, 18.

325   **and sit for two sessions with the home circle** Stewart wanted to make sure I understood that there were no guarantees that anything would happen at the séances—sometimes they are blank, or very little happens, he told me,

and he can never predict. He was worried that I would travel all that way, and then be disappointed, and expressed that to me numerous times, as he does every time I travel to the UK to join the group.

325 **"or in the presence only of a dim red light"** Alexander, *An Extraordinary Journey*, 14–15.

325 **sensitivity to light heightened as the depth of her trance increased** Carrington, *Eusapia Palladino and Her Phenomena*, 334.

325 **"invariably telekinetic in character and of simple nature," he wrote** Ibid., 329.

325 **"and disrupt any excessively fine and subtle body"** Ibid., 330.

326 **"the injurious action of light in materialization séances"** Geley, *Clairvoyance and Materialization*, 14.

326 **"but that it happens at all," he wrote in his foreword** Alexander, *An Extraordinary Journey*, 15.

326 **"nature of the phenomena associated with his mediumship"** Ibid., 16.

328 **consciousness can be separated from it** Katie Halliwell, *Experiences of Trance, Physical Mediumship and Associated Phenomena with the Stewart Alexander Circle, Part One: Evidential Survival After Death* (Saturday Night Press Publications, 2008), 84. For anyone who wants more exposure to what occurs during the séances of Stewart Alexander, I recommend Halliwell's three short books. (Any profits on sales go to charity.) They were written during her eleven years of observations within the circle, and include transcripts of séance excerpts from 1999–2010. CDs of these excerpts can be ordered to accompany the books, which are available on Amazon.

329 **"Do you feel the strap, ma'am?" Walter asked** All quotes and details from the séances I attended are reported here from the audio recordings of the sessions.

330 **showed no signs of pressure or abrasion** R.G. Medhurst, *Crookes and the Spirit World* (Souvenir Press, 1972), 125.

330 **providing sufficient energy for it to occur** Halliwell, *Part One*, 82.

332 **"that are connecting themselves to the trumpets, dear," she said** Ibid., 85.

332 **"created in seconds within the séance room"** Ibid.

332 **"the object may perhaps be raised above the heads"** Carrington, *Eusapia Palladino and Her Phenomena*, 317.

333 **it is exceedingly difficult and the structure is unstable** Katie Halliwell, *Physical Mediumship and Associated Phenomena with the Stewart Alexander Circle, Part Two: Home Circles and Public Sittings* (Saturday Night Press, 2008), 102.

333   **hollow ectoplasmic tube into the smaller end of the trumpet** Katie Halliwell, *Physical Mediumship and Associated Phenomena with the Stewart Alexander Circle, Part Three: The Etheric Connection* (Saturday Night Press, 2011), 44.

335   **it could not possibly have belonged to anyone in the room** On some occasions, Stewart has placed his hands on the edge of the table during this experiment; at other times every sitter in the room has placed their hands around the table to make them visible. Ibid., 37.

336   **"So I have to slow down my vibrations"** Halliwell, *Part Two,* 56.

336   **and then faded off back into the cloud** Medhurst, *Crookes and the Spirit World,* 119.

336   **"I think I see the creases in the skin"** Richet, *Thirty Years of Psychical Research,* 524.

336   **"Then it retreats, diminishes in size, and disappears"** Geley, *Clairvoyance and Materialization,* 187.

337   **Many people, including David Fontana** Fontana, *Is There an Afterlife?,* 350.

337   **while strapped in his chair, often waking up** Halliwell, *Part Three,* 136. D. D. Home, as reported by Crookes throughout his research, was levitated during his séances.

338   **or like wearing a heavy, wet overcoat** Halliwell, *Part Two,* 20.

338   **dwelling in that room was almost indescribable** In describing only four séances, I have not been able to do justice to the full scope of Stewart's mediumship. There is so much more, as described by Halliwell and in many other accounts. For example, members of the home circle were allowed to witness ectoplasm in red light, just after it emerged from Stewart's mouth; Halliwell was invited to physically touch the ectoplasm in its various stages (from a cold draft of air to warm snowflakes to a solid ball); the group saw materialized forms create their own "spirit lights" in their hands, allowing the sitters to see their hands as they walked around the room. All of these strange events were witnessed by the full circle. It's hard to believe, but this is all true.

339   **I contacted Violet to confirm** Violet Eccles, email communication, March 3, 2016.

340   **"the séance would be closed," Leone told me** Leone Holdsworth, email communication, March 2, 2016. The account was written to me in an email by Leone and confirmed by Stewart and members of the Circle.

341   **Robin says he has no more symptoms** Robin Hodson, email communications. On November 15, 2015, Robin provided a written report on what happened; he answered my follow-up questions on November 25, 2015.

343 **I have no reason to doubt his integrity** Kevin Kussow provided a detailed written report on the book test on June 3, 2016, and I interviewed him by telephone on June 16, 2016.

CHAPTER 26: A LIFE IN TWO WORLDS

345 **Whilst I am not in any way religious** I consider religion to be a belief in, and a worship of, a supreme divine deity—a system of faith and devotion. To me this has absolutely no connection or relevance to spiritualism, which, at best, can demonstrate the absolute reality of survival beyond death and communication between the living and the so-called dead. That the movement has, this past half century, been transformed into a religion to accommodate many faiths, sadly (in my view) presents to the world a spurious image. Man's final destination owes nothing to a belief in a mythical God.

349 **very few people will ever experience the wonders of the séance room** Therefore I produced a double CD, *Physical Séance Room Recollections*, from my audio archives. They contain a series of fascinating firsthand physical séance room accounts presented by people privileged to sit with mediums whom today we can only read about. All the speakers personally witnessed and experienced the manifestations they described and took the time and trouble to record them in audio form for future interested parties. That they did so prior to their own transition, has left us a marvelous historic legacy. Often exceeding the "boggle factor," their amazing séance room recollections bring back to life the wonders of the past and thereby keep alive that which must never be forgotten. For orders and inquiries, email sue@finka.karoo.co.uk.

350 **an exhaustive study of the history of physical mediumship** Leslie Kean suggested I provide a list of my most highly recommended and favorite books. Of course there are many more—but these stand out:

Arthur Findlay, *On the Edge of the Etheric* (Rider & Co., originally published 1931)

Gladys Osborne Leonard, *My Life in Two Worlds* (Cassell & Co. Ltd., originally published 1931)

Harry Emerson, *Listen My Son* (Casdec Ltd., originally published 1946)

Maurice Barbanell, *This Is Spiritualism* (Herbert Jenkins Ltd., originally Published 1959)

S. Ralph Harlow PhD, *A Life After Death* (London/Victor Gollancz Ltd., originally published 1961)

Leslie Flint, *Voices in the Dark* (Macmillan London Ltd., 1971)

Paul Tabori, *Pioneers of the Unseen* (Souvenir Press, first British edition published 1972)

Guy Lyon Playfair, *The Indefinite Boundary* (Souvenir Press, 1976)

Elizabeth Jenkins, *The Shadow and the Light* (Hamish Hamilton Ltd., 1982)

David Fontana, *Is There an Afterlife?* (O Books, 2005)

Louie Harris, *Alec Harris: The Full Story of His Remarkable Physical Mediumship* (Saturday Night Press Publications, 2009)

350   **critics totally ignored remarkable phenomena** Wooden rings made of different types of wood were brought to the séances by the researchers. At the end, the rings were linked. Additionally, the researchers constructed a soundproof box, weighing over a hundred pounds, containing a condenser microphone surrounded by soundproofing and exterior sheathing. The voice of Walter, Margery's spirit control, seemed able to get inside this locked box and to speak clearly into the mic buried deep inside. The voice would be inaudible to the sitters in the séance room but audible to other sitters in a distant room, who heard it through a connected loudspeaker.

356   **"our world is a world of ultimate reality"** Halliwell, *Part Three*, 154.

CONCLUSION

358   **"both sources operate within the same domain"** Daniel Drasin, personal communication, November 17, 2015.

358   **"a reasonable basis for believing in personal postmortem survival"** Braude, *Immortal Remains*, 306.

358   **not experienced any phenomena he is convinced are genuine** Braude, personal communication, January 25, 2016.

358   **"intuitive certainty about our real nature"** Fontana, *Is There an Afterlife?*, 471.

359   **"that confer justification of their belief in survival"** Michael Sudduth "Personal Reflections on Life and Death," *Cup of Nirvana*, August 7, 2015.

361   **"little more than posturing and dishonest bluffing"** Braude, *Limits of Influence*, preface. All quotes in the proceeding paragraph are from the same preface.

362   **forced upon one—as they were forced upon me** Carrington, *Eusapia Palladino*, ix–x.

Acknowledgments

I benefited from the help of many people while working on this book. First and foremost, I'd like to thank Gary Jansen, a senior editor at the Crown Publishing Group, for his insightful comments and superb edits of the manuscript. They improved the book tremendously. An accomplished author as well as a skilled editor, Gary has always been there for me when events in my life necessitated an extension of deadlines, and he guided me through the many phases of the publishing process with great expertise.

I'm also very grateful for the ten outstanding contributors whose original chapters add such a richness and strength to the narrative. Their insight stemming from many years of work and experience is profound, and I commend them for their deep involvement in areas that are not readily accepted by the mainstream. Much appreciation goes to Bruce Leininger, and also to Jeffrey Kane, Jane Katra, Laura Lynne Jackson, Sandra O'Hara, Mark Lewis, and Russ Stratton, for their extensive communications, which were crucial to the stories and cases being presented.

A special thanks to my literary agents, Phyllis Wender and Allison Cohen of the Gersh Agency, who believed in this book from the beginning and helped give it birth. Having worked with me on my previous book, *UFOs*, Phyllis and Allison have been an essential part of my team, and I would not be where I am without them.

I had a number of outstanding advisers and consultants during the three years I worked on *Surviving Death*. I especially want to thank Stephen Braude for providing me with historical documents and references; engaging in numerous Skype discussions, which challenged my thinking; and for inviting me to Germany as part of his team studying the mediumship of Kai Muegge. In addition, Jim Tucker, Stewart Alexander, Alan Gauld, Julie Beischel, and Michael Sudduth gave of their time and knowledge freely in so many ways, which helped inform and shape the narrative. Filmmakers Daniel Drasin and Tim Coleman provided valuable material and input, including exclusive interview transcripts, and gave me useful feedback; Dan upgraded the quality of the book's photographs with great proficiency, which was essential for their publication.

In addition, many thanks to Katie Halliwell, Robert Narholz, and Barrie Coleman for their excellent line drawings within the text; Bob and Phran Ginsberg of the Forever Family Foundation for answering my endless questions about mental mediumship and scoring readings; Kai Muegge for his trust and invitation to study his mediumship; Howie Abraham and Ken Saari for their steadfast support and for making helpful connections; Jon Beecher of White Crow Books for providing some of his valuable books and photographs; Larry Landsman for initiating a documentary film to be made on this topic; Kevin Kussow, Violet Eccles, and Leone Holdsworth for their reports on experiences with Stewart Alexander; and Cyndi Hammons for inviting me to her home and helping with research.

I am especially grateful to members of Stewart Alexander's Home Circle—especially Ray and June Lister, Carol Petch, Chris and Jane Jackson, and Lisa Clifford—for accepting me so warmly into the Circle. Ray and Carol have engaged me in many informative discussions. Katie Halliwell, a long established honorary member of the Circle who spent many years documenting the phenomena in the séance room, has generously shared her knowledge to my benefit. And Alf and June Winchester, longtime associates of the circle and supporters of Stewart's mediumship, have also been very helpful.

At Crown, associate publisher Campbell Wharton was instrumental in moving the project forward when I first proposed the idea for this book. I also thank Molly Stern, publisher; Elizabeth Rendfleisch, director of interior design; Kevin Garcia, production manager; Nicole Ramirez, production editor; Robin Slutzky, copyeditor; Alane Gianetti, jacket designer; Tricia Boczkowski, vice president and editorial director; Tammy Blake, vice president of publicity; Maya Lane, publicist; Julie Cepler, director of marketing; and Christina Foxley, marketer.

I appreciate the additional help provided by John Alexander, Carlos Alvarado, Ralph Blumenthal, Yves Bosson, Will Bueche, Annette Childs, Samir Coussa, Tatiana Daubek, Paul Gaunt, Ann Harrison, Sandy Ingham, Robert Mitchell, Peter Mulacz, Marisa Martyn Rosenblatt, Erika Ruehlman, Leo Ruickbie, Ralph Steiner, and Lisa Trump. Also, many thanks to the Montreal-based creators of the *Surviving Death* website—Raj Ramtuhol for tech support and programming work, and Sheela Ramtuhol for graphic design.

Lastly, I am grateful for the personal support from my son, Paul McKim; my friend Jose Lay; and close family members, who helped sustain me throughout the unusual, often solitary journey of researching and writing *Surviving Death*.

Index

ABOUT THE AUTHOR

LESLIE KEAN is an independent investigative journalist and author of *UFOs: Generals, Pilots, and Government Officials Go on the Record* (Crown Publishing Group, 2010), a *New York Times* bestseller. She helped produce a 2011 documentary based on *UFOs* for the History Channel, made by Breakthru Films, an award-winning film company. Kean has been featured on CNN, MSNBC, FOX, *The Colbert Report*, and NPR and in *USA Today*, *US News & World Report*, and the *Columbia Journalism Review*, among other media. She has written articles for the *Huffington Post* since 2012.

Kean was also a producer and on-air host for a daily investigative news program on KPFA radio, a Pacifica station in California. She has contributed articles to dozens of publications here and abroad including the *Boston Globe*, *Philadelphia Inquirer*, *Atlanta Journal-Constitution*, *Providence Journal*, *International Herald Tribune*, *Globe and Mail*, *Sydney Morning Herald*, *The Nation*, and *Journal for Scientific Exploration*. While spending many years reporting on Burma, she coauthored *Burma's Revolution of the Spirit: The Struggle for Democratic Freedom and Dignity* (Aperture, 1994). She has contributed essays for a number of anthologies published between 1998 and 2009.